TENNESSEE!

The seventeenth thrilling episode in the *WAG-ONS WEST* series—a riveting tale of love and adventure by a special breed of American, true heroes ready to fight with their rifles and their dreams to protect a birthright of freedom and justice for all.

★★★★★★★★★★★★★★★★★★★★★★★★★★★★★★★★

WAGONS WEST

TENNESSEE!

**An America in crisis pitted the brave
against the bad, as violence exploded
from the mighty Mississippi to Memphis Town**

TOBY HOLT—

With gun, saber or bare fists he had the skill to best any
foe . . . but he had no armor for his heart as a dangerous mission brought him face to face with a dual threat—a
brutal renegade general and a beautiful woman he could
not resist.

CLARISSA HOLT—

Left behind with only her memories and empty arms,
she yearned for the husband she adored, but as absence
made the nights too long to bear, would she risk her
marriage for a moment's pleasure?

JAMES MARTINSON—

Haughty son of a railroad tycoon, he wanted all the
power his money could buy by blackmail, greed, and a
daring plan to make him not just a politician . . . but
President of the United States.

MARTHA—

Voluptuous, dazzlingly beautiful, her mysterious past
tied her to the infamous criminal kingpin, Domino, but
her dreams joined her with Toby Holt . . . and what
Martha wanted, Martha got.

★★★★★★★★★★★★★★★★★★★★★★★★★★★★★★★★

★★

EMIL BRAUN—

Brilliant in the military arts, but with a twisted mind, he turned his genius against his native country in a demented quest for his own kingdom and the death of Toby Holt.

HANK BLAKE—

A West Point cadet asked to make a heartbreaking sacrifice for his country—a secret mission that could cost him the woman he loved, his career . . . and his life.

EDDIE NEFF—

Ruggedly handsome and ruthless, he operated outside the law and took his orders from Domino . . . and his orders were to steal Clarissa Holt's heart.

WHITE ELK—

An Indian boy thrust into a snakepit of cruel desperados, an act of bravery would make him a man and a proud inheritor of the best of both the red and the white man's worlds.

DOROTHY WHITE—

Her hunger for money would lead her down the path of seduction and crime, and her blond beauty would lead the way to a powerful man's heart.

★★

Bantam Books by Dana Fuller Ross
Ask your bookseller for the books you have missed

INDEPENDENCE!—Volume I
NEBRASKA!—Volume II
WYOMING!—Volume III
OREGON!—Volume IV
TEXAS!—Volume V
CALIFORNIA!—Volume VI
COLORADO!—Volume VII
NEVADA!—Volume VIII
WASHINGTON!—Volume IX
MONTANA!—Volume X
DAKOTA!—Volume XI
UTAH!—Volume XII
IDAHO!—Volume XIII
MISSOURI!—Volume XIV
MISSISSIPPI!—Volume XV
LOUISIANA!—Volume XVI
TENNESSEE!—Volume XVII

WAGONS WEST ★ SEVENTEENTH IN A SERIES

TENNESSEE!

DANA FULLER ROSS

 Created by the producers of
White Indian, Children of the
Lion, Stagecoach and
America 2040.

Chairman of the Board: Lyle Kenyon Engel

BANTAM BOOKS
TORONTO • NEW YORK • LONDON • SYDNEY • AUCKLAND

TENNESSEE!

A Bantam Book / May 1986

Produced by Book Creations, Inc.
Chairman of the Board: Lyle Kenyon Engel

ISBN 0-553-25622-X

Published simultaneously in the United States and Canada

Bantam Books are published by Bantam Books, Inc. Its trademark,
consisting of the words "Bantam Books" and the portrayal of a
rooster, is Registered in U.S. Patent and Trademark Office and in
other countries. Marca Registrada. Bantam Books, Inc., 666 Fifth
Avenue, New York, New York 10103.

PRINTED IN THE UNITED STATES OF AMERICA

O   0 9 8 7 6 5 4 3 2 1

Missouri

Illinois

Indiana

Missouri River

ST. LOUIS

Mississippi River

Wabash River

Ohio River

CAIRO

· ALONG THE TENNESSEE RIVER ·

NASHVILLE

Arkansas

TENNESSEE

MEMPHIS

Tennessee Ri

VICKSBURG

Mississippi River

Mississippi

Alabama

NATCHEZ

Louisiana

Florida

NEW
ORLEANS

Gulf of
Mexico

© BOOK CREATIONS INC. 1985

★ TENNESSEE ★

JISVILLE

West
Virginia

Kentucky

Virginia

Holston River

KNOXVILLE

North Carolina

CHATTANOOGA

*French
Broad
River*

South
Carolina

Georgia

Atlantic
Ocean

· MEMPHIS, TENNESSEE ·

RON TOELKE 85

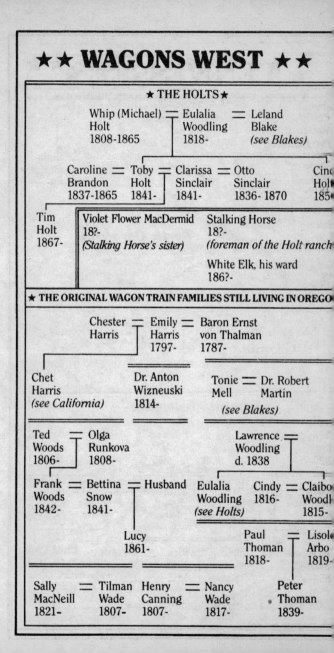

★ ★ WAGONS WEST ★ ★

★ THE HOLTS ★

Whip (Michael) ═ Eulalia ═ Leland
Holt   Woodling   Blake
1808-1865   1818-   *(see Blakes)*

Caroline ═ Toby ═ Clarissa ═ Otto   Cind
Brandon   Holt   Sinclair   Sinclair   Hol
1837-1865   1841-   1841-   1836- 1870   185

Tim Holt 1867-

Violet Flower MacDermid
18?-
(Stalking Horse's sister)

Stalking Horse
18?-
(foreman of the Holt ranch

White Elk, his ward
186?-

★ THE ORIGINAL WAGON TRAIN FAMILIES STILL LIVING IN OREGO

Chester ═ Emily ═ Baron Ernst
Harris   Harris   von Thalman
     1797-   1787-

Chet
Harris
(see California)

Dr. Anton
Wizneuski
1814-

Tonie ═ Dr. Robert
Mell   Martin
   (see Blakes)

Ted ═ Olga
Woods   Runkova
1806-   1808-

Lawrence ═
Woodling
d. 1838

Frank ═ Bettina ═ Husband
Woods   Snow
1842-   1841-

Eulalia
Woodling
(see Holts)

Cindy ═ Claibo
1816-   Woodl
    1815-

Lucy
1861-

Paul ═ Lisol
Thoman   Arbo
1818-   1819

Sally ═ Tilman
MacNeill   Wade
1821-   1807-

Henry ═ Nancy
Canning   Wade
1807-   1817-

Peter
Thoman
1839-

★ ★ FAMILY TREE ★ ★

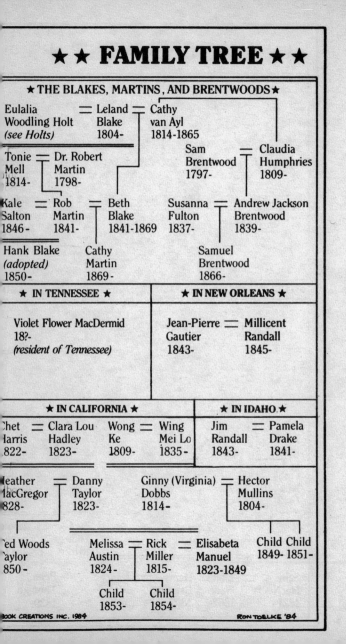

★ THE BLAKES, MARTINS, AND BRENTWOODS ★

Eulalia Woodling Holt *(see Holts)* = Leland Blake 1804- — Cathy van Ayl 1814-1865

Sam Brentwood 1797- — Claudia Humphries 1809-

Tonie Mell 1814- = Dr. Robert Martin 1798-

Kale Salton 1846- = Rob Martin 1841- = Beth Blake 1841-1869

Susanna Fulton 1837- = Andrew Jackson Brentwood 1839-

Hank Blake *(adopted)* 1850-

Cathy Martin 1869-

Samuel Brentwood 1866-

★ IN TENNESSEE ★

Violet Flower MacDermid 18?- *(resident of Tennessee)*

★ IN NEW ORLEANS ★

Jean-Pierre Gautier 1843- = Millicent Randall 1845-

★ IN CALIFORNIA ★

Chet Harris 1822- = Clara Lou Hadley 1823-

Wong Ke 1809- = Wing Mei Lo 1835-

★ IN IDAHO ★

Jim Randall 1843- = Pamela Drake 1841-

Heather MacGregor 1828- = Danny Taylor 1823-

Ginny (Virginia) Dobbs 1814- = Hector Mullins 1804-

Ted Woods Taylor 1850-

Melissa Austin 1824- = Rick Miller 1815- = Elisabeta Manuel 1823-1849

Child 1849- Child 1851-

Child 1853- Child 1854-

BOOK CREATIONS INC. 1984

RON TOELKE '84

TENNESSEE!

I

On the north side of Lafayette Park, a long stone's throw away from the White House, stood one of the District of Columbia's most imposing dwellings. The handsome mansion was among the showplaces of the nation's capital. Built by the late railroad magnate and financier John Martinson, it was on the sightseeing itinerary of every tourist.

Martinson's son, James, had inherited the house and made the most of the stature that being its owner gave him. Standing by the bay window of his study, which gave him a clear view of the executive mansion in the early morning sunshine, Martinson gave vent once more to his envy and impatience. No matter how fine his present dwelling, he reflected, he would not be satisfied until he exchanged it for the White House. For years, only one ambition—becoming president of the United States—had dominated his life. Now, at last, he felt that he actually was coming closer to that goal.

His first major move, two years earlier, had been to win appointment as assistant secretary of the Treasury. This post was perfect for him: It brought him into relative prominence in the upper echelons of government without placing him in so high an office that his lack of qualifications would attract attention. He had won the appointment by making a major contribution to the campaign fund of President Ulysses S. Grant when the general was first seeking office. Now, after years of conniving, scheming, and planning, he saw himself in a position to take another step toward achieving the presidency for himself.

Turning abruptly from the window, he tugged at a bell rope, then seated himself at his highly polished mahogany desk, an heirloom from his father's estate. Burrows, the butler who had spent his professional lifetime with the Martinson family, answered the summons promptly, as usual. Entering the study unobtrusively, he cast a critical eye at his employer, who seemed absorbed in the papers he was reading.

The old butler had to admit that James Martinson was good-looking. His features appeared to have been chiseled out of stone. He exuded an impressive aura of virility, and when he wished to take the trouble, he could be quite charming. All the same, in the butler's opinion, he was hardly the man his late father had been. The younger Martinson lacked the elastic nimbleness of mind that had won a great fortune for the old pirate, though he matched him in ruthlessness and in single-minded purpose.

Diplomatically, Burrows cleared his throat. Martinson looked up but continued to hold a document in front of him, thus giving the appearance of being engrossed. "Yes, Burrows," he said sharply. "As you know, I am entertaining a guest at noon dinner. I wish to go over several things with you."

"Very good, sir."

"It is Milton Plosz who is coming. Please be sure you use our best Spode—"

"We have entertained Mr. Plosz many times, sir," the butler interrupted in an aggrieved tone. "Not only in your time but, as you will recall, in your father's day as well, sir. I am sure we know how to entertain him properly."

Martinson ignored the remark. "Use the Bohemian

crystal, please, and the heavy silver bought from the duke of Cumberland's estate."

"Very good, sir!" Burrows replied stiffly.

"We'll begin with a she-crab soup," Martinson continued. "Then a lightly prepared fish—grilled sole, perhaps, if it can be found in the market—followed by the very best cut of beef the chef can obtain. Plosz is incapable of appreciating style or quality, but I wish to impress him and put him in a receptive frame of mind. I will leave the wine and other details of the meal to you and the chef. I know I can rely on you, Burrows. This is a very important occasion."

"That's kind of you, sir," Burrows muttered.

"While you're about it, send a magnum of champagne to Plosz at his hotel, and why not order a young woman to report to his suite at about two-thirty, following our meal. I assume his appetites are still insatiable." He dismissed Burrows with a wave of his hand.

The butler nodded stiffly and withdrew.

Martinson returned to his plans, reviewing them again. He paused to examine each step, looking for possible holes or faults in his scheme. Unable to discover any, he began to feel reassured. After his meal with Milton Plosz, his dream of becoming president would be much closer to being realized.

He stood up and walked out of his study. Glancing at himself admiringly in the mirror in the center hall, he clapped his tall hat on his head and departed to keep morning appointments at his office diagonally across the park.

Milton Plosz prided himself on looking like a gentleman. His features were fundamentally gross; nevertheless, with his barber's and tailor's assistance, he managed to achieve a reasonably clean-cut and civilized appearance. His clothing had been tailored in London to fit his ample build, and across his waistcoat hung a chain of solid gold. He exuded the confidence of a man who had achieved success. No casual observer would have guessed that he had been a gambler and a cardsharp, a notorious womanizer, a hard drinker, and, when necessary, a killer.

A native of Memphis, Tennessee, Plosz had gambled up and down the Mississippi River as a young man, then drifted from city to city, making money any way he could. At the start of the Civil War, he had settled into a government job in Washington, D.C., making himself right at home. In this post he accepted huge kickbacks from prospective government contractors and enjoyed frequent contact with Union Army officers, many of whom made a point of seeking his company when they visited the capital. He had come to old John Martinson's attention as a skillful manipulator, utterly lacking in conscience, who would do anything for money. He had eventually left his government job to go to work for John Martinson, doing all his dirty work for him, and after the old man's death he stayed on, acting in the same capacity for his son.

At their dinner meeting, James Martinson listened, until the dessert course, to Plosz's long-winded tales of his exploits with women. Plosz broke into a broad smile of anticipation when Martinson told him he could expect to find a female guest awaiting him in his hotel room.

Then Martinson decided to get to the point. Glancing keenly across the table, he asked, "Milton, would you like to pick up an extra ten thousand dollars? As a matter of fact, considerably more money is involved. The first phase of the job alone will pay you ten thousand. The next step should net you at least that much more. I daresay the initial sum will be at least tripled before you accomplish the entire mission."

Plosz's genial smile of anticipation evaporated. His manner quickly became hard and cold. "For that kind of money, James, I'm your man," he answered. "As always, I just need to know the situation and what you want—and that the money will be there. It's money, as you happen to know, that makes the mare go."

Martinson rose, then went swiftly to the door to the butler's pantry and peered through its small window to make sure that no servant was eavesdropping. "I have a certain operation in mind," he said, returning to the table. "It will involve the formation of a select group of military men—a kind of elite corps. You'll take charge of it, and you alone will be responsible for the operation and its success. You will report only to me, of course. However, under no circumstances is anyone to know of our association. After you leave today, you're not to come here again."

Plosz nodded in agreement.

"To begin the first phase of your operation," Martinson went on, "you'll need to acquire a sizable area of land and choose one or two key subordinates. Here is the address to which you are to send your reports." He handed Plosz a folded sheet of paper. "Memorize the address and then burn this. Tell me regularly by mail what you need and, above all, what you are doing."

"I understand," Plosz said neutrally. "But what's the purpose of this? I need to know—"

"It is not at all necessary that you do," Martinson told him sharply. "I am not explaining the entire plan at this time. We've worked together long enough for you to do what I'm asking without unnecessary questions. It's enough for now that you know I want you to find a site large enough for the training of at least a regiment. Such a place must be sufficiently isolated that the authorities will not be asking questions. Then, having found the site, you or your subordinates can begin looking for the men for the regiment. I want no greenhorns, no raw recruits. Preferably, select only veterans of the Union and Confederate armies, perhaps malcontents, men unable to adjust to civilian life even after these several years."

Plosz took no notes but nodded from time to time.

"Choose the officers—particularly a commanding officer—from the same group of men. Your selection of the commander is particularly important. He should be your front man, assuming all public responsibility for raising this regiment. He can provide his own explanations, whatever they may be, if he's asked."

"I think I know just the man we need," Plosz replied. "His name is Emil Braun. He was a colonel in the Union Army, and he ran up a distinguished record in combat. The various regiments he led all had good records. Unfortunately for him, he never was promoted from colonel to brigadier general. He was always too quarrelsome. Subordinate officers liked him and willingly followed him, but he frequently quarreled with his equals and his superiors. I suspect he would be delighted to join up in this enterprise."

"He sounds just right to me," Martinson agreed.

Plosz became increasingly enthusiastic. "Braun lives in Baltimore, and—"

"If you want him, get him!" Martinson answered coldly. "All details are strictly your business now."

"One matter I need to clear with you," Plosz interjected. "What is your reaction to Tennessee as a site for training this regiment? Through an acquaintance in Memphis, I've learned of some excellent land deals, large farms that face foreclosure. There's one in particular I have in mind. I believe we can acquire it without much trouble."

"Once more," Martinson replied, "do what I've requested expeditiously and discreetly. You've heard my conditions. As for Tennessee, I have no objection to it. And it has the added advantage of being a relatively central location, which could be useful at a later stage. But we're going too fast now. I prefer to proceed one step at a time."

He reached into a pocket of his jacket and withdrew an envelope. "This," he said, "contains an initial payment to you personally of ten thousand dollars in hundred-dollar bank notes. It also contains a sum to be used in establishing your training ground, retaining your commander and his officers, and recruiting your regiment. Let me know where I can keep in touch with you, and I will have a bank account opened in a city near that address. You are to use the account for guns, clothing, ammunition, wages, and anything else that you find necessary. Exactly how you allocate the money is up to you. Results are what I care about."

Not wishing to appear greedy, Plosz reached slowly for the envelope and tried to speak offhandedly. "Thank you very much," he said. "I'm sure the matter will work out to your satisfaction."

"I hope so," Martinson answered dryly.

Raising his glass, Plosz held it so that sunlight streaming in the window reflected on the red wine sparkling in it. "Here's to me and you!" he exclaimed. "And to the regiment, which will have absolutely no connection with either of us!"

A half hour later, as Plosz walked back to his hotel and the woman he knew would be awaiting him there, he was busily planning ahead. After the woman left, he would telegraph instructions to an associate in Memphis, authorizing proceedings against the aged widow who owned the property he had in mind. And in the morning, he would take an early train to Baltimore to begin making arrangements for recruiting Emil Braun. Plosz did not know what use Martinson had in mind for such a regiment, but he was sure of one thing: Ten thousand dollars was a welcome prospect indeed, and there was more in the offing. He intended to wring out every penny that might come his way in the transaction. The fact that Martinson had waved off, with growing irritation, any effort by Plosz to gain further information didn't bother him at all. Despite the unanswered questions, he had neither doubts nor qualms.

Pale and frightened, the dark-haired woman confronted the unwelcome caller at the doorway of her modest dwelling. Her fingers fumbled at the tie of her frayed cotton dress as she blinked at him.

"I'm sorry, sir," she said, "but my husband isn't home. He's never here at this time of day."

"Do you have any idea where I could possibly locate him, ma'am?" Milton Plosz inquired politely.

Laura Braun shook her head vehemently. Her one desire was to be rid of this prying stranger as soon as possible.

Before seeking out Braun, Plosz had taken the precaution of disguising his appearance by shaving off his mustache and dying his normally pale brown hair and eyebrows a deep black. He also wore black rimmed spectacles. "My name is Jonas—M. P. Jonas," he told Laura with a show of patience and sympathy. "I'm looking for Colonel Braun," he added, pointedly employing the man's former military title, "because I have a position to offer him—an important position."

A hopeful expression crossed the woman's tired face. Her resolve to keep her mouth shut vanished. "You'll find him at Mike O'Brien's saloon on the harbor waterfront," she said. "He goes there around this hour every day."

"Thank you very much, ma'am!" After saying goodbye, Plosz returned to the light carriage he had rented when he arrived in Baltimore. He drove rapidly toward the harbor district, stopped once for directions, and then proceeded to O'Brien's saloon. After tying his horse to a hitching post, he stepped inside. His attention was drawn immediately to a card game at the corner table. One of the players was a brawny, broad-shouldered man, who held a fistful of cards in one hamlike hand. Perched on his lap was a young woman in a tight-fitting dress with a low neckline and a slit skirt. Henna had given her hair an orange tone. The expression in her heavily made-up eyes was almost bovine in its vacantness. She was holding a half-empty tumbler to the man's lips, while his free hand roamed over her body, patting and caressing. His opponent, a middle-aged man of nondescript appearance, was studying his cards as though his life might depend on his ability to memorize them.

Suddenly the stocky man bellowed with rage and jumped to his feet so unexpectedly that the woman tumbled from his lap and went sprawling on the floor. He reached across the table and roughly grasped his opponent's wrist. The man's cards were scattered across the table.

"Damn you, Flanagan!" the larger man shouted. "You cheated! I saw you take a card from your sleeve and slip it into your hand."

Flanagan tried to protest, but his accuser would have none of it.

"Shut your lying mouth!" he went on, "or I'll shut it for you for good!" Twisting the slender man's arm behind his back, he brought it sharply upward. The man moaned with pain.

The rotund bartender approached and exclaimed loudly, "Here now, Emil! We'll have no more exhibits of your temper today. I've warned you that you've got to control yourself if you want to be welcome in my saloon." He clasped his arms around the brawny man's chest, pinning his arms to his sides, and pulled him away from his slender foe.

Emil Braun's temper cooled, and looking almost sheepish, he twisted around in the bartender's grasp. "Sorry, O'Brien," he muttered. "I do try to keep my temper, but that damn Flanagan cheated, so naturally I saw red."

"Maybe you saw him cheat, and maybe you didn't," O'Brien replied quite gently. "Frankly, I think you saw nothing of the sort. You always suspect that someone is cheating you. The best way to solve that is by not playing with him anymore. Come to think of it, I'm going to make a new rule: You're not to play cards at all in this establishment. Maybe that way we can keep the peace around here." He turned to the slender man. "As for you, Flanagan," he advised, "if you know what's good for you, you'll put some distance between yourself and Braun. You know he's got a vicious temper, and it serves you right for playing with him."

Flanagan silently straightened his coat and withdrew with as much dignity as he could command.

Far from being chastised, Braun reached for the woman and, pulling her back toward him at the now vacant table, slid his hand over her breasts as she settled on his lap. Turning to the bartender, he ordered, "Marie and me will have a couple more ales."

"Coming right away," O'Brien replied cheerfully, as if the recent violent scene had never occurred.

Milton Plosz walked toward the table. "I'll pay for those ales," he offered as he approached. "And while I'm about it, I'll have one myself."

Braun and the woman looked at him questioningly.

"Colonel Braun," Plosz went on without pause, "I've come from Washington for the express purpose of seeing you. My name is Jonas—M. P. Jonas."

O'Brien arrived with three mugs of ale. The woman seized one and quickly drained it. Braun raised his mug in mock salute. "Thanks for the drink, Mr. Jonas."

"You're certainly welcome," Plosz replied. "I hope that drink serves as a suitable introduction. In fact, I am eager to speak to you in private on a matter of considerable importance, to you as well as to me."

Braun put one of his palms against the woman's bottom and lifted. She found herself unexpectedly standing. "Go to the back room, Marie," he instructed. "I'll join you there after I finish my business with this gentleman."

She departed, and Plosz promptly ordered another mug of ale for O'Brien to take to her in the back room. Then he turned his complete attention to Braun, who was eyeing him suspiciously.

"You achieved a remarkable record for yourself during the late war, Colonel Braun," he said. "You deserved to win a promotion to brigadier general."

"I had too many enemies in the War Department," Braun replied bitterly. "Men who were jealous of me."

In a much lowered voice, Milton Plosz continued. "Suppose I offered you a commission as a brigadier and command of your own brigade. Maybe even rank as major general. Would you be interested, Colonel Braun?"

Braun's eyes narrowed, and he leaned toward Plosz. "Don't joke with me, Mr. Jonas," he warned. "Not on such a subject!"

"I assure you I'm hardly joking, Colonel," Plosz replied earnestly. "You come highly recommended. And in the short time since I came in, I like what I've seen. I'm prepared to offer you not only the rank of a general, but a salary equal to that paid by the United States to officers of that rank. I'm further prepared to offer you the sole command of a thousand men or more. You will recruit and train them yourself, employing both Union and Confederate veterans. I'll provide the grounds for your encampment and training facilities. And I'll pay all the expenses."

Braun could not control his excitement. "What use do you plan to make of this corps?" he asked.

Plosz, of course, was still ignorant as to the purpose of the mission. It still annoyed him that Martinson had chosen not to confide in him. It bespoke a lack of trust, which piqued Plosz's vanity. But he had no intention of revealing his feelings, so he merely said, "I prefer that we proceed one step at a time. All I ask is that you supervise the training of your corps and provide the best preparation possible for field action. Beyond that, I expect you to notify me when you consider your men ready for action."

"The prospect is almost too good to be true," Emil Braun answered slowly. "I've dreamed for years of commanding a brigade and wearing a general's stars. So far, I find the offer greatly to my liking."

"It would be necessary," Plosz cautioned, "for you to agree to several rules. Since I prefer to remain strictly in the background, whatever attention the corps creates will be centered on you. I'll expect you to avoid publicity, but if it isn't possible, you must conduct yourself with dignity suitable to your rank. For example, you would be expected to bring Mrs. Braun to your military headquarters. A doxy like the one waiting for you in the back room would not be a suitable companion for an officer who wants to win respect."

Braun was incapable of tolerating a reprimand. "I'm well aware," he replied heatedly, "of what conduct is considered befitting a general. Rest assured I will bid farewell to any woman who has been my part-time companion during this period of enforced retirement from the military. You need have no fears regarding my conduct."

"I'm relieved to hear it," Plosz told him, then launched into a detailed discussion of the requirements for establishment of a training camp and the beginning of Braun's recruiting campaign.

Plosz was pleased at his success thus far. And in Memphis, he knew, the land agent should be taking the first steps in acquiring the farm.

Tennessee, sixteenth state of the nation, was a land of impressive contrasts. From the rugged mountains in its northeastern sector, through its dense, dark forestlands and its large, sun-dappled fields where corn and hay grew in abundance, to the cotton-raising plantations in its southwest, the state was many things to many people. Rich in tradition, it numbered such giants as John Sevier and Andrew Jackson among its illustrious heroes. James K. Polk, one of the greatest of presidents, had come from Tennessee, as had President Grant's predecessor, Andrew Johnson, whose true worth was yet to be realized.

The industrial revolution had begun to come to the larger cities—Nashville, Memphis, Knoxville, and Chattanooga. But elsewhere the state was still largely agricultural, and most people, following in the traditions of the early Scottish-Irish settlers, lived close to the soil. This was true of Violet Flower MacDermid, an elderly, full-blooded Cherokee, one of the few members of her illustrious Indian tribe still living in the state. Long the wife, and more recently the widow, of a sturdy farmer of Scottish descent, Violet lived on the property she had inherited from him. On her plot of over a hundred acres, she grew cotton and corn, her "cash crops," while maintaining an extensive vegetable garden for her own use.

Proud of her Cherokee heritage, she was especially fond of her brother, Stalking Horse, who many years earlier had gone off with Whip Holt to make history as an explorer, scout, trapper, and hunter in the West. After that, Stalking Horse had become the foreman on the horse ranch in Oregon now owned by Whip Holt's illustrious son, Toby. Violet, who kept in touch with her brother by letter, was justifiably proud of his accomplishments.

No detail was too small to attract Violet's complete attention. On this day, as she did every day, she spent much of the morning working in the field with her three permanent farmhands, Edward Bruton and the Calloway brothers, James and Matthew. They were hardworking young men who stayed with her because she treated them fairly and paid good wages. She allowed them to see to the hiring of temporary help during peak seasons, and they appreciated this sign of her trust in them. Unmarried, they lived together in a small cottage on the property.

Nearly an hour before mealtime, Violet returned to the house to heat some beef and vegetable soup for the hands and herself. She put the pot on the wood stove and then busied herself setting the kitchen table.

As she glanced out the kitchen window, she stiffened, and her expression became stern and disapproving. The county land agent, Thaddeus Belcher, was tying his horse to a hitching post and then limping slowly toward the house. Belcher claimed to have suffered a wound while serving in the Union cavalry, but Violet knew he had not served in either army; his background was questionable at best. Hired when manpower was very scarce, he was rumored to accept bribes from the wealthy and to act against the interests of small, struggling farm owners. Violet believed that the scandalous stories were true.

She was composed, however, when she greeted him at the kitchen door. Her calm expression successfully concealed her feelings.

Unbidden, Belcher seated himself at the kitchen table, lighted a cigar, and drew a legal-looking document from a pocket. "Miz MacDermid," he said without preamble, "I have here a court order that says I can foreclose on you because you still haven't paid your annual land fees. They were due . . . let's see, on the fifteenth of last month."

"That's correct," she replied calmly. "I've been short of cash because of the improvements we are making this year. I arranged with the tax assessor to be as late as six weeks, if need be. I'm preparing to pay the full amount of the assessment, as I always have, even though I will be slightly tardy."

"The assessor has no right to go making any such deals," Belcher challenged, chomping on his cigar and enveloping the room in smoke.

"My record and my husband's for many years speak for themselves, Mr. Belcher," Violet objected indignantly. "He never failed to pay one penny of what was due, and since his death, I have kept up his tradition. The books are clean, and you can be sure I owe nothing to anybody."

"The law is the law," he replied firmly. "Under the law, I am entitled to take action against you, and I have a choice. I can take you to court and request that your property be confiscated, or, on behalf of a generous party, I can see that you are offered a reasonable sum. I advise you to be sensible. The assessor didn't put a word of your agreement on paper, and you know blamed well that the court is not going to stand for any tall tales that some Indian is going to bring in. So I urge you, rather than lose everything, to accept a reasonable offer that I can promise you will be made for this here property."

She steeled herself. "How much?"

"Four thousand. Cash."

Violet was stunned. Only two years earlier she had been offered more than twice as much for the property, and improvements made since that time would have increased its worth.

"Take the offer or leave it," Belcher went on implacably. "It's all the same to me. If you want to go through a long fight in court that you're certain to lose, do that. It will cost you more than this blasted property is worth. You'll spend every penny you own—and then some—and still wind up on the short end of everything." He drew a pen from his pocket and indicated a place on a printed form that he was holding. "Just sign your name right here," he urged. "Now! And I'll see that you get the money right away."

He was so insistent and his attack was so clever that Violet felt almost faint. In spite of the pressure Belcher was putting on her, however, she could not bring herself to sign away her property so quickly.

Belcher, seeing that she was not ready to sign, decided to modify his tactics slightly. With a show of affability, he offered her twenty-four hours to accept or reject his proposition. Adding that he hoped that time would bring her to her senses, he left the house.

In the hours that followed, Violet agonized over her decision. By the time she retired that night, a sense of helplessness had overcome her, and she realized that she could do almost nothing to keep from losing her property. As she lay in her bed, unable to sleep, she thought of every possible solution, but the longer she pondered, the more she recognized that she was trapped by forces she could not defeat alone.

Suddenly she became aware of the smell of smoke. Alarmed, she jumped out of bed, put on a robe and slippers, and raced to a window.

She caught her breath when she saw that a large storage shed was on fire. The shed was some fifty yards away, so she could see little danger of the house catching fire. But the shed held a large quantity of seed corn, stored until the selling season, and it would all be destroyed. She had counted on the proceeds in order to survive.

It was imperative that she try to salvage what she could of her property. If she lost the corn, her financial situation would be even worse than it now was.

Responding instantly, Violet ran outside, where she saw that the hired hands were already at work. James and Matt Calloway had found buckets and were bringing water from the well pump to throw on the flames. Ed Bruton was working with an ax to clear away nearby small trees and brush, so as to keep the fire from spreading.

Immediately Violet raced to the barn, seized another bucket, and pitched in alongside the Calloways, trying to douse the fire. With each soaking, the flames sputtered and subsided briefly, but to Violet's dismay they quickly flared up again and continued their advance.

After she and the men had been working feverishly for several minutes, they were joined by two neighbors, Frank Daly and Carl Swenson, who lived on farms on the other side of the main road past Violet's place. Their houses were close enough to hers so that they had been able to see the light of the fire. They had brought buckets and joined the others.

By now Ed Bruton had cleared a small area around the shed so that the fire would be contained. But the entire shed was in flames, and because the wind was rising, the fire was burning even more furiously.

"Let the shed go, Violet," Frank Daly finally advised. "There's nothing we can do to save it."

Violet nodded dully as she watched the flames leaping high in the air.

Suddenly a strong arm encircled her shoulders. Violet turned and recognized Elizabeth Daly, Frank's handsome wife.

"Come along," she said gently. "What you need right now is a bracing cup of strong coffee." Guiding Violet, she led the way down the road to her own house, where Rebecca Swenson was waiting, with hot coffee and buttered bread, to greet them.

Violet sat at Elizabeth's kitchen table and, between sips of coffee, tried to eat some of the bread. She remained very quiet. Neither Elizabeth nor Rebecca forced her to talk, but instead offered occasional words of comfort. They were joined a while later by Frank and Carl, who had stayed behind to see that the fire burned itself out safely. They stood in the kitchen now, awkwardly trying to express their sympathy.

At last Violet felt able to speak. "I'm ruined," she said starkly. "There's nothing anyone can do to save me." Speaking in a small, cracked voice, she described her session that afternoon with Thaddeus Belcher.

Swenson and Daly exchanged a long, significant look, but it was unnecessary to put their thoughts into words. Both had the same idea: This fire was not accidental but had been set by people in Belcher's pay to increase the pressure on Violet. With her corn destroyed, she had no other source of cash available.

"It's a damn shame, Violet," Elizabeth Daly exclaimed, "but what can we do about it? All of us are in the same boat, more or less. We've known Belcher to do this to other farmers who were in no position to help themselves."

"It's useless to wish for a lot of money to fight a battle like this," Rebecca Swenson added wistfully. "You'll be better off to give up before you lose your health and your mind."

Frank Daly agreed. "The burning of your shed was a warning," he said. "That was Belcher's way of saying he's going to make it tougher for you day by day until you sign. Get out while you can, before you suffer even worse losses."

The next morning, when Belcher returned, Violet signed his form, her hand trembling and tears forming in her eyes. As soon as he had left, she steeled herself to break the news to Ed Bruton and the Calloway brothers.

The three farmhands, exhausted after their hard night's work, listened with sympathy and stunned outrage to Violet's explanation of what had occurred. Then, because they would no longer have either employment or a place to stay, they packed and left, intending to look for work over in Arkansas or in Missouri.

In the following days, numb with depression and fatigue, Violet assembled her possessions and prepared to move out. She would have to find other quarters. She knew that both the Dalys and the Swensons would be glad to take her in, but, proud as she was, Violet refused to consider that possibility. When Elizabeth Daly called on her two days after the fire, offering her a place in the Daly home, Violet instead asked her friend to help her find a house of her own in the neighborhood. Elizabeth agreed, adding that she would also seek buyers for most of Violet's livestock.

It was only after many days that Violet regained sufficient composure to realize that there was one other thing she could do in her present situation: She could write to Stalking Horse and ask for his assistance. Though her own fierce self-reliance had made her reluctant to admit the need to ask for his help, she realized that she had no choice. It was not fair to her neighbors to lean on them; she would seek help from her only living relative.

The two-year-old colt reared and pawed the air violently with his front legs. Then, his head descending close to the ground, he kicked his hind legs angrily. His rider, a tall, lean, sandy-haired man of thirty, remained calm and easily kept his seat. He winked at the little boy perched on Stalking Horse's shoulder outside the corral.

Tim Holt was wildly excited. "Hurray for Papa!" he cried. "Ride him, Papa! Ride him!"

The colt regained his breath, and with it, his energy. He dashed from one side of the corral to the other, rearing and plunging, bucking ferociously, and doing everything in his power to throw his rider.

Toby Holt not only stayed on, but made the doing appear easy.

Clarissa Holt, a handsome, large-boned woman, smiled at her husband, then turned to the gray-haired Cherokee standing beside her. "How does he do it, Stalking Horse?" she asked softly, running a hand through her red hair.

"He is very much like his father," the Cherokee replied. "He does not know the meaning of fear. And he is teaching the horse that he is the master. When I break in a colt, which I do whenever Toby is absent for a time, it takes me as much as three times as long to break it. I can't describe what he does or how he does it. I know of no one who is his equal."

The horse had stopped bucking and had begun to walk around the corral, the picture of docility. Expertly handling the training reins, Toby stopped the colt several times and started him again. The fight had gone out of the animal, who now obeyed every pressure Toby exerted.

Leaping nimbly to the ground, Toby patted the colt's nose, then took an apple from his pocket and held it in his palm. "He's all yours, boys," he called to the ranch hands sitting on the corral fence. "You might work him a little bit more to polish him around the edges, then let him go until morning. Be sure you put him through his paces first thing tomorrow, though. At this stage of his training, we don't want him to forget what he's learned."

Climbing through the corral fence, he waved to his

wife, then took his son from the Cherokee's shoulder and hugged him. He pulled out his pocket watch and glanced at it.

"I've got a job for you, White Elk," he said to a young Indian boy, Stalking Horse's adopted child, who had strolled up and joined the small party. "And for you, too, Tim. Climb aboard your ponies and ride to the front gate. The mail should have arrived by now. Bring it back, and we'll take a look at it over dinner."

With approval, he watched as the ten-year-old Indian boy and his own four-year-old son mounted and went cantering off. Both were accomplished riders. "It won't be long," he said to Clarissa, "before those two are breaking in colts."

Clarissa asked Stalking Horse to stay for the noon meal, and the Cherokee promptly accepted, walking back to the house with her and Toby. Clarissa busied herself at the stove, frying potatoes and preparing beef-steaks for broiling, while the men seated themselves at a spacious table, discussing the training program for colts.

When the boys returned from the mailbox, White Elk, proud of his ability to read, brandished a letter. "This is for you," he said to Stalking Horse. "It's from a lady named Violet Flower!"

"My sister!" Stalking Horse exclaimed. "I have not heard from her in a long time." He took the envelope, opened it, and eagerly began to read the letter. He frowned and reread it, this time more slowly. It was obvious he was disturbed.

"What's wrong?" Toby asked.

Stalking Horse handed him the letter, and as Toby began to read it, the Cherokee explained his sister's predicament to Clarissa, who looked on sympathetically from her place at the stove.

"Oh, dear!" Clarissa exclaimed when Stalking Horse had finished. "What will become of her?"

"She's relatively fortunate," Toby remarked as he read the letter, "in that she's been able to rent a cottage from a neighbor not too far down the road. She can even keep a few of her horses and some poultry." He turned to Stalking Horse. "You read the postscript?"

"Yes, she says the land agent turned her farm over to a stranger. Now men are showing up there, and they've begun to build a large barracks, apparently to house them. They are said to be doing military drills, even shooting at targets."

Clarissa raised an eyebrow. "Are they connected with the United States Army in some way?"

"All that my sister and her neighbors know is that there seems to be no connection. She has no idea as to the identity of the men. It seems to be quite mysterious."

Clarissa looked at her husband, a question in her eyes.

Toby spoke emphatically. "I don't like this at all. There's a bad smell to it."

"Violet has asked for my help, and that is unusual in itself," Stalking Horse said. "For the first time since she was a child, she admits she needs me. Even when she was married to Walt MacDermid, she always was one to expect to do for herself. If it is all right with you, Toby, I would like to go to Tennessee immediately. I would take White Elk. The ranch is in good shape and—"

"Never mind the ranch," Toby interrupted. "We can manage somehow without you. You go to Violet right away and do everything in your power to help her."

"I will. Thank you," Stalking Horse said. "I will go into Portland right after dinner and make arrangements for travel."

"Do you need any money?" Toby inquired.

"No, thank you. I have enough."

"Be sure to keep us informed of developments," Toby urged firmly. "If you need help of any kind, just let me know. There's something very wrong about the way your sister has been treated. What's more, I don't like the idea of mysterious armed men parading and practicing target shooting on her property. Let me know all the details. I'll expect you to ask for assistance, if you need it".

II

Gazing at the countryside as the transcontinental train chugged eastward from San Francisco, Stalking Horse marveled at the changes that had taken place in three decades. To him, it seemed only yesterday he had ridden ahead of the wagon train, ranging far into virgin wilderness, reporting at sundown every evening to Whip Holt, the wagon master. The pioneers who crossed America to Oregon had faced untold hardships. Subjected to the elements, to the hazards of the great prairies and the sky-high mountains, to the dangers from hostile tribes and from enemies of their nation, they had pressed on and on, determined to reach their goal. They had known thirst and starvation, floods and blizzards, and all the other perverse elements of nature. But they had kept on—and they had won.

Now, those who crossed the continent could sit in relative comfort, as Stalking Horse and White Elk were able to do. Sturdy railroad cars sheltered them from cold and heat, rain and snow; and armed guards on every train protected passengers from bandits and from renegade Indians. Best of all, the journey lasted little more than a week, compared with the many months it had taken the first wagon trains to creep slowly across America.

Stalking Horse gazed at White Elk, who was absorbed in the passing scene, the foothills of the Rocky

Mountains in eastern Colorado. Though jointly the ward of Stalking Horse and Pamela Randall—a Holt family friend in Idaho—the boy was spending more and more of his time these days in Stalking Horse's care, an arrangement that thoroughly satisfied the Cherokee. He enjoyed his company and never ceased to marvel at the boy's capacity to learn.

White Elk sat with his nose pressed against the window, his eyes riveted on the rolling hills, the intermittent stands of tall trees, and on occasion, the lone farmhouse etched against a pale blue sky.

It was not difficult to imagine how the boy felt, Stalking Horse thought. Closing his eyes, the Cherokee imagined that he could breathe in the pure air and enjoy the invigorating breeze that swept down from the majestic heights of the Rockies.

White Elk's urgent whisper cut into his reverie. "Look!" the boy exclaimed in an awed voice.

Stalking Horse opened his eyes, and in the distance he saw a small herd of buffalo, including a bull, several cows, and many calves, who were grazing peacefully.

"Buffalo!" White Elk said ecstatically. "Are they really buffalo?"

Stalking Horse successfully fought a desire to smile. "Yes, boy," he said solemnly, "they really are buffalo."

"I'd give anything if we could ride on the cowcatcher and shoot buffalo from there. Do you suppose we could do that?"

Stalking Horse shook his head. "The railroad would not permit it," he said. "They would tell you it was too dangerous, and I am afraid it would be. Besides, shooting from a moving train is not like a real buffalo hunt."

He wondered whether the day of the genuine buffalo hunt would be ended forever by the time White Elk had grown to manhood. Although it was hard to believe, the boy might never know the thrill of being in

the midst of a stampeding herd of wild beasts racing
madly past him, barely skirting him, so close that he
could feel their hot breath. On more occasions than he
could remember, Stalking Horse had participated in a
buffalo hunt and had been rewarded with a steak of the
juicy meat, broiled over an open fire. The coming of
civilization had made daily life far simpler and less
difficult in what had been the frontier lands. But at the
same time, the joys he had experienced in his youth
were fast disappearing.

He sighed, and his bony hand fell on the youngster's narrow shoulder. Stalking Horse let it rest there
as he stared with unseeing eyes at what had been the
great wilderness of North America until he and men
like him had tamed it.

It was dusk when Stalking Horse and White Elk
arrived at Violet's small house. She immediately cooked
and served her guests a simple but hearty supper. Then
she put White Elk to bed and rejoined her brother in
the tiny kitchen. Busying herself at the stove, she filled
two cups with a steaming brew and sat down opposite
her brother.

As Stalking Horse sipped his drink, tears appeared
in his eyes. When he spoke, he addressed Violet Flower
in their native Cherokee tongue. "I have not tasted
such good sassafras tea," he said, "since it was brewed
for us by our mother when we were children. You
learned the art from her well, my sister. It tastes just as
it has tasted in my memory all these years."

"That is good," she said, replying in the same
tongue. "Many things change in this life, but much that
is important remains as it has always been."

For a time they drank in silence, then Stalking
Horse shifted to English. "What new developments
have taken place," he asked, "since you wrote to me
about the men who have taken possession of your farm?"

"The leader appears to have plenty of money to pay whatever was necessary for him to take it over," Violet replied, "because the neighbors tell me he keeps adding new buildings. Newcomers seem to arrive two or three days a week. Essentially, though, I have learned nothing beyond what I wrote to you, nor have my neighbors."

Stalking Horse finished his tea, pushed back his chair, and buckled on a weapons belt, which had a repeating pistol hanging from one hip and a double-edged knife on the other. "It is time that this mystery is solved," he said. "I am going out to the farm and learn what I can."

"Wouldn't you be wise to wait at least a day until you have had a chance to rest properly?" Violet protested.

Her brother smiled. "I had nothing to do, other than sleep and rest, all the way on the train. I must stretch my muscles again."

He set out at once, following the road until he approached the farm. Here he made his way in the dark into a copse of trees and walked silently, taking care to leave no trail. He remained under cover until buildings came into view in the moonlight, then followed the edge of the woods in a half circle to his left. At last he came to a hill and peered out into the open, where he could make out several man-sized dummies. He judged this to be a target practice area, so he settled down in thick foliage, making certain he was invisible from beyond. There he waited for daylight.

Long experienced in reconnaissance, Stalking Horse felt completely relaxed. He fell asleep, dozing until daybreak, when the rising sun lightened the sky over the trees sufficiently to awaken him. He felt a cold chill move up his spine when he heard the notes of a bugle sounding, followed immediately by a rumble of voices. From his vantage point, he watched as what appeared to be several hundred men, clad in dark green uni-

forms, marched in formation to a long, low building.
There, his nose told him, they were receiving a breakfast of bacon and eggs.

Later they scattered, and about fifty, led by two
others, approached the hill adjacent to the area near
Stalking Horse's hiding place. Paper targets were pinned
to the wooden dummies, and an officer wearing the
insignia of a major, whose voice betrayed a drawl when
he shouted instructions, outlined the objectives for his
men. They were to storm the hill, firing at the dummies as they went. A second officer, wearing the bars of
a captain and speaking in a distinctive New England
twang, warned them to be sure to hug the ground as
they advanced. He threatened to shoot down any soldier who remained completely upright. This warning
was greeted by nervous laughter.

Stalking Horse assumed that the officers, obviously
accustomed to command, were veterans of the Confederate or Union armies. He watched with interest as the
men went through the exercise, dashing up the hill one
at a time and firing at the dummy targets as they
advanced. Most of them crouched low; however, two
apparently had forgotten the captain's warning. He fired
warning shots directly over their heads, forcing them to
double over as they ran.

After watching for three-quarters of an hour, Stalking Horse had seen enough. Silently, using the skills
that were second nature to him, he retraced his steps,
noting another company of men in close-order drill on
what appeared to be a parade ground. Other troops
were busily cleaning their rifles.

When he left the farm, he did not return to the
road for another half mile. Only then did he venture
into the open.

By that time, he had decided on a course of action.
He knew that he lacked sufficient evidence to persuade

authorities to act, for even though he had seen military training, he could not put his finger on anything illegal. Nevertheless, a sixth sense told him that the troops who were undergoing such intense training were up to no good.

A realist, Stalking Horse knew he had stumbled onto a situation too complex and potentially too important for him to handle alone. He was, after all, an Indian, whose credibility and influence in the white man's world would be limited. He needed the services and expertise of someone like Toby Holt. The more that Stalking Horse thought about it, the more convinced he became that only Toby would know what to do.

Stopping briefly at his sister's house, where he declined to eat until his return, he saddled a horse and rode off at once for Memphis. Arriving there by noon, he went to a telegraph office and dispatched a long message to Toby, cloaking the most telling references in a code Toby would recognize.

Stalking Horse assured himself that Toby would know what needed to be done. For the first time since receiving Violet's letter, he felt a reasonable measure of peace of mind.

Toby Holt was preoccupied on the short journey from his ranch to Fort Vancouver on the Washington Territory side of the Columbia River. Accompanied by his wife and son, he crossed in a boat sent by his stepfather, Leland Blake, commander of the Army of the West. When they reached the far shore, they found a carriage manned by a master sergeant awaiting. Toby remained silent and distant on the drive to the house of his mother and stepfather.

While young Tim celebrated his increased fluency of speech by jabbering incessantly, his father occasionally nodded absently, not listening to a word.

"Timmy," Clarissa suggested, "why don't you wait until we get to Grandma and Grandpa's house, and then you can tell all these wonderful things to Grandma. Daddy is very busy thinking about business right now. He can't really pay much attention to what you're trying to tell him."

"Thanks, my dear," Toby said apologetically. "I'm sorry, but that telegram from Stalking Horse really has my mind in an uproar. I won't be able to relax until I've discussed it with the general in detail."

"I know, dear," she answered, and reaching out, she put a hand over his. "I know, too, how you feel about going off on your various missions and leaving Tim and me at the ranch. I just want to assure you that you're free to do whatever you feel necessary. At least you're not going as far as China this time. I won't stand in your way."

"Clarissa, I know I can always count on you to recognize what has to be done," he replied.

"Why don't we wait until we hear how the general reacts?"

He agreed, and they both fell silent. Tim resumed his nonstop jabbering, but neither of his parents paid much attention to his words. At last the carriage drew up before the spacious house of the commanding general on the Fort Vancouver grounds.

Eulalia Blake, still a beautiful woman with only a few streaks of gray in her abundant dark hair, was the first to greet them at the door. She kissed her son and daughter-in-law, then gathered Tim into her arms. As the little boy hugged her, the tall, trim figure of General Blake appeared. Seeing him, Tim gravely raised his hand in a military salute. The general returned the salute before taking the child from his wife and hugging him.

"Thank you for having us here on such short notice," Toby said to his mother. Then he turned to his stepfather. "We just got word on something important earlier today, and I thought it best to talk with you as soon as possible."

General Blake put his grandson down. "Come into the study with me, Toby," he said. "We'll have a chance to chat before dinner."

In the study Toby first took out the letter that Stalking Horse had received from Violet. "The best way to begin is to show you this," he said. "It's a letter Stalking Horse received from his sister, a widow who lives in Tennessee. Until very recently, she made her home on a large farm that she and her late husband owned. The letter speaks for itself, I believe." They sat, and General Blake carefully read the letter.

"What's all this about a military camp?" he asked in some bewilderment. "The army has no installations in the vicinity of Memphis."

"For some time I knew only what Violet wrote in her letter," Toby replied. "Stalking Horse left promptly for Tennessee, and I've been waiting for his report. Now I have it, and I'll show it to you."

"Meanwhile, if you don't mind, Toby," the general said, "I will retain this letter in order to have a clean copy made that I can send on to the War Department. I expect to send an overnight wire about it to the chief of staff. You've done the proper thing in calling this matter to my attention."

"The worst is yet to come," Toby said. "It's in the report that I received only today."

"Our country and its leaders look with disfavor on armed conspirators, you may be sure," the general went on. "What you have shown me so far brings up a number of questions. Who is behind this group, and who is financing it? Who is the commanding officer, and where are the troops being recruited? For what purpose is this group being established? It disturbs me greatly. Before I see Stalking Horse's report, let me ask: Do you think he's qualified to investigate and obtain the whole story?"

"Having known him all my life," Toby said, "I trust him anywhere, any time, but I can't necessarily swear he's capable of carrying out a military intelligence function. Someone with more training may be needed. The message I received today only confirms that fact. I see the need to become personally involved." He handed over the telegram.

General Blake read it in silence, his jaw tightening. "This confirms our worst suspicions," he said. "Are you willing to make yourself available to accept another government assignment?"

"If you're concerned about my leaving Clarissa again while I perform a service for the government, dismiss it from your mind. She seems to be as upset as I am; this wire convinces her, as it does me, that Stalking Horse really isn't capable of handling this problem alone. So, regardless of whether or not I have an official assignment from the army, I intend to leave for Tennessee immediately."

"You would also conduct an official investigation, then?"

"Of course," Toby replied.

"You may prefer to operate on your own, at least at first," the general said. "But feel free to call on local authorities if you need assistance. The secretary of the army will be notified, of course, and you may rest assured that authorities for the district that includes Tennessee will be instructed to cooperate with you, if you find it advisable to call on them."

"Do I gather correctly that I have the freedom to handle the matter in the best way I see fit?"

"By all means," General Blake assured him. "You

will have the full financial support of the government, I feel confident. And at least until we learn more about the formation of this private armed force and the reason for its existence, confidentiality seems highly advisable."

"You can count on me, sir!"

"We always do," Lee Blake told him, smiling. "It has become a habit for the United States to call on Toby Holt whenever an emergency threatens the country's well-being."

General Blake's transportation officer arranged for Toby's travel with a military courier from Portland to make connections with a train from San Francisco.

"Are you sure you'll be able to run the ranch with both Stalking Horse and me away?" Toby asked Clarissa uncertainly.

She pondered the question and finally replied. "As nearly as I can judge, I should be able to manage. The hands are capable, as you know, and every man knows his job. If anything unexpected comes up or if an emergency arises that I can't handle, I can go to a lot of our friends for advice and help. And I can always turn to your mother and the general."

"If difficulties become too great to handle," he urged, "send me a wire and I probably could be back within a week."

Clarissa nodded as though she agreed, but in actuality she already had made up her mind: Under no circumstances would she take Toby away from his newest task.

He smiled, hoping to reassure her. She returned his smile, silently telling him in that way not to worry about her or the ranch. She wanted him to have nothing other than his mission to concern him.

When the time came for him to leave, Toby put his arms around her, drew her to him, and they kissed.

She was prepared for another separation, but in spite of her attempt to be brave, she sighed tremulously.

"I love you," he murmured tenderly yet passionately.

"I love you, too," she whispered in reply, then raised a finger to his lips. "We have no need to say anything, Toby. I know how you feel, and you know how I feel. We've so often sworn that each separation will be our last, but the country's need for you is too great, and this time, more than the country's need is at stake. Stalking Horse, whose loyalty to you is greater than that of anyone else on earth, requires your help for his sister's sake. So you and I have no choice. We can't let our own selfish desires get in the way of what must be done."

"You're right," he said, setting his jaw firmly.

All the way to San Francisco, he carried an image of Clarissa in his mind, her huge eyes on the verge of tears, her lips trembling as she held one hand raised in a farewell salute.

Stalking Horse met Toby's train when it arrived in Memphis. As they rode out to Violet's cottage, they discussed her situation and the discoveries that Stalking Horse had made on his reconnaissance journeys to the farm.

"I have made three visits to the property," Stalking Horse reported, "all without anyone's knowledge. The last two simply confirmed my first findings. It is definitely a military camp, and troops certainly are being trained. But so far, I have not learned anything about who commands them or the reasons they were organized. Because Violet is my sister, I have refrained from probing too far, for fear I might be discovered and then found to have a connection with her."

"I much prefer to have you keep watch on the

perimeters of the camp," Toby said, "and especially to watch the entrances and exits for anyone who might be recognizable. I'll take over the rest."

When they reached the cottage, Violet greeted Toby warmly. "You're not alone, Violet," he said to her reassuringly. "We're here to help. I have the names of competent attorneys in Memphis who could bring court actions against the land agent and the people who have taken over your property. Before we attract attention by doing that, however, I'd like to do some snooping around on my own, to see what I can learn about the gang that's camped on your land."

Anxious to start right away, Toby took time only for a light meal, then prepared to leave for the farm. He would need a mount for the ride, so he was pleased to find that Violet had been able to keep several of her prize horses, as well as a fine saddle, bridle, and other equipment he required.

As he was saddling a horse, Stalking Horse appeared at his side. "Watch your step," the Cherokee urged. "I would hate to have anything happen to you."

"I'll be careful," Toby assured him, and, mounting, he rode off in the direction of Violet's old property.

When Toby approached the main entrance to the farm, he was not surprised to see a sentry post just inside the gate. Four young men in dark green uniforms were standing sentry duty. One approached and barred Toby's way with a rifle. "Sorry," he said, his manner neither churlish nor friendly, "but no visitors are allowed."

"I have come to see the person in charge," Toby answered firmly, unimpressed by the rifle and not yielding an inch.

"What do you want to see him about?" the soldier persisted.

"That's my private business," Toby replied, dismounting with a show of casual unconcern.

"Wait here," the man said, then disappeared into a nearby shack. A few moments later, a burly man emerged, adjusting the visor of his field cap. He, too, wore a dark green uniform, but on his shoulders were the twin bars of a captain in the U.S. Army. He peered at Toby, his manner belligerent.

"What do you want?" he demanded.

"As I've told your friend here," Toby replied, refusing to use military forms of address, "I've come to see the person in charge."

"What about?" The officer's voice was antagonistic.

"A private matter that concerns only him and me," Toby told him quietly.

"He has no business with the likes of you." The officer waved menacingly, his hand resting for an instant on the open flap of his holster.

Toby continued to hold his ground. "May I know his name?"

"No, you may not!" The captain was working himself into a rage. "See here, mister! I tried to be polite, but I guess you don't understand polite talk. Now I'll tell you plain. Either you'll get the hell off this land and stay off, or you'll never have a chance to go anywhere under your own power again. Do I make myself clear?"

The officer started to reach for his weapon, but before he had a chance to draw it, he found himself staring into the muzzle of a repeating pistol. Toby had drawn with lightning speed.

"You listen to me," Toby said amiably. "Keep a civil tongue in your head when you're addressing me, or you'll have no opportunity to address anyone, ever again. Right now, you can order your friends to throw their rifles to the ground. It makes me a mite nervous when rifles are being pointed at me."

The captain gave the necessary order in a surly voice, and the men obeyed immediately.

"Now, hold your own pistol by the barrel and hand it to me," Toby said.

The officer did as he was told, and Toby, using his free hand, took the pistol. Still keeping the man covered, Toby opened the cylinder and emptied out the bullets; then he handed the weapon back, butt first. "Here's your toy," he said to the humiliated officer.

"The next time you threaten somebody," Toby told him in a seemingly friendly way, "make sure your firearms are operable and you know who your enemy is." He turned and mounted his horse; then, tipping his broad-brimmed hat, he showed his contempt for the sentries by abruptly wheeling his mount around, turning his back on them, and moving away at a slow trot. The men were so startled that not one ventured to fire a parting shot.

Red Leary was an ordinary-looking citizen, neither old nor young, tall nor short, fat nor thin. But everyone in Memphis recognized him as head of the Mackerels, a gang that ruled the city's underworld with an iron hand. Having disposed of two other rival organizations, the Mackerels had recently emerged as the only remaining gang of importance in Memphis. As their leader, Red Leary was universally feared and respected.

In one gambling establishment, the proprietor and several blackjack and poker dealers were relaxing when Leary strolled in. Three subordinates casually followed behind him. It was not yet noon, too early for a gaming house to be open, and no customers were on hand.

" 'Morning, DeWitt," Leary called out in a casual tone, but with a hint of menace.

"Good morning, Mr. Leary," the proprietor replied nervously. "How are you?"

"Oh, I have no complaints," Leary told him, "except that you've welshed on me once too often. I can't have you deciding, all by your lonesome, when and whether you are going to pay me for all I have done for you. The fact is, you've been cheating me for months."

DeWitt stared at him, white-faced. "I'll pay up," he promised, panic-stricken. "And I'll do better in the future."

"You'll pay, all right," Leary said calmly, "but you also have a lesson to learn about what happens to cheaters and deadbeats in this town."

"No!" the proprietor shouted. "Look, I said I'd pay. There's no reason to take it out of my hide—"

Red Leary waved a hand to silence him, then beckoned to two of his henchmen. "Take Mr. DeWitt into the back room," he said icily, "and see if you're able to persuade him to change his ways for keeps."

The pair moved forward purposefully, each grasping DeWitt under one arm and dragging him off.

From another room, several loud thumps could be heard, followed by a scream. A moment later, the two gang members returned, still dragging the proprietor, who had blood dripping down his face onto his collar. One eye was closed.

"He's persuaded, Red," one of his men said.

Leary held out his hand. "I'll take that payment now, if you please. You know the amount, but you'd better be sure you don't try to cheat me."

The proprietor went to a safe and took from it a stack of bills. Counting them wearily, he handed the bills to Leary.

"Thanks, DeWitt." Leary tipped his hat politely and wandered out onto the street, still followed by his men. "I think we'll go home for a bite of dinner, boys," he said. "A morning's work always gives me an appetite. We'll continue to make the rounds after we put some food into our bellies." They walked a short distance to an imposing brick building, the headquarters for the Mackerels, though few people knew it.

Once inside, they proceeded to the dining room, and after downing three straight shots of whiskey, they sat at the table and immediately were served their meal. No sooner had they started, however, than yet another member of the gang entered the house and asked for Leary.

"Send him in," Leary ordered brusquely. A small, insignificant-looking man sidled into the dining room. "What's on your mind, Gibby?" Leary demanded.

Gibby shuffled his feet and tugged nervously at the open collar of his shirt. "You said I was to keep track of what's goin' on with Miz MacDermid and that there property she lost, and that's what I been doin'," he said nervously. He was one of Leary's operatives charged with helping him keep fully informed of unusual developments anywhere in the Memphis area. The activity of Braun's men had quickly fallen into that category.

"Well, some real fireworks started poppin' today, and I thought you better know right off," Gibby added.

Leary took an oversize bite of food. "What kind of fireworks?"

"Toby Holt has come to town," Gibby said, "and he's started snoopin' around out at the MacDermid farm."

Red Leary promptly forgot his meal. "Are you sure it was Holt?" he asked.

Gibby was indignant. "You think I'm a damned fool or crazy or somethin'?" he complained. "Of course I'm sure. About six months ago, when Domino was passin' through town on his way north and Toby Holt was with him, I got a good look at Holt. I couldn't ever forget what *he* looks like."

"Tell me what's happened," Leary ordered.

Gibby took the liberty of lowering himself into a chair. "Miz MacDermid is a sister of an old Indian who works for Holt on his ranch. He must have rung an alarm bell, to get Holt to come chargin' in here all the way from Oregon. And now he's snoopin' around. I happened to be watchin' today when the sentries apparently tried to get tough with him, and he pulled his pistol on them before they could move. They didn't want to let him onto the property, but they didn't hurt him none, neither. He just rode away leaving them with their mouths open."

"What happens next? Any idea?"

Gibby shrugged. "Who the hell knows? I got a good look at Holt's face when he went ridin' off. He was disappointed, but he wasn't too riled up, except that he had a funny look in his eyes. A look that I thought meant business, and you can bet he's goin' to keep up until he finds out more about that place. Them soldiers said he couldn't enter, but he ain't goin' to let that stop him, not for a minute."

Leary gazed at the ceiling and sighed quietly. "Domino will want to know about this right off," he said, referring to the gang overlord who was the leader of an all-powerful band of criminals in New Orleans. "He and Holt are old chums. They've worked together before."

He spoke accurately. Although Toby and Domino stood on opposite sides of the law, they had cooperated in eliminating common enemies. In the process, they had become friends, establishing a degree of mutual trust and even admiration.

"Get me a pen and paper, somebody," Leary directed. "I'm going to get off a wire to Domino right now!"

That same evening, Domino was having dinner with an extraordinarily attractive young woman in the dining room of his New Orleans home. As always, with her red hair falling below her shoulders and her luminous eyes of intense green, she looked lovelier than anyone Domino could remember having seen, other than her mother. The great secret of their relationship was that the young woman, Martha, was his daughter. For business purposes, as well as personal reasons, no one else in the world knew that.

Their meal was interrupted by the arrival of the most trusted of Domino's lieutenants, Eddie Neff, who entered the dining room without apology, took a chair adjacent to his superior, and handed him a telegram. Domino read it immediately, then shook his head and muttered, "Damn!"

"What's the matter?" Martha asked.

"Toby Holt may be in trouble. He's probably biting off more than he can chew this time!"

Martha was instantly concerned. Intimately associated with Toby in some of his joint ventures with her father, she was pleased that their acquaintance had ripened into a complex friendship. She was reluctant to admit, even to herself, that she liked Toby too much for her own good. She knew he was married, and he had made it plain on a number of occasions that he was devoted to his wife. That knowledge, on the other hand, in no way diminished her feelings toward him.

She tried to conceal her alarm. "What's this all about?" she asked Domino.

"A disreputable county land agent cheated an old woman out of her farm and has turned the property over to someone who has about a thousand men training for military operations on the farm." Domino spoke rapidly as he explained the situation. "Toby has shown up in Memphis because the woman's brother is the foreman of his ranch, and I suppose the old woman wants his help."

"That seems logical," Martha observed.

"Toby's too proud to ask for help," Domino went on, "but I suspect he'll need it, whether he wants it or not."

"I'm going to Memphis!" Martha announced. "I'll take the northbound boat up tomorrow."

Domino and Neff exchanged helpless glances.

"Think twice," Domino told her, "before you do anything rash."

"I've already done all the thinking that's necessary;" she replied firmly. "I'm going!"

"What makes you think you could be of greater help than anyone else I might send?" her father demanded.

"I'm a crack shot, both with pistol and rifle," she reminded him, "and I enjoy the advantage of having watched you in operation. What's more, a woman can do things that a man can't."

"Won't you at least ease my mind by taking someone along, to help you in case of an emergency?" Domino countered.

"Definitely not," Martha replied emphatically. "I appreciate your concern, but it's really best that I work alone."

Domino knew it would be a waste of time to offer further arguments. Martha had obviously already made up her mind and would pay no attention to anything he might say.

Domino glanced at Eddie, rolled his eyes upward in surrender, and said to her, "And don't hesitate to ask for reinforcements if you feel they're necessary. Oh, yes—and be sure that Toby understands that your joining him is your idea, not mine."

Red Leary was numb, transfixed by the impact of Martha's beauty. Blushing and stammering like an infatuated schoolboy, he invited her to dine at one of the better restaurants in Memphis, and he was elated when she accepted. Not until they had eaten their main course did she reveal her reason for having approached him.

"Domino sent me here to try to help Toby Holt," she said. "He may be a famous investigator and a wonderful operator, but I know him well, and he's too stubborn to recognize the odds against him. Your wire seems to suggest he might be up against something big."

"The man in charge out there, according to my men, is a bad one. He's mean and he's tough, and he seems to have lots of money."

"What else do you know about him?" Martha persisted.

Leary shrugged. "If you mean why is he training men out at the MacDermid place, I'm damned if I know. He keeps his reasons close to his chest. From some loose talk, we've managed to learn his name— Emil Braun—and that he hails from Baltimore. In the war he was an officer in the Union Army, of all things. His wife came with him from Baltimore, and she lives with him in the MacDermid farmhouse.

"For some reason she looks scared to death of her own shadow, much less him. She appears to be a follower of the Reverend Dennis Dillon. She's been attending his services ever since she and her husband arrived in the area."

"The name Dillon sounds familiar," Martha mused.

"He's a mighty popular preacher hereabouts," Leary said. "Also, he's a mystic. Claims to be in touch with the dead, and receives all kinds of messages from them. He mixes his mysticism with his religion, and the people who go to his church eat it up. I suspect he's a phony, but I don't know much about those things."

She was frowning, but suddenly her brow cleared. She remembered that her father had done a considerable favor for a clergyman named Dennis Dillon some years earlier. The minister had been a patron of a bordello owned by Domino at the time the police raided it. The clergyman had been able to avoid considerable embarrassment when one of Domino's men sneaked him out a back door.

"Dillon is indebted to Domino," she said, not bothering to explain. She lightly fingered her necklace. Two tiny jade dominoes set with diamonds hung from a gold chain. This was her form of identification when meeting associates of Domino. "I think I'll just go to his church on Sunday, and we'll see what progress we can make from there. I'm not even going to let Toby know I'm in Memphis until I have some specific information to offer."

III

The Reverend Dennis Dillon's congregation was made up mainly of local farmhands and factory workers. On this particular Sunday morning, they had something other than the sermon to think about.

In their midst sat an incomparably beautiful redhead. Her grooming was immaculate, and the other churchgoers realized that her clothes, modest yet somehow revealing, were worth a fortune. Everyone in church watched her all through the service.

Mr. Dillon could not take his eyes from her, either. Had she wandered into his church by mistake? He was conscious of her every move, of every change in her expression as he preached on his favorite subject, communication with the afterworld.

After the service, almost everyone continued to watch her as she stood patiently in the long line, waiting to exchange a word at the door with the minister. Perhaps, some of the worshipers thought optimistically, she would be only the first of many upper-class residents of Memphis to attend their services; they had visions of the church's attaining a far greater financial stability, thanks to contributions from new and well-to-do parishioners.

At last the young woman stood in front of the clergyman. Shaking his hand, she addressed him in such a low tone that even members of the congregation

who strained to make out what she was saying could not
understand a single word.

"I come from Domino," she told him. "I'm sure
you remember the favor that his representative did for
you a number of years ago in New Orleans."

He flushed violently. "I remember him well," he
muttered. "What can I do for you?"

"I am eager to exchange a few words with you in
private," Martha said.

"Of course," he replied very quickly. "Perhaps you
would be good enough to stand to one side while I
exchange the morning's greetings with the rest of my
congregation."

When they saw the woman waiting for the clergyman and then strolling with him to the parsonage, the
remaining worshipers shook their heads and whispered
to one another. One young parishioner even suggested
that their minister might be having a romance or an
affair with the beautiful stranger, but others rejected
this notion.

After the minister and his guest entered his sparsely
furnished home, he offered Martha a seat and lowered
himself into a rocking chair opposite her. He picked up
a Bible and held it in front of him as though it were a
shield to ward off whatever evil she might be intending
to perpetrate.

"I'll be grateful," Martha said, coming to the point
at once, "for any information you can give me about a
man named Emil Braun."

"You are speaking, I believe, of dear Laura Braun's
husband. I regret to say that General Braun doesn't
belong to my church. He is not a believer."

"*General* Braun?" Martha inquired gently.

He smiled slightly. "To be sure, General Emil
Braun. Dear Laura is a relatively new but devout member in excellent standing, I am pleased to report. She
converses from time to time with her late mother in

seances that I hold. Many years ago, Laura and her mother owned a black poodle named Inky, and whenever Laura hears what she considers to be Inky barking at night, she comes to me the following day. We communicate together with her mother at that time."

Martha was certain that the clergyman was a charlatan, but her face remained expressionless. "Then it should be a fairly simple matter to hold a seance," she suggested, "and learn the nature of General Braun's business in Tennessee."

Conscious of the hold that this beautiful young woman had over him, well aware that she could ruin him if she chose, Dillon nodded eagerly. "I have no doubt," he said, "that I could arrange for precisely that."

Martha stood and began to pull on her gloves. "Then I shall be in touch with you again in a few days. Thank you for your help. You are indeed doing the Lord's work."

He saw her to the door, and she hailed a carriage-for-hire that took her to Red Leary's headquarters. Not until she was seated with the gang leader did she indulge in a laugh. "I don't suppose you know of any trick dogs that I could rent for an evening," she said, after she had explained the situation.

Leary chuckled and then suddenly struck his desk with an open palm. "I can do better than that," he told her. "I'll get Clancy to work with you."

"Who is Clancy?"

"He's one of my men," Leary explained. "He does dog imitations, barking and whimpering so you'd swear it was really a dog. He's done it only at parties so far as I know, but I don't see any reason he can't imitate Mrs. Braun's late poodle."

That same night, when darkness fell, Martha and the diminutive Clancy, a middle-aged man with a lively sense of humor, stood just outside a fence that marked the perimeter of the MacDermid farm. On the opposite side of the fence was the house that had been Violet's. Lights were visible in two rooms.

Martha kept watch on a second-floor room. It was presumably a bedchamber, and because a light could also be seen in another second-floor room, she hoped Braun and his wife occupied separate rooms.

The bedchamber window was opened wide, and by the light of an oil lamp, Laura Braun was revealed at the window, clad in a voluminous flannel nightdress, which she clutched about herself. After breathing in fresh air for a few minutes, she turned back into the room and extinguished the lamp.

No sounds could be heard but the faint chirping of crickets in the distance and the tramp of a sentry's boots as he made the rounds not far away.

Martha waited ten minutes, then motioned to Clancy, who went into action, barking, whimpering, and yipping at great lengths. His imitation of a small dog was perfect. Martha had to press her finger above her upper lip to prevent herself from laughing aloud.

The performance was effective. A lamp was lighted in the bedchamber and then was carried into the interior of the house as Laura Braun hurried to what apparently was her husband's room.

Martha and Clancy had no way of knowing just how excited Laura Braun was. She burst into her husband's room, "Did you hear that, Emil?" she cried. "Did you? My dear Inky was barking. Surely you heard him! That's the signal that my mother wants to speak to me!"

Heavy, black drapes shut out the bright sunlight, and the special room of the parsonage was in total darkness. Laura Braun and Dillon sat at opposite sides of the rickety table, which tilted dangerously. It was too dark for Laura to see the clergyman, but she felt his presence and was comforted. The more active the table became, the worse were the cold chills that ran up and down her spine.

"Your dear mother greets her beloved daughter," Dennis Dillon said in a deep, sepulchral voice. "She is pleased to see you looking well, and she not only envelops you in her loving arms, but she says her Inky is beside himself with joy and is leaping up around her with his tail wagging."

"Are you well, Mother, dear?" Laura asked tremulously.

The table trembled and shook.

"She is always well in the afterlife," Dillon assured her. "But she summoned you to this meeting because of her deep concern for you. She is worried about you and about your relationship with your husband. She had never liked Emil Braun, and she does not like him now."

"Oh, dear," Laura whimpered.

"She wants to know why you came to Tennessee, why you are living here. What is happening at the MacDermid farm that keeps your husband so busy? She must have the answer to these questions."

The table tilted so drastically that it almost landed in Laura's lap.

"You've never liked General Braun, Mother," Laura said in a whining voice. "You never have understood him. If you did, you would be proud of him, as I am."

The table continued to tilt.

"Answer the questions," Dillon prompted in his normal voice.

"Emil has told me nothing about his activities," Laura said, "but I have pressed my ear to the heat register and heard him speaking to officers in the living room. In this way, I found out about his activities, and I know what he's doing. He is no longer a colonel; he has been promoted to general and is commander of his own private army. His subordinate officers are former officers for the North and also for the South. Most of his troops are veterans, and they are united in their obedience to Emil. I gather that he is putting them through a rigorous training course, and when he is finished they will be prepared for combat. They will be able to fight anywhere, at any time."

Dennis Dillon was so interested that he almost neglected to disguise his voice for his role as a medium. "What is the purpose of this brigade?" he asked. "Why has it been formed, and what will it do?"

"I don't know exactly." Laura sounded somewhat bewildered. "Emil tells me little, so all I can tell you, Mother, dear, is that it will be used to assist certain governmental officials in this country. And Emil will keep advancing in rank and in power. He will be the leading soldier in the country. Just as President Grant was the greatest soldier of his day, so will Emil be the hero of all America!"

Dillon was satisfied with the information. He had suspected that a heathen like Emil Braun would be up to no good, and his wife had now inadvertently confirmed that he was engaged in what had the earmarks of a very strange enterprise.

Braun, the clergyman reasoned, had to be a very wealthy man in order to pay the salaries of his troops, support them during their training, and provide uniforms and arms. Perhaps, Dillon reflected, Braun would be killed if his troops ever went into action. At the very least, he could face arrest and imprisonment for conspiracy against the United States. That meant that Laura might be a widow, or at least would be able to obtain a divorce from a man who might turn out to be a criminal, even a traitor. When Laura left him, she would fall heir to that money, either through his death or because a court would confiscate his fortune and turn the funds over to her.

The more Dillon thought about Laura as an heiress, the more attractive she seemed. He saw it as a fairly simple matter to persuade her to marry him after she had rid herself of Emil Braun. He should begin to prepare the way immediately.

"I'm sure you understand my reason for not talking about Emil's activity, Mother, dear," Laura continued. "I don't really understand what it is he's doing, but I don't feel that I could betray him by going to any authorities about it. Do you agree?"

The table swayed gently now, and when Dillon next spoke, his voice was soothing. "Indeed, she does understand," he said. "And she says that you are to tell no one about the confusion and uncertainty you feel concerning your husband, but wait patiently for his plans to develop. You will be rewarded in ways that you scarcely know, and cannot even dream about as yet. She urges you to put your trust in me and heed my advice and assures you that you will not be sorry. Her parting words were to continue to treat your husband's business affairs as a secret entrusted only to you."

The table swayed again, then suddenly halted.

Dennis Dillon jumped to his feet and opened the drapes. Sunlight came streaming into the room. Laura blinked as she tried to adjust to the light.

Dillon seized her hands. "I shall try," he said humbly, "to live up to the trust that your mother has placed in me. For the present, I can only echo her good advice. Say nothing to anyone about General Braun's activities, and do nothing about them. In due time, you will receive a sign telling you what needs to be done and when you are to do it."

Her eyes shining, Laura looked at the clergyman. "I'm so grateful to you, Mr. Dillon!" she said, gushing. "I will do exactly as my dear mother suggested in your seance. I will rely on your advice and will keep Emil's information to myself. I will say and do nothing!"

*   *   *

James Martinson sat in his study, smiling benignly
at his visitor. G. D. Atkins, gray-haired and florid-
faced, was a caricaturist's delight: A cigar smoker, overweight, and almost bald, he resembled the public's
concept of a political boss. Some said he exercised
control over his party's congressional delegations from
New York, New Jersey, Pennsylvania, and Delaware,
but no one had ever been able to prove it. He held no
public office but was on close terms with many members of the Grant administration, and his power was
regarded as virtually unlimited.

"I will gladly contribute an initial twenty-five thousand dollars to the party's election fund," Martinson
said. "But I make the contribution on one condition."

"What's that?"

"As usual, I wish absolutely no attention. I don't
want a single word mentioned publicly about this, and I
will leave it up to your discretion to notify each candidate that I'm giving him financial support on a highly
personal and confidential basis. It's quite enough that
you know that I am behind you with virtually unlimited
support."

"That's wise," Atkins commented. "Damn smart of
you, Jim. I wouldn't be the least bit surprised if you are
considered as our candidate for president yourself one
of these years."

You can bet I will, Martinson thought. *I'll be president a damn sight sooner than you think!*

They rose and shook hands. Martinson saw his
visitor out, then returned to his study, where he went
over a list of officeholders and prospective candidates
he particularly wished to assist in return for support
that he could anticipate receiving from them. He was
still reviewing the list when his butler came to the
door. "I regret to interrupt you, sir. A gentleman is
here to see you. He insists."

Martinson was very annoyed. He had given strict instructions that he was not to be disturbed after Atkins's visit.

Close on the butler's heels came a man whom Martinson at first thought was a cheeky stranger. Then, with a shock, he recognized him. It was Plosz! The absence of the mustache, the hair and eyebrows darkened to black, and the spectacles he wore all contributed to a total change in his appearance. As Plosz entered, his right hand extended, the butler discreetly vanished.

Martinson ignored the outstretched hand. "I thought I gave you instructions to stay away from here," he said angrily. "And what is the meaning of this weird disguise?"

Plosz appeared unperturbed. "My appearance has changed so much that even my own mother wouldn't know me," he replied cheerfully. "How do you like these glasses? They have plain glass instead of lenses, but they do add greatly to the overall deception, don't they?"

"What's the big idea?" Martinson demanded.

"It's quite a story," Plosz said. "The brigade is forming rapidly, and your plan is moving along with commendable speed."

"I'll be glad to hear about it," Martinson replied impatiently. "And while you're at it, tell me what that has to do with this strange disguise you're wearing."

"Well, word is getting around in the right places in several cities that Braun has posts to offer good men, and at attractive terms," Plosz said. "The response has been very enthusiastic so far. Braun is giving every man who enlists a bonus of an extra month's pay, and every officer also is getting a bonus, depending on his experience. They've taken over a farm I obtained near Memphis. Braun has them working out on a regular training schedule, and the brigade is actually taking shape. Braun himself is gratified to be called a brigadier general."

Martinson's irritation eased, but he remained curious. "You still haven't told me yet why you—"

"I'm coming to that," Plosz said. "These days, I am Mr. M. P. Jonas. As Plosz, I have no visible connection whatsoever with General Braun and his army. I supply funds, but only Braun knows that, and he thinks of me as Jonas. He's a strange egocentric, and by this time he's convinced himself that he alone is responsible for what has occurred. No one could trace the financing to me as Milton Plosz, and it's totally impossible to track it through me to you."

"That's pleasing to know." Martinson relaxed and smiled broadly. "What does your captive general think is our purpose?"

"He isn't asking," Plosz said with a grin. "I led him to believe, or at least I have not discouraged the idea, that he's going to take over the government of Tennessee. He sees it as becoming his private realm. I've let him go on believing that. He's so taken with himself that he accepts it."

"That's fine," Martinson said, chuckling. "Continue to encourage that idea, and while you're about it, keep your distance from the operation. I am glad it's progressing without your being active. The more remote your association with it is, the better. No one must be allowed to make the connection to you, much less to me."

Martinson's plan, which he had revealed to no one, was exceedingly simple. When the appropriate time came—that is, when Braun's brigade was trained and ready for action—Martinson intended to reveal its existence to Congress, the press, and the public, though not his connection with its origin. So much the better, he reasoned, if Braun and his men fought arrest and efforts by the government to disband them. A corps of even a thousand men could not constitute a genuine threat to the security of the United States. But the mere existence of such a force on American soil, without the President's knowledge, would be a source of deep embarrassment to Grant as the nation's chief executive. Martinson, on the other hand, would be credited with foiling an insidious plot; his plan to become president would be far advanced. The sum he was paying for the opportunity to become a hero was a relatively small part of his fortune and well worth every penny.

"How are you fixed for money these days?" Martinson asked.

"Funds are growing a mite short," Plosz said. "Starting such an organization from scratch has proved to be an expensive business."

Martinson pulled twice at a bell rope, and a moment later, his private secretary entered. Wilma Peterson was thirty years old, brown-haired, and would have been exceptionally attractive were she not so thin and pale. She coughed behind one hand, a clue to something Martinson did not know: She was in an advanced state of consumption. She had said nothing to him about her condition because she was the sole support of a six-year-old son, Freddy. She was determined to keep working as long as possible to help provide for the boy's future after her death. Also, as seemed evident from the way she looked at Martinson, Wilma was devoted to him, and imagined that she loved him.

Having been associated with the Martinsons for years, Plosz knew that James was using Wilma for his own ends, probably including bedding her on occasion.

Stifling another cough, Wilma struck a provocative pose. She knew that if Martinson realized she was sick, he would get rid of her promptly and hire someone else. "You rang, sir?" she inquired brightly.

"Bring me twenty-five thousand from the upstairs safe, please. From the general expenditures packet, if you will."

The young woman left the room and returned with

a.thick bundle of money, which she placed on his desk. Then, leaving his study, she engaged in the suggestively swaying walk that she knew he appreciated.

"Here's enough to keep Braun operating for at least another month," Martinson said. "Feed it to him slowly so he doesn't get the idea that the supply is endless. And here's another five for you. Let me remind you that there will be more, a great deal more, if you keep on doing such good work."

Plosz thanked him as he stuffed the money into his pockets. As he left the mansion he thought this was the best job he had ever held, the best he could possibly imagine. Braun was doing all the work, and he was reaping all the profits.

Martinson, too, was satisfied and well pleased with himself. Others took the risks, while he spent nothing except money, of which he had more than enough. Each day brought him that much closer to the presidency.

Again he pulled twice on the bell rope, and when Wilma came into the office, he waved her to a chair. "I gather," he said evenly, "that you could use some extra money."

She froze, her stomach muscles contracting. *Has he been reading my mind, or has he learned of my consumption?*

"What makes you think that I have a need for extra money, James?" She used his given name only when they were alone.

"Your face gave you away when you were handing me that bundle of cash," he said shortly. "And I thought of an easy way you can pick up as much as a thousand for yourself—if you want it."

"I can't imagine anyone not wanting an extra thousand dollars," she said uneasily.

Martinson laughed and folded his hands on the desk. "Your sister, Dorothy White, is still a secretary at

West Point?" She nodded. "She still works for General Pitcher?"

Again Wilma nodded. "Yes, sir, she's secretary to General Thomas Pitcher."

"Pitcher is an important man in the army," he reminded her. "He not only is superintendent of the academy, but he's a member of the board of review, which General Sherman heads. It has only a half dozen other members, all senior major generals. As I understand it, the board passes on every important procedure the army undertakes."

"I wouldn't know anything about that," Wilma mumbled.

"What's more, General Pitcher, as a member of the board, receives General Sherman's weekly confidential review of matters coming before the board for study and decision."

"I doubt that my sister would mention something like that," Wilma said, knowing that Martinson surely had some matter of importance in mind.

"I'll not only pay you a thousand," Martinson went on, "but I will deposit twenty dollars into an account bearing your sister's name every week that she sends a copy of General Sherman's report to a certain address here in Washington. Fifty-two such reports are sent in a year, so she could earn over a thousand a year, provided she sends all the reports."

Wilma was stunned. Her prayers for financial aid were being answered, but she recognized that Martinson's offer was extremely risky. Documents of the U.S. Army Board of Review must be exceedingly confidential, she reasoned, and if any of the information was leaked deliberately, a prison term would surely result for the person who had revealed the information. Nevertheless, she felt that her best choice would be to try to persuade her sister to go along with the generous offer.

"You've been looking a little peaked lately," Martinson said in a sudden show of considerateness. "Why not take a few days off? Take your son with you and go up to West Point to visit your sister. If you are able to accomplish what I suggest, you can receive your thousand dollars immediately. Money can be deposited into Dorothy's account the very week that her first report is mailed. I have your welfare at heart, as well as hers, or I wouldn't make these suggestions."

As secretary to the superintendent of the U.S. Military Academy, Dorothy White was the sole occupant of a tidy, five-room house on the academy grounds. She was young and good-looking, with long, blond hair and inexhaustible energy. She had dreams of a comfortable and happy future; complete with a doting husband, fine clothes, and a beautiful home. Her proximity to so many military officers fed her dreams and kept them alive. She was determined to get ahead in the world rather than frittering away her life as she believed her older sister had done.

Dorothy was glad to see Wilma and Freddy when they appeared for a visit of a few days. After the boy was in bed the first night, she and Wilma settled down for a talk.

"You look like hell," Dorothy remarked bluntly.

Wilma coughed behind her hand. "I've been known to feel better," she said. "I'm a little tired these days." She had no intention of admitting, even to her sister, that she was suffering from a disease that was almost sure to take her life before long.

"You still jump whenever that tightwad Martinson cracks his whip, I suppose," Dorothy said sarcastically.

Wilma shook her head. "Really," she said, "he's not nearly as bad as you make out. He's thoughtful and generous, and anything but a skinflint."

"He always reminds me of the villains in Dickens.

If you want to work for a real dear, try General Pitcher. I never put in a full day's work for him."

"He's still a member of the U.S. Army Board of Review, I suppose?" Wilma asked.

"Of course. He'll hold that post automatically until he retires."

"I hope you're prepared to eat your words about Mr. Martinson's lack of generosity," Wilma said. "Listen to this. He will pay you twenty dollars every week for almost nothing. All you'd need to do would be to mail a copy of General Sherman's weekly report for the board to a Washington address."

Dorothy stared at her sister in openmouthed astonishment.

"I realize how upset you must be," Wilma said, "but please remember there's nothing really illegal about this offer. Mr. Martinson is assistant secretary of the Treasury, and as a member of President Grant's so-called Little Cabinet, he learns many official secrets."

"I'm not in the least upset," Dorothy responded. "I'm surprised, that's all. Why does Martinson want the board's reports? If you ask me, they're so dull they'd make any normal person scream."

"I have no idea why he wants them," Wilma said primly. "I didn't ask, and he didn't tell me. He suggested that I make you the offer, and that's exactly what I'm doing." She deliberately chose not to mention the large sum of money she would earn by setting up such an arrangement.

"Actually, I don't know of anyone in the Grant administration," Dorothy volunteered now, "who has a better reputation for being an upstanding citizen."

"Exactly!" her sister said triumphantly.

"The army is terribly chary of outsiders seeing any board of review information," Dorothy said. "Are you sure that his motives are all honest and aboveboard?"

"Naturally!" Wilma snapped. "In all the years I've

been associated with him, I never have known him to do one dishonorable thing. His word is good, and he has been honest and upright in all of his dealings." Her manner conveyed sincerity about his character, though behind her back her fingers were crossed.

Dorothy, far less intense than her sister, was thinking of the additions to her wardrobe the extra income would make possible.

"It sounds just fine to me," she concluded. "We'll let General Sherman fight it out with Mr. Martinson if they get into an argument about who is entitled to the reports and who isn't. Sure, Wilma, tell him that I'll be glad to oblige him. I can easily transcribe them mornings before I even start to work for the general."

"Here's the Washington address," Wilma told her. "Memorize it and then burn this paper."

Amused by the secretive precautions, Dorothy giggled. "You make me seem like a spy."

"On the contrary," Wilma corrected. "I'm sure everything is being done for a good cause."

"In that case," Dorothy replied airily, "I'll inaugurate the new procedure tomorrow. You can tell your Mr. Martinson that I take back all the unkind things I may have said about him. I'm going to find his money very useful."

IV

Toby Holt hated to admit, even to himself, that he was feeling stale and that his time was not being used to best advantage. Every day, he and Stalking Horse kept the armed camp under surveillance. He had soon learned the training routines and was able to predict when any given unit would be on the parade ground or at the shooting ranges. Keeping watch from the woods outside the tightly patrolled perimeter of the MacDermid property, Toby saw the veterans as they perfected their use of the new rifles and pistols that had replaced the Civil War weapons with which they were familiar.

A few days after Toby's arrival in Tennessee, he and Stalking Horse had ridden in to Memphis, to call on the sheriff.

"I understand what you're saying," the sheriff told them, after listening to their story. "But I'm afraid there's not a whole lot I can do. The purchase of your friend's land was to all appearances legal. You can challenge it in court if you like—that's your privilege— but it's not a criminal matter. Even if the new owner chooses to have men engaged in military drills on his private property, that's not my concern, unless I'm given clear evidence that this activity poses a threat to the safety of the public at large."

Toby was sorely disappointed. He had hoped that through a visit to the sheriff, he and Stalking Horse

might gain some additional information about the mysterious strangers on Violet's land, or that the sheriff
might be willing to do something about the military
operations. But for the time being, it appeared they
had no alternative but to resume the watch on Violet's
farm.

One day, while concealed behind the camp's
fence, about forty feet away from men who were
firing pistols at dummy targets, Toby decided to
join in the practice. Leveling his pistol, he timed his
shots to coincide with those of various soldiers who
were aiming at the dummies. Each time he fired, he
put a bullet into the forehead of the dummy figure. The
officer in charge was delighted by the improved accuracy of his men.

Later, Toby saw Mrs. Braun leaving the farm in a
carriage. Apparently bound for Memphis, she reached
the open road, then her carriage suddenly drew to a
halt. She climbed down in consternation to look at it;
one wheel had come loose and was almost falling off.
Her reaction was to wring her hands helplessly.

Toby saw a chance to obtain some information
about her husband, so he strolled out of the woods and
down the road toward her.

"Good morning, ma'am," he called, tipping his
broad-brimmed hat politely. "Is something wrong?"

Terrified, Laura Braun shrank from him. Toby saw
several marks on her face, and he recalled what Stalking Horse had reported about noises from the farmhouse on the previous night. Evidently Emil Braun had
beaten his wife.

"If you have some tools in the buggy, ma'am,
maybe I can fix it for you."

Laura responded by raising one hand to her throat
in fright and taking a quick backward step. Toby removed his hat. "Ma'am," he said, "I'm not a highway-

man. Do I look like a robber? I'd like to help you if you need help. But if not, I'll go my own way."

"I think you will find tools under the seat," she murmured, barely audibly.

"You do want some help then?"

Having seemingly exhausted her powers of speech, she could only nod assent.

Toby found a wrench and began to tighten the nuts on the wheel. "I hope," he said, "you are enjoying life in Tennessee, ma'am. Plenty of good fresh air here, lots of rich earth and green meadows, as well as rivers and friendly woods. A heap sight better than you'll find in the big cities back East."

"Yes," Laura murmured, "it *is* very pleasant here. I like it."

"What about General Braun?" he asked casually. "Does he like living here, too?"

Once again she retreated into her shell.

Toby could see that Laura was useless as a source of information. She was too frightened and too shy to speak freely. He realized he could not gain information from her.

In silence he finished tightening the carriage wheel, and when he was done, he merely tipped his hat again and then went on his way down the road.

That same day, he decided to adopt new tactics. "So far, we've achieved almost nothing," he said to Stalking Horse. "The number of men on the farm continues to increase, and the men are becoming more proficient in their military skills. We know quite a bit about them, but we still must find out about the origins of the organization and its purpose. We've got to get to the bottom of the story—why they chose Violet's land for their headquarters, for example. We must adopt a new approach."

"I am ready to try anything," the Cherokee replied. "It makes me sick when I see those troops marching where Violet grew her crops and when I think of the planting season she will be missing because those scoundrels are occupying her land."

"I can't predict whether this idea will work or not," Toby said, "but beginning tonight, let's work together as a team. We'll go over every inch of the farm's perimeter and see if any sector remains unguarded. If so, we'll go in and start snooping around. Maybe Braun has some correspondence or other documents that might give us a lead to the people behind him. The money in this venture isn't his, you can be certain. The funds for an enterprise this large come from people of considerable means. Anyway, we'll try to find out what we can."

At sundown they left the cottage to begin exploring the farm's borders, leaving Violet to the task of preparing supper. She was absorbed in cutting up vegetables when young White Elk arrived home. He had been enrolled in a local school at Violet's suggestion, to supplement the education he was receiving elsewhere in the white man's ways. He was carrying his books, held together with a strap and slung over one shoulder. In his other hand were a fishing pole and a string of trout.

Violet looked up as the little boy came into her kitchen. "I thought," she said, trying to sound severe, "that you were coming straight home from school so you could repair the leak in the roof."

"Oh, I fixed the roof this morning before I went off to school," White Elk replied. "I didn't have much homework tonight, so I went fishing in the brook after school, and I brought some trout home for supper."

Violet relented and looked at the fish admiringly. "You sure do have a talent for catching plump trout, White Elk," she said, "and for snaring rabbits and catching turtles, as well."

White Elk grinned in response to her praise.

"You do have some homework?" Violet asked him.

The little boy hesitated. "Well, some," he admitted.

"All right," she told him. "You get started on it while I fix the fish for supper. Get moving, now!"

An hour later, after White Elk was persuaded to go out to the pump for water to wash his hands, they sat down at the supper table.

White Elk was pleased because he had made a substantial contribution to the meal, and Violet was glad for him. Stalking Horse, who had never married, was doing a superb job of bringing up his ward, Violet reflected. The boy was learning Indian ways, and it was also plain that he was acquiring the best traits of the white settlers of the American West. Stalking Horse had told her how much both Pamela Randall and the Holts had taught the boy; with so many loving adults looking after him, his happiness seemed assured.

After supper White Elk brought in two buckets of water for Violet, one of which she heated in order to wash the dishes. The boy returned to his homework. They finished about the same time, and White Elk was glad to call it a day when Violet suggested that they go to bed. The little household got an early start every morning.

Using a spill, White Elk lighted an oil lamp from the kitchen fire, and after saying good night to Violet, he climbed up the ladder to his own quarters, a loft above the sitting room.

White Elk put his fishing pole and his skinning knife onto a small table beside his bed, and crawling into it, he pulled up the covers. Before extinguishing the lamp, he looked for the last time at his pole and knife. He was being very much a little boy to keep them nearby, but he felt better knowing that they were within easy reach at all times. Soon he dropped off to sleep.

At that very hour, in the living room of what had been Violet MacDermid's farmhouse, a decision was

being made that would profoundly affect White Elk's
life.

Emil Braun sprawled in an easy chair, taking substantial sips of gin and water as he conversed with Dick
Collins, his Civil War regimental adjutant, who was
adjutant general of his brigade, with the rank of colonel. "Think hard, Dick!" he urged. "You have a great
mind for detail, so I want you to go over everything
we're doing and tell me where you see any weak places
or any leaks."

Collins, weary of the exercise, took a swallow of his
drink. "We've reviewed every aspect very carefully,
General," he said, "and I'm damned if I can spot anything wrong."

Braun was not satisfied. "Something is niggling at
me that I can't put my finger on, although it ought to
be obvious to us. But hold on!" He continued to sip his
drink, snapping the fingers of his other hand. Suddenly
he sat bolt upright in his chair. "I've got it! You saw the
papers the county land agent brought out here the
other day," Emil explained. "The papers make me out
to be the owner of this property, which I allegedly
bought from a woman named Violet MacDermid. Well,
that's just fine, and the land agent assures me the
documents are all legal. But I'm damned if I can take
his word for it. I see a possible weakness in our position. I've never met this Mrs. MacDermid, and she's
never set eyes on me. I wonder whether, if she ever
decided to go to court for the property, she could
embarrass us. I'd have to prove to the court that I
negotiated with her and bought the place from her. I
did nothing of the sort, so she possibly could make hash
out of my story. We'd have to find another location and
move, and we'd lose stature, which is most important. I
want the American people to admire and respect us,
not to snigger at us behind their hands. You get what I
mean?"

Collins drained his drink. "I really don't see what you're driving at."

Braun sighed, pulled himself to his feet, and re-filled both glasses. "If this old woman, Violet MacDermid, goes to court to get her property back, Dick, she could be in a position to damage us. How would it look in print to see that we kicked an old Indian woman out of her home?"

Collins thought hard. "But how do we persuade her to keep her mouth shut and not to go shooting off about us?"

"That's a serious question," Braun said, "and it deserves a good answer, but I don't know the answer. I have no way of persuading her not to talk."

"So she's like a bomb that may detonate and leave us in a shambles at any time," Collins said gloomily.

"At last," Emil Braun said in relief, "you've got the whole picture."

"I've got it, but now I need to figure out what to do about it," Dick Collins said. "Any ideas, General?"

"None." Braun spread his hands in front of him.

Collins reached for the gin bottle and poured himself a fresh drink. "You know where the old woman lives?"

"Sure," Braun replied, "and so do you. You know the cottage that lies on the far side of the property fence beyond the meadow that we use for overnight campsites? That's the place."

"I've seen it plenty of times, but I never knew who lived there. Does this woman live by herself?"

"As far as I know." Braun began to smile.

"This problem might not be so hard to solve after all," Collins said. Taking a knife from a sheath attached to his belt, he began to clean his fingernails with the point.

"Some things in this world I don't want to know

about," the general said. "In fact, it's best all around if I never hear of them."

Collins's grin deepened. He was sure of himself now and knew precisely what was expected. "Don't worry, boss," he said. "I'm not going to say a word, and even this little discussion is a talk we never held."

"That's the idea." Braun paused for a moment and then added, "If you plan to leave the base at any time in the near future, Colonel Collins, I urge you to change into civilian clothes. Not that you will see anybody or be seen, mind you, but it's always best not to take chances. Oh, as a final precaution, if you intend to leave the property at some time soon, leave all your identification here. You never know when something might drop out of your pocket and embarrass you."

Collins ran his thumb along the edge of the knife blade, testing its sharpness. "Don't you worry about a thing, General," he said. "I know enough to change into other clothes and to leave my identification in camp." He stood and drained his drink. "You can stop worrying about the woman talking out of turn. You might even say she's going to be as silent as a grave."

Laughing at his idea of humor, Collins left the farmhouse and went to his own quarters in one of the new buildings. There he changed from his uniform into a nondescript woolen shirt and a pair of shapeless, heavy cotton trousers, after which he put on heavy-soled boots. He took care to attach his sheath to his belt and to insert his knife into it.

Thick banks of clouds, blowing from the direction of the Mississippi, obscured the moon and stars, and Collins was grateful that it was dark. He deliberately waited until the sentries, whose schedules he knew, had passed the fence nearest him, and then he climbed over it. It was best, he thought, if even the troops had no idea that he had a major errand to perform outside the camp.

After a short walk he came to the MacDermid cottage and circled it slowly, inspecting it and the grounds. No lights were burning in the little house, and Collins was relieved when he saw no sign of a dog. This task was going to be even easier than he had expected.

He moved close to the house and peered in through the window. There was no sign of movement. The old woman was alone and asleep, he concluded.

Drawing his knife, Collins raised the latch with his free hand, stepped inside, and silently closed the door. Then he cautiously began to look around.

The small sitting room was unoccupied, as was the kitchen. Peering through an open door, Collins made out the outlines of a chamber with two beds in it, both empty. He had no way of knowing that this room was used by Toby Holt and Stalking Horse, who at this moment were still off scouting the perimeters of Violet's old farm.

The sound of even breathing drew him back to the sitting room, and he looked through an open door into another bedchamber. He could make out a single bed, in which someone was lying, obviously asleep. He could not have arrived at a better time if he had planned his arrival, he thought, and he grinned wolfishly as he crept inch by inch toward the bedroom.

Suddenly, unexpectedly, Collins tripped over a hardwood ball that Stalking Horse had made for White Elk and that the boy had inadvertently left lying on the sitting room floor. The man stumbled and fell to one knee, cursing under his breath. However, there was no sound or movement coming from the bedroom; Violet MacDermid continued to sleep.

The sound of Collins's stumble and fall did rise to the loft, however, and penetrated the layers of White Elk's sleep. The boy woke up, his instinct telling him something was amiss. He reached for a tinderbox and flint on the bedside table in order to light his oil lamp, but a sixth sense warned him not to do so. He climbed silently out of bed and peered down from the loft. What he saw below froze his blood.

The dark figure of an unknown intruder loomed below. In the dim light coming through one window, the boy could see the man was holding a knife. It was apparent at a glance that this stranger intended great harm to Violet!

The boy threw himself into action immediately, not stopping to weigh the consequences. He snatched up his skinning knife from the table, hoping it would be sturdy enough. As he crouched at the edge of the loft, peering down, White Elk knew it would be useless to climb down and engage the man in combat, for he could not hope to win such a duel. Only one alternative remained, and he did not hesitate. Raising his knife high over his head, he jumped, aiming for the man's back.

His feet landed on Collins's shoulders, and his weight sent the man staggering forward. At the same instant, White Elk brought down his knife with all his force and plunged it into the left side of the intruder's back. Collins crumpled to the floor and lay still, in an ever-increasing pool of his blood.

Realizing he had probably killed the man, White Elk clambered to his feet and began to shout for Violet.

When she awakened, she was amazed by what she saw at the entrance to her room. She was even more astonished by the explanation that poured out of White Elk. She was questioning him when Stalking Horse and Toby returned home after a fruitless search of the farm's perimeter. They praised White Elk for his courage and for the speed with which he had responded to save Violet's life. Then Toby rode off to the nearest deputy sheriff's office, while Stalking Horse stood guard at the cottage.

Over an hour later, Toby returned with two deputies, who took copious notes. They returned the boy's knife to him after removing it from the intruder's body. After examining the body, they reported that the man had not been carrying any identifying papers, nor could they identify the dead man by his clothes.

Eventually the officers left, taking the body of the stranger with them. Toby promised White Elk a pistol of his own, as a reward. Then, when all the hubbub had died away and the house had been cleaned up, Toby and Stalking Horse returned to their bedroom.

"I don't like the looks of this situation," Toby said.

"Neither do I," Stalking Horse told him. "Who do you suppose the fellow was?"

Toby shrugged. "It's useless to speculate. I'm reasonably sure of one thing. I don't believe it was accidental that he carried no identification; that was deliberate. Without identification, there's nothing we or the sheriff or anyone else can do."

"I cannot imagine why anyone would want to kill Violet," Stalking Horse said. "She has already lost the only thing of value she's ever owned—her farm."

"Until we find out who's trying to kill her and why," Toby said, "you and I would be wise to take special precautions. Suppose we take turns standing guard over her and don't let her out of our sight."

"That will be wise, I think," Stalking Horse replied.

"I feel so helpless," Toby said, clenching his fists. "This is the first case I've had in years where there haven't been any clues or leads. We're surrounded by enemies, both personal and national, and I can't think of a thing we can do to control or trap or eliminate them. This is the strangest situation I've ever seen. And I don't like it!"

The next day the Memphis newspapers carried articles about the mysterious stranger killed by a little boy while the man was stalking Violet MacDermid in her cottage. The articles stressed the child's heroism and speculated on the intruder's identity but came to no real conclusions. The sheriff's office was quoted as saying that an investigation was under way, but that the case was unlikely to be solved.

Only one person knew for certain that the dead man was Colonel Dick Collins, and that was Emil Braun. Braun, of course, kept the information to himself and quietly appointed a new officer to the vacant post.

Collins's body remained unclaimed and unidentified, and eventually he was buried in a pauper's grave.

When Martha, still lingering in Memphis without Toby Holt's knowledge, read the newspaper account, she went straight to the headquarters of the Mackerels, where she announced her wish to see Red Leary.

Flustered by the announcement that the woman to whom he had lost his heart wanted to see him, Leary shaved quickly, nicking his chin, and then hastily put on a clean shirt and his best suit in order to make a favorable impression on her.

Aware of his mounting interest, Martha was determined to keep a space between them, so when Leary showed her to a table, she sat opposite him. Leary ordered coffee for her, and Martha handed him the newspaper articles. "What do you know about this case, Red?" she asked.

"Only what I've read, same as you," Red replied, perusing the articles. "I do try to keep up on what's going on over there."

"This bears out what Domino and I have believed from the outset," Martha said. "Toby and his friends are in grave danger. It's a sad state when the safety of their lives must depend on the intervention of a ten-year-old boy."

"How did Holt react?" Leary inquired. "Didn't he take you seriously?"

"I haven't spoken to him about it yet," Martha replied. "In fact, he doesn't know that I'm in Memphis."

Leary's face showed his surprise.

"Toby is a strange, proud man," she explained. "I have no intention of letting him know that I came to help, until I can present him with specific suggestions that would benefit him and Mrs. MacDermid. He'd reject my offer to help otherwise. That's why I'm waiting and trying to uncover something that would really assist him."

Leary studied Martha quietly and at length. "I'm sure it's no secret to you," he said at last, "that I'm very much taken with you, Martha."

"I know," she murmured.

"I took one look at you, and it just happened. I've fought the feeling," he went on, "because I haven't wanted my life complicated by a lot of romantic twaddle. I'm far too busy for that, but it hasn't done me any good. I can't control my feelings."

"I am aware of it," Martha replied, "and, frankly, I've been dreading this conversation, Red. I'm terribly sorry." She reached across the table and covered his hand with hers, then quickly withdrew it.

He continued to watch her intently. "I don't stand a chance. Is that what you're telling me?"

"Yes, Red," she said. "I'm truly sorry. I don't know what might have developed if life had been different, but it isn't." She paused and went on firmly. "I learned long ago that it's useless to speculate on what might have been. We must be realists in this world and accept life as it is."

"I know." He was silent for a time. "This is none of my business, and you don't have to answer if you don't want to, but—you're sweet on Toby Holt, aren't you?"

Martha nodded solemnly. "I'm more than sweet on him," she admitted. "I'm hopelessly in love. Ridiculous, isn't it? I've fallen in love with perhaps the one man on earth I can't have, one I can never have. I've never felt this way before, and I'll never feel this way about any man ever again. It's once in a lifetime for me, and it's all so futile. Toby is so in love with his wife he doesn't know that any other woman in the world even exists. Every time I see him, his commitment to Clarissa, his wife, is stronger. I know I'm being foolish, but what can I do? I'm no more capable of controlling the way I feel than you are. The only thing I can say that's good about all this is that I'm sure Domino knows the way I feel, but he's had the good sense not to say a word about it. He knows, as I do, that I'll just have to live with my feelings and get over them."

"I'm willing to wait," Red said.

"I wish you wouldn't," she replied.

He grinned. "Oh, I have no intention of taking a vow of celibacy," he said. "I intend to lead a normal life, and I'll take my chances that some day you may get tired of waiting for Holt. If that day comes, I'll be around."

"That's fair enough," she said.

"As a matter of fact," he added, forcing a smile, "I'm growing up. A few years ago, I would have seen to it that Holt had a fatal accident, and then I would have taken my chances of persuading you to marry me. But I've learned a few things, and I'll do my damnedest to protect him now, in spite of his own desire not to be protected."

"Last night's murder at the MacDermid cottage," Martha said, "brings matters to a head even faster than I had anticipated. I'm going to take drastic steps to gain information from Mrs. Braun about her husband."

"How do you do that?"

Martha smiled mysteriously. "I'd rather not go into details," she said, "but I'd like to borrow Clancy tomorrow."

"Sure," he replied. "What else can I do?"

"Keep watch on Violet MacDermid, without her knowledge, of course, and without the knowledge of her brother and Toby Holt. That won't be easy, but I'm sure you can manage it."

"We'll try," Leary said.

Martha was very much relieved. "Thank you, Red. It's a relief to know that if the people who are trying to kill Violet MacDermid make another attempt, you'll have men there to block them. Now, if my plans for tomorrow work out, we should know a great deal more about Emil Braun's intentions, and then I can let Toby know I'm here."

"Just remember I'll be nearby if you need me. And I'll be hanging around if you ever decide that you're tired of waiting for Toby Holt to be free."

The seance that Dennis Dillon had arranged for Laura Braun was unlike any he had held for her previously. They sat opposite each other at the same table in the darkened "seance chamber" of his house, but what made the occasion different was the secret presence of Martha and Clancy in the adjoining room. Martha was sitting with a handkerchief held in front of her mouth in order to muffle her voice.

A cotton drape separated the occupants of the two rooms, and Martha clearly heard everything, as did Clancy, when Dillon escorted Laura into the seance room. He called on the "spirits of the departed dead" to heed his call and to return in order to communicate with the living.

Finally, after judging that Dillon's exhortation had gone on long enough, Martha nodded to the little man who sat beside her. Clancy launched into his imitation of a barking dog.

Martha could not help marveling at the man's talent. If she had not known otherwise, she would have sworn that a real dog was in the room.

They could hear Dillon trying to soothe "Inky" with gentle words. Clancy obediently stopped barking and began to whimper joyfully. He did not stop until the clergyman called on the spirit of Laura Braun's late mother to rise up and join them.

"Thank you for summoning me, dear Mr. Dillon," Martha said. "Darling Laura, you look well. Life in Tennessee agrees with you, and especially your close association with dear Mr. Dillon." Martha was relieved that Laura seemingly was not disturbed that for the first time her mother's message was audible, rather than being relayed by the medium.

The exchanges of amenities continued for some time, and Martha took pains to include greetings from an aunt and two cousins who had been fond of Laura and who had died in fairly recent years, according to information provided by the minister.

Uncertain as to how long she could maintain her precarious role and refrain from giving herself away by laughing, Martha said quickly, "As you know, I've never liked or approved of Emil. I do hope he's not creating difficulties that will cause more problems for you with the authorities."

"He's so busy I hardly see him, Mother, dear," Laura replied. "In any event, you'll be pleased to learn that he's going away for a couple of weeks. I've been listening at the heat register again, and he and three of his officers are going up to St. Louis by paddle-wheel steamer a week from Friday. Then they're going to take the steamer all the way down to New Orleans before they return here. The whole trip is being made on the one ship."

Here, at last, was specific information that could be of great value! "Why are Emil and the others making this trip, Laura, dear?" Martha asked innocently.

"Emil and his staff members," Laura said, "are intending to try to locate certain men who have been mentioned as outstanding candidates for his brigade. Emil and his associates will decide which men are to be hired."

This was the only concrete information Martha had been able to acquire about Emil Braun since she came to Memphis. She questioned Laura sharply, trying to learn details, but it soon became evident that the woman had revealed all she knew about her husband's plans.

Therefore, Martha bade her "daughter" farewell until their next meeting, and Clancy brought the seance to an end by once again barking. The pair was silent while Dillon conducted Laura from the seance room and to the front door. Only when they were sure Laura had left did the two impostors emerge.

"Thank you for your cooperation and help, Mr. Dillon," Martha said. "I've finally been able to put together enough information to enable me to go to Toby Holt. At last we may be making progress!"

V

No matter how he tried to reject the feeling, Toby Holt was discouraged. He felt he had let down Stalking Horse and his sister. Only the courageous intervention of White Elk had saved Violet MacDermid's life.

Equally depressing to him, he had failed to acquire information of significance for the United States government. His opponents were proving exceptionally clever, and so far, he doubted that what he observed could be used against them.

Toby felt reasonably sure of only one fact—that Emil Braun could not be the brain responsible for the organization. Toby had sent the War Department the names of Braun and as many of his officers as he had found it possible to ascertain. The list was very short.

Two days earlier, a courier from the army's district headquarters had brought a communication containing Braun's complete army record. Braun was described as having been courageous in battle, though lacking in imagination. The letter went on to say that he often inspired confidence among his subordinates, and so his regiment distinguished itself in the field. At the same time, however, he rarely gave anyone besides himself credit for his victories, and he was quick to blame others for his mistakes. He had a quarrelsome nature and a vicious temper, and he occasionally gave vent to his opinions in outbursts that displeased his superiors.

He was also a notorious drinker. Regarded as head-strong and unreliable, he was never seriously considered for promotion beyond the grade of colonel.

The information supplied by the army made Toby even more anxious to find out who was behind Braun and why the troops had been organized. Having spent hours observing the training, he had learned nothing. Meantime, while he had been moving ineffectively, Violet MacDermid had almost been killed, very possibly by the same enemies who had stripped her of her farm.

Making his way down the road to Violet's cottage after spending the better part of the day watching men in training, Toby told himself that either he must make demonstrable progress very soon, or he would be forced to admit failure. In that case, he would have to pull out and return home to his ranch. Before giving up the case, though, he would contact General Blake or possibly authorities in Washington, to see if they could send someone to help him ferret out the truths that seemed to elude him.

As he walked along, the sweet-smelling meadow ended abruptly and was replaced by a heavily wooded area on both sides of the road. He paused to look at the trees—particularly the sycamores, oaks, and hickories, so different from the foliage of Oregon—before he moved on. Instantly he became aware of someone in the road ahead, facing him. He instinctively reached for the pistol in a holster at his side. He was so startled that he could only stare, openmouthed; his mind refused to function.

There, looking at him and smiling, a light shining in her deep green eyes, not a red hair out of place, was Martha. She was wearing a snugly tailored traveling dress that was tasteful but also showed off her lovely curves, and her feet were in stylish high-heeled shoes. Her makeup, as always, was neither too heavy nor too light and brought out every angle, every plane of her beautiful face.

"Hello, Toby," she called quietly, her tone suggesting she thought it quite natural to be greeting him in the forests of western Tennessee, hundreds of miles from her home and thousands from his.

He shoved his pistol back into his holster. "I don't believe in ghosts," he said, "but I find it hard to believe that it's really you, Martha." He advanced rapidly, so amazed to see her that he even failed to question how and why she was there.

She raised her face to his, and he grasped her by both shoulders and brushed her cheek with a light, friendly kiss.

She knew she had to be satisfied with the token sign of friendship. She had been foolish to expect more, to hope she could tempt him to kiss her full on the mouth.

"I have a horse and buggy parked in a little clearing a short distance from here," she told him. "Will you ride into Memphis with me? I have a suite at a hotel."

Thoroughly surprised and intrigued by her presence, Toby followed her to her carriage. Martha, he reflected, was perhaps the most unusual person he had ever known. Climbing onto the seat beside her, he watched her as she competently took the reins. Soon she had maneuvered onto the road and started off for the city.

"How long have you been in these parts?" he asked.

"Actually, I arrived in Memphis a few days after you did."

He peered at her. "You knew I was here? How?"

"Domino knows everything of consequence in cities under his jurisdiction."

Toby laughed. "Of course," he said. "Domino has an intelligence-gathering organization that can make the government's system look sick by comparison." He glanced at her sideways; she could feel his eyes boring into her.

"Do I gather correctly that you came to Memphis because I'm here?" he asked.

"You're too much for me, Toby Holt," Martha said, sighing. "You have an uncanny ability to read my mind. It isn't fair! A woman has a right to keep some things secret."

"I asked you a simple, direct question," he said quietly, "and I believe I'm entitled to a simple, direct answer."

Martha sighed. "If you must know, Domino was very much worried about you," she said, making no mention of her own deep concern. "He considers you an honorable person, and he was concerned for you, seeing that you were involved with an element with which you perhaps can't deal for once."

"I can deal with them as soon as I know what these people are up to and why they're doing it," he said, defending himself.

"Anyway," Martha lied, "Domino sent me here to help you."

"I see."

Martha's dazzling smile would have melted almost any man. "Let's wait until we get to the hotel before we discuss such things. We have many things to talk about." She smiled again and inquired after his family.

Toby replied at length, as she knew he would, and, without his realizing it, she guided the conversation until they arrived at the hotel. After they reached her suite, Toby refused a drink but readily agreed to a cup of tea.

Eventually Toby told her what he had learned about Emil Braun from the War Department records.

"I've learned quite a bit more about him than that," Martha replied, and explained her connection with Dennis Dillon and how she and a member of the local gang of Mackerels had assisted the clergyman in obtaining data from Laura Braun. "Her husband's something of a monster, I gather," she said. "I know she's frightened half to death of him. He drinks too much, which corroborates what you learned through the army, and he has incredible self-confidence. He's also maniacally dedicated to what he believes is right."

"All those things may be true," Toby said, "but I still feel frustrated. I don't know why this organization that he's leading is being formed, and who, if anybody, is the real force behind it. I can't seem to find out a blamed thing."

"I have a new lead that may prove useful," Martha said, and told him in more detail about the seance.

Toby sat rigid, his tea forgotten, as he listened.

"He and several of his lieutenants are going to be on board a paddle-wheeler for about two weeks," Martha said. "If we could work out some way of being on board the ship for that time, we might get any number of leads from him. It should be easier on board a ship than trying to pick up crumbs outside a fence that's guarded by sentries."

"Do you have any idea when the paddle-wheeler is going to put into port here?" Toby asked.

"She's due tomorrow afternoon and will be back again a week from Friday. That's when Braun will board her," Martha replied. "I've sent a telegram to Domino explaining and asking for his advice. I know he has some connections in the steamship company. I should have a reply by tomorrow morning."

"Thank you, Martha," he said. "I'm in your debt."

She inclined her head graciously but, knowing how proud he was, did not want to make an issue of her contribution. Instead, she stressed the importance of his role. "By tomorrow," she said, "I'm sure you'll know what to do."

"I'm inclined to take your suggestion and already be on board the paddle-wheeler when Braun boards her," Toby said. "Maybe if I stay close to him, I'll learn something."

"You mean *we'll* learn a great deal," she replied, smiling. "I'm coming with you."

"It's too dangerous," Toby replied.

"I'll be the judge of that," she responded quickly. "Besides, either I come with you or I'll wire Domino to forget about the arrangements."

"You have me there," Toby conceded, grinning. "You'll go if I do. The only thing is, I'm worried about Violet. She's had a narrow escape, as you undoubtedly know, and I don't want to leave her unprotected. Her brother will be nearby, of course, but Stalking Horse isn't as young as he once was—and as brave as White Elk is, he's only a boy. I don't know what the two of them could do to hold off a determined enemy."

Martha had no intention of admitting she had already arranged for Violet's protection; she was afraid that he might feel she had acted presumptuously. But she saw no reason not to use the arrangement to her own advantage, as a means of winning his gratitude. "Perhaps," she said, "I could talk to Red Leary, the leader of the Mackerels, between now and tomorrow morning, and arrange with him to have some of his men set up a twenty-four-hour-a-day guard over Mrs. Mac-Dermid."

"It would be wonderful if you could make such an arrangement," Toby said gratefully. "That would give me the freedom to devote my whole time to tracking Braun and company without having to worry about Violet's safety. Again, I'm in your debt."

She smiled but made no reply.

"Come to think of it," he said, "the debt is already so big there's no way I can possibly repay it."

Martha knew of a way, she reflected, but she hesi-

tated to mention that fact to him. She could only hope
that their proximity might cause him to forget his wife
long enough to turn to her.

No sooner had Captain Waldo Hummel of the
paddle-wheeler *Tennessee* put into port at Memphis, en
route downstream to New Orleans, than he was notified
that a telegram awaited him.

He read the message from Domino twice. Less
than an hour later, he sat in his quarters off the prome-
nade deck and looked at the young couple who had
called on him. The woman, who was strikingly beautiful, wore a necklace with jade and diamond dominoes.
Her escort was handsome in a rugged way. "My old
friend Domino has urged me to find temporary employment on board this ship for you two," the captain said,
removing his spectacles and running a hand through his
graying hair. "I'd like to oblige him because he's been a
very good friend for many years. But positions in the
crew aren't easy to create." He directed his full attention to the young man. "Tell me frankly, Mr. Holt, do
you consider yourself capable of running the gambling
saloon on board ship?"

"That all depends on what would be required of
me," Toby replied.

"Your principal duty," Captain Hummel told him,
"would be to act as the dealer in the poker games that
are held in the saloon. You'd make yourself available to
play with any passenger who wanted to pass the time
that way."

"It doesn't sound too rough," Toby said. "I've been
playing poker off and on since I was a youngster, and
my game is fair enough, I guess. How large a percent-
age of wins do you expect from a dealer?"

"The management of this shipping line is very
reasonable," Captain Hummel said. "We aren't trying
to make a large profit from poker. We're offering it to

our passengers merely as a way of passing the time on a long, possibly dull voyage. We don't object to our dealers making a small profit for us, and we certainly prefer not to lose money, if that can be avoided. Does that answer your question?"

"Then I'll give you an unqualified reply, sir," Toby said. "Yes, I can handle the job of a poker dealer."

"Good." It was obvious that Captain Hummel was troubled as he turned to Martha. "I'm sorry to say that we have only one staff opening for a woman at present, young lady. Would you care to be a waitress in the gaming saloon? You would be expected to wear a costume that encourages the passengers to relax and drink, and you would serve alcoholic beverages from the bar."

"I accept," Martha replied promptly. "As Domino undoubtedly explained to you in his telegram, it's very important to us that we temporarily join the staff of the *Tennessee*."

"As you no doubt can imagine," the captain said with a slight smile, "Domino was very persuasive in his telegram, but frankly, I prefer not to know your reasons. The less I know about your private matters, the more satisfied I'll be."

Toby thought his attitude was typical of many citizens: preferring ignorance to knowledge as a way of avoiding trouble.

The captain frowned. "I see one obstacle, I'm sorry to say, in the way of my adding you to my crew, and you may find it an insurmountable obstacle. We're very short of space. Business is booming lately, and we're selling out on every voyage, which means we have no cabins to spare. I have only one cabin available. You would have to share it. If you find that objectionable, I'm afraid I can't do anything for you, and I'd let Domino know accordingly."

Martha smiled blandly. "There's no problem," she

said. "One cabin will be just fine for our needs. After all, we *are* married."

Toby stared at her in astonishment.

In the meantime, Captain Hummel had accepted her statement at face value. "In that case, you're quite right. There is no problem, Mrs. Holt. And I will expect you to be on hand for work in, say, six hours. Can you do it?"

Martha had not expected to start work on board quite so soon, and she knew that Toby felt as she did. This would, however, give them the opportunity to break in on their jobs before Braun boarded the vessel. She was quick to confirm the agreement. "That will be just fine, Captain," she said. "We'll be here this evening. In fact, we'll show up a little early."

The captain then described for them some of the many conveniences offered to passengers of the *Tennessee*. At last he rose and shook hands with them, and they departed.

"We'll telegraph Domino at once, telling him of your kindness to us," Martha said. "I'm sure he'll appreciate it—as we do." She took Toby's arm, and they left the *Tennessee* together.

Toby was still so stunned that he remained silent until they reached the shore and were making their way across the dock. "I can't believe you told the captain that we're married and will share a cabin," he said at last.

Martha, still holding his arm, looked up at him, and when she spoke, her tone was sharp. "Would you have allowed prudery to disrupt our plan and prevent us from obtaining employment on the ship?" she demanded. "Surely you haven't forgotten that we're hoping to find out some important information about Emil Braun and his men!"

"I realize all that," Toby said, "but you're forgetting that space in a ship's cabin is very crowded, and for us to live in such intimacy for a period of weeks can be—well—embarrassing."

"It will be embarrassing only if we allow it to become so," she replied briskly. "We had a choice, and I took it. If you're dissatisfied, we'll call off the whole plan."

"No," Toby said, "we'll go through with the deception. We've got to find out something about Braun's activities, and our backs are to the wall."

At six o'clock that evening, Toby left Violet Mac-Dermid's cottage to pick up Martha in Memphis and report with her to the *Tennessee*. He was leaving Stalking Horse to watch over Violet during his absence, but he felt much better when he saw two of Red Leary's men in the underbrush near the cottage.

Toby was disturbed by the potential problem that he knew he would face when he and Martha shared a cabin, but he did his best to put the matter out of his mind. The problems would arise soon enough, and he saw no point in unduly anticipating them.

Their future together was called to his immediate attention, however, when he stopped at Martha's suite to pick her up en route to the ship. He noted at once that Martha was wearing a diamond ring on her left hand to enhance the role she had chosen to play as his wife. She made no mention of the ring, but she saw him look at it, and she smiled enigmatically. It was best, he decided, not to discuss the subject and thereby give it greater importance than it deserved.

Unfortunately, Toby knew that his situation was complicated by the undeniable fact that he was drawn to Martha. He not only found her exceptionally attractive, but also he could not help admiring her keen mind and her ability to analyze complicated matters. In most respects, she was unlike any other woman he had ever known. That was part of her appeal, and it also became

a danger to his home life. Among other things, her
standard of morality was different from most people's.
Her actions, consequently, were unpredictable.

They hired a carriage and driver for the short ride,
with their luggage, to the pier where the *Tennessee* was
tied up. As they approached the waterfront, Toby studied the paddle-wheeler that would be their home. The
Tennessee was a long, graceful ship with a square prow,
which was the most practical for river travel. If need
be, it could push fallen trees and other obstacles out of
her path. Locomotion was provided by the huge paddle
wheel at her stern, which was powered by a steam engine
fed with coal. Three decks were available to passengers.
The uppermost was open to the elements. Above it
stood the glass-enclosed wheelhouse, and in front of
this stood the bridge, which was for the exclusive use of
the captain and his officers.

From the captain's description, Toby knew that on
one deck were located the ship's extensive restaurant,
the gaming room, and behind it, the bar, the ship's
library, and several writing rooms. The *Tennessee*, a
new type of ship, was to be used exclusively for passenger travel. Earlier vessels also had carried freight, but
these days, cargoes, such as logs and produce, were
consigned to ships built specifically to carry such
products.

Uniformed porters took charge of the luggage, and
Martha followed them down the stairs to the cabin,
while Toby went directly to the gaming saloon to inspect his new domain.

Awaiting him there was the chief steward, Arnold
Simmons, an exceedingly tall man who was almost totally bald, although still in his thirties. He showed Toby
where the playing cards and poker chips were kept, and
also called his attention to a concealed bell rope behind
a drape. "This is for emergency use," he explained. "If
any card player drinks too much or becomes overly

excited, just pull this rope, and in a minute or two you'll have all the help you need to get the situation under control again."

"I doubt I'll be needing much help," Toby replied, smiling. "I think I can manage to control most situations myself." He opened his coat to reveal his repeating pistol in its holster at his side.

"The captain," Simmons said, "disapproves of any staff member using weapons to threaten or control passengers."

"I'm sorry," Toby said firmly, "but the captain will have to trust my judgment in the use of firearms, and so will you. I'm never without my gun."

Simmons was inclined at first to dispute the matter, but he changed his mind when he saw the expression in the clear blue eyes of the new gaming saloon master.

At last Toby knew the inevitable could be postponed no longer, and he asked for directions to his cabin. He took his time in descending the broad staircase, then started forward along a narrow hallway. He noted that the nearest bathroom was directly opposite the door of his cabin. He halted, took a deep breath, and tapped lightly at the door.

"Come in!" Martha called in a light, cheerful voice.

His misgivings increasing, Toby opened the door, stepped into the cabin, and was so startled that he felt paralyzed.

Directly in front of him was Martha, clad in a gown of green, clinging silk with a daringly low-cut neckline and a slit in her long skirt that revealed the better part of a shapely thigh whenever she moved. The effect she created would have been startling anywhere. In this confined space, it was overwhelming.

"This is the costume I'm to wear when I'm serving drinks in the gaming saloon," she said. "What do you think of it?" She pirouetted for his benefit.

"It's all right, I guess," he replied. "What there is of it."

"Now you sound just like a husband," Martha said, and laughed.

He forced a small smile in reply and looked past her at the cabin. There were two small easy chairs with a little table between them. On the wall were a washbasin and a number of shelves. The cabin was dominated by a bed—only one, he saw, and his discomfort became acute. However, he did not want to give any sign that he regarded the situation as other than normal. "It's time that we report for work," was all he said.

"Give me a few seconds to check my makeup," Martha replied, and showed no self-consciousness as she reached into her handbag for mascara and lip rouge and began to apply them.

"Here we go in our first public appearance as husband and wife," Martha said, putting the makeup back in her handbag. Preceding him out of the room, she laughed quietly as she took his arm and they started off together down the corridor. Passengers had returned to the *Tennessee* from shore excursions in Memphis, and as the couple made their way up to the gaming saloon, Martha was subjected to intense scrutiny. Her beauty caught the eye of everyone who saw her, and Toby wondered how he would feel if he were actually married to such a woman. He wondered if he would find intolerable the degree of attention that she attracted.

While he removed two decks of cards and a container of multicolored poker chips from their hiding place, Martha went off to the adjacent bar to become acquainted with the bartender with whom she would be working.

She returned after a short time, smiling mischievously as she carried two glasses filled with ice and a brown liquid. "The captain neglected to mention to us," she said, "that we get free drinks with these jobs.

The bartender has just mixed each of us a mild whiskey and water. I know you drink next to no alcohol, so yours is mostly water." She placed one glass on the table beside Toby, and when she perched on the arm of the adjacent chair, her skirt fell away from her legs.

Toby frowned but decided not to mention that in his view she was exposing too much. What she did was really none of his business.

Martha noticed his frown, however, and discreetly drew her skirt around her legs.

"I hope," Toby said, "that these disguises will pay off for us. If they don't, we're going to be in a very tough situation. We know so little about Braun and his intentions."

"I'm confident," she replied, "that we'll learn what we need to know. After all, we're ideally situated here. Domino couldn't have planned it better if he had known that these jobs existed."

She was truly a remarkable person, Toby reflected. She was worldly-wise in the ways of human beings and their weaknesses, yet she had an essential sweetness that disarmed friends and foes alike, making it possible for her to achieve more than she otherwise could. Her optimism was based on solid reasoning; she was never guilty of romanticizing or of wishful thinking. He had seen her behave with cool competence in emergencies, and he knew she was valuable as an ally, more reliable than almost any man.

But she was not a man, and he would forget that fundamental fact at his peril. He had great respect for her as a colleague, but at the same time he knew he wanted her badly as a woman, and he knew he must never give in to his ever-present desire.

Equally important was his strong suspicion that Martha felt as he did. In fact, he wondered about the alacrity with which she had stated to Captain Hummel that they were married. He could not rid himself of the realization that Martha was in all probability available. He knew she would not fight him if he tried to take her. On the contrary, he believed she would be eager to join in enthusiastic lovemaking.

Under the circumstances, it was proving exceptionally difficult for him to keep his mind on business and his hands to himself. Although he loved Clarissa, she was far away in Oregon. Temptation was proving more and more difficult to resist.

Circumstances, however, forced Toby to put his personal problems out of his mind, at least temporarily. Returning passengers were delighted to find a dealer on hand in the gaming saloon, and Toby promptly became involved in a series of poker games that lasted until well after the *Tennessee* cast off and resumed her voyage down the Mississippi.

Martha, too, was kept busy, supplying drinks for customers who thronged to the gaming saloon, and she exchanged only a few words with Toby as the evening progressed. Eventually the last card players gave up for the night, and Toby was able to engage in some simple arithmetic. He found that he was ahead a few dollars, and he was pleased that, although he had not played poker for some time, his instincts had not deserted him.

Toby knew the confrontation he had been anticipating could not be avoided any longer, and he started slowly down the aft staircase toward the cabin that he and Martha were sharing. He could feel the vibrations caused by the constant, powerful turning of the ship's huge paddle wheel, and the sensation contributed to his sense of displacement. It was as though he were cut off from the world that he knew and was floating, not down the Mississippi, but through space toward a distant, unimagined goal. His footsteps lagged as he approached the cabin, and eventually he stood in front of it. Taking a deep breath, he tapped gently at the door.

"Come in, Toby," Martha called. And as he opened the door she added, "There's no need for you to knock, you know. You live here, too." He shut the door behind him and stood still. She was sitting in one of the room's easy chairs, sipping a drink. She was clad in a filmy nightgown and negligee of black lace that left little of her body to the imagination, and Toby's heart beat hard at the sight.

Martha smiled up at him, her green eyes luminous. "Join me in a nightcap," she suggested. "I brought both of us drinks from the bar upstairs."

Somewhat relieved by the temporary respite, he hastily sank into the cabin's second chair. Picking up his glass, he raised it in a silent toast.

Martha lifted her own glass in return, then eyed him over its rim as she sipped her whiskey and water. "It strikes me," she said, "that we need to have a talk to clear the air."

"By all means," Toby answered cautiously.

"Through circumstances beyond our control," she said, "we're forced to pose as husband and wife while we try to get evidence that will incriminate Emil Braun. That means that for the time being we're going to be living in very confined quarters. I know you, Toby, and I'm sure you have an idea of spending your nights in the chair in which you're now sitting."

He grinned at her, acknowledging the accuracy of her observation.

"You can't do it, Toby," she told him flatly. "I know that you're stronger than most and that you have great endurance, but you can't spend your days and evenings living normally if you're going to sleep only in a chair all night. You'll need your wits about you if you intend to nail Braun."

"What do you suggest?"

She gestured toward the double bed. "That's big

enough for both of us," she said, "and I see no reason why both of us don't use it."

"I know of one very good reason," he replied. "I already have a wife—a lawful one."

"Surely you're not suggesting we're both so lacking in self-control," she said, "that we would deliberately complicate our lives by behaving contrary to our own expectations."

"I'm not suggesting anything," Toby answered. "I do know that you're the most beautiful woman I've ever seen in my life. And I don't want to tempt fate by getting into close quarters with you, quarters so close that I don't leave myself room to retreat."

"Let's not make problems where there may not be any," Martha said. "Why don't we try sleeping in the same bed? At the very worst we'll recognize that we're tending to fail to keep our distance, and if that begins, it'll be time enough to reconsider and seek alternatives."

Toby was silent for a moment. He was reluctant to admit to her, almost as much as he disliked admitting to himself, that he was so lacking in discipline that he could not curb his desires in her presence. "All right," he said at last. "I'm willing to take the chance if you are."

Again she toasted him. He smiled, and they touched glasses.

A short time later, when Toby returned from the bathroom, he found Martha already in bed. Lying on her side, she had turned her face toward the far bulkhead. He undressed quickly, and after changing into his nightshirt, he extinguished the oil lamp. Then he climbed into bed, being careful to avoid touching her and to stay on his own side. Uncertain whether or not she was asleep, he said softly, "Good night, Martha."

Her voice sounded disconcertingly close as she murmured, "Good night, Toby."

Both slept lightly, and the night passed without

incident. In the morning Martha was still asleep when Toby woke up. He shaved and washed quietly, then dressed, and did not awaken her until he was about to leave the cabin. Then he went up to the gaming saloon, where he waited until she joined him, and they went on together to breakfast.

Toby felt relieved that they had passed their initial test without incident. His confidence was vastly increased. Perhaps, he reflected, they *could* avoid embarrassment or complications, after all.

The gaming saloon remained deserted during the morning, so they had little to occupy them. Sitting together at one of the poker tables, they talked at length about themselves, their hopes and their ambitions, and Toby learned a great deal about Martha.

For the first time, she confirmed what he had begun to suspect might well be the case—that Domino was in fact her father. Her mother, after whom she was named, had once been an ambitious young woman employed in one of the first brothels Domino had owned. The young couple had fallen in love, and the elder Martha had retired, devoting herself instead to the pursuit of music, art, literature, and philosophy. She had acquired an extensive library, which the self-educated Domino had read over the years. His wife had died when Martha was quite young, leaving him to rear his daughter. Martha had been sent north to attend college, and after her graduation only a few years before, she had returned to New Orleans as her father's informal associate in his business enterprises.

People began to gather at the poker tables after supper that evening, and Toby was busy for hours, as was Martha. After they were finished with their work, they repeated their experiment of the previous night, and once again Toby was relieved that they could avoid temptation. He raised the matter at their second breakfast together, and Martha expressed confidence that they had overcome whatever problem existed. "I don't want to speak prematurely," she said, "but I honestly believe we have learned to handle the situation."

"I hope you're right," Toby said.

Any remaining tensions vanished, and thoroughly enjoying each other's company, they chatted on and on. At the noon meal, Martha reddened, and Toby felt distinctly uncomfortable when they overheard a woman at an adjoining table remark to her companions, "Just watch them and see how much they enjoy being together. You just know at a glance that they're happily married! Probably newlyweds, in fact."

By the fourth day of the voyage, Toby found that their routines were sufficiently well established that they seemed able to take each other for granted much of the time. He relaxed even more, becoming convinced that they had reached a point where each no longer felt the effect of the other's physical appeal. He mentioned this notion to Martha, who nodded in reply.

That night, the gaming saloon was relatively uncrowded because the *Tennessee* was due to put into port at New Orleans late the following morning, and most of the passengers no longer were interested in whiling away their time at games of poker. Only two or three players were on hand, trying to recoup losses from earlier in the day. Martha, too, was eager to reach New Orleans and see her father, and Toby was looking forward to seeing Domino again.

At midnight, when Toby and Martha were free to do as they pleased, they followed their now-customary routine: He closed up the saloon while she preceded him to the cabin and changed into night attire before he arrived.

Scrupulous in observing the routine they had established, Toby and Martha cautiously refrained from touching, or even looking at each other as they retired. She soon went to sleep, and he, lulled by her even breathing, dropped off, too. It was quiet and peaceful in the cabin.

Later that night—he had no idea of the hour—Toby dreamed that he and Clarissa were making love. Their bodies were pressing close together, their legs were intertwined as they kissed passionately. Their hands roamed freely, and Toby knew that Clarissa was as eager as he to consummate their lovemaking.

Gradually he awakened, just enough to realize that he was holding the seminude body of Martha in his arms. Clarissa was in far-off Oregon.

At that same moment, Martha, whose eyes were still closed, pressed one hand against the back of his head, pulling him still closer, and a shuddering sigh seemed to envelop her whole frame as she gave herself to him.

Toby could fight his own desires no longer. He was making love to a woman he had long considered beautiful; she was also someone whom he admired and respected, and she was his for the taking. Already aroused by the time he had discovered his error, he knew it was too late to back away, just as it would have proved impossible for Martha to have called a halt.

His caresses became more urgent, and she responded in kind. "Darling," Martha whispered.

Toby was too far gone now to worry about the consequences of his actions; the future would have to look after itself.

He took her then, gently but firmly. They began to move in unison, rocking, thrusting, their actions increasingly convulsive.

As Martha reached a climax, she moaned once and dug her long fingernails into the bare flesh of Toby's back. Her reaction triggered him, and he, too, obtained release. Time stood still, and they drifted for an eternity in a void.

Then slowly, familiar objects in the cabin took shape again, and at last the couple returned to earth.

"I'm sorry, Martha," Toby said. "I thought I had myself under control, but it's quite evident I didn't. It does no good to apologize, but I do, nevertheless, for whatever problems I may have created for you."

She looked at him, her green eyes wide open, the expression in them candid. "I'm not in the least sorry," she said. "I'm happier than I've ever been before. For a very long time, I have believed that I love you, and now I know I was right. This experience fulfills me and makes life worth living. It's something that no one can take from me. I'm sorry for only one thing: I know that I've caused you to be unfaithful to your wife."

"You didn't cause it," he said. "I alone am responsible, and I accept that responsibility. I don't know yet how I'll handle all this, but I won't lie to Clarissa; I've got to tell her the truth. But for now all that will have to wait, until I can think clearly again. I don't want to hurt her. And I won't hurt you, either, any more than can be helped."

VI

Domino grinned steadily as he looked first at Martha, then at Toby. "Well! Well!" he said, at a loss for words. Although he was urbane and cosmopolitan, he was so overcome by their unexpected visit that he did not know how to express his surprise and pleasure.

At his insistence they joined him for a late breakfast, even though they had already eaten before the *Tennessee* docked in New Orleans. Questioning them closely about developments in Memphis, Domino listened intently to their replies, bobbing his head frequently but keeping his opinions to himself. Finally, when they were having second cups of coffee, Eddie Neff entered the room. He and Toby, who had not seen each other since they had worked together tracking the villainous Karl Kellerman some months earlier, greeted each other boisterously. At Eddie's suggestion Toby went off with him to see several other of Domino's men with whom he had been associated in the past.

Father and daughter were alone at the table.

Domino peered at his daughter. "What's really new, Martha?"

"Red Leary proposed to me," she reported with a smile, "but I turned him down."

"For what reason?"

"I didn't love him, and he's not the type I could ever love."

"A very good reason," he commented. "What about you and Toby Holt?"

She could feel the color rising to her cheeks and burning. "I—I don't know what you mean," she stammered.

Domino smiled gently. "Martha," he said, "I've been looking after you for many years. I daresay I know you and understand you even better than you know and understand yourself. It became apparent a short time after I saw you and Toby today that you've slept together. It has also become very clear that you're very much in love. Don't deny the obvious."

Martha clenched her fists and faced him defiantly. "All right, I won't deny a word. In fact, I admit that everything you've deduced is absolutely true. What about it?"

Domino refilled his cup from a silver coffee pot. "You don't seem particularly happy for a woman in love," he observed mildly.

"I walked into this situation with my eyes wide open," she said, "and I have no one but myself to blame. Mind you, I didn't connive or trick Toby into going to bed with me. It just happened. Before we ever got together, I knew that he loved Clarissa, his wife. And I know it still, at this very moment, for all the good it does me."

The gang leader sipped his coffee, then tapped his fingers lightly several times on the highly polished surface of the dining room table. "Ever since you were little, Martha, I've tried my best to compensate for bringing you up without a mother. I've given you the best education possible, and over the years I've denied you nothing. I don't intend to now. If you want Toby Holt, you shall have him."

Martha smiled bitterly. "I could never be satisfied with life as Toby's mistress," she said. "I truly love him, and I'd have to be his wife. I think you don't understand what I said. He's married already! He has a wife!"

Domino did not reply in words. He merely looked at his daughter, and a smile spread slowly across his face.

A hand flew to her mouth. "Oh, no!" she cried. "You can't."

"What are you forbidding me to do?" he asked lightly, a hint of laughter in his voice.

"You can't have Toby's wife killed. You mustn't! I know how your mind works, and it would be wrong, a terrible tragedy, to have her put out of the way in order to clear a path for me!"

"You don't know the workings of my mind nearly as well as you may imagine," he said. "Toby is my friend. We have worked together, and I would do nothing against his interests. I promise you the present Mrs. Holt won't be physically harmed in any way. She won't be killed. Or injured. You have my word on it."

Martha was very much relieved.

"Put the problem out of your mind," her father said, "and we'll see what develops naturally." He deliberately changed the subject and began to talk about a local political problem that was becoming increasingly complicated.

A short time later, Toby and Eddie Neff came back into the room, and Domino immediately rose to his feet. "I'll see you youngsters at dinner," he said. "I have work to do this morning. Come along, Eddie." He went off to his office with Neff following, leaving Martha and Toby in the dining room.

"Close the door," Domino directed when he and Eddie had reached Domino's study. "What I have to say to you is strictly confidential, to be repeated to no one."

"Yes, sir," Eddie said, struck by the sudden note of gravity in Domino's voice.

"On the day after tomorrow," Domino said, "as soon as Martha and Toby leave on board the *Tennessee* to start their sail north up the Mississippi, I want you to catch the first train to San Francisco. Find whatever transportation will take you to Portland, Oregon, quickly. There you'll find Toby Holt's wife, Clarissa, living with their small son on the Holt ranch somewhere outside of town. I want you to get well acquainted with her in a hurry."

"Yes, sir," Eddie said. "For what purpose?"

"I can give you directives in this matter only in general terms," Domino said. "Understand, I want no harm of any kind done to Mrs. Holt. She's not to be killed or subjected to physical injury, either deliberately or inadvertently. Martha would never forgive us if anything happened to the woman."

Eddie nodded.

"The easiest and best way of obtaining our objective in this matter," Domino continued, "is to persuade Mrs. Holt to fall in love with you."

Eddie was so startled he did not know what to say or how to react.

"At the same time," Domino went on, "I'll expect you to arrange in some way to have concrete evidence that can be offered to Toby Holt of his wife's intimacy with you. This is to be used only if absolutely necessary. I think it likely that, being the type of woman she is, she will agree to dissolve her marriage rather than have him told."

Silence prevailed in the office for some moments, and then Eddie spoke slowly. "I've worked for you for a long time, boss," he said. "And I've done all kinds of jobs for you. I've never done one like this before. All I can say right now is that Toby is my friend—and I thought he was yours. I can't do anything that's going to harm him. It rubs me the wrong way. Very much so!"

"Toby is my friend, too," Domino replied firmly. "You've known Martha for a long time. You know how I feel about her, and I think you believe that my affection for her is justified."

"It sure is," Eddie said. "She's a wonderful person."

"Suppose I were to tell you that what you're going to be doing in Oregon will free Toby to marry Martha," Domino said. "How would you react to it?"

After another long silence, Eddie ran a hand through his blond hair. "That's different," he said. "That changes the whole picture."

When the *Tennessee* put into Memphis again, one of several stops on her long northward voyage, Toby went ashore just long enough to assure himself that Violet, Stalking Horse, and White Elk were all right. Stalking Horse had little to report, but he confirmed that Braun and three of his associates were ready to leave on a voyage. Knowing that a confrontation was close at hand, Toby returned to the paddle-wheeler.

Martha also went ashore and proceeded to the headquarters of the Mackerels, where Red Leary told her that his men had been keeping a close watch on Braun's headquarters. But they, too, had nothing of note to report, other than that Braun was preparing to leave on a trip.

By the time Martha returned to the *Tennessee* for the trip up the Mississippi to St. Louis, Braun and his associates were on board. Early that evening, two of the officers came to the gaming saloon and engaged in a game of poker with Toby, ordering drinks from Martha. They drank heavily as the evening progressed, and with increasing frequency they grabbed at Martha, drunkenly trying to caress her as she waited on them.

Martha tolerated their boorish conduct as best she was able, adroitly sidestepping their advances without creating a scene.

Toby did his best to avoid an involvement, but finally, when one of the men slid an arm around Martha's waist and she tried in vain to disengage his hand, Toby felt compelled to intervene. Reaching out suddenly, he struck the man's wrist with the edge of his open hand. The blow hurt, and the man promptly dropped his arm to his side and blinked at his unexpected attacker.

"This lady," Toby said in a firm voice, "is employed to procure drinks from the bar on demand, even for you, but at no time and in no way is she required to tolerate your pawing insults. I strongly advise both of you, for the sake of your continuing good health, to keep your hands to yourself henceforth and let this lady work without interference."

Something in the manner of the poker dealer stayed the hands of the men. As military officers they had become fairly astute judges of human nature, and they suspected that this steely-eyed young man meant exactly what he said. They did not molest Martha further.

Later, after they had returned to their own cabin, Toby told Martha, "I didn't like interfering, but I'd had enough of those louts grabbing at you."

She was pleased, thinking that he was jealous of the attention she had been getting, and for her purposes that was a good sign.

The following day they ate an early midday meal, and shortly after they had finished, Emil Braun appeared in the gaming saloon, accompanied by his three subordinate officers. Laughing and joking with his officers, he was in a boisterous mood, and it was evident that he relished being called "General."

When Braun ordered a round of drinks from Martha, Toby noted with grim satisfaction that the man was extremely polite to her. His companions undoubtedly had warned him not to make advances, that he would incur the dealer's wrath if he did so. At least, Toby reflected, it was not likely that he would have trouble with Braun because of Martha.

Seating himself at the card table, Braun took out several bills, which he handed to Toby in exchange for chips. Then he lighted a cigar. "Let's get started, Mr. Dealer," he said. He beckoned to his companions. "Gather round, boys, and I'll give you a lesson in the way poker ought to be played."

Toby smiled politely and dealt himself and Braun five cards.

Braun picked up his cards, winked at his companions, and announced, "I'll take just one card, thanks." He moved a card facedown toward the center of the table and was dealt a replacement.

"I'll take three," Toby said, and dealt himself three cards.

Braun chuckled, exhaled noisily, and pushed a stack of white chips, worth one dollar each, in front of him. "I'll open with a bet of ten dollars."

Toby remained polite. "I'm sorry, sir," he said, "but the *Tennessee* has a hard and fast rule that no opening wager is to exceed five dollars."

Braun's laughter boomed across the room. "I see," he said. "They don't want you going broke too fast?"

His men laughed. Toby, whose dislike for the man was growing, did not even smile.

Braun pushed five white chips into the center of the table, and Toby did the same. Then, after a moment's pause, Toby said, "I believe I'll raise you five." He threw an additional five chips into the pot.

Braun grinned wolfishly. "Fair enough," he said, "and I'll raise you five."

"Done," Toby said, matching his bet. "And I'll call you." Braun laid his hand on the table, revealing a single pair of aces. Toby put down his own hand and had three fives. He smiled politely and then gathered in the chips. Braun scowled ferociously, cursed under his breath, and muttered something about the luck of the house dealer.

That was the start. Toby was a somewhat better than average poker player, whose innate caution led him to take few risks. Braun, however, had an exaggerated opinion of his own worth and took chances that no sensible gambler would ever take. Occasionally luck favored him, but in the end he lost far more than he won. After more than an hour's play, he was completely out of chips.

"Damnation!" he exclaimed. "My luck's bad, but it's bound to change. Boys, give me a scrap of paper and a pencil."

He wrote an IOU for five hundred dollars and handed the slip to Toby. "Now give me more chips!" he demanded.

Toby glanced at the slip of paper, then braced himself for trouble. Braun had been drinking heavily while playing, and Toby anticipated a violent explosion. "I'm sorry, sir," he said, "but the management of the *Tennessee* accepts no promissory notes. The house is pleased to give passengers the opportunity to play poker, but all chips must be paid for in advance."

Braun glowered at Toby but was too concerned with his own status to make a real issue. He was determined not to jeopardize his new reputation. At the same time, he did not wish to lose face in the eyes of his companions, by acceding to the demand that he pay cash for chips. Accordingly, he abruptly rose from his chair and stamped off. His companions followed him out.

That evening, Braun and his men launched what appeared to be a scheme to recoup their leader's losses. They appeared one at a time in the saloon and sat down to play poker, apparently hoping to win enough to even the score.

All three were inferior poker players, however, having no real understanding of the game. They lost consistently, and by the time the evening ended, they had dropped an additional five hundred dollars.

Adding up his day's winnings, Toby found he was more than a thousand dollars to the good. That gave him a margin for future games. For the first time, he felt thoroughly comfortable in his temporary position.

"Go down to the cabin, and I'll join you there shortly," he told Martha, who was finishing the task of clearing away beverage glasses. "I want to put the cards away and make the night's winnings secure until I can turn the money over to the purser tomorrow."

After Martha left, he locked away the cards and chips. When he was finished with all other duties, he made certain no one was within sight, then quickly opened a wall safe concealed behind one of the pictures in the saloon, deposited the money inside, and closed the safe again.

The gaming room had been filled with cigar smoke for so many hours that Toby felt a craving for fresh air. Turning out the oil lamp, he stepped outside to the deck and walked to the starboard rail.

The weather had been fair at supper time, but subsequently the wind had abated, and a deep fog had settled in, covering the Mississippi from bank to bank and making it so dark that it was impossible to see the prow of the ship from the stern. A drizzle accompanied the mist, and the deck was wet, its wooden planks somewhat slippery.

As nearly as he could tell, he was the only person on board, either passenger or crew member, who was not inside. Standing at the rail, he inhaled the damp air.

Suddenly his senses, always alert, warned him that he was not alone. On the open deck, someone was behind him, and another person was ahead of him. He peered through the fog, and his superior eyesight enabled him to identify the pair. One was a burly man who had taken part in the evening's play, and the other was a slender, spidery man who also had played and lost. They inched closer, and Toby saw that both were carrying long swords.

Leaving his pistol in its holster, Toby drew his knife.

The thin man acted as the spokesman. "We don't want to hurt nobody," he called. "We just want our money back. We ain't accusing you or nothin', but it seems damn funny that the general and us—every last one of us—got our socks beat off playing with you. Maybe you cheated us, and maybe you didn't. We're not going to make any complaints to your bosses, and we're not going to get you fired from your job. All we want is our thousand bucks back. And we want it right now!"

"I don't have it," Toby replied honestly. "I'm not carrying a cent with me."

"Don't hand us that," the burly man said angrily. "We was keeping watch outside the gaming saloon after we finished playing there tonight, and no one went anywhere near the purser's office."

Toby had no intention of telling them what he had done with the thousand dollars. "Sorry," he said, "but there's no way I can oblige you."

"Just remember," the thin man told him, "you're asking to be sliced to shreds. The general wants us to get that money back, and what the general wants, he gets!"

They began to advance, slowly and simultaneously.

Stalling for time, Toby retreated a few paces, and as he did, his eyes fell on a long oaken spar across a coil of line. Relatively unfamiliar with ships, he did not fully understand the use of the spar, but he saw that it was a sturdy, slatlike pole about four feet long. It had a loop at one end and a slight point at the other. Sheathing his knife, he snatched up the spar, and taking the initiative, as he always did when possible in combat, he swung it hard in a vicious circle around his head.

The pair stepped backward in alarm. Then the thinner man, endowed with greater courage, raised his sword and advanced again.

Toby knew now exactly what needed to be done. Taking hold of the spar by its looped end, he brought it down full force on the man's wrist. The blow was so sharp and well delivered that the sword clattered to the deck, and the man was temporarily rendered helpless.

The second man had no intention of being caught in such a trap. Backing away rapidly and still gripping his sword with one hand, he hastily drew his pistol with the other.

Toby wanted to avoid a pistol duel at all costs—it would call the attention of everyone on board ship to the confrontation. So far, he had learned nothing new about Braun's activities, and he wanted no attention that could interfere with his mission.

Grasping the spar in both hands, he pointed the other end at the larger man and raced toward him, driving the pole into his chest with full force.

The man skidded backward across the deck, unable to halt his reverse motion, and the small of his back struck the rail. He grunted, fell over backward, his feet flipping up into the air, and before Toby could reach him, his opponent had disappeared overboard.

Toby raced to the rail, as did the thin man, enmity momentarily forgotten as they peered through the fog at the muddy, swirling waters of the Mississippi.

For a moment Toby saw the white face of the man who had been knocked overboard beneath the surface

of the water a short distance from the ship. Then the
fog closed in again, and Toby could no longer see him.

Suddenly he remembered his remaining opponent
and turned to face him, finding him again clutching his
sword.

Toby quickly scooped up the sword dropped by
the other man. With the odds more nearly equal, he
could almost enjoy a duel.

"Don't for a minute think you've won," the thin
man gasped venomously, "just because you've gotten
rid of poor old Jules. The general told us to recover that
thousand dollars tonight, and it'll be recovered. You
can bet your life on it."

Toby gestured with the borrowed sword, inviting
him to duel. The officer, who seemed to be no stranger
to swords, judging from the way he handled the blade
in his hand, advanced slowly.

At that moment the *Tennessee* swerved suddenly
in order to avoid hitting some object that had loomed
up before it in the fog. Both combatants were thrown
off balance, the thin man sliding and tumbling into a
mass of tarpaulins, while Toby bumped into the railing,
which kept him upright. They gripped their blades
more tightly and approached each other slowly, both
aware of the treacherous footing.

They circled one another cautiously, each seeking
an opening, each waiting for a move by the other.
Suddenly the officer began the combat, but his blow
was not a typical thrust. Instead, he brought his sword
high above his head, ready to smash down with it, as
though wielding a powerful flyswatter.

Had Toby Holt been an ordinary swordsman, he
would have ducked and simultaneously raised his own
blade to ward off the coming blow. As it happened, he
did neither.

Reacting instantly, he sprang forward until he was

face to face with his foe. He was close enough, in fact, that he caught hold of the lapels of his opponent's suit and twisted them hard, forcing the man to lose his balance.

Before the startled swordsman quite knew what was happening, he found himself on one knee. He stared up at Toby for a moment, then spat full in his face.

Toby wiped off the spittle. "So be it," he said. "*En garde!*"

He fought hard from the outset, lunging and parrying, striking and thrusting, constantly on the move, shifting from an active attack to a seemingly passive defense, and then going into another attack without warning. The officer proved to be reasonably proficient, too, and for a while he gave as good as he received. The odds seemed fairly even.

Occasionally, as the grim battle proceeded, one or the other stumbled over some object on deck as the ship lurched, but he quickly regained his balance, and the duel was resumed.

Toby, fully aware his opponent would settle for nothing less than his death, gradually applied more pressure. The thin man tried to do the same, but his skill was no longer the equal of Toby's. He did not falter, but his eye and his hand became less sure. He was bothered by the swirls of fog that rolled across the deck. When he slipped, he took longer to regain his balance. He was obviously tiring.

Toby at last found an opening, and just as he lunged, the ship again lurched and pushed him forward with far greater force than he intended. His sword penetrated the left side of his opponent's chest, and the swaying of the *Tennessee* forced the blade still further into the man's body.

The defeated officer crumpled backward onto the

deck, sword in hand, and slid headfirst beneath the rail into the Mississippi. His descent was so quiet that the splash was barely audible on the deck above.

Toby stood very still for a long moment, lost in thought. Once again he had triumphed over the forces of evil, but he felt no elation or sense of accomplishment. He had done what was necessary for survival, nothing more. Suddenly he threw his sword, hurling it as one would a javelin, high over the rail of the ship. It struck the water and vanished beneath the surface of the great river.

For a long time, Toby continued to stand motionless, and he roused himself only when he realized that a heavy rain was starting to fall. By the time he reached cover, the rain had become a deluge. He made his way quickly down the stairs to his cabin, and there he found a deeply concerned Martha awaiting him. She had brought a cup of tea for him, and it sat beside his chair. As he entered the cabin, she looked at him anxiously. Before she could question him, he launched into an account of what had happened.

Martha was no stranger to stories of violence, but she was nevertheless startled. "Do you mean to tell me they actually wanted to get back the money they had lost to you at poker?"

"Apparently," Toby replied.

"From the first time I heard of Emil Braun, I didn't consider him very sensible," Martha said, "but he must be even more foolish than I imagined."

"He's somewhat lacking in wisdom, I think," Toby conceded as he sipped his tea.

She looked at him curiously. "Where did you get a sword so you could engage in a duel with them?"

"I neutralized one of them with a long spar," Toby explained, "and I took his sword."

She nodded thoughtfully. "Obviously you were a match for the remaining foe."

"I appear to have been," he said mildly.

She shook her head in wonder. "You're astonishing, Toby, you really are. You're the best shot I've ever seen. You make my father and his men look incompetent by comparison. You can throw a knife accurately, you use a lasso, and now it develops that you're also a swordsman. Aren't there any limits to your accomplishments?"

"As a matter of fact," he replied, grinning modestly, "I have many failings. It just happens that I learned how to use a sword, along with firearms, when I was quite small, and I kept up with the art when I grew older."

"I don't suppose Emil Braun will learn from this experience not to cross you again."

"Braun seems to be the type that never learns from experience," Toby said. "And, in any event, I'm not going to tell him what happened to his followers. He can make his own assumptions and jump to whatever conclusions he wants."

Toby began to pace, restless. "Sometimes I wonder why we came on this trip," he said, a note of annoyance in his voice. "It seems as if we've spent days and days cooped up on this boat, with nothing to show for it."

" 'Nothing'?" she repeated archly at him. "Is that all you think of our time together?"

"No, that's not it at all!" he replied hotly, then broke into a grin when he realized she was teasing him. "What I mean is, we've very little to show for our efforts to learn something about Braun."

"That may be," she said calmly, "but that doesn't mean we shouldn't have tried. If you hadn't taken this trip, you would always wonder what you might have learned, if you had. Now at least you know. If it seems you've accomplished little—well, that's life. Most things worth doing require endless patience."

"I suppose so," Toby replied.

By common consent they changed the subject. A short time later they went to bed and made love for the first time in several nights. It was not planned or premeditated. It seemed to grow naturally out of the dangers to which Toby had been exposed and which he had successfully overcome.

The next morning, the *Tennessee* put into the port of Cairo, Illinois, where it was scheduled to remain until noon, on its run to St. Louis. The absence of ship's motion and the noise of passengers disembarking and arriving awakened Toby and Martha, and they arrived early in the ship's dining room for breakfast.

Seated at a nearby table were Emil Braun and his one remaining aide, so deeply engrossed in conversation that they failed to notice the arrival of the couple. They continued to talk, their voices clearly audible.

"Where the hell *are* those two?" Braun demanded roughly.

"I've searched the entire ship for them, sir, and I haven't found any sign of them. I checked with the chief steward shortly before we came down here, and he conducted a personal search. His opinion is that they are nowhere on board."

Braun looked disgusted. "Then they must have jumped ship when we put into Cairo."

"I guess so," his companion said miserably.

"They must have had it all planned," Braun said in an outraged tone of voice. "They waited until we pulled into Cairo because it was such an early hour, and they went ashore as soon as the gangplank was let down. They left most of their belongings, just in case we woke up and happened to notice they were missing. They wanted to give themselves plenty of time to get away."

"You must be right, General—as always."

"I'll be damned if we're going to waste any time looking for them," Emil Braun said. "When we get back to camp, we'll issue a notice to all companies, and from there we'll let nature take care of itself. If either of them is captured, he'll go before a court-martial board, be found guilty immediately, and be executed by a firing squad."

"Are we authorized to take such action, General?" the aide asked in a somewhat awed tone of voice.

"Authorized?" Braun boomed. "Hell, yes! Every officer who serves under me has signed a contract, under the terms of which he submits himself to military disciplines and to court-martial procedures in the event that he exceeds them. If I ever get my hands on those two, they're as good as dead!"

Toby and Martha exchanged a long, significant glance. They still had no idea why Emil Braun was going to the trouble and enormous expense of raising an armed force, but they knew beyond all question now that he was running a strict military organization.

Toby and Martha exchanged only a few words at the breakfast table. When they were through, they assured themselves that Braun and his adjutant were remaining on board rather than going ashore in Cairo. Then they retired to the security of their own cabin to analyze what they had learned.

"As I see it," Martha said, "we face a very serious situation. Braun wouldn't speak in terms of executing supporters whom he accuses of treason if he were merely leading some patriotic veterans group in a series of exercises. He's forming his group for a definite purpose. And I'm afraid that purpose isn't good for the United States."

"You're right," Toby replied. "Even the way Violet MacDermid's property was seized indicates that Braun isn't hesitating to go beyond legal bounds. Whether the force he is amassing and training has an evil purpose remains to be seen, but I wouldn't be surprised if they're breaking many laws. The real test of our investigative prowess will begin when we arrive in St. Louis. We'll have to exercise great caution every step of the way to avoid being uncovered, but the results can be well worth the risks we'll be taking. In fact, I'm hopeful we can gain enough information to cripple Braun and put a real crimp in his outfit, once and for all!"

VII

The rugged, well-dressed young man stood in the open doorway of the Oregon ranch house and smiled engagingly. "I regret to disturb you, ma'am, but I'm looking for Mr. Toby Holt."

"I'm sorry to tell you," Clarissa said, "he has gone to Memphis. In fact, so has Stalking Horse, our foreman."

Eddie Neff held his forehead. "Don't tell me I've come out here for nothing!"

Clarissa liked his looks and smiled at him. "Perhaps I could help you, sir. I'm Mrs. Holt."

"Eddie Neff's the name. I came out from New Orleans on other business, so I thought I would come here to look over your horses, if you have any for sale. I'm interested in yearlings, and your ranch was recommended to me by a man named Domino, as having the finest stock in the country."

Because she recognized Domino's name, Clarissa promptly invited the visitor into the house, never stopping to wonder how he planned to transport horses to New Orleans. She seated him in the parlor, then brewed a pot of tea, which he said he preferred to wine or any other beverage. They talked for some time, with Eddie commenting at length about the differences between the Columbia River Valley and New Orleans. He explained that he was hoping to buy the yearlings and

117

ship them east by rail; he named an agent in Portland who, he said, would make the necessary arrangements.

Clarissa, having recovered from her initial surprise at having anyone show up unexpectedly from such a distance, accepted his story without question.

Eddie was very much taken with her, and to his surprise, he discovered that he liked her company as much, in fact, as she seemed to be enjoying his. He found that carrying out Domino's instructions was no chore at all.

Before darkness fell, Ty Granby, one of the ranch hands, was summoned to take Eddie to see the horses. Together, the two men walked out to the stables behind the house.

"The Holt horses," Granby said, "are considered rather extraordinary—not only hereabouts, but all over the country. For our horses, the period of suspension in a gallop—that is, when all four feet are off the ground—is longer than for most mounts."

As the men walked past the stalls, Eddie, who knew something about horses, carefully examined each one. "This strawberry roan is a handsome animal," he said, pausing before one stall. He moved on. "That buckskin dun is extraordinary, too," he said, pointing to a yellowish horse with a black mane, tail, and dorsal stripes, and fanned zebra stripes on its legs.

He stopped again to examine a blood bay, reddish-brown with black mane, tail, and lower legs. "This one is magnificent!" he exclaimed.

"They're all great," Granby replied. "We started with a small number of horses. We used to capture them in the hills. But now we breed our own stock, and we're up to fifty mounts or so, depending on sales patterns. It's a great business, particularly for anyone who loves horses the way all of us here do."

Eddie finally returned to the house. He meant

every word of his praise when he said to Clarissa, "Your stock is outstanding. I've not seen better-looking horses anywhere, including the bluegrass region of Kentucky."

Clarissa, who had taken advantage of his absence to change into what she considered a more attractive dress, smiled broadly at the compliment. Before she had a chance to reply, little Tim raced into the room and unhesitatingly threw himself at the stranger.

"Well! Who do we have here?" Eddie demanded. Within moments he and the boy were engaged in boisterous play.

"Leave the gentleman alone and let him catch his breath, Timmy," Clarissa ordered at last. "You'll have to excuse him, Mr. Neff. He misses his father, and that's why he's behaving so with you."

"No need to apologize, Mrs. Holt!" Eddie said, and turned back to the child. "Boy, do you want to ride with me tomorrow when I try out some of these horses your mother is selling me?"

"You bet! I can ride," Tim said proudly. "I have my very own pony."

"So much the better."

They resumed their play, and they were having such a good time that Clarissa, acting on impulse, invited Eddie to stay for supper.

He accepted with alacrity, for he could recall having met very few women who seemed as charming, intelligent, and delightful as Clarissa.

Tim ate supper with the adults at the big kitchen table. After he went to bed, Clarissa and Eddie walked to the parlor for coffee.

Clarissa poured Eddie a liqueur, but he was enjoying their conversation so much that he left the drink untouched. Surprised to discover they both originally came from Philadelphia, they were additionally astonished by the coincidence that they had attended the same grade school there. Their talk was wide-ranging, and they found they had a number of acquaintances in common.

It was late when Eddie, after promising again to return in the morning, finally rode back to Portland on the horse he had hired. He felt refreshed to have enjoyed so pleasant an evening with Clarissa, whom he discovered was clever and wise, with a lively sense of humor. She was exceptionally attractive, without being flashy. Her attitudes were feminine, yet he was pleased that she was not cloying. In brief, she was endowed with all the attributes he could ever want in a wife, and he was pleased at the thought of seeing her again the next day.

As Clarissa watched him go, she positively glowed.

Toby's frequent absences from the ranch made her "ripe" for a romantic interlude, she realized, but she did not view Eddie Neff in such terms. It was enough that she liked him and that she looked forward to the prospect of their next meeting. She liked him because he had a quick, incisive mind and a wit to match. Certainly he was not in a class with Toby as a specimen of manhood, but, nevertheless, he was moderately good-looking and exuded an air of solid masculinity. It was evident that, like Toby, he refused to stand for non-sense from anyone who might try to deceive him.

Early in the morning, Eddie hired a horse again and returned to inspect some yearlings he had not seen the previous day. He did not forget his promise to Tim, however, and later he took time to pick him up and ride around the property with him. The outing culmi-nated in a "race," which Tim took pride in winning.

Clarissa invited Eddie to stay for the noon meal. He demurred, saying that he was imposing on her, but she finally prevailed, and they lingered at the table almost an hour after eating.

By the end of the day, Eddie had signed a contract for eighteen horses. When Clarissa proposed that he remain for another meal, he countered with the suggestion that she accompany him into Portland for supper, and he was so persuasive that she finally agreed. It would be her first evening in town since Toby left for Tennessee, and she arranged for Barney, a droll and patient ranch hand, to entertain Tim for the evening. In fact, it was to be her first social occasion with anyone except Toby in the years of her marriage, and in spite of herself, she found the prospect an exciting one.

In honor of the occasion, she selected a gown of pale beige silk that she had worn only once. It was snug-fitting with a low, square-cut neckline.

Eddie, meanwhile, supervised the polishing up of a carriage from one of the barns, and the hitching up of two fine mares he felt confident of handling on the trip into Portland. They rode gaily and in high style to the Hotel Oregonian. It was known as the most luxurious establishment in town, and everyone of distinction celebrated festive occasions there.

The handsome furniture in the dining room had been manufactured locally, but the thick Oriental rug was from China, and the huge crystal chandelier had been made in San Francisco especially for the hotel.

Clarissa's arrival created a minor sensation, and many of the guests greeted her. Among them were Toby's close friend and business partner, Rob Martin, and his lovely wife, Kale. They were delighted to see her, and Clarissa was pleased to introduce Eddie Neff as a prospective purchaser of some of the Holts' fine horses. The Martins liked him on sight and sat down for a few minutes at the table to join in a drink. It soon became evident, even to the few who wondered about Clarissa's presence with a man other than her husband, that nothing clandestine was going on.

Pleased by the companionship of an attentive, attractive male, Clarissa relaxed and had a most enjoyable evening. She had badly missed their social life during Toby's latest absence, and she wished with all her heart that he was sitting across the table from her. But she knew he was elsewhere, doing his duty, and Eddie Neff was a reasonable substitute under the circumstances.

Clarissa had merely picked at her food for weeks, but on this night she had a hearty appetite and ate a large, satisfying dinner. She and Eddie shared a bottle of a good Rhine wine. Color returned to her cheeks, her eyes sparkled, and she laughed frequently.

Observing Clarissa, Kale Martin said quietly to her husband, "I'm beginning to wish Toby would come home soon. Clarissa is far more lonely than we had realized. With him away, she could be vulnerable to such a man."

Encouraged by Eddie, Clarissa talked freely of her life. She told of her first, unhappy marriage, and then of the subsequent joy she had found with Toby, only to have her hopes nearly dashed when her first husband, Otto Sinclair, had unexpectedly appeared again. She spoke of his attempts to blackmail her and was frank in telling him that Sinclair finally had met death at her hands.

Eddie listened intently and was convinced that she was one of the most courageous, as well as loveliest, women he had ever encountered. Now it was his turn to reveal his background, and although he ordinarily was chary of talking about himself, this night was different. He spoke without reservation about his past and was as honest as Clarissa had been.

He told in detail how he had been virtually adopted by Domino, when as a young man he had turned up penniless in New Orleans. Subsequently, he had been established as the gang overlord's first lieutenant, handling all manner of problems and making decisions on his behalf.

Today, Eddie confessed, he had more power than he felt comfortable with. Like Domino, he operated outside the boundaries of the law, but also like Domino, he tried to be fair in his business dealings.

Because people demanded the opportunity to gamble, Domino operated a number of honest gambling halls, and since men insisted on visiting brothels, he owned a string of bordellos that paid decent wages, protected the customers, and were medically supervised. It was true that Eddie, like Domino, had a reputation for toughness, even ruthlessness, when the occasion demanded it. But in managing some of Domino's interests, he was hard only in his dealings with those criminals who tried to acquire some of the substantial sums that Domino earned.

"I hope you're not apologizing for what you do," Clarissa commented. "Domino is Toby's friend, and that's good enough for me. Besides, you have become my friend, and friends don't judge each other."

Eventually, Eddie drove Clarissa back to the ranch, and the evening came to an end, regrettably for both of them. They shook hands good night, holding each other's hand longer than was necessary, and then Eddie returned to the hotel.

As Clarissa went to sleep, she couldn't help wishing he would prolong his visit to Oregon and that she could see much more of him in days to come.

The elusive Karl Kellerman had been a detective sergeant in the St. Louis Police Department before he turned to a life of crime. Consequently, Toby Holt, his nemesis, had dealt in the past with the commissioner of police in that city. The commissioner welcomed Toby now to his office in the St. Louis city hall, and after a brief exchange of civilities, Toby explained the reason for his visit, telling about Emil Braun and the organization that he was training.

"Let me get this straight," the commissioner said at last. "If I understand you correctly, you would like me to assign a couple of Civil War veterans to be interviewed by this fellow, Braun, and to find out as best they can just what he has in mind."

"Exactly right, sir," Toby said. "I'm proceeding largely on a basis of hearsay so far. I need something more concrete to go on."

The commissioner assigned two members of his department who had been Union officers. They went off to the hotel where Braun was conducting interviews. Telling Braun that they had heard from friends that he was in town to hire veterans, they showed him their army discharge papers and applied for commissions in his corps.

Later that day, the commissioner again received Toby in his office. "I've gathered at least some information for you, Mr. Holt," he said. "Why don't you sit down."

Toby sat opposite the commissioner at his oversize desk.

"One of my men was rejected by Braun rather quickly," the commissioner related. "Although he'd been a captain of artillery with a fine record, he's a married man with two children. That put him out of consideration."

"Are you saying," Toby asked, "that Braun wants only single men?"

"Apparently so," the commissioner replied. "He didn't say this in so many words, but he made it plain that he's interested in men who have no family commitment. In this way, he seems to feel he has a force that would be freer to take greater risks on his behalf than would men with dependents on their minds."

On the basis of what he had learned so far, Toby was able to conclude that Braun had some reckless ventures in mind for his men.

"As it happens," the commissioner went on, "the other officer is a bachelor. He was a captain of infantry and was decorated for valor. Braun appeared to be much impressed by him and offered him a bonus of a hundred dollars in cash, together with a promise he would be commissioned as a major."

"Did your man find out what Braun is up to?"

The commissioner shook his head. "He tried, but Braun was tricky and wasn't in the least forthcoming. All he said was that if anyone wanted action, he'd get enough to keep him thoroughly satisfied for a long time to come. He gave no hint as to the nature of any such action and no indication of what he has in mind."

Toby knew now he was on the track of a major plot of some sort. A man who was prepared to pay a recruit so generously for signing on with him must have considerable financial backing. The whole affair appeared more than ever to be worth pursuing.

Eddie Neff needed no excuse to linger in the Portland area. Even after he had completed his purchase of horses from the Holt ranch and his Portland agent had seen to their shipment, he stayed on and saw Clarissa daily. She gave her ready approval, only vaguely aware that she was causing complications from which she might find it difficult to extricate herself. She mentioned Eddie's presence to Toby's mother and stepfather, and they, learning that he was a friend of their son's, promptly invited him to Sunday dinner, along with Clarissa and Tim. On Sunday noon a small boat was dispatched on General Blake's orders, and manned by eight oarsmen headed by a sergeant, it awaited them at the Oregon shore of the Columbia River.

They were rowed across the broad, swiftly flowing river, and on the Washington shore the general's aide was on hand with a carriage drawn by matched bays. At Fort Vancouver, Eulalia and Leland Blake extended a warm welcome to Eddie Neff, as did their daughter, Cindy Holt, home on holiday from her college, where she was in her senior year.

Eddie made no attempt to keep secret his association with Domino. As a matter of fact, General Blake was already acquainted with Toby's collaboration with the New Orleans gang leader.

For a time conversation centered on Cindy's coming marriage to General Blake's adopted son, Henry Blake, who was soon to graduate from the U.S. Military Academy. The young couple had been privately betrothed for a long time, but now that Hank was in his final year, they were permitted to officially announce their coming marriage. Cindy could talk of little else.

Brief mention was made of Toby's current assignment, but Eddie knew few details, and the general was keeping to himself the little he had learned from his stepson.

In the midst of a loving family scene, Eddie was enjoying himself but felt ashamed of the role that Domino had assigned him. Following orders, he had intended to arouse Clarissa's interest in him, but he could not tell whether or not he had succeeded. He was well aware, however, that his interest in her was genuine and had reached a high pitch. He realized he had lost his heart to her.

No useful purpose would be served if he confessed that he had started their relationship for the wrong reason. He was paying a heavy price for that error. The question that loomed largest in his mind was what he should do now. He wanted her, it was true, but he respected her too much to cause her to break her marriage vows. On the other hand, he found it painful to bear the thought of returning to New Orleans, never to see her again.

Eddie needed time to seek a solution to this dilemma. He wished he could discuss it frankly with Clarissa; perhaps they could find some way of reaching an answer satisfactory to everyone concerned. He could not quite get up his nerve, though, to approach her and speak candidly.

That Sunday afternoon was the most pleasant interlude he had ever enjoyed, and he was unhappy when it drew to a close. When Eulalia invited him to return the following Sunday if he was still in the area, he wanted to shout that he would make it his business to be there. Instead, he thanked her quietly, said his farewells, and after shaking hands with the general, wished Cindy happiness in her forthcoming marriage.

Clarissa was unusually quiet on the drive back to the embarkation point on the Columbia. Watching Eddie in the home of her husband's parents, chatting with them, had created a distinct shock for her. For the first time, she realized that her emotional involvement was far deeper than she had suspected.

Not for a moment did she forget she was Toby Holt's wife and that her love for him was great. Of that much she was certain.

All the same, there was a special place in her heart for Eddie Neff, and he rested there securely. Was it possible, she wondered, that she was in love with two men at the same time? A few days before, she would have insisted that such an idea was impossible. Now she was not nearly so sure.

She suspected that her loneliness, including her physical craving for a normal sex life, was largely responsible for her attraction to Eddie, but all she knew for certain was that she liked him very much and was happy to be near him. Beyond that, her mind refused to function.

After a busy day, Tim was drowsy, so Eddie picked up the little boy and carried him as they boarded the boat for the return trip.

The sergeant in charge pointed to a broad seat slightly forward of the center of the craft. Eddie helped Clarissa climb over other seats in order to take her place. Then, before sitting beside her, he handed her son to her. Tim's head drooped as he rested against his mother.

The crew members sat at their places beside the oarlocks, and they pushed off when the sergeant gave the order.

It was apparent from the outset that the ride would be rougher than the one in the opposite direction. The wind had freshened, the current was stronger, and the river was choppy. The craft bounced up and down on the waves and occasionally was knocked sideways as a wave slapped against her hull.

The crew members used all their skill and strength to keep the little vessel moving smoothly. But in spite of their efforts, the voyage was slow and torturous. Clarissa, accustomed to such changes in the temperament of the Columbia, paid scant attention to what Eddie regarded as a crisis.

Suddenly a large wave slapped against the port side of the prow, jolting them with considerable force. Tim, who had been resting in his mother's light grasp, was jarred loose. Before Clarissa could recover, he seemed to fly out of her arms. He dropped overboard into the dark, menacing water.

Even as Clarissa's terrified scream cut through the night, Eddie tore off his suit jacket, kicked off his boots, and jumped into the river.

Reacting sharply to the sergeant's orders, the crew

swung the boat about and held it close behind Eddie in the churning water.

Eddie had learned to swim as a boy in the upper Schuylkill River, outside Philadelphia, and he had been a strong swimmer ever since. He hoped his experience would serve him well now.

Swimming steadily with powerful strokes against the strong current, he quickly reached the spot where Tim had fallen overboard. Then he dove beneath the surface and strained his eyes as he tried to see through the murky, churning water. Off to one side he caught a glimpse of the child, arms and legs waving feebly. Swimming to him, Eddie gathered the boy up with his left hand.

Rising to the surface and holding Tim's head out of the water, Eddie swam back toward the boat. The sergeant took in the situation at a glance, and directed the oarsmen to swing the boat around, bringing the craft alongside them. Strong hands lifted Tim into the boat, and while he was given first aid, water being pressed from his lungs, Eddie was helped aboard. The crew immediately hurried on again toward the Oregon shore.

Soon Tim began to whimper, and by the time the boat reached land and Clarissa took her son into her arms to disembark, he seemed none the worse for his adventure.

Before they transferred to waiting horses from the ranch, the sergeant shook Eddie's hand gratefully. "We're indebted to you, Mr. Neff," he said. "I'd never have been able to face General Blake if you hadn't saved his grandson!"

Comforted and cuddled by his mother, Tim fell asleep on the homeward ride, and when they reached the ranch house, he was put straight to bed.

Then, at Clarissa's insistence, Eddie was taken to a guest room, where she provided him with dry clothes.

"There's no question about it," she said. "You simply must change. It wouldn't do at all for a hero to become ill with pneumonia!"

After Eddie changed, he went down to the parlor, where he found Clarissa had built a blazing fire in the fireplace and had mixed a hot rum toddy, which she instructed him to drink.

"No matter how long I may live," she said, looking at him with shining eyes, "I'll always be in your debt."

Embarrassed by her extravagant praise, he smiled and waved self-deprecatingly.

"I mean it," Clarissa continued. "You saved my son's life at the risk of your own. What more could any woman ask of a man?"

"The boy was in trouble, so I reacted," Eddie answered. "I did no more than any other man would do. Let's please drop the subject, if you don't mind."

Clarissa began to speak of other matters, but it was plain that her attitude toward him had intensified. Everything she had felt previously was now magnified, and Eddie could not help but be aware of the difference in her response to him.

He deliberately confined himself to a single toddy, fearful that a second might cause him to lower his inhibitions and lose self-control.

Eddie sensed that the right pressure would persuade Clarissa to allow him to spend the night with her. But for the first time, he disobeyed Domino's orders. He knew he could not live with himself if he seduced this proud young woman, though he was deeply in love with her. For the first time in his life, he cared enough for a woman to put her honor above all else.

They talked until after midnight, when Eddie suddenly jumped to his feet and announced harshly, "It's late; time for me to go back to the hotel." He knew that he was weakening, his resolve was breaking down, and that he might begin to make love to her if he stayed longer.

Clarissa was experiencing a similar reaction. She started to protest his decision but suddenly broke off and agreed that it was proper for him to go.

They walked together to the front door, and there they lost what vestiges of self-restraint they had retained. Suddenly they were embracing and kissing. As their lips met, Clarissa's passion flared, and her reaction instantly sparked Eddie's.

They wrenched themselves apart with difficulty, and as he started back to Portland, he knew that the next time they met—if they met again—they would find it more difficult than ever to avoid having an affair.

Emil Braun and the one remaining member of his staff accompanying him, Lieutenant Colonel William Gilman, sat silently together in the dining room of the *Tennessee*. Braun was morose over what he regarded as the defection of two staff members. Gilman had been unable to cheer him by pointing out the success of their most recent stop, in St. Louis, where he had signed up three promising new officers.

As the two men were talking, Toby and Martha entered the room and sat at their regular table directly across the room.

It was the height of the dinner hour, and as always, the room was filled with diverse groups of people. At one table, five men were enjoying themselves enormously, boisterously swapping stories and laughing uproariously. Nearby was a family with two small children, a boy and a girl, who were under sharp restraint from strict parents who insisted on decorous behavior. Facing them was an obvious honeymoon couple, completely lost in each other. The bride smiled at her husband with misty eyes, regardless of what he said or did. An old lady was traveling with a middle-aged companion, who was clearly making an effort to be agreeable.

Braun and his companion, however, paid no attention to any of the guests except Toby and Martha.

Gilman sat facing them, with Toby directly in his line of sight. He stared at him for several moments. Suddenly he snapped his fingers and exclaimed, "By God, I've got it!"

Braun looked up from his plate. "What the hell are you talking about?" he asked.

In a low voice, Gilman said, "As you know, General, my home is in the District of Columbia. One day, about a year ago, maybe it was a year and a half, I went to a ceremony where President Grant himself presented a medal to an officer by the name of Toby Holt. Seems this fellow was a big hero. Colonel Toby Holt and the poker dealer in the gaming saloon on this ship are one and the same person!"

Braun stared. "You must be dreaming."

"You know my memory for faces is blamed near perfect, General," Gilman whispered earnestly. "I never forget a face, and as sure as I'm sitting here, that fellow is Toby Holt."

"What's a fellow who was awarded a medal by the President doing as a poker dealer?"

"Damned if I know! You tell me, General."

Braun sat in silence for a time, brooding and drumming his fingers on the table, his meal forgotten. Suddenly he slapped the table with his palm. "The answer is obvious," he sputtered, keeping his voice down despite his anger. "The government has set spies onto us. They're frightened of us! From western Tennessee, word already has gone back to Washington that we're training an armed force. This fellow Holt has been hired as a government agent."

The rationale was too pat, the reasoning too glib,

but Gilman knew better than to argue with his stubborn superior. "You may be right," he said cautiously.

"I know goddam well I'm right!" Braun insisted. "We're at war, Gilman, and we've got to act accordingly. I want you to treat Holt as a spy and get a confession from him, if you can. But in any event, dispose of him."

"Yes, sir!" Gilman said. "When do you want me to act?"

Braun spoke decisively. "As a rule, only a few people come to the gaming saloon during daylight hours. Pick a time when Holt is alone there. Get his confession and perform the execution then. Be sure you do it today!"

They finished their meal in grim silence.

Toby and Martha had not noticed the intense but private conversation between Braun and his associate, and they had no idea of the drama in store. After they finished their meal, they returned to work, with Martha changing into her provocative costume. A couple from Mississippi came in to have drinks and play poker, and they whiled away an hour, then wandered off after losing a modest sum. Martha removed their empty glasses and took them into the nearby bar.

Toby was momentarily alone. Suddenly, Colonel Gilman appeared from behind. "Don't move, Holt," he said. "I've got a pistol on you, and if you make one move, it'll be your last."

Toby froze.

At that moment, Martha came into the saloon, carrying two glasses of ice water. Almost directly facing Gilman, she took in the situation at a glance and instantly proved that she was Domino's daughter. She hurled the contents of one glass into the man's eyes, momentarily blinding him. At the same moment, she hurled herself at him, catching him off balance and knocking him to the floor while his pistol clattered across the room.

At the same moment, Toby whirled and threw himself onto the man, but he was too late. Gilman had landed on the back of his head, striking the hard wood with a loud crack. His eyes were open, but he stared emptily into space.

Martha knelt beside him and felt for a pulse in his wrist. To her astonishment she could discern no beat whatsoever. "He's dead!" she whispered.

Toby felt beneath the man's coat and waistcoat and confirmed that her diagnosis was accurate. Rising to his feet, he hauled the corpse upright. In the meantime, Martha cleared up all signs of the struggle. She put both glasses on the table, and picking up Gilman's pistol, she dropped it into Toby's pocket. Then she moved forward and took her place on one side of the colonel, while Toby, with an arm around the dead man's waist, supported him from the other side.

They shared the burden between them and slowly made their way to the open deck. Any passerby who noted the trio from a distance probably would have assumed that the man in the center was intoxicated or ill. If someone came close, however, the truth might become obvious.

As Toby realized, and as Martha guessed, the risk they were taking was enormous. For the bodies of Braun's dead associates to slip overboard in a heavy fog late at night was one thing. It was far different to take a corpse to the rail and heave it into the Mississippi in broad daylight when two hundred passengers were free to roam the ship, any one of whom could appear at any moment. Nevertheless, the risk had to be taken. If the man's death were known, doctors and police would be called in. The manner of his death would be revealed, and Toby would be forced to admit his identity and

Martha's. It was essential to his mission that he keep this information secret as long as possible. He was disturbed that the dead man knew him by name. He recognized the possibility that Braun was also aware of his identity, but he had no way of knowing that for certain. For the moment he would have to proceed on the assumption that his secret was safe. There was nothing else he could do.

They stood at the rail, Gilman still in the center. His feet were planted apart, his elbows rested on the rail, and he appeared, as did Toby and Martha, to be looking westward at the far bank of the Mississippi, about half of a mile distant. All three stood with their backs to the deck.

Two middle-aged couples who spoke with southern accents were sauntering down the deck together and called a cheerful greeting. Martha replied with a smile but was careful not to speak. She, too, had a southern accent, and she knew that if the two couples heard her, they would be likely to stop, inquire as to her home and her relatives, and try to find friends in common.

Toby breathed more easily when they moved on. He and Martha seemed to be engaging in a lively conversation but actually were spouting sheer gibberish for the sake of any other passengers who might happen to notice them. Both were afraid that potential poker players would appear and would request Toby's presence in the gaming saloon.

He spoke urgently. "The deck is clear, both fore and aft," he said. "Not a soul is in sight. Are you ready?"

Martha nodded.

"We heave him overboard," he directed. "Quick now!" He bent down and took hold of one of Gilman's legs.

Martha needed no instruction to do the same thing.

She grasped the other leg, and they lifted him into the air and thrust him forward simultaneously. He slid silently beyond their reach into the water below.

Martha shuddered, and Toby took a step closer and put an arm around her shoulders to steady her. Then they watched Gilman's body floating as the ship moved past it.

Suddenly the body was struck by one of the huge blades of the paddle wheel, and the entire vessel shuddered as though an underwater rock had been encountered. That was the only noticeable disturbance. The paddle wheel continued to turn, and the man's body was battered beyond recognition before sinking below the underwater level of the wheel.

Ostensibly taking their time, Toby and Martha returned to the gaming saloon, where they conducted a rapid, thorough search for any clues that would reveal the dead man had been there. Finding nothing, they quickly went down to their cabin. There Toby examined the man's pistol and found it was a single-shot Colt of pre-Mexican War vintage. It was loaded, however, and was capable of doing great damage.

"Guns like this," he told Martha, "were manufactured nearly forty years ago and are very old-fashioned. They were issued during the Civil War only to artillery officers. That means he probably was an officer in the field artillery." He grinned as he slipped the weapon into a jacket pocket. "I'll take charge of this, and I'll throw it overboard late tonight. I don't want to take the chance of anyone's finding it and suspecting that its owner met an unexpected end."

As he spoke they could feel the ship veering to port. Martha became alarmed.

Toby smiled and shook his head. "No cause for concern," he said. "We're putting into a town where we'll be taking on more food and fuel. We shouldn't be here for more than a couple of hours."

She sighed in relief. "We got rid of the body just in time."

Toby put his hands on her shoulders. "I can't even begin to thank you," he said. "You saved my life, you know. He came up behind me with his gun and called me by name. That's when you came in, and I must say, you didn't hesitate for as much as a second."

"I reacted without thinking," she said. "That's what comes of having been through several tight spots with my father."

She was as valuable in a crisis as any trained, experienced man could have been, Toby thought, and her value was even greater because of the various guises she could assume.

"Once more, I'm in your debt."

"In the business that we're in, there's no such thing as debts between us. You save me one minute, and I do what I can for you the next. Both benefits and hazards come in working together in a dangerous game."

Toby looked at her, his expression thoughtful, and then he spoke huskily. "Call your help what you will," he said. "You saved my life. If you hadn't come in at the exact moment you did and if you had given a second's thought to your own safety, which you didn't, I would be a dead man now."

"You've intervened more than once on my behalf, Toby," she told him. "Let's say that, if you insist on speaking in terms of debts, I was merely repaying one debt to you. We can go back and forth like this indefinitely, and the way this case is developing, it wouldn't surprise me in the least if that's just exactly what we do."

He grinned, and as he did, he discovered that his sense of guilt was very much relieved. He had been depressed by the realization that he had allowed physical cravings to get the better of him and that he had been unfaithful to Clarissa. Now, however, he felt that his affair with Martha had more or less justified itself. He had no way to measure the favor she had done him or to weigh the risk she had taken on his behalf. He found it increasingly difficult to weigh the good and the bad, to differentiate between them and make his decisions accordingly. Martha was much more than provocatively lovely. She had exhibited a true nobility of character, and his admiration for her made him desire her more than ever.

Not stopping to think, much less to measure the consequences of his act, he took a single step toward her, swept her into his arms, and kissed her with all his might. She returned his embrace and kiss with a passion and devotion that matched his.

Time once again stood still for both of them. They were locked together in an embrace so all-encompassing that the issues of right and of wrong no longer existed. They were a man and a woman meant for each other; everything else was forgotten.

At last they moved apart and looked at each other with burning, mounting passion. Their eyes continued to lock as Toby reached to bolt the cabin door. They would have two hours or more completely to themselves while in port; neither was on duty during that time, so they were free to do as they pleased. Neither spoke as they removed their clothes, taking their time, drawing out the process in order to prolong the delicious suspense that hung over them.

A searing passion swept over and through them, engulfing them, and they responded to it like two drowning creatures exposed to pure oxygen. They clung to each other, stroking and touching, and quickly they became one, with Martha screaming aloud in sheer ecstasy. Her cry was matched by his, and they reached a climax together.

Afterward, they lay side by side, looking deep into each other's eyes. Their passion had subsided, but in its place was a feeling far deeper, far more lasting, a sense of security and more. Each knew that he or she could depend on the other in any emergency, for any help that was necessary, regardless of the cost, the circumstances, or the risks. They were united in every sense of the word.

Martha was at peace within herself. She loved Toby and was convinced that he loved her. She had no idea of the depth of his feelings for Clarissa, but she strongly doubted that he could truly love her. In his lovemaking, it seemed to her, he had proved that he cared deeply for only one woman on earth. He was too honest to play games, and she was positive that the moment would soon come when he would be forced to reevaluate his relationships.

They dressed together in a tender silence and made their way to the gaming saloon as the *Tennessee* pulled away from the dock and resumed her voyage. When Toby reached the saloon, his own desire was to get rid of Gilman's pistol as soon as he could, but fate was against him. A passenger from St. Louis was waiting to play two-handed poker. Toby not only had to play for more than an hour, but was forced to concentrate and pretend to enjoy the company. He felt only relief when the game finally came to an end.

No other passengers came into the saloon before supper time, and Toby waited until dark to go out onto the open deck. Then, with Martha standing guard, he hurled Gilman's pistol into the deepest part of the river.

When they went down to the dining room, they could see Braun eating, conspicuously alone. All other tables had two or more occupants. After glancing at him, Martha commented, "He seems very much out of sorts."

"Yes," Toby replied with a slight smile. "He may

be angry because his companions appear to be deserting him, one by one."

As a matter of fact, Emil Braun was furious over the disappearance of Gilman. In his chaotic and suspicious state of mind, he jumped to the conclusion that his operations officer, like his other two subordinates, had deserted when the ship had put into port. It seemed that these officers had accepted his bonus money, stayed with him while it suited their purposes, and then had decided to vanish when they found it convenient.

To hell with all of them, Braun thought angrily. He would carry out his mission with his newly signed officers, and without any help from his veterans, if need be. One way or another, he would force all America to respect Emil Braun.

VIII

As the days passed, the disappearance of his man Gilman began to eat into Braun. It could not be accidental, he finally concluded, that three of his officers had vanished and that all of them apparently had deserted. Someone was responsible, and he could not help suspecting that the man in charge of the gaming saloon, whom Gilman had identified as Holt, was somehow involved. As for the waitress who seemed generally to be in his company, Braun figured that she could be made to talk. She was a red-haired temptress if ever he had seen one, and everything in her demeanor indicated that she would be an easy mark for a seduction followed by some adroit questioning. Completely forgetting earlier warnings by his subordinates to steer clear of her, he began to anticipate the pleasure of interrogating her, smiling to himself and rubbing his hands together at the prospect.

Timing his move perfectly, Braun waited until a short time after noon dinner, when the passengers were occupied elsewhere.

Captain Hummel had invited all passengers to visit the bridge in small groups and observe the operation of the vessel as she made her way down the Mississippi. Virtually everyone had responded with enthusiasm, and groups had clustered in animated conversation near the steps to the bridge, with the result that other areas of the ship were virtually deserted.

Braun therefore had the saloon to himself. He sauntered in, saw that no one else was present, and sat down. He lighted a cigar and waited with as much patience as he could muster for the redheaded waitress.

When Martha entered the room, she stopped short inside the door. She knew she was in trouble from the moment she saw Braun staring at her, his eyes taking in every detail of her body. Certainly his presence in the saloon was not accidental, and she had good reason to suspect that he was not there for any legitimate purpose.

Nevertheless, she had a task to perform, and she went through the motions with crisp efficiency. "Good afternoon, sir," she said cheerfully. "Would you care for a drink?"

Braun nodded and grinned. "Yes, but there's something I'd like better," he said, "though there's no need to rush. Most people seem to be occupied with the captain this afternoon."

"I'm not surprised," she replied. "The captain's invitation was most generous. In fact, I doubt we'll have much gaming business before supper time."

"I'm in no hurry for that drink," Braun said, and patted the cushion adjacent to him on the divan. "Why don't you sit down and rest your feet, and we'll chat for a while before you go traipsing off to the bar for it."

Pretending to be cordial, Martha seated herself but took care to sit in a chair opposite him.

"Tell me about yourself," he demanded.

She smiled at him and replied with seeming innocence. "What is it you'd like to know?"

"Anything you care to tell me," he replied. "I'm fascinated, and I'd love to know why a lovely lady like you happens to be working here as a waitress."

She smiled sweetly, and her reply was both rapid

and glib. "My husband and I signed on together for a number of voyages," she said. "He's in charge of the gaming saloon, and as you know, I serve drinks. We keep each other company, and we both earn money we need."

She could tell he was disconcerted by the look in his eyes when she mentioned the fact that she had a husband, but his expression did not alter.

"I've changed my mind," Braun said suddenly. "I think I'll have a nip after all. I'd like a plain whiskey with a little water on the side."

"By all means." Glad to escape, Martha jumped to her feet, and smoothing her provocative skirt, she quickly left the room. When she returned with the drink a few moments later, she noted that Braun was on his feet, pacing up and down the saloon. His restless energy reminded her of that of a caged animal.

"Here you are, sir," she said, and put the tray containing the two glasses on a table.

Braun picked up the shot glass that held the liquor and extended it to her. "You didn't bring one for yourself," he said. "I was hoping you would, but you can share with me instead."

She prudently kept her distance. "I'm sorry, sir," she said, "but we're not allowed to drink with the guests. It's a rule."

She could see a hint of evil intent in Emil Braun's smile. He continued to hold the glass out to her. "You don't think I'd be stupid enough to tell the ship's officers that you've broken one of their foolish rules," he said.

Martha took a cautious backward step so he would not be able to come too close to her.

Braun then swallowed the contents of the glass in a single gulp. Placing the empty glass on the tray without bothering to drink the water, he instead swung around quickly, and reaching out a brawny hand, he unexpectedly caught hold of Martha's wrist. Jerking on it with considerable force, he caused her to lose her balance.

His movement was so swift and sudden that he caught her off guard, and she could not stop herself from falling against him. This was precisely what Braun was trying to achieve, and his heavy arms encircled her, drawing her close. In the meantime, his moist hands began to move across her body.

Martha realized that physical resistance was useless, that, in fact, it actually encouraged Braun to go further, so she went limp and did not resist him.

He pulled her still closer, and she could feel one of his hands sliding across her breasts.

In her anger at being mistreated, she stiffened and, reaching out, slapped him hard across the face.

Angered, Braun caught her shoulders and began to shake her. Then he released her so unexpectedly that she staggered backward and fell onto the couch. As she looked up, she realized what had happened. Toby Holt had come into the room and had clamped a hand on Braun's shoulder, turning him around.

Never had she seen Toby in such a mood. His face was grim, and his eyes blazed. He held Braun at arm's length with his left hand and at the same time drove his right fist with full force into the man's face.

"Keep your hands off my wife!" he said, enraged.

Martha found herself wishing anew that she *were* his wife. Only in that way could she be assured of his constant attention and guidance, his ever-present protection.

Toby reached out again and drove his right fist into Braun's cheekbone and then planted his left with such force in the man's midriff that Braun doubled over.

Emil Braun, a powerful man, knew how to use his fists, but he was no match for an infuriated Toby Holt. Braun tried to assume a defensive position, but his own fists were knocked aside, and he took a frightful drubbing as Toby's fists crashed repeatedly into his face and body.

Martha knew that Toby's control was legendary, that he always had a purpose behind every move, and that he never acted without having thought it out first. But his manner now was that of a very angry man, a husband whose wife had been mauled by a boorish stranger. His fists lashed out with such speed that Martha could scarcely follow them, and she heard nothing but their thudding against the man's face and body.

She had no way of telling how long the beating would have gone on, but the first and second mates, walking the deck en route to the bridge, saw the altercation and immediately stepped in.

The second mate came up behind Toby and threw his arms around him, pinning Toby's arms against his sides, while the first mate came between the two antagonists.

"What's the meaning of this, Mr. Holt?" the first mate demanded frostily.

Toby shook off the restraining hands of the second officer and answered coldly. "This man dared to insult my wife."

The first officer looked at Braun, and the battered, bleeding man could only nod in reluctant corroboration.

"I would advise you, sir, to retire to your own cabin immediately," the first mate said to Braun. "And if I were you, I wouldn't think of pressing any charges. You're fortunate to have escaped with a thrashing."

Emil Braun had no choice, and after looking at Toby for a long moment, he turned on his heel and staggered off down the corridor.

That look was all that Toby needed to know that he had a new and permanent enemy in Emil Braun. And because it was a virtual certainty now that the man knew his identity, Toby knew he would have to be on his guard at every moment. A dangerous, unbalanced fanatic such as Braun was capable of doing anything in order to eliminate his enemies.

Eddie Neff, having concluded his legitimate business at the Holt ranch, no longer had any valid reason for visiting the place. Nevertheless, he continued to appear every day, sometimes showing up only late in the afternoon, but always arriving in time to take Clarissa out for supper. No longer did he care about obeying Domino's mandate to stay in Oregon until he succeeded in seducing Clarissa. Such considerations were far from his mind now. His love for the young woman was genuine; never before had he cared so much for anyone.

As for Clarissa, she accepted his attentions, while assuring herself constantly that she was still in love with her husband. She nevertheless looked forward to Eddie's daily visits. So far, she had remained faithful to Toby, but she had to admit to herself that she was strongly tempted to give herself to Eddie and that the temptation became harder to resist every time she saw him. She knew full well that she was playing with fire, but at the same time, her inner being demanded relief from the lonely existence that had become her lot for month after month during Toby's prolonged absences from the ranch. What was more, her body craved the natural outlet that Eddie could offer. But while her instincts urged her to give in to him, her basic consciousness of morality also became firmer, and she became trapped in a dilemma of her own making. The result was that she procrastinated, making no decision, hoping that the issue would be taken out of her hands and that in some miraculous way a painless, satisfactory decision would be made for her.

One night Eddie appeared at the ranch a short time after sundown, and he and Clarissa enjoyed a predinner drink while he played with Tim, who was, as always, delighted to see Eddie. Then, after Clarissa put her son to bed, leaving him in the care of one of the ranch hands, they went by carriage to an inn outside Portland. They had a quiet dinner, during which they chatted incessantly. Their words, like their thoughts, were in total harmony.

After dinner they returned to the ranch, and the night being warm, they retired to the gazebo behind the house, hoping to catch a glimpse of Mount Hood in the moonlight. Eddie sat on a bench while Clarissa went into the house to check on Tim and to let the man caring for him know that he could go home.

The night was humid; thunder began to rumble, with streaks of lightning appearing in the sky off to the west, heading their way. Mount Hood would eventually be obscured by clouds. But for the moment, the storm was still some distance off.

When Clarissa rejoined Eddie, she brought drinks for both of them. She handed one to him, and they sat side by side on a bench in the gazebo. They remained silent for several minutes, enjoying the breeze, for the night seemed rather stifling.

Finally Eddie raised his glass in a silent toast and said solemnly, "I must talk to you about something of great importance. At least, it's important to me."

Struck by the seriousness of his tone, she looked at him intently.

"As I'm sure you realize," he said, "I finished my business here many days ago. I could have found excuses to stay on, but I've made none. I have stayed for only one reason—I lack the strength to say good-bye and stop seeing you."

She met his gaze, but her voice faltered when she replied. "I know. I felt just as you have, and I've been glad for each day as it has come and found you still here."

"Mine is the very worst mistake that a man can

make. Not only have I fallen in love with a lady who is
married, but she happens to love her husband."

Her smile was bitter. "And I've made the worst
mistake that a married woman who loves her husband
can make. I'm attracted to another man, and I don't
know what to do about it."

The thunder sounded closer, and the flash of lightning lit up the sky, but they were too intent on their
problem to pay any heed to the weather.

"All I know," Eddie said brokenly, "is that I love
you. A dozen times I have tried to give you up, to say
good-bye, and to disappear from your life. But I'm too
weak. I lack the courage to turn my back and to walk
away."

"I'm glad you couldn't do it," Clarissa murmured,
"because again and again I have been on the point of
sending you away. I tried to tell you that I love Toby
and that you have no place in my life. But the words
stick in my throat, and I'm unable to utter them."

They looked at each other, and the tension grew
until it became a physical presence. The wind freshened, and the rumble of thunder grew louder. A flash
of lightning crossed the horizon nearby, but the couple
continued to ignore the elements.

"What are we going to do?" Clarissa murmured. "I
can't betray Toby, but I don't have the strength to give
you up, either."

As Eddie looked at her, many answers came to
mind. He tried in vain to find one that was suitable,
one that would offer her comfort and yet would leave the
door open for their desires. He could think of nothing
to say. Instead he made a tentative move toward her,
his arms extended.

Swiftly, scarcely aware of what she was doing,
Clarissa slid into his embrace. Her lips were raised to
his.

Just at that moment, the entire sky was lit up,

and almost simultaneously a great clap of thunder sounded directly overhead. Startled, they looked up. The air seemed charged. Not moving, they sat for a moment, staring into each other's eyes.

Another streak of lightning and a peal of thunder broke the stillness of the night.

Eddie started to speak, but before he could do so, Clarissa raised a finger to his lips, to silence him. Then she leaned forward to kiss him.

Before their lips touched, the air around them seemed to explode, as a bolt of lightning ripped down out of the sky and struck the topmost point of the gazebo. Clarissa screamed as Eddie tried to shield her. But the falling timbers of the collapsing gazebo struck them both hard, and they were killed instantly.

The bodies of Clarissa and Eddie, still locked in an embrace, were pinned beneath the wreckage. The rain poured down, soaking their clothes and their lifeless forms.

Their bodies were found at dawn when the ranch hands reported for work. The acting foreman went at once to Fort Vancouver, taking Tim to his grandparents' home and giving General and Mrs. Blake the unhappy news.

The general, accompanied by his personal aide-de-camp, went off to the ranch at once and spent the better part of the morning there. When he returned home at noon, Eulalia accompanied him to their private sitting room.

"How bad was it?" Eulalia asked.

"Brace yourself," her husband said. "The only way I can explain this to you is to let you have the unvarnished truth. As you heard earlier, Clarissa is dead, and so is Neff, the fellow she brought here to dinner. They were in the gazebo when a bolt of lightning apparently hit it. It collapsed, and they were killed. It distresses me greatly to have to tell you that they were embracing when lightning struck and they died that way."

Eulalia drew in a deep, quick breath and clenched her fists tightly. "Were they lovers?"

"I don't know," was the general's blunt reply. "I don't deal in conjecture. I can tell you that they were fully clothed."

Eulalia shook her head. "I just can't believe it of Clarissa," she said, "and of that young man we thought was so nice. I'd have seen it then if they had any real romantic interest in each other. I swear I would. Perhaps she was frightened by the storm and sought out his company for reassurance."

"What difference does it make?" the general demanded harshly. "They're both dead, and the facts of their relationship—whatever it may have been—will be buried with them."

"For Toby's sake, I'd like to know."

"If you want my advice," her husband told her, "you will mention nothing about the association of this other man when you write to Toby or speak to him. If there was an affair, Clarissa and the man were very discreet about it. Say nothing to Toby, and for the sake of his little boy's future, let the whole question be buried with Clarissa."

"I suppose you're right."

"I've started to make arrangements for a funeral to be held tomorrow."

She could not help interrupting. "Toby can't possibly get here from Tennessee."

"Under the circumstances, we won't wait for him," the general said gruffly. "We'll see to it that she and the man are both given appropriate respect. I'll get a wire off to Domino, as well as to Toby. We'll keep Tim with us until Toby comes home to stay and makes other arrangements. I don't want to interfere with his assignment, and frankly I think it's probably just as well that he doesn't quit in midcourse. If I know him, he'll find solace in hard work, so if he wishes to keep going on the case till it's solved, then I feel we should do nothing to discourage his making that choice. As a matter of fact, I've already spoken with the acting foreman at his ranch, to be sure that there's a drawing account to meet the payroll and take care of things until Toby returns."

"It's so like you to think of everything," Eulalia replied, "and I suppose you're right about Toby's not coming home now. All the same, it breaks my heart. And poor Cindy. I'll have my hands full in consoling her after I tell her this dreadful news. You know how close she and Clarissa have always been."

The general kissed her. "Keep your chin up. We must go back to Cindy and Tim soon and break the news to them in the best way we know how. If you'll speak to Cindy, I'll take care of Timmy. We'll see the next few days through together. Then, I'm afraid, you'll have to get along without me for a while. I must make that trip to the War Department, as you know, without further delay. And then it's my plan to come home by way of West Point. I'll take the sad news to Hank at that time."

Eulalia braced herself, and they went downstairs to present a united front to Cindy and their grandson.

The worst part of her present situation, Violet thought, was that she had too little to do, too little to keep her occupied. Keeping the cottage in order took only a few hours each day, and she did the work automatically. She no longer had fields to till and weeds to remove and plants to nurture, so she spent most of the day doing nothing but sitting in the sunlight and daydreaming about her return to the life she had once known.

She sat now in the midmorning sunlight, rocking gently and keeping her eyes closed. Perhaps if everything went well, she thought, she might be able to return to the life that she had known and loved for so many years.

Opening her eyes, she caught a glimpse of Stalking Horse and beyond him saw two of Red Leary's men partially concealed in the underbrush. She was protected, she knew, and she thought that ironically her protection was so complete now that she was quite isolated.

As that thought occurred to her, she recalled that she was far from completely alone. Her former neighbors, the Dalys and the Swensons, had called on her several times, and each visit had cheered her up considerably. Of course, now that the season was advancing, they had plenty of work on their own farms to keep them busy, so their visits were becoming more infrequent. Violet could hardly begrudge them their work, inasmuch as she was a farmer herself and understood such things; still, she could not altogether fight down a twinge of self-pity at being neglected of late.

While she was immersed in these thoughts, she heard a carriage thumping on the road that approached the cottage. A few minutes later, a dusty cabriolet pulled to a halt, and Jedidiah Maynard, a young man who had just moved his family into the area, stuck his head out and grinned at her.

" 'Morning, Miss Violet," he called. "Hope I'm not disturbing you."

"As you can plainly see, Mr. Maynard," she replied tartly, "I am not doing a thing except drying my old bones in the sunlight."

He laughed heartily at her little joke and then explained, "Here, Miss Violet. My wife baked you this cake that she hopes will make things a bit easier in the kitchen for you, and while we're at it, I've brought this young man back home." He opened the door, and a grinning White Elk tumbled out of the carriage, followed by a boy of about his own age.

"What's all this?" she demanded in surprise.

"I told Tommy Maynard," White Elk said eagerly, "that if he would come back here with me, my grandpa would be glad to show him how to use a bow and arrow."

"By all means," Violet said, knowing her brother would be delighted. White Elk, at least, was being kept busy.

"Do you want us to bring your son back home later in the day, Mr. Maynard?"

"Thank you, ma'am, but that won't be necessary. I've got to go into town, and if it's all right with you, I'll stop off and pick Tommy up on my way home in the afternoon. That is, if you don't mind feeding him lunch."

"I think we can manage that without too much difficulty," Violet said with a smile. "Go along with you, boys. Stalking Horse is over yonder, White Elk. It wouldn't surprise me if he has a bow and arrows with him, so you can get straight to your lessons."

The two little boys went racing off to the area where they would find Stalking Horse, and as Violet watched them, she shook her head. They were so young, so innocent, so free of the evil that filled their elders. She couldn't help wishing that everyone she knew was as free of guilt and sin.

The private office of James Martinson, the assistant secretary, was located on the third floor of the U.S. Treasury Building across from the White House. Like the private sanctums of all highly placed government officials, the office was comfortable, handsomely furnished, and impressive. It occupied a corner overlooking the executive mansion. Behind Martinson's desk stood two flags, one of the United States, the other the Treasury Department's ensign. His desk was fashioned of highly polished mahogany, his visitors' chairs were of glove leather. Government pamphlets and other official documents were placed in neat piles on a large table near the desk, but the desk itself was uncluttered. In an adjoining room, Wilma and her assistant worked against the unending flow of government paperwork and kept Martinson's desk unusually clear.

Martinson sat back in his chair, taking his time as he read the latest secret army high command report that had been forwarded to a Washington post office box by Dorothy, Wilma's sister. As usual, she had done a first-rate job of copying the contents, and Martinson found two items of particular interest in it.

Picking up a scratch pad, he scribbled a few notes to himself, notes indecipherable to anyone else. Then he crossed the office to the fire burning in the fireplace and threw the report into it. For a time he watched it burn, then prodded the brittle remains with a poker until the entire document disintegrated.

Returning to his desk, Martinson paused at the large double windows, and jamming his hands into his trouser pockets, he stared out at the nearby White House. He could discern no sign of activity other than the armed sentry patrolling the entrance. Smoke curled from chimneys, and a flag, flying from a pole above the colonnades that formed the front entry, informed the world that President Grant was in residence.

Martinson smiled to himself in satisfaction. His plans were proceeding on all fronts, and he saw the day drawing closer when he would take up residence in the White House as the new president.

Emil Braun's brigade was making good progress in its formation and training, according to Milton Plosz's reports. Plosz apparently had done an excellent job to date. Martinson was additionally pleased that the work was going ahead with the desired secrecy. Not a word had appeared in print about it.

In revealing the existence of the army when the time was ripe for his own plans, he would create a sensation. He could accuse his government colleagues of criminal negligence in allowing such a force to be formed, for it would be only too evident to an alarmed nation that President Grant had failed to learn of the threat to the country and act promptly and decisively, as he should have, to put an end to it.

Some finishing touches remained, however, and his mind was busy with them. He wanted to take no needless risks. As his father had always preached: "When a man wants to make certain that a deal will succeed, he covers every possible angle in advance, and in that way, he guarantees his own success."

His mind racing, Martinson reached into a desk drawer, drew out a checkbook, and wrote a check for five hundred dollars. Then he pulled the bell rope that summoned his secretary.

Wilma, concealing her illness as best she could with an increased use of cosmetics, came into the office and stood inside the door. "You rang, James?"

"I did," he said. "Close the door and come over here and sit down."

She obediently shut the door, then approached his desk and sat in a straight chair opposite him, a pencil poised over her dictation pad.

Martinson shook his head. "I'm not giving you a letter at the moment," he said. "Here's a check I've just written for five hundred dollars. I want you to cash it. Half is for you, and the other half is for your sister. These are bonuses because of the splendid work she is doing."

"But I've had nothing to do with what Dorothy has accomplished for you," she protested feebly.

"Nonsense," he replied. "You set up the arrangement, and that's what counts. I have a little additional chore for your sister. If she carries it off successfully, there'll be two thousand dollars in it for her. I'll give her half of it for merely undertaking it. And on the same condition, you will receive a hundred dollars."

"You're too generous, James," she murmured, relieved at the flow of extra money that was helping to pay her medical bills as well as supplementing the fund she was trying to set aside for her son.

"My requirements are quite simple," he said. "I want Dorothy to find a cadet at the academy—preferably an upperclassman who is an honor student and who is willing to give up his career as an officer. Instead, he would form an association with a group that he will be told about later in greater detail. The right cadet will be launched on a career that will prove far more lucrative than any in the army. Also, he'll be paid a thousand dollars in cash the moment he leaves the academy."

Martinson had no intention of explaining in any greater detail what he had in mind. Actually, however, his plan was a simple one. When he exposed Braun, he would also reveal at the same time that the traitorous elements had infiltrated the student body at the U.S. Military Academy and had actually recruited a cadet in good standing to accept a commission in their armed forces. This would strengthen his own hold on the imagination of the American people and win him greater admiration for having uncovered and exposed the plot. Every move he made would go that much farther to discredit President Grant and others in the present administration—except for an alert and heroic assistant secretary of the treasury.

Even though Wilma had no idea what her employer had in mind, she felt uneasy. She knew that he was interfering in government affairs that were none of his business. Furthermore, her sister was assuming great risk in doing his bidding, although they had never met and had no direct contact. On the other hand, Wilma's need for money continued to be pressing. Consequently, she felt she had no real choice but to agree to act as an intermediary for Martinson, by presenting his request to Dorothy.

That weekend, as it happened, Dorothy made a trip to Washington to visit her sister. On the first evening of her stay, when Freddy was in bed, the sisters shared a bottle of wine and settled down for a confidential talk.

Wilma realized that Dorothy had changed appreciably since her agreement with Martinson had begun. Always attractive in a healthy, country-girl way, now she looked chic and positively glamorous. She had been on a diet, and this was partly responsible. Far more important, however, her hair was now dyed a shade of blond that made it resemble a field of ripe wheat. She wore expensive clothes, silk gowns that clung to her figure and increased her seductiveness. Her silk stockings and high-heeled shoes added to her appeal. Equally striking was her subtle but pronounced use of cosmetics. Her brown eyes, which had been ordinary, now looked large and sparkling. Her mouth was bright red and was made up beyond its natural lines to give it a provocative, pouting appearance.

Dorothy saw her sister studying her and absently fingered a long, dangling earring as she said, "Obviously, you find something out of the ordinary in the way I look."

"Out of the ordinary doesn't quite describe you," Wilma told her. "You look breathtakingly attractive. I never knew that I had such a beautiful sister."

"Thank you very much, dear," Dorothy said complacently.

"I'm surprised that the academy authorities haven't complained about the way you look," Wilma said. "After all, you have hundreds of young males on the grounds, and they must go mad when they see you."

Dorothy gave a slight giggle. "I guess the answer,"

she said, "is that the superintendent likes the way I look. The cadets stare at me until their eyeballs are ready to fall out, but they're so well disciplined that not one of them would ever dream of causing any trouble."

"Do you have any access to the corps of cadets?"

Her sister looked somewhat confused. "I'm not sure I know what you mean."

"I'll begin at the beginning." Wilma took her handbag from a nearby table, opened it, and counted out two hundred and fifty dollars in cash, which she presented to Dorothy. "This is a nice little bonus from your generous benefactor. He's very pleased with the reports, and he wanted to express his appreciation."

"What a nice way to show appreciation," Dorothy replied. "I think he must be a very considerate person."

"Indeed he is," Wilma assured her, "and he has an additional assignment for you if you're willing to perform it."

"I'm all ears."

"He wants you to subvert a cadet, preferably an honor student, and persuade him to resign from the corps. He'll be paid a thousand dollars for leaving, and he'll be employed in a way that the skills he has acquired will be well utilized."

"In what way?"

Wilma regarded her stonily. "That's none of your business, just as it's none of mine. Frankly, I don't know, and I wouldn't dream of asking. Once you have arranged for the cadet to defect, you are to arrange an appointment for him with someone who will fill him in on the details."

In the quiet of the room, Dorothy twirled the stem of her glass, looking into the dark red wine that filled it. "I can't imagine a more difficult task," she said. "The corps of cadets is made up of the most dedicated young men in the entire United States. Those in the top ten percent, the honor students, are absolute zealots. To persuade one of them to go back on his oath and to abandon his commission would be damned near impossible."

"Perhaps I neglected to mention," Wilma said softly, "that if you were to succeed in this enterprise, you would be paid an additional two thousand dollars."

Dorothy stopped twirling her glass and sat bolt upright. "Did you say two thousand?" she asked in wonder.

Wilma nodded. "Better than that, in fact. Whether you succeed or fail, you'll be paid a thousand just for making the effort. And once your mission is completed, you'll receive an additional thousand."

Dorothy's mascara-laden eyes became hard. "I assume," she said, "you're not joking."

"Indeed I'm not."

"My benefactor," Dorothy murmured, "has far too much money and doesn't know what to do with it. But as long as he keeps paying it out, I have no objection."

"Well," Wilma asked lightly, "what shall I tell him?"

Dorothy took a large swallow of her wine. "Tell him," she said emphatically, "that I accept the challenge of his offer. I have no idea how I'm going to carry this out, but one way or another, I'm going to do it. An extra two thousand is worth any extra effort and whatever sacrifice is needed!"

The next morning Dorothy left Washington by train, bound for New York and West Point, carrying with her the money James Martinson had given to Wilma to pay Dorothy for accepting his proposed mission. Wilma had assured her that the second installment would be sent off the moment Martinson received word of the resignation of a cadet. On the train ride, Dorothy amused herself by planning ways to spend her increasing fortune.

*   *   *

First-class cadet Henry Blake was surprised in mid-week to find a note in his mailbox asking him to call at the apartment of General Pitcher's secretary on Saturday evening at six o'clock. The time interfered with the cadet's normal supper hour in the mess hall, but Hank regarded the summons as seriously as though coming from the superintendent himself, so he presented himself at Dorothy's apartment promptly.

He was startled when she answered his knock in a black, floor-length gown, her hair tumbling loosely around her shoulders. The musky odor of perfume was strong in the air, and the cadet felt somewhat giddy.

Dorothy welcomed him with an inviting smile. "Please come in, Hank," she said, using his nickname.

"Thank you, ma'am," he replied stiffly.

"Not 'ma'am,' " she told him gently. "Just call me Dottie." She took his uniform cap and cape and led him into the living room, where she had prepared a whiskey and soda.

Hank looked at the glass and hesitated. He wanted to tell her that he was unaccustomed to alcoholic beverages. Reminding himself, however, that this was the general's secretary, he steeled himself, picked up his glass, and after toasting her, took a sip.

"It occurred to me," Dottie said, crossing her legs in such a way that her skirt was pulled up so as to reveal her well-turned ankles and shapely legs, "that I asked you here at just the wrong time of day. Ordinarily you'd be at the mess hall right now, so perhaps you'll allow me to compensate by offering you supper."

Hank sat straight on the edge of his chair. "I—I wouldn't want to impose on you, ma'am—I mean, Dottie," he stammered.

"It's no imposition, I can assure you," she said smoothly. "We'll consider the matter settled. Is your drink all right?"

He nodded. "It's just fine, thank you." He won-

dered why she had invited him to her apartment, but
he could not bring himself to ask.

Dorothy seemed to read his mind. "You know,
Hank," she said, "you've appeared in so many reports
that the general has dictated to me. You rank number
one in your class consistently now. I became curious
about you and decided that I simply had to know you
better. I therefore took the liberty of inviting you to
join me here."

He was flattered, and his embarrassment was so
great that he floundered when he tried to reply.

Utilizing her physical charms and her femininity,
Dorothy worked hard to put Hank at his ease. Gradually she succeeded, particularly as he slowly downed
the contents of his glass. As soon as he had finished his
drink, she swiftly refilled it, not bothering to ask if he
wanted more.

The liquor seemed to loosen Hank, and Dorothy
silently made a mental note of that fact for future
reference.

Eventually Hank relaxed sufficiently to talk about
his recently announced engagement to Cindy Holt, and
he spoke at length, too, of the pride he took in his
adoptive father, Major General Blake. He was at ease
now, and Dorothy served him a dinner calculated to
win a young soldier's heart. Knowing that the academy
fare was hearty but plain, she had prepared a meal that
included a number of delicacies, and she knew she was
on the right track when Hank ate everything on his
plate.

She was also pleased to note that he drank two
glasses of wine with his meal. Combined with the liquor he had drunk before supper, it had a pronounced
effect on him.

Although Dorothy was warm and friendly, she kept
her distance, not wanting to frighten him away. When
she became convinced that she had won his confidence,

she said lightly, "This has been great fun. I hope you'll come again and have supper with me next Saturday—a week from tonight."

He demurred and seemed puzzled by the second invitation.

Dorothy exerted still more charm, to override his objections. "You seem to forget," she said, "that I lead a lonely life here at the academy. I can't go out on many social engagements because of the nature of my position, and I'm forced to spend most of my evenings alone. I know you're engaged to be married, and I have no designs on you, you may be sure. But you're an intelligent young man, and I really do enjoy your company. So you'll be doing me a great favor when you come again next week."

Under the circumstances, Hank could not refuse her invitation, so he accepted with all the grace he could muster.

IX

The following week passed quickly, and the normal routines of life at the academy were interrupted only by a very brief letter for Hank from his stepfather, who informed him that he would be arriving for an overnight visit within a few days after he made a report in person to the War Department in Washington.

On Saturday night Hank again went to Dorothy's apartment for dinner, bringing his hostess a bouquet of flowers and a small box of candy. As far as he was concerned, this was to be a pleasant visit with a new acquaintance, and he had no thought of any kind of involvement, in view of his engagement to Cindy. The date of their marriage was set for the day of his graduation in June.

He managed to convince himself, therefore, that nothing was wrong in accepting Dorothy's invitation. She had proved herself to be a good but casual friend, nothing more, and he could see no harm in the relationship.

However, he noted subtle differences in the atmosphere. The drink Dorothy prepared was much stronger than the drinks he had been served before. When Dorothy sat and her skirt fell away, her legs were even more enticingly revealed. Her gown fell from one shoulder, revealing an expanse of smooth, creamy skin. Dorothy seemed to be totally unaware of this mishap and seemed not to notice that Hank was fascinated, unable to tear his eyes from her bare shoulder.

By the time that Hank had finished about half of his second drink, he became rather hazy on developments. Somehow he found himself sitting beside Dorothy on the couch with their glasses on a coffee table in front of them. His arm was stretched across the back of the couch behind her, and the next thing he knew, she was leaning up against him. It seemed only natural for him to lower his arm, and his hand happened to come in contact with her bare shoulder.

The feel of her soft, smooth skin beneath his fingers electrified him, and he found himself unable to resist the temptation of caressing her. The next moment they slid naturally into a full embrace, their bodies pressing together.

Hank realized that Dorothy was scantily attired beneath her gown, and that knowledge added to his excitement. He pressed closer to her. When he felt her hand beginning to roam, searching and caressing, he lost all vestiges of self-control.

He loved Cindy, and it was true that he had never as much as looked at another girl romantically since he had met his future wife. But he lacked experience with women and his control was limited, particularly as a result of the spartan conditions under which cadets lived. Here was a provocative young woman, who was making it clear that she was not only available but eager to participate in a sexual adventure. He never could remember just when they both undressed, but he recalled only too well the excitement of holding her and feeling her caresses matching his own.

The thought flickered through his mind that perhaps she had some ulterior motive for being so amenable. He was inflamed, and partly intoxicated, but that thought clung. Even in their ardent lovemaking, he did not lose sight of the question.

When they began to simmer down, still wrapped in a close embrace, Dorothy began to murmur in dulcet tones. "You're wonderful, Hank," she whispered. "You're wasted as a cadet, and you'll be wasted still more as a second lieutenant trying to live on the tiny pay that you'll receive in the army."

He chuckled indulgently. "It's a bit late to think of that now, isn't it?"

"I'm serious," she replied. "I can get you a thousand dollars, free and clear, and I can promise you a position that will make use of all the training you've had at the academy and yet will pay you a salary several times the amount that you could earn after graduation. Are you interested?" She accompanied her words by softly stroking the back of his neck.

A warning bell sounded in Hank's mind. He knew that he would have to proceed with the greatest care, making certain he did not frighten her into silence while he pumped her for further information. "I guess I could be interested," he said slowly. "What you say sounds too good to be true."

"I know it does, but it is true," Dorothy replied earnestly. She caressed him as she spoke. "I don't pretend to know what this offer is all about, but I do know for certain that it's legitimate. When my source promises payment of a thousand dollars, you'll get the full thousand promptly, not a penny less! And when he promises a position that will require you to use your experience and knowledge, I give you my word that he means every word of it."

"Who is this fellow, and where do I get in touch with him?"

"Not so fast," she replied cautiously. "I can't tell you anything more without a commitment on your part. If you accept the offer, I'll give you information on how to proceed from there. Until then, I can say nothing."

Something was very wrong with the offer she had

made, Hank thought, and he needed to know much more about it. "I've spent more than three years as a cadet," he said, "and I've worked hard in all that time to maintain a high average. Naturally, I'm very much interested in what you've had to say. The offer sounds very attractive. But I'm not so sure I want to give up my commitment to the army in order to take on something new that I know nothing about. If you don't mind, I'll need some time to think about it."

"Of course, honey," she replied, cuddling closer to him and kissing him. "Take all the time you need. I'm sure that the more you think about it, the more attracted you'll be to the offer."

When they were dressed again, they enjoyed a light supper, and Dorothy made no further mention of the proposition. Although he was almost overcome with curiosity, Hank refrained from asking her any questions. Not until he announced that it was time for him to return to the barracks did she bring up the subject again.

Handing him his cape and visored cap, Dorothy asked gently, "How soon do you suppose you'll reach a decision on the matter we were discussing earlier?"

"If it's all right with you," he said, "I'd like to mull it over for at least the next few days."

"Can you make up your mind by next Saturday?" she asked quickly.

He thought for a moment, then nodded.

"Good," she said. "We have an engagement for next Saturday. You'll come here for supper, and I'm sure we'll have ample opportunity to talk and to keep busy in various ways."

On Sunday afternoon Hank was surprised and delighted when his stepfather appeared unexpectedly early at West Point, having concluded his business in Washington and having then come north without delay.

Father and son spent the afternoon together, and Hank inquired at length about the health and state of mind of his fiancée. Eager to learn everything the general could tell him about her, he was at the same time curiously reserved, appearing to be even somewhat embarrassed by his own questioning.

General Blake also took this opportunity to tell his stepson about Clarissa's death, specifically refraining, however, from any mention of Eddie Neff. Hank, shocked, assured his father that he would write to Toby at the earliest opportunity, to express his condolences.

At dinner that night, Hank finally confessed what had happened at Dorothy's apartment the preceding evening. The general listened carefully.

When Hank was finished, the general asked, "Are you seriously contemplating accepting this offer of money and a position from the man who's been using this woman as a go-between?" he asked quietly.

"Hell, no!" Hank exploded, and then deliberately calmed down. "I'm sorry, sir. What I meant was—no, sir, I haven't given it a second thought."

His stepfather smiled. "That's what I assumed, of course. I know you're angry and upset with yourself for giving in to the young woman's wiles and going to bed with her. You undoubtedly think that you've betrayed Cindy—"

"Don't rub it in, Dad," Hank said miserably. "I feel just awful about it."

"Dismiss that thought from your mind," the general replied forcefully. "You were deliberately seduced by a woman who used sex as a means of softening you up and making you more amenable to her proposal. That will never be mentioned at home, and I see no reason for you to tell Cindy about it. She would just be hurt, and I doubt that she could understand."

"I'm not so sure I understand it myself, Dad," Hank said, looking down at the table.

The general reached across and patted him on the shoulder. "Let's concentrate on more important matters. Are you willing to see this whole business through to a logical conclusion?"

"Something very odd is going on," Hank said. "I wouldn't be surprised if a conspiracy of some sort against the United States is what's afoot. I'll be glad to contribute whatever I can to solving the riddle."

"Good boy!" General Blake said. "We'll go see General Pitcher in his quarters as soon as we finish dinner."

Hank froze. He was reluctant to tell his story to the austere superintendent, but he knew that the issue was out of his hands now. The next steps had to be worked out by those with experience in handling treasonable matters.

They walked the short distance to the superintendent's house and there found Mrs. Pitcher and her two teenage daughters with the superintendent in the living room. Mrs. Pitcher greeted General Blake cordially, but she and the girls soon made their excuses and left the room. General Pitcher, a genial host, poured whiskeys for himself and his colleague. Hank was so nervous, however, that he even declined an offer of tea and sat rigidly on the edge of his chair like a new cadet undergoing hazing by upperclassmen.

"Tom," General Blake said, "my son has a fascinating story to tell. Hank, repeat to the superintendent what you were telling me at dinner."

Deeply embarrassed, Hank dug his short fingernails into the palms of his hands and manfully repeated the story of his experience the previous night with Dorothy.

General Pitcher was silent as he listened, and his face remained expressionless. When the cadet finished, he whistled softly under his breath.

Lee Blake broke the silence. "What do you think, Tom?"

General Pitcher tugged at his uniform tunic. "To say I'm surprised is to put it mildly. I've known Dorothy as an excellent secretary, and I'm astonished to find her implicated in something that plainly has many ramifications. Now that I think about it, however, she has changed a great deal in recent months. My wife has noticed that she's wearing a far more expensive wardrobe than usual. That's the sort of thing a woman would see, where we wouldn't. I have observed, however, that Dorothy is considerably 'flashier' than previously." He turned to Hank. "She said nothing about the associates who were making this offer? She gave you no clues to their identity?"

"No, sir," Hank replied. "I've repeated everything she said."

"I wonder," Lee Blake said, "whether Dorothy's offer has anything to do with that strange operation in Tennessee. There may well be a tie-in, and if so, that would be the break we've been looking for. As you know, my older son, Toby, is working on the case, but so far, he's not been able to come up with the real reason behind this operation."

Pitcher shook his head. "There's no more able operator in the country than Toby Holt," he said. "But you're right. This may be the opening wedge." He turned back to Hank. "Are you willing to see this through, regardless of the consequences, young man?"

Hank was bewildered. "I'm afraid I don't understand, sir."

"What we're about to reveal to you is strictly confidential," General Blake said. "We've been on the trail of an armed force that's being organized by a former infantry colonel in the Union Army, Emil Braun. He's recruiting and training a substantial force in western

Tennessee near the Mississippi. We know nothing about his financial backers, and we're in the dark as to the use he plans to make of his corps."

General Pitcher picked up the burden of the explanation. "You've been made an offer that we are hoping comes from someone connected with Braun, as seems quite possible. Are you willing to go through with this recruiting plan, accepting the cash offer and presumably accepting an appointment in that outfit, as well?"

"I'm prepared to follow orders, sir," Hank replied stolidly. "I'll do whatever I'm told is in the best interest of the country and the army."

The generals exchanged brief, satisfied glances, and then Lee Blake again addressed his son. "Don't make any hasty decisions, Hank. Weigh this fully before you make up your mind. You would be called on to make some major sacrifices, and life would not be easy for you for some time to come. You would be very unpopular, and I wouldn't be able to do anything to protect you or intervene on your behalf."

"In fact," General Pitcher added, "you'll be operating on your own, completely alone."

"I was on my way to becoming a no-good gunslinger and all-around hoodlum when General and Mrs. Blake took me in and then adopted me," Hank replied. "That adoption, combined with the years I've spent here at the academy, changed me and gave me a future, a whole new life. I'd be pretty damned selfish if I didn't respond in the best way that I possibly can, even if I do have to make sacrifices. I have enough confidence in America to know that whatever I suffer will only be a temporary loss. Just tell me what you expect of me, and I'll do it!"

General Blake hitched his chair forward. General Pitcher checked the doors to make sure they were closed and bolted and then returned to his seat. Between them, the two senior officers spoke for nearly three hours, making meticulous plans and taking notes so they could make an accurate report to General Sherman at the War Department. The possibility that they had uncovered a key to Emil Braun's operation invigorated them, and they were taking no chance on making an error that would spoil their chance to end whatever threat Braun might pose to the United States. General Blake even vowed that he would not disclose any information to Hank's mother and fiancée, and added that in order to preclude any leaks that could endanger Hank, he would delay sending word of this new development to Toby in Tennessee.

The following Saturday night, Hank again went to Dorothy's apartment. As soon as she had greeted him with a kiss, he broke the news to her. "I've decided," he said, "to accept your friends' offer. How soon do I get the money?"

Acting on the suggestion reluctantly offered by the generals, Hank made love to Dorothy so she would not suspect that he was inclined to do anything other than carrying out her bidding. Later, over dinner, she told him the next step in the drama in which he had become a principal actor. He was to offer his resignation from the corps of cadets. As soon as it was accepted, he was to inform her so she could send a telegram to Mr. M. P. Jonas at the Astor House in New York. Then he was to travel to New York, where he would meet Mr. Jonas at the hotel and learn more about his future.

Hank agreed to everything, as he had been instructed, and the evening, which had seemed interminable to him, came to an end. No sooner did he leave for the cadet barracks, than Dorothy sat down and wrote a letter to her sister. She had succeeded in her mission, she said, but in order to carry it off, she had found it necessary to go to bed on two separate occasions with the subject. Consequently, she felt compelled to request not only that the additional thousand dollars that was due her be placed promptly in a bank account maintained in her name, but also that it be matched by a like amount.

On Sunday, Hank reported to his father about the previous night's developments. With the general making pointed suggestions as to the content, Hank painfully wrote a letter to Cindy, announcing his decision but providing no details and making no attempt to justify it.

Then, in the privacy of General Blake's room at the West Point Hotel, father and son said good-bye. The general was taking a train to New York City, where he would make a connection with the first of the trains that would carry him to the West Coast.

"Good luck to you, boy," General Blake said, holding Hank by the shoulders. "You'll need all the luck you can scrape together. Just keep your chin up and keep your mouth shut and remember the procedures to follow in the event of emergency."

"I won't forget them, Dad," Hank promised.

"I'll do the best I can to attend to things at home," the general said. "I'm not going to pretend that this is going to be easy on your mother, or anything but hell for Cindy. But they'll have to tolerate the conditions as best they're able. You'll just have to leave that end of it to me."

"I will, Dad, and thanks very much," Hank said quietly.

"I'm proud of you, Hank," General Blake said, gripping the young man's shoulders hard. "I'm proud of you as a father is proud of his son, and I'm proud of you as a senior officer in the army is proud of an outstanding junior officer. You've done well for yourself, and you're going to do better. I'm proud you've chosen the military as a vocation, and I predict that the hardships you

are to suffer are merely a prelude to the glory years that
will be yours."

Hank felt choked up when he realized there were
tears in his father's eyes.

Not another word passed between them as they
parted company. Hank spent an almost sleepless night,
and Monday afternoon he was called out of a class in
military tactics and was summoned to the office of the
superintendent in response to a request he had left
there earlier for an interview. There, General Pitcher
awaited him, as did the brigadier general who was the
commandant of the corps of cadets. Dorothy smiled and
winked at him as he made his way into the general's
inner office, but he was so tense that he failed to see or
acknowledge her greeting.

What occurred in the next half hour was a military
secret, reserved for inclusion in Hank's confidential file.
The report, written in General Pitcher's own hand,
then was locked away in his safe.

Hank emerged from the office white-faced, and as
he passed Dorothy's desk in the outer room, he inclined his head a fraction of an inch.

That was the only signal she needed to know that
the scheme she had presented to Hank was proceeding
smoothly and that his resignation had been accepted.
She had no way of knowing that an intelligence officer
would be dispatched from Washington to West Point
that same day for the purpose of observing her.

A short time later, the entire corps of cadets was
summoned to a brigade muster on the parade grounds.
Hank was called forward, and while he stood facing his
colleagues, some of whom had been his close friends for
nearly four years, the commandant read the charge
against him. First-class cadet Henry Blake had renounced
his pledge to remain at the academy until graduation
and accept a commission as a second lieutenant in the
United States Army. As a consequence, he was being

dismissed in disgrace from the corps. Effective immediately, he was to be treated as though he had never existed.

The superintendent personally cut the metal buttons from Hank's tunic and ripped the gold eagle from his uniform cap. Then, while Hank stood at rigid attention, a tear trickling down his face, the cadets paraded past. Some looked at him without seeming to see him. Others looked above his head. He had become a non-person to those who had been his closest friends and associates. The experience was enough to break a man's heart.

Less than an hour later, Hank, now attired in civilian clothes and carrying a small valise that held his belongings, walked out the gate of the academy. No one said good-bye. No one even appeared to notice that he was leaving.

As Hank left the academy grounds, he had to go through a small patch of woods before he emerged onto the road that led into West Point. When he entered the woods, something stirred directly ahead of him, and his grip on his valise tightened. Suddenly his old friend, Reed Kerr, stepped through the screen of trees wearing his gray undress uniform. Ever since the day that they both entered the academy, Hank and Reed had engaged in a friendly rivalry for first place in their class, and out of that rivalry had grown a firm friendship. Both were the sons of generals, and they had a great deal in common. Hank was so embarrassed he did not know what to say.

"I'm breaking regulations by meeting you like this," Reed said, "but I had to do it. I couldn't just stand by and let you leave the academy without shaking your hand and wishing you the best of everything. I just want you to know that, to me at least, you're not a pariah."

"Thanks, Reed," Hank said, deeply moved and finding it difficult to find his voice.

They eyed each other in silence for a minute. Then Reed said, "I don't know what in tarnation happened to you, Hank, or what this is all about, and I'm not asking you to tell me anything about it. That's your business. Let's just say that I didn't want you to leave until I could tell you that as far as I'm concerned you're the best man the academy has had in one whale of a long time. That's based on fact, not conjecture, and I'll tell you flatly, nothing can change my belief. You would have been a great officer, and the army is going to miss you badly."

Deep chagrin, combined with a feeling of gratitude to his generous friend, made Hank mute.

"Wherever you go, Hank, and whatever you do, I hope you'll consider me your good friend for life and that you'll call on me if I can ever be of any help to you, just as I know I could call on you."

Hank Blake's eyes misted, and he blinked them to clear them.

Reed silently extended his hand, and Hank took it. They shook firmly, both too moved to speak.

Cadet Reed Kerr stood stiffly at attention and raised his right hand smartly to the visor of his cap. He was actually saluting a friend who seemed to deserve no salute.

Although Hank was in civilian clothes, he, too, stood at attention and returned the salute. Both then executed smart about faces and marched off in opposite directions, Reed Kerr returning to the academy and Hank heading toward an unknown destiny.

Silent and morose, Hank took the train to New York City. Arriving in the metropolis, he followed instructions Dorothy had given him and went straight to the Astor House, one of the finer hotels of New York.

There he announced his identity to a desk clerk and inquired after the whereabouts of Mr. M. P. Jonas.

"He's expecting you, Mr. Blake. Go right up to suite two hundred twelve."

Still carrying his suitcase, Hank climbed the stairs to the second floor and walked down a long corridor to the suite.

Milton Plosz came to the door in his shirt-sleeves, the odor of whiskey heavy on his breath. "Come in, Blake, come in," he said cordially, shaking hands with enthusiasm. "I've been waiting for you, and I want to be the first to congratulate you on having made a very intelligent choice."

"Thank you, sir," Hank replied, and although he tried to match the other's jovial enthusiasm, he failed markedly.

"You'll have dinner with me here and spend the night in my suite. I've made arrangements with the hotel for that. Tomorrow you'll begin your new life. Come in and sit down. You must be anxious to find out what's in store for you."

"Yes, sir, I sure am," Hank said, as he accompanied the older man into the living room. They sat down opposite each other. Plosz offered him whiskey, which Hank refused.

"Tomorrow," Plosz said, "I'm giving you a railroad ticket that will take you to Nashville, where you catch a connecting train to Memphis. There you will go out into the countryside and report to a military training camp under the command of General Emil Braun."

"Is this a U.S. Army camp?" Hank asked in evident surprise.

Plosz smiled. "It's an army camp, all right, but it's not the U.S. Army. It's a private corps that's being trained by General Braun. He needs officers, and I've arranged that you will join him with the rank of a captain. You also will receive the full pay and benefits of a captain."

Hank, carefully coached, replied, "That sounds pretty good to me."

"Do you have any questions I may be able to answer?"

"Yes, sir. To whom does this corps owe its loyalty?" Hank asked ingenuously. "From whom does it take its orders?"

"You'll take your orders from General Braun," Plosz replied sharply. "That should be sufficient for you. Like all military organizations, it's a self-contained unit. Officers, as well as enlisted men, obey their superiors."

"I understand, sir," Hank murmured. As a matter of fact, he did not understand in the least, but his attempt to learn more about the organization had failed, and he did not want to press too hard or too quickly. Perhaps when he arrived at the camp, he would find answers to some of the questions his father and General Pitcher wanted to know.

"Do I buy any uniforms or weapons before I join the corps in Tennessee?" he asked.

Plosz shook his head emphatically. "You'll be supplied with all that you need once you arrive at the organizational headquarters," he said. "There won't be need for you to buy anything. By the way," he added with a broad wink, "we're going to do some fancy celebrating of your new commission. Once you reach camp, you can expect to be pretty much restricted to the grounds for the foreseeable future. I'm sure you'll want to get in a little hell-raising before you leave for military service."

Not knowing what he had in mind, Hank made no comment.

"Don't ask me about the military life you'll be leading," Plosz said. "You already know far more about that subject than I do. That's not my field, after all."

"May I ask you, sir," Hank inquired respectfully, "just what your connection is with this organization of General Braun's?"

"Of course," Plosz smiled easily. "You might say that as a friend of the whole project I'm interested in doing what I can to help it succeed. Which reminds me—" He reached into his waistcoat pocket and pulled out a folded piece of paper. "This is a check for a sum of money that I believe was promised you for volunteering your services in our cause."

Unfolding the paper Plosz handed him, Hank gasped in spite of himself. It was a bank check in the amount of a thousand dollars, the exact sum Dorothy had promised he would receive.

"Cat got your tongue, boy?" Plosz inquired genially. "Well, no matter. Suffice it to say, we keep our promises."

Hank noted that the check was made out to someone named Milton Plosz. He had no way of knowing who this man was, nor could he have had any inkling of Martinson's existence, since the wealthy politician had ordered his bank to prepare the draft, rather than write a personal check himself. When the check had been drawn up, Martinson had been unaware of who, in fact, the recipient would be; accordingly, he had ordered it payable to Milton Plosz, carelessly forgetting the man's alias, M. P. Jonas. In any case, all that had remained to seal the arrangement was for Plosz to endorse the draft, which he had promptly done.

Hank was not worried about the name on the check, in any case. The main thing was that he was on his way toward fulfilling the secret mission with which he had been entrusted.

He deferred any further effort to question his host about his upcoming military duties. He decided he would learn nothing more of value until he reached

Braun's camp; Mr. Jonas was too slick and too secretive to reveal anything of importance.

After a time, they went down to the hotel dining room for supper. Hank had the appetite of a young, athletically inclined man, but even so he was astounded by the quantities of food that his host consumed. Suffering from the humiliation of his farewell from the academy, Hank ate a much smaller meal. Plosz began his meal with an order of imported French pâté, followed by a rich lobster bisque. Then he ate one of the biggest steaks Hank had ever seen, together with a large baked potato, and with it he consumed at least half a loaf of bread and a salad, then topped it all off with a wedge of apple pie and a mound of ice cream. Hank was sickened by the sight.

Back in the suite, they no sooner had made themselves comfortable in the sitting room than an insistent knock sounded at the door. Hank was surprised when two blowsy young women came into the suite. One of them had dyed blond hair, and the other was a dyed redhead. Both were gaudily attired in clothes that seemed too small, and both reeked of cheap perfume.

The redhead, whose name was Gussie, established her claim to Hank immediately. "I like the looks of the young one," she said. "I'll take him!" Plosz poured gin for all of them, and then he and the blonde settled down on the divan together.

Hank now understood what the man had meant by "hell-raising," but he wanted no part of it. He left his drink untouched on the table and deliberately seated himself in a small easy chair that offered no room for anyone to sit beside him.

Gussie, after tossing off half her drink in a few quick gulps, threw herself onto Hank's lap, sliding back and forth in a crude attempt to arouse him while she slid one arm around his neck. "You can loosen up around me, my friend," she said. "After all, you and me are going to get better acquainted before this night's over, an awful lot better acquainted!"

Hank was uncertain as to the best way to treat her, but he knew that he lacked the slightest desire for her. Accordingly, he saw no reason to conceal his feelings. "Lady," he said, "you and I are going to get along just fine if we keep our distance. I suggest you move to that empty chair over yonder, where you'll have more room to make yourself comfortable. You can even have my drink as a reward."

She looked at him, her heavily made up eyes narrowing. "What's the matter with you, sonny?" she demanded. "Don't you like girls?"

He had to laugh. "Yes," he said, "I like them so much that I'm about to marry one, and she's spoiled me for anybody else." He guessed how his host had obtained her services and spoke accordingly. "Don't you worry," he said. "You'll get paid your full fee, even if you and I don't get chummy."

She jerked herself to her feet and glared at him. "Of all the no-good, rotten spoilsports I've ever met, you're the worst, sonny!" she said scornfully.

Hank was so relieved to be rid of her that he grinned. "Here," he said. "Drink this and you'll feel better." He offered her his glass. Gussie snatched it and downed the contents, then belched loudly.

They were alone in the room by now. The man Hank knew as Mr. Jonas had disappeared with the blonde into an adjoining bedroom. Hank, feeling in control of the situation now, became relatively expansive.

Exercising good humor as well as showing firmness, he kept the young woman at arm's length for more than an hour. By then Gussie was sufficiently intoxicated that she no longer constituted a problem.

Before the women left, Plosz handed each a twenty-dollar bill from a thick wad. Hank made a mental note that the man seemed to be well supplied with funds, and he mentioned that fact in the detailed report he wrote later that night. With the report, he included the bank draft he had received, suggesting that even though it could be evidence someday, it ought to be cashed in order to avoid suspicions about his intentions. He mailed the envelope at a nearby post office early in the morning.

After breakfast Mr. Jonas gave him his railroad tickets and enough cash to buy his meals and take care of other expenses on his journey to join General Braun. Almost as an afterthought, he handed Hank a pistol, suggesting it might be well to carry one on his trip.

Hank hired a carriage to the railroad station and soon was on board a train that would take him to Nashville on the first stage of his momentous journey.

Hank's unpleasant sojourn in New York City was ended, and he consoled himself with the thought that, at the very least, he had picked up several tidbits that he had been able to pass along to General Pitcher. With any luck, after he reached his destination, he would learn a great deal more about Emil Braun and would have material of substance to contribute to the army high command.

Not until Hank was gone did Plosz begin to worry about the bank check that had been made out to him in his own name. He realized that he had made a serious mistake and was in considerable danger. Even though Hank knew him only as M. P. Jonas, the entire secret of his own complicity in Martinson's nefarious scheme would be revealed if the details of the check became public knowledge.

It was urgent, Plosz decided, that he get together again with Hank in order to emphasize that under no circumstances must he ever mention the name of Milton Plosz to anyone.

Only after his return, with Martha, to the Memphis area did Toby receive the message from his stepfather, announcing the unexpected death and burial of his wife, Clarissa. The news struck him with the force of the lightning bolt that was responsible for her death.

Looking gray-faced, old beyond his years, Toby sat in the cottage of Violet MacDermid, the message in one hand as he stared into the flames of the fire burning in the hearth. White Elk had gone to bed, Violet had diplomatically absented herself, and only Stalking Horse was present as a witness of Toby's great grief.

The Cherokee knew better than to intrude at such a time on his lifelong friend's thoughts and emotions. He sat silently on the floor, cross-legged, as he, too, looked into the fire. He was present in case Toby wanted or needed him.

Practical decisions had to be made, and Toby tried to dispose of them as best he could. "I couldn't possibly have been home in time for Clarissa's funeral," he said. "In fact, my stepfather had no way of reaching me aboard the *Tennessee*, so the telegram was delayed. She was already buried before I even received it. My absence made it that much worse."

Stalking Horse nodded sympathetically.

"Tim is still much too young for me to try to look after him without a woman's help," Toby went on. "I think he's far better off with my mother looking after him for now."

"Mrs. Blake will take better care of your son than anyone else in the world could," Stalking Horse assured him. "You are very fortunate to have such a wonderful woman as a mother."

"You're right," Toby replied. "And my stepfather has been very thoughtful, too. He told me not to worry about the ranch. He's seen to it that everything will remain in order until we return."

Toby covered his face with his hands. His thoughts were not centered on the ranch, or his family, but were elsewhere. At the moment, he was in the grip of a far more primitive emotion, caused by an overwhelming sense of guilt. He had been unfaithful to Clarissa.

The fault, he told himself, was his alone; Martha was not to blame, and he had to assume the full burden. The nature and extent of that burden were plain for him to see.

Divine justice had intervened, and Clarissa had been snatched from him in an accident so rare, so freakish, so frightening that it left him cold. He prided himself on his lack of superstition, but the coincidence was too great to be ignored. Trying to sort out his thoughts, he managed to reach several conclusions.

Foremost among them was the realization that it would be wrong for him to see Martha now. Until he resolved his confused and conflicting feelings, both about his wife's death and about his recent affair aboard the *Tennessee*, it would not be fair to Martha to subject her to his company. He resolved to stay clear of her.

At the same time, he knew it would serve no purpose for him to abandon his mission and return to Oregon. Clarissa was gone, and nothing he could do would bring her back. He could be assured that Tim's grandmother would take excellent care of the small boy. Therefore, he would be wise if he remained true to the trust placed in him. It was up to him to follow through on his investigation of the mysterious army. That came first.

Feeling somewhat better, now that his priorities were clearer, Toby sat down and drafted a telegram to his mother in Washington. Then he immediately wrote out a long letter, expressing his shock and grief over Clarissa's death and thanking his mother for looking after Tim. This done, he rose, and asking Stalking Horse to watch over the cottage, he went outside and saddled his horse for the ride into Memphis.

He would send his telegram and letter, he thought as he rode toward the city, but more than this he could

not do. He must remain here; only after he acquired
the information on Braun's army that the government
so urgently wanted would he be free to go home, to
pursue his own concerns and resume whatever life was
left for him. Until then, he had only his duty to sustain
him.

Martha paced the floor of her suite at the Memphis
hotel. She was grieving, but at the same time, she was
angry, so angry that it was difficult for her to think
clearly.

No more than an hour earlier, she had received a
wire from her father in New Orleans that had changed
her whole life and threatened to influence it permanently. Domino had told her the shocking news that
Clarissa Holt and Eddie Neff had been killed as a result
of a freak bolt of lightning on the Holt ranch in Oregon.

Martha did not for an instant doubt the validity of
her father's message. She knew that he was telling her
the truth, that a strange accident of nature had killed
Toby Holt's wife and Eddie in a single, savage blow.

What shocked Martha was the fact that Eddie, as
well as Clarissa, had been killed. What was her father's
trusted aide doing so far from home? How did he
happen to be present on Toby Holt's ranch in Oregon?
And how did he happen to be in the presence of Toby's
wife when both of them had been killed?

Martha knew her father well enough to recognize
his subtle hand in the developments. Eddie's presence
in Oregon had been no accident, no coincidence. He
had been sent there by Domino, who undoubtedly had
given him orders to make himself attractive to Toby's
wife and to seduce her.

Knowing that Martha had fallen in love with Toby,
her father had acted in typical fashion and had chosen
his own unique way of trying to assure that the road
was clear so that Martha would be able to win Toby's

affections permanently. Eddie must have been sent to Oregon with orders to remove Clarissa from Martha's path. He had succeeded in that mission in a way that far exceeded even Domino's expectations.

Now Martha was furious with her father. He had unwittingly placed her in a situation from which it would be all but impossible for her to escape.

Conscious of Toby's strong attraction to her from the outset, she had also known that he had felt guilty from the first moment that he had engaged in an affair. She had risked her whole future on the hope that since she was meeting Clarissa on equal terms, Toby would come to prefer her to his wife and would choose to spend the rest of his days with her. Now, however, by losing her own life, Clarissa had won.

Though Toby was a courageous, fearless leader, at the same time he was an exceptionally sensitive human being. Martha felt certain that he was overcome by a sense of guilt, and that it might well take years for him to rid himself of it. During that time, Martha knew, he would refuse to see her or to have anything to do with her.

Even if Domino produced evidence that Clarissa and Eddie had indulged in a romance, Martha reflected, that would have no bearing on Toby's attitude. He expected to hold himself to the highest standards, and he would not forgive himself for his conduct while his wife was in the final days of her life.

Certain in her own mind that Toby would take great pains to avoid her, Martha was tempted to give up the struggle, leave Memphis, and return to New Orleans. But she could not go. She was the victim of the ironic situation that had been created.

She loved Toby with all her heart, all her soul, all her mind. She cared more for him than for life itself. She felt compelled to stay on in Memphis on the remote chance that somehow they would be able to find a way to get together. He was free now and could marry her if he chose to do so, but she knew that the greatest obstacle of all existed in his mind and that only a miracle would overcome it. Her love forced her to pray that somehow this miracle would occur and that Toby at last would turn to her.

That was her only hope of achieving the happiness she craved so desperately.

X

The sergeant in charge of the sentry detail at the main gate had been briefed, so as soon as Hank identified himself, he was admitted to the military compound.

"Follow the path that goes off through the trees to the left, sir," the sergeant instructed him, "and you'll come to the barracks where you'll live. You'll be issued your uniforms there, instructed as to your command, and so on."

"Thank you very much," Hank replied. Picking up his valise, he started down the path the sergeant had designated. The patch of woods was small, and beyond it, to his right, he saw a large parade ground on which two companies of infantry were engaged in close-order drill under the command of sergeants whose loud, barking voices he could hear. To his left was a target practice range for both pistol and rifle fire that appeared to be almost as extensive as the one at West Point. Directly ahead were barracks.

The military surroundings felt comfortably familiar, and as a result Hank's tension eased somewhat. As he came to a two-story barracks, he saw a captain and two lieutenants standing and conversing. They wore smartly tailored, gray-green uniforms, but their insignia were very close to those worn in the United States Army. When he approached, they stopped talking as all three looked him up and down.

"Excuse me, gentlemen," he said, "but am I right that this building is the officers' barracks?"

One of the lieutenants, a beefy, red-faced man, answered curtly, "So it is, but what's it to you?"

Hank ignored the rudeness. "I've just joined the corps," he said, "and I've been told to report here for uniforms and initial instructions."

The lieutenant shoved him in the shoulder with a large hand. "You're going to be an officer, sonny? I don't believe it. You don't even look like a soldier."

Hank kept his temper and replied civilly, "Nevertheless, that's what I am, and I'd appreciate a reply to my question. May I also warn you, sir, to keep your hands to yourself."

The lieutenant laughed loudly, as did his companions. "Suppose I don't," he said. "What are you going to do about it?" He accompanied his words with another hard shove.

Hank's response was immediate and explosive. He cocked his fist, drew back his arm, and delivered a lethal punch to the lieutenant's jaw that sent the officer sprawling backward.

As the lieutenant fell, the captain scowled and reached for the pistol in his holster. He was no match for Hank. Known for his lightning-fast draw since the days before he had gone to the academy, he had his pistol in his hand before the officers even realized that he was armed. Grateful that Mr. Jonas had forced it upon him in New York, he fired just once, shooting the pistol out of the captain's hand. As it fell, shattered, to the grass, Hank smiled and returned his weapon to its holster.

Before Hank or the officers could escalate the encounter, a bulky man wearing the twin stars of a major general on each shoulder suddenly appeared in their midst. All of them, including Hank, jumped to attention.

"Who are you?" Emil Braun demanded.

"Henry Blake, sir. I'm reporting for duty."

"Oh, yes, Blake. I was expecting you, but wasn't sure when you'd arrive. I saw this whole incident, and I'm rather impressed. I believe you were contracted to join my force as a captain."

"Yes, sir."

"With reactions like yours, the rank isn't high enough. You'll be a major, effective immediately. I'll give the word to the adjutant."

"Thank you, sir," Hank said. Although he was in civilian clothes, he nevertheless saluted.

The captain, whose hand was throbbing from the impact of the bullet hitting his side arm, and one lieutenant also saluted. The lieutenant who had started the brawl was still stretched on the ground, dazed and semiconscious.

Hank looked down at him without pity, and when he spoke, his voice was cold. "You accused me of being wet behind the ears," he said, and walking several feet to a nearby pump, he picked up a pail and filled it with water. He returned to the prostrate officer, stood above him, and then emptied the contents of the bucket onto his head. "Mister," he said, "you're the one who's wet behind the ears now." Throwing the bucket aside, he picked up his valise and went on into the barracks, leaving the captain and the lieutenants silent and awe-stricken. General Braun smiled grimly and turned away.

Mail was delivered early at General Blake's house on Saturday mornings. His aide-de-camp brought a stack of letters into the dining room, where the general, who had just returned from his trip, was having breakfast with Eulalia and Cindy.

Cindy, a slender woman of just twenty-one, with sandy blond hair and pale blue eyes, was more subdued than usual this morning, the general thought, as he

observed her picking at her meal and discussing with
Eulalia the well-being of Tim Holt, who had finished
his breakfast and gone out to play.

The general distributed the mail, bracing himself
when he handed Cindy a letter from Hank. It had
actually been written by Hank with his own help during
the last hour of his visit to West Point.

Cindy read the brief letter quickly, gasped, and
unable to speak, burst into tears.

Eulalia Blake looked at her daughter, then reached
for the letter, and she, too, read it swiftly. White-faced
and trembling, she handed it to her husband, who felt
miserable as he saw his stepdaughter dissolved in tears.

Hank had followed the theme that his father had
suggested: He had left the U.S. Military Academy after
being dishonorably discharged. He was writing from
West Point before leaving to begin a new, related career that was full of promise, and he would write about
it in greater detail after he became settled.

Cindy made no attempt to curb the hysteria that
washed over her. "I can't believe it! This doesn't sound
like Hank—it makes no sense!"

"I don't know what to say," Eulalia replied in a
trembling voice. "You're right, dear. This doesn't seem
like Hank at all."

The general remained silent for the moment. As an
architect of Hank's secret plan, he could say nothing
without being hypocritical, and he waited for an oppor-
tune moment to try to calm both women.

Finally Cindy began to regain sufficient control to
wonder about the nature of the position that Hank
would be taking. Her mother wondered, too, and they
speculated at some length without arriving at any realistic conclusions.

"I was dreaming of the day when I'd be an officer's
wife," Cindy said at last, fighting the tendency to start
weeping again. "All that apparently is finished now. I

don't even know that I'm going to be marrying Hank, much less finding out about the kind of life we're going to lead together."

General Blake knew the time had come for him to intervene. "You're too hasty in jumping to conclusions, Cindy," he said. "I see nothing in Hank's letter to suggest that you won't be married, that he's given up any plans to become your husband in June."

"If he's not in the army," she wailed, "it won't be the same."

"I'll grant you that much," he replied, "but again, let's take all this one step at a time. Perhaps when you find out what this is all about and hear his whole story, it won't be nearly as bad as you're afraid it will be."

Eulalia knew her husband well enough to hear something in his tone of voice leading her to believe that he might know more about Hank's conduct than he had admitted so far. She peered at him. "Do you know something about this that you're not telling us?"

Leland sidestepped her question with as much grace as he could muster. "I'm going strictly according to what Hank has written to Cindy, no more and no less. He's reticent about details, including the reasons for his dishonorable discharge. I think that, loving him, we've got to give him the benefit of the doubt until we hear his complete story. I refuse to sit in judgment on him until I know a great deal more than he has written in this one letter."

Eulalia was certain now that he was concealing something. There was a small smile on her face as she studied him. She felt strangely comforted by the thought that there must be far more than met the eye in the unexpected situation in which Hank was involved.

Cindy, however, accepted her stepfather's statement literally and did not try to look beyond it. "I won't be able to eat, sleep, or breathe until I find out what this is all about," she cried.

"Have faith in Hank," the general insisted. "That's all I can tell you, and I'll keep repeating it until we are given facts to the contrary."

He was speaking very positively, which Eulalia knew he did whenever he had all the facts in hand. She reached across the table and grasped her daughter's hand. "Papa is right, Cindy," she said. "Your whole future with Hank is being put to the test, in a strange way. All you can do is to trust in him and support him. And know that whatever he is doing must be right."

Her husband smiled at her gratefully.

Cindy picked up her glass of water, took a sip, and did her best to compose herself. "I'll try, Mama," she said. "This is the hardest thing I've ever had to do in all my life. But for Hank's sake as well as my own—I'll try!"

Toby and Stalking Horse reverted to their previous practice of alternating in keeping watch on the activities inside Emil Braun's military camp. Between them, they kept watch for the better part of twenty-four hours a day. Although they discovered little, they continued their patrol in the hope that sooner or later they would see some significant action. Eventually, Toby hoped, Braun or some high-ranking member of his staff would make a mistake that would provide the key to the mystery.

Under the best of circumstances, surveillance was dull, monotonous work. As Toby concealed himself in the woods outside the camp and peered through the barbed wire fence, he had ample opportunity to ponder his own life and the many mistakes he felt he had made. His feeling of guilt did not lessen day by day. In addition, he felt ashamed for neglecting to get in touch with Martha in nearby Memphis.

As he knew, she was there only because of him. She wanted to help him in any way she could to solve the riddle of Emil Braun's activities. He was repaying her loyalty by his silence and by turning his back to her. He was wrong, he knew, erring almost as badly as when he became involved in an affair with her.

As the days passed, Toby convinced himself that he was acting contrary to his basic nature and was being cowardly. He was being unfair to Martha by ignoring her, he reflected. She deserved better.

Shortly before dawn one morning, after he had been on watch outside the encampment all night, Martha was very much in his thoughts. He made up his mind that he would see her within the next twenty-four hours and explain how he felt. He owed her that much, if not a great deal more. He began to compose the explanation he would offer her.

It was perhaps his concentrating on Martha that made him less vigilant than he otherwise would have been. Possibly he was tired and his nerves were blunted after spending so many hours on surveillance duty. Whatever the reason, he was taken completely by surprise when four men jumped on him from the rear and, pinning his arms to his sides, made him a prisoner before he could fight back.

The soldiers who had captured him kept a tight grip on his arms as they hauled him to his feet. He felt the muzzle of a pistol pressed into his back as they marched him through a small gate in the barbed wire fence that surrounded the compound. They took him to a whitewashed building where, after tying his hands securely behind his back, they removed his pistol and his knife before they left him alone in a cell-like room furnished only with a cot and a chair.

No one came near Toby for hours. This he interpreted as an attempt on the part of his captors to break his nerve.

He sat in the chair and occasionally got up and roamed from one end of the room to the other, but that was the extent of his activity. The window was barred, and from the little he could see, troops were engaged in drill on a corner of the parade ground. No one brought him anything to eat or drink, or even came near him.

Finally, at what he believed was about noon, a key turned in the lock, and Emil Braun came into the room, followed by three officers—a colonel and two majors. Toby continued to sit until two of the officers, responding to a gesture from Braun, pulled him to his feet. Toby was astonished beyond belief when he saw that one of the majors was Hank Blake.

Hank remained silent and gave no sign that he recognized Toby. Taking his cue from his stepbrother, Toby did not reveal that he had ever seen him before.

The officers stood Toby against the far wall, facing into the room, while Braun approached him with a scowl.

"So we meet again," Braun said. There was a slight sneer in his voice. "You disguised yourself as a poker dealer on board ship, and today we've caught you red-handed snooping around my camp. It's obvious that you've been spying, and equally plain that you were doing a lousy job of it. Now it's my turn to get information from you." He paused, and taking a cigar from his pocket, he lighted it with a phosphorous safety match imported from Sweden. "Who are you working for? What kind of information have you put together about my organization? And what is it that you're under orders to learn?"

Planting his feet apart, Toby quietly clenched his bound hands behind his back and remained silent.

Braun blew a blue cloud of cigar smoke into the prisoner's face. "It won't do you much good to keep quiet, Holt," he said. "I know ways to make you talk, lots of ways."

Toby remained silent, his face wooden.

"I don't think you quite understand the position

you're in," Braun said, "either the nature of it or the fact that it's very precarious. Let me make our relative positions very plain to you. As you can see, I'm in command of a trained force that is preparing to carry out my will. As my men already know, and as millions of other people in this country are going to learn soon enough, I consider that a state of war exists. You were caught in the act of spying on me, a hostile act by a government I no longer acknowledge. I suppose you know what happens to spies in time of war."

Toby unblinkingly returned his glare.

"If there happened to be any doubt about your activities," Braun said, "I would order you before a court-martial board, but you were caught in the act of spying, so there's no doubt about your guilt. Therefore, I urge you to talk freely and tell us everything that you know in order to save your own skin. If you fail to cooperate, I regret to inform you that it will be necessary for me to condemn you to execution."

Toby saw that Braun was serious and concluded that the man was mad. He actually believed that he and his little outfit were at war, presumably with the United States, and that he had the right to execute anyone he caught "spying," including legitimate U.S. government agents. Toby knew only one way to treat him, and that was with the silent contempt he deserved. So, Toby continued to regard Braun steadily, his expression unchanged.

"You're a stubborn bastard, Holt, but I can't believe that you're so anxious to die," Braun said. "Maybe you need a little time for the facts of your situation to sink in." His face was momentarily hidden in a cloud of cigar smoke. "Your execution will take place at midnight unless you give me the information I want. Maybe between now and then you can be made to realize the gravity of the fix you're in."

Hank Blake spoke for the first time. "General," he

said, "I come from out West, same as Holt, so I can speak his language. Give me a chance to have a few words with him, sir, and maybe I can talk some sense into that thick head of his."

Emil Braun chuckled. "By God, I like your style, boy," he said. "Sure, help yourself. Just be sure that you leave a couple of guards to keep him under watch when you're through dealing with him." Without another look at Toby, Braun went to the door and left the room, trailed by his other officers.

Hank pulled the door closed. Approaching Toby from behind, he quickly loosened the thick bonds around Toby's wrists. Toby would be able to slip free at a moment's notice. Then Hank leaned close to Toby's ear and spoke in a low voice. "Give me an hour," he muttered, "to settle in at the officers' barracks so I can establish an alibi for myself. When you leave, head to your left. You'll be closest to the property line, and all you'll need to do will be to go over the fence. I'll try to hold down the number of guards I assign to watch you."

"Thanks, Hank," Toby muttered. "But I don't want you taking any risks for my sake."

"I know you're wondering why I'm here, in Braun's camp," Hank replied. "I'll tell you about it, when there's more time. The important thing is that we're on the same team. In fact, I've been wondering for quite a while how to get in touch with you, and now that problem has been solved. If you get clear and can get word to me, I'll meet you any night at the clump of white birches at the fence you're going over."

Toby nodded in assent. Hank started to move toward the door, then stopped and turned back. "By the way, Toby, I'm sorry—about Clarissa, I mean. Dad told me about it."

"I appreciate your concern," Toby replied, turning aside lest his face betray the full extent of his emotions. "It was a crazy accident."

"I know. Sometimes there's no fathoming these things."

Both men were silent for a moment, then Hank spoke up. "I'd better get along. Don't want Braun's men to think something's wrong in here. I'll say good-bye for now." He patted Toby on the shoulder. Then Hank went to the door, opened it, and called to soldiers in an anteroom.

Two troopers came into the room, both armed with rifles, and stood at attention before Hank.

"Keep watch on this prisoner for me," he ordered. "Ordinarily he might be dangerous, but I think he has learned a lesson, so you have no need to get rough with him. Just keep an eye on him. You'll be relieved after four hours."

"Very good, sir," a corporal replied, and both saluted.

Hank stalked out without a backward glance.

Alone with the corporal and his companion, a private, Toby leaned back against the nearest wall, taking care to make his guards think that his wrists were still tightly bound together.

He had recovered from his initial surprise at discovering that Hank was an officer under Emil Braun, but he knew that his many questions would have to wait. His immediate concern was his escape.

His pistol and knife had been taken from him, but he was not overly worried. On his long sojourn in China not long before, when he had been helping the imperial government break the power of the tong that was preying on innocent Chinese-Americans, he had learned the martial arts. As a consequence, he knew he could defend himself with his bare hands and his feet. The only question was a matter of timing. He knew he had to wait for enough time to pass to give Hank the opportunity to establish an alibi so he would not be suspected of complicity in the prisoner's escape. Therefore, Toby yawned, leaned against the wall, and closed his eyes.

The private finally took pity on him. "You don't have to stand up, buddy," he said. "You can always sit down on the cot yonder and stretch out."

Toby answered without opening his eyes. "I'd rather stand for a while," he said. "I find it's easier to stretch my muscles this way."

His reply seemed to satisfy the pair, and they were silent for another quarter of an hour.

Then the corporal broke the silence. "You want a drink of water, or something?" he asked.

"That would be a good idea eventually," Toby replied. "I don't need any water just yet, though."

For a long time, no one spoke, and Toby could hear no movement. After a short while, he deliberately yawned again, opened one eye, and peered at the two soldiers. Both of them had somewhat glazed expressions, and both had relaxed their vigil, lowering their rifles so the butts rested on the floor. They were staring into space rather than keeping the prisoner under close watch. The time had come to take action, Toby decided.

He had no idea how many other rooms in the building might be occupied, so he reasoned that his success would depend on the speed and the silence with which he could reduce the efficiency of the two guards. Even if he had firearms, he could not use them now. Freeing his wrists of their loose bonds and gathering his strength, he balanced himself and then shot out his right foot in a vicious, straight-legged kick. It caught the corporal under the chin and knocked him backward into the wall behind him, stunning him as he slid to the floor.

At the same time, Toby leaped forward, his arms flailing, and caught the private with a sharp blow, delivered with the edge of his hand on the side of the neck. The man staggered, and as he did so, Toby delivered a similar blow with his other hand against the bridge of the soldier's nose. He whimpered and crumpled in a heap.

Not wasting as much as a second, Toby took the corporal's knife from its sheath, pulled up the man's shirttail, and slashed off long strips of cloth, which he used to bind both men's ankles and wrists. Then he stuffed gags into their mouths. At the very least, he knew they would be incapacitated for a quarter of an hour.

He debated with himself whether or not to take their rifles and decided to leave the men in possession of their firearms. If he started firing shots while still inside the boundaries of the camp, he would only call attention to himself. He needed to utilize stealth above all and could not depend on his prowess as a marksman under the circumstances. Taking the knife as a precaution and sliding it into the top of his boot, he left the room, quietly closing the door.

The corridor was deserted, and as he made his way cautiously toward the entrance, he heard no sound from any of the rooms on either side.

When Toby reached the door, he slowly raised the latch, then opened the door no more than an inch and peered outside. Standing directly in front of the door, with his back to it, was a sentry armed with a rifle and bayonet, which he held at arm's length by its barrel, the butt resting on the ground. He stood with his feet apart and seemed to be staring out across the parade ground at a platoon of recruits drilling on the far side. The shouts of the drill sergeant could be heard faintly.

Toby always regretted the taking of a human life, but at the moment he had no choice. He had to kill or run the risk of being killed. Drawing the knife he had taken from the corporal, he pulled the door wide open and plunged the blade deep into the back of the sentry. As the man fell forward, Toby caught him, and after

swiftly removing the knife, he hauled the body inside
the entrance and closed the door. The entire incident
had taken no more than a minute.

Momentarily free, Toby followed the directions that
Hank had given him and started off toward the small
patch of woods to his left. He found that from his own
surveillance, the terrain was familiar. He walked rapidly, not daring to break into a run for fear of calling
attention to himself. In the distance he could see as
many as twenty or thirty officers and men walking
around in the compound, and he wanted to avoid their
notice at all cost.

He breathed somewhat easier when he reached a
clump of woods just this side of the fence. He paused
beneath a large maple tree in full leaf and, on sudden
impulse, decided to climb it to see if any sentries were
on guard. From it, he knew he could also gain a better
view of his immediate surroundings and check what
enemies might be below in the wooded area. He climbed
about thirty feet before he finally halted and began to
scrutinize the area.

Forcing himself to take his time, he studied the
ground around him, searching for any men who might
be camouflaged or any sentries who might be in the
woods. At first he found no one, but after a few minutes
a guard appeared, carrying his rifle and apparently marching a predetermined route.

As Toby watched him, the sentry appeared directly
below him and continued on his rounds. Toby noted
the clump of birch trees that Hank had mentioned, and
he realized they were actually on the boundary, growing on both sides of the fence.

The sentry was the most immediate problem. Toby
kept his eyes riveted on the man, who went off into the
open area beyond the woods, circled back, and appeared again directly below the maple tree as he repeated his rounds.

As Toby recognized, time remained the most important factor in his escape. With each passing moment, the possibility increased that the body of the sentry he had been forced to kill would be discovered and that the two guards he had incapacitated would recover sufficiently to break their bonds and give the alarm. In either event, every officer and man in the camp would be assigned to finding the escaped prisoner and either killing him or returning him to captivity. The sooner that Toby put himself on the far side of the fence, the better off he would be. He began his descent from his observation post to a limb not far above the ground, though still out of sight.

His eyes narrowing as he watched the sentry below approaching again on his rounds, Toby knew that he had to act immediately. He braced himself, and waiting until the man was within a single pace of being directly beneath him, he leaped feetfirst from his perch.

His timing was perfect. His feet crashed into the back of the sentry, just below the shoulders, sending the man plummeting forward facedown with such force that his rifle flew out of his grasp and skidded along the ground.

The blow had knocked the breath out of the sentry, who was groggy, but he still was able to look around to learn who or what had attacked him.

Toby gave him no chance to recuperate and strike back. Removing the corporal's knife from his belt as he landed on the ground, Toby brought the blade down with all his strength, driving the steel deep into the sentry's body. The man struggled hard for a few moments, then shuddered and lay still.

Leaving the man's body where it lay, Toby wiped the knife blade on the sentry's uniform and then dashed toward the stand of white birches.

To his utter astonishment, he found a gap in the wire fence that extended from one end of the clump of

trees most of the way to the other end. There was no
fence for a distance of nearly eight feet.

Possibly, Hank had known of this lapse in security
when he suggested the birches as a convenient meeting
place for Toby, from outside the perimeter, and for
himself, inside it. Why Toby had not also known of it,
from his own surveillance, he was at a loss to say, nor
could he fathom why Braun's men had not repaired the
fence. On the other hand, perhaps the fence had previously been intact, and Hank had found a way to
remove it just within the past few hours.

Whatever the facts, he had no time to speculate
further. All that mattered was that he put distance
between himself and the encampment. He had little
doubt that Emil Braun would pursue him and deal
harshly with him, so he ran at top speed, not bothering
to conceal whatever tracks he might be leaving in the
woods. He reasoned that few members of Braun's group
would be able to track him through any patch of wilderness. Most military men lacked experience in wilderness lore.

Toby continued to put as much distance as he
could between himself and the perimeter of Braun's
military compound. After running for another quarter
hour, he began to feel somewhat safer, but suddenly he
grew tense when, thanks to his keen hearing, he made
out the sounds of someone approaching rapidly through
the forest ahead. He could not imagine how any of
Braun's men could have circled around him in the short
time that he had been gone and could be approaching
him head-on. Nevertheless, he was determined to take
no chances. Drawing the knife he had killed the guard
with, knowing he had a backup blade in his boot, he
walked softly, scarcely making a sound as he went forward through the heavily wooded area.

Suddenly the tall, spare figure of another man
appeared out of the woods directly ahead of him. Toby

stopped and sheathed his knife in his belt and grinned as he recognized Stalking Horse. The Cherokee, still gripping the tomahawk that he had been prepared to throw, came forward rapidly, and he, too, grinned. They embraced silently.

"You ran into some trouble," Stalking Horse said.

"Yes, I had a mite of it," Toby confessed. "It was my own fault. I let them take me prisoner by being careless, and I had to kill two of their soldiers in order to get away, so I'm trying to put some distance between me and their headquarters. I met Braun again, and that only confirmed my impression that he's a mean one. He'll be out for my blood now."

Stalking Horse nodded, and they trotted in single file until they came to the road that cut through the woods. They slowed their pace somewhat and followed it to Violet's cottage. She and White Elk were away on an errand, so Toby sat down to a belated meal of bread and cold sliced meat as he told the story of what he had experienced.

Stalking Horse had known and seen so much throughout his long life that he was almost immune to surprise, but he sounded incredulous as he asked, "Are you sure it was Hank Blake you saw and who helped you?"

"It was Hank," Toby said. "I thought at first when I saw him that I was dreaming, but I wasn't. We actually exchanged a few words after he loosened my bonds and before he took off. I can't imagine why he left the academy and how he obtained a commission from Braun, but we'll learn all that in good time, I suppose. The important thing now is to establish contact with him." He went on to explain that Hank had told him about the clump of birches as a rendezvous point, and he added that, through accident or design, there was an opening in the fence near the trees.

"Is it possible," Stalking Horse asked, "for Hank to

communicate with General Blake and with other officers in the army?"

"You're assuming," Toby said, "that he has reason to communicate with them. At the moment we have no way of knowing anything for certain. It seems unlikely, but it's just possible he left West Point under a cloud and then got together with Braun. I've got to get more information on the subject. I'm going into Memphis and will send a telegram to my stepfather. After we learn more about Hank's status, we'll be better able to judge what to do. All we know now is that he has won Braun's confidence, but whether or not he may even be trying to evade the authorities is still a mystery."

As soon as he finished eating, Toby wrote out a wire to General Blake and then translated it into a code that they had used for years. "I'll be back in time for supper or, at the latest, in time to spell you so we can keep the camp under constant observation," Toby said before he saddled one of Violet's horses to ride into Memphis.

When he reached the city, he first went to the telegraph office, where he dispatched his message to his stepfather. Then he resolutely headed for the hotel and, leaving his mount at a hitching post outside, went in and climbed the stairs to Martha's suite. He was determined to act on his conviction that he could not in good conscience simply turn his back on her and never even offer an explanation.

When she came to the door, Martha seemed pleased to see him, but her greeting was noticeably subdued. She was simply dressed, wore almost no cosmetics, and her eyes were suspiciously puffy and red.

"You've been very much on my mind," Toby said bluntly. "May I come in?"

"Please do." She stood aside to let him enter, closed the door, and then preceded him into the sitting room of her suite.

He put his hat on a table and watched as she seated herself. Then, jamming his thumbs into his belt, he squared his shoulders and said, "You may have heard that my wife died in a freak accident."

"Yes, I know," Martha replied, folding her hands in her lap and meeting his direct gaze. "I had a wire from my father. I hesitated to get in touch with you because—well—it would have been rather awkward, under the circumstances."

"I understand."

At that instant Martha made a decision; Toby should not be spared the whole truth if their own relationship was to go forward honestly and with genuine hope.

Toby was silent for a time, and then he was shocked to hear Martha say, "She wasn't alone. The same bolt of lightning that knocked down the gazebo also killed my father's assistant, Eddie Neff."

Toby took a deep breath. "I don't suppose you happen to know what Neff was doing in Oregon," he said, "how he happened to be there, and how it came about that he was with my wife on our ranch at the time lightning struck?"

"I don't actually know," Martha said, "but I can guess. I know my father and the way he thinks and operates. When you hear what I have to say, you may hate me even more than you already hate me."

Clenching his fists, Toby shook his head. "I don't hate you," he said. "I couldn't, Martha. After what we've meant to each other and what we've had between us, I'm incapable of feeling anything but a deep and abiding love for you."

Her gaze was piercing as she looked at him. "Do you mean that?"

"Completely."

She was silent for a moment, and then she looked down at the floor, absently twisting and plucking at a small lace handkerchief in her hands. "When you and I were in New Orleans together," she said, "my father saw us, and he jumped to the conclusion that we were in love. He didn't have to be a magician to see it. It was written all over both of us, I guess, and I know him. I'm sure he sent Eddie to Oregon in order to entice your wife into becoming romantically involved with him. He figured that if Eddie could win her affections, she would ask you for a divorce, and then you and I would be in a position to marry."

"I'm not surprised, and I'm certainly not shocked," Toby said. "You see, I've come to know and understand Domino pretty well, and I have a fairly good idea of how his mind functions and of the way he operates. I don't blame him for sending Neff to Portland. And in the event that Clarissa did become involved with him, I can't blame her in any way for it. I've been away much of the time for several years now, and she didn't lead an easy life."

"You're being generous," she said softly.

He shook his head, and his smile was bitter. "It's easy to show generosity toward someone who's no longer among the living. That's the least of my troubles. What bothers me is what I feel toward you."

"When I learned what had happened to Clarissa," Martha said, "I knew you needed me, but at the same time, I recognized your even greater need to be alone and to work things out by yourself."

He swallowed hard. "Thank you."

"Unfortunately," Martha continued, "I've known all too well just how you feel, too. You've blamed yourself for our lovemaking, and you feel that the Almighty punished you by taking Clarissa from you."

"That's almost exactly how I felt," Toby admitted.

She spread her hands out before her. "In my opinion, such thoughts are nonsense, but you have to live with yourself before you can live with any woman. It's what goes on in your mind, not in mine, that matters.

You're still suffering from shock and hurt, as well as from guilt, and it would be bad for both of us if we continued to see each other at present. I think it would be wrong for me, as well as for you. We might begin to nitpick, and before we knew what was happening, we could find ourselves involved in arguments and all sorts of unpleasantness. You need time for your wounds to heal.

"For several days," she went on, "I was on the verge of going back to New Orleans. I didn't want to be in your way or to complicate your life, but I changed my mind. I can do neither of us any good if I go back to my father's house now. I'll stay here on the off chance that you may need me and want my help in working out your assignment. You should know that you need only call on me and I'll do anything in my power for you."

He inclined his head in thanks but was so touched that he momentarily lost his powers of speech.

"After your wounds have healed," she continued, "you'll be in a far better position to think about your future. By then you'll know whether you want to go on with me or whether we were doomed to failure, whether we were maimed for life by the same bolt of lightning that caused the deaths of Clarissa and Eddie. I'll be right here whenever you make up your mind. All you'll have to do is tell me, and then I'll either rejoin you, or I'll quietly go off to New Orleans.

"Go now," she said after a pause, "while I'm in a mood to relinquish you freely. Go quickly, before I change my mind and persuade you to stay, as I'm afraid I may do."

Toby knew that words would be inadequate to express his gratitude to her, but at the same time, he realized that if he touched her, both of them might lose their self-control and they would find themselves in a far worse predicament. He bowed to her from the waist, and then, picking up his hat, he walked out of the suite, not daring to look back.

He had work to do, and problems to solve. Thanks to Martha's understanding, their future would have a chance to resolve itself in the weeks and months ahead.

XI

General Blake's telegram answering Toby was sent in code from Fort Vancouver. It was a detailed explanation of Hank's presence in Tennessee and his status. Now that he understood the situation, Toby was delighted that he had a reliable ally in the camp.

That evening Stalking Horse went to the clump of white birch trees, and concealing himself just outside the clump, he settled down to wait.

Demonstrating the same patience that the Cherokee tribe had displayed for centuries, Stalking Horse remained quietly hidden. He was ready to repeat the stakeout night after night until he and Hank made contact. As it turned out, he was rewarded that same night.

Thanks to his acute hearing, he heard someone approaching. Stalking Horse gripped his tomahawk and waited. Finally he could make out a single form drawing near. Soon he was able to recognize Hank. Dressed in the field uniform of an officer in Emil Braun's brigade, he bore the insignia of a major on his shoulders. Smiling to himself, Stalking Horse gave his expert imitation of a cricket chirping in the night.

Hank replied with his own chirp, and although his effort was less smooth than that of the Cherokee, at least it was recognizable.

They moved forward simultaneously toward the

midst of the trees, where no fence separated the compound from the outside world. There they clasped hands warmly. Hank owed much of what he knew about the wilderness to the elderly Cherokee, and they had been devoted companions in the years before he had gone off to the military academy.

Stalking Horse wasted no words. "Toby," he said, "has learned your whole story from General Blake. It is his wish that you work closely with us from this time forward."

"Has he been given the job of bringing about the downfall of this organization?"

Stalking Horse nodded gravely.

"What does Toby want me to do? I'll follow his orders, naturally."

"Is it possible," Stalking Horse asked, "for you to arrange a position for me over there? Your commander cannot know me, or have any idea that I am Violet's brother. Toby's idea is that it would be good if I had a post that would enable me to come and go from your camp as I please. In that way, you and he would be kept in touch, through me."

Hank was puzzled. "I know of no post that would enable you to come and go as you please," he said. "Once someone joins this outfit, he seems to be confined to the post, except under rare conditions."

"I am too old to become a soldier in your corps," Stalking Horse rejoined, "but it is Toby's thought that I might find employment with you as a scout."

Hank thought for a moment and then grinned broadly. "That's it!" he exclaimed. "I'll speak to the general tomorrow morning. We can meet at the front gate at noon. Upon your arrival, ask for me, and I'll show up to act as your escort."

They shook hands, and Stalking Horse glided away, the first step of the new plan accomplished.

When Stalking Horse appeared at the gate promptly at noon the following day, Hank was already on hand.

"I'll take full responsibility for the admission of this man to the encampment," Hank told the lieutenant in charge of the guard. "I'm escorting him to headquarters, where he has an appointment with the general."

The rifles of the sentries were lowered, and Stalking Horse was admitted to the camp. "I'll do the talking," Hank said, as they made their way across the interior of the compound toward the headquarters building. "Say no more to General Braun than is necessary. I've told him that I've learned you are an expert tracker and are the most valuable scout we could possibly hire. If he asks for a demonstration of your skills, you'd better try to oblige him."

Stalking Horse nodded but made no comment.

Braun surrounded himself with the full pomp of a major general in the regular army. Hank went in first, stood at attention, and saluted. Stalking Horse, who followed him, indulged in a traditional Indian gesture of greeting by raising his hand, palm outward.

Braun, clearly taken with his own importance, barely inclined his head in return. "So you're a scout," he said deprecatingly. "Major Blake tells me you have a reputation as having no equal as a scout anywhere in the United States."

Stalking Horse thought the claim was exaggerated, but he bowed his head modestly.

"Can you give me a demonstration of this supposed great skill of yours right now?"

Again the Cherokee lowered his head slightly.

Accompanied by Hank and the general's aide, Lieutenant Taylor, they walked out to the adjacent corral and mounted horses. They rode to the far side of the property, where heavy woods extended a considerable distance beyond the boundary. There they dismounted, and Braun instructed his aide. "We'll give you a few minutes' head start. Try to lose yourself in the woods, and we'll see if this Indian is smart enough to find you."

The lieutenant, who had been a platoon commander in Braun's Civil War regiment, grinned and promptly disappeared into the woods. Stalking Horse stood with his back to the spot from which the lieutenant had departed.

Braun took a cigar from his pocket, jammed it into a corner of his mouth, and not bothering to light it, chewed on the end, seeming to enjoy the taste. He stared at the landscape for several minutes and then said suddenly, "Don't be impatient. I want to give Taylor all the time he needs to get away from you and hide. He's damned clever."

Stalking Horse made no response.

Finally, it was Braun whose patience proved to be limited. "All right," he said at last. "Let's go!" He gestured toward Stalking Horse. "Find him if you can."

Stalking Horse walked to the edge of the woods, where he stood very quietly. Looking ahead with his head slightly bent, he examined the terrain. Then he began to walk with graceful, quiet confidence, never hesitating, moving with surprising speed. Braun and Hank followed at a distance of several feet.

Stalking Horse led them deep into the forest, without pausing once. Finally, he halted abruptly before some very thick foliage. Reaching in swiftly, he closed his hand over something and tugged it.

A sheepish Lieutenant Taylor, his face beet red, emerged from the bush.

Not satisfied with his accomplishment so far, Stalking Horse reached out, and with lightninglike speed and adroitness, he disarmed the officer and handed his pistol to Emil Braun.

"Damned if you're not as good as Blake says you are!" Braun exclaimed, chuckling.

He was about to add something more but fell silent when Stalking Horse gestured sharply and plunged into the brush. He emerged a moment later, his tomahawk grasped in one hand; with the other, he held the bloody carcass of a porcupine. How he had sensed the proximity of the animal was impossible for the others to fathom.

Braun was awed. "How in hell did you know that animal was lurking there in the underbrush?" he demanded.

A flicker of a smile appeared on Stalking Horse's lips.

"You're hired, Indian," Braun said. "How much wampum do you want?"

Stalking Horse preferred to ignore the insulting remark.

"I'll give you two dollars a week." Braun tried to make the offer seem magnanimous.

In order to maintain the mystery of his identity, Stalking Horse deliberately replied in his own tongue.

Hank pretended to translate for him. "The Cherokee," he said, "will offer himself for employment to General Braun in return for wages of five dollars per week. It is understood that when he is not needed in the field to lead the army toward its enemy, he will live in his own home, and he will report for duty here each day."

As he spoke, Stalking Horse folded his arms and held them chest high while he stared into the distance, his expression wooden.

Emil Braun looked thoughtful, then apparently decided it was beneath his dignity to haggle. "Agreed," he said. "You will start tomorrow. Make the necessary arrangements, Major Blake. This man will be very useful to us. We have a need for an expert scout."

Toby Holt was pleased when he heard the news. With Stalking Horse as well as Hank working for Braun, the chances were double that he could gather enough evidence to break up the illegal organization and send Braun to prison.

Milton Plosz was worried. Ample cups of coffee and a suprisingly hearty breakfast in the hotel dining

room had compensated for his night of debauchery with
the blonde. After his meal, he had retired to his room
with the morning newspapers under his arm and had
been completely calm until one item struck him with
the force of a thunderbolt.

The article was datelined West Point, New York,
and the opening was a bombshell:

> First-classman Henry Blake of Washing-
> ton Territory, the son of Major General Le-
> land Blake, commanding general of the Army
> of the West, reportedly has been dismissed
> from the United States Military Academy at
> West Point. No reasons were given for his
> abrupt departure. Spokesmen at the academy
> rejected all inquiries, and former Cadet Blake
> is no longer in residence there, so it was im-
> possible to seek confirmation from him.

Plosz was extremely dismayed because of the unexpected publicity. This made it all the more imperative
that he get in touch with Hank, to ensure that he
remained silent about the name he might have noticed
on the bank check given him. It was just possible, of
course, that Hank had deposited the draft without noting the name or caring anything about it. But Plosz
knew that he could afford to take no chances, particularly now that the newspapers were showing an interest
in the story. He could foresee further snooping around
by reporters, and he had to find a way to ensure
Hank's silence. Only if Hank kept his mouth shut would
the authorities find it impossible to connect Jonas and
Plosz.

Still uncertain whether or not to use threats or
bribes when he saw Hank, Plosz purchased a railroad
ticket and caught the next train to Memphis. When he
arrived there, he hired a horse and carriage and drove

out to the military encampment, where he insisted on seeing the commanding general without delay.

Emil Braun was annoyed that the man he knew as Jonas had come to the camp, but his irritation eased when he learned the purpose of the visit. If Jonas succeeded in persuading young Major Blake that he had not actually played any part in recruiting him from the cadet corps, Braun would be pleased. It would be another step bolstering the general's own pose as the sole motivating force behind his organization. Consequently, he readily gave his approval for the proposed meeting with Hank.

Not wishing to be seen with Hank, Plosz ate dinner with Braun in the general's home. After the meal, Hank was summoned, with the purpose unstated.

Surprised to see his New York contact at the camp, Hank nonetheless agreed to go off with him in the carriage for a private conversation. He left his sword behind but carried a repeating pistol. The two men engaged in only desultory conversation as the carriage followed the road around the inside of the perimeter of the encampment. When they came to the woods at the farthest side from the buildings, Plosz dismounted and suggested that Hank come with him for a short walk in the woods.

Plosz was very conscious of the differences in their physical condition. He was flabby and overweight, the result of indulgence and easy living, while Hank was well-built and fit.

Suddenly Plosz felt a sharp pain in his right foot, a pain so intense that he groaned loudly. Hank looked at him in considerable concern. Plosz's agony was so great that he fell to the ground.

"Hold on!" Hank ordered. "Let me help you." He bent down and pulled a board containing a long, rusty nail away from the sole of Plosz's right shoe. Plosz had failed to see the board lying in the tall grass, much less the nail sticking upright from it.

"Damn whoever left that around!" Plosz exclaimed angrily. In fact, the workmen who constructed the camp were so hurried that they often dropped pieces of lumber and left them strewn about, a hazard to the soldiers and to everyone else.

Hank smiled sympathetically. "Will you be all right?"

Plosz nodded weakly. Cursing his luck, he considered his situation in light of the changed circumstances, measuring what he should do. As he did so, he was relieved to find that his foot felt somewhat better. He decided to press on with the business that had brought him to this meeting with Hank.

Slipping a hand into an outer pocket of his jacket, Plosz shrugged back the cape that covered his arm and felt a sense of relief as his fingers closed around the butt of the small, single-shot pistol he carried there. "You and I," he said, "need to talk about an extremely serious matter."

Hank was amenable, even though he had no idea what the man could have in mind. "Sure," he said. "I'll talk about anything."

"I was somewhat negligent at the time of our first meeting in New York," Plosz said. "Or it could be that I erred in not spelling things out more precisely for you. Be that as it may, I wouldn't be at all surprised if the government is on our trail. Yours as well as mine."

"What do you mean?" Hank asked.

"I can only say that I may come under investigation for my part in helping General Braun. Your identity is no secret to the authorities, so if they learn where you are, they may well question you. They'll want to know how you happened to come here and become associated with Braun. If that happens, I hope you will be very discreet and reveal nothing about any dealings with me."

Hank chose to pretend he was thick-witted. "If the government sends any investigator to question me," he said, "I see no reason not to speak the truth. I'll gladly tell anybody who asks that I was paid a whopping bonus for resigning from the academy when I did. My new rank of major here speaks for itself. Thanks to you I'm a field-grade officer, whereas I would have been no more than a second lieutenant if I'd stayed to graduate."

Plosz became agitated. "That's precisely what you must *not* do!" he said. "Our financial arrangements were strictly private business, and the government has no right to any of the details."

Hoping to learn more, Hank pushed his seeming stupidity one further step. "I don't see what harm it could possibly do," he declared, "for me to tell the truth. All the government would have to do is inspect my bank account in order to learn the facts, so I see no reason not to admit it. I did nothing illegal, and I'm not ashamed of anything. I see no reason to hide behind a pack of lies like a criminal!"

His companion's annoyance turned to outright anger. "Don't be so stubborn!" Plosz said loudly. "Just do what you're told, and keep your mouth shut!"

"I don't take orders from civilians," Hank told him calmly, and waited for an even more violent outburst that might reveal more information.

It never came. Instead, Plosz—seeing that threats would avail him nothing with this stubborn young man— resorted to an abrupt change in tactics.

Trying to ignore his injury, Plosz somehow managed to smile. He knew nothing about acting, but nevertheless he gave a sterling performance. No one looking at him would have realized that he was actually in discomfort. "We have no basic disagreement," he said placatingly. "I feel sure that if you're questioned by the authorities, you'll know what to say and won't take any steps that could cause trouble for one who has befriended you."

Hank shrugged but made no reply, and as they

drove back, they exchanged only a few words. When they reached the officers' dwelling, their good-byes were abrupt and cool. Plosz saw it was useless to try to persuade Hank to act against his conscience, and Hank clearly would resent any additional attempts to influence him.

Plosz's foot was throbbing increasingly as he drove back to Memphis, and he hastily changed his plans. Instead of taking the next train for the return trip, as he had intended, he decided to stay at a Memphis hotel until he felt better.

He took a room at a commercial hotel near the Mississippi waterfront. There he remained for the better part of a week, spending most of his days and nights sleeping, and eating only infrequently. He knew he would be wise to see a doctor who would attend to the wound, but he procrastinated, not wanting to have to answer any difficult questions, and eventually he abandoned the idea. The virulent infection that had set in was not only draining his strength but appeared to be affecting his reasoning.

During his lonely sojourn in Memphis, Plosz unexpectedly reached one conclusion: He wanted nothing more to do with James Martinson. For years he had done Martinson's dirty work, just as he had served Martinson's father in the same way earlier. Enough was enough. He had earned sufficient money from them to consider retirement, and he had continued to work only because of greed. Now, however, with the possibility that the government might be looking for him, he realized that the time had come for him to retire, assume a new alias, and disappear.

Only one step remained before he left his dubious career behind. He would go to Washington, see Martinson, notify him of his intentions, and say good-bye. While he was about it, he would also collect a large "farewell" bonus. Martinson would find it advisable to pay him, in order to guarantee that he would keep his mouth shut.

Breathing somewhat easier in spite of his continuing physical discomfort, Plosz took the train from Memphis to Nashville, where he transferred to a sleeper that took him to Washington.

James Martinson was disconcerted. His secretary, Wilma, had reported sick on Tuesday morning. On Friday, word came that she had died suddenly.

His new secretary was less than efficient and had her hands full taking care of visitors who filled his reception room, hoping to see him on matters ranging from banking problems to treasury loans. Therefore, he had to fend alone with his schedule, which ordinarily had been efficiently handled.

Now, to compound matters, Milton Plosz had appeared unexpectedly at his office in the Treasury Department, once more ignoring his instructions never to show his face there. Rather than allow the possibility of a scene in his outer office, Martinson consented to see him, grateful that he had happened to intercept the man as he arrived, instead of having had him announced by name.

Plosz's complexion was gray and mottled, and he had lost considerable weight. His eyes were glazed and watery, one of the visible effects of the poison in his system. Beads of perspiration stood out on his forehead, and he walked with a distinct limp. He appeared to be in considerable pain, and he winced as he moved. He was obviously unwell.

"Milton," Martinson said sourly, "you look like the devil."

"I've been a trifle under the weather lately," Plosz said, choosing not to go into detail, "but I'm much better now. I know you prefer me not to come here, but this is an urgent matter."

"What's on your mind?"

"I've decided to retire," Plosz said, "effective immediately. As a going-away gift, I'm counting on you for an additional ten thousand dollars. Then we'll call it quits."

James Martinson was stunned. Plosz's present assignment was far from complete. As for his demand for an additional payment, it was blackmail, and Martinson had no intention of tolerating it. He had rarely resorted to physical violence, but he knew that he would have to permanently silence this opportunist.

Rising from his desk, he said, "Some matters we can't discuss here. Let's go outdoors, where the walls have no ears."

The Washington weather being cold and inclement, he donned a long scarf, his greatcoat, and a hat, as well as a pair of gloves. Plosz waited, a half smile on his face. He had anticipated a strong objection from Martinson, but he was both surprised and pleased by the ease with which his employer seemed ready to consider his demand.

They walked together to the stable behind the Treasury Department building and picked up a carriage and a team. They climbed onto the padded seats and Martinson took the reins. He directed the horses through the downtown streets and toward Rock Creek Park. "I've had a particularly bad morning," he said. "I need a little fresh air and exercise. This will be a good opportunity."

When they reached the outer rim of the large park, Martinson pulled the carriage to the side of the road and suggested they walk.

Because of the season of the year and the time of day, the park was deserted. As they put a distance between themselves and the road, Martinson puffed nonchalantly on a cigar. "It grieves me, Milton, to learn that you want to quit," he said. "I'm engaged in a very big project, the biggest I've ever undertaken, and I certainly have valued your help."

"I've helped you to the limit of my capabilities," Plosz replied, limping as he walked. "Now I've got to think of myself. That's why I'm retiring. You'll just have to get along without me."

"If you say so," Martinson said with a show of regret. "But I wish you'd think it over."

"I've been thinking of little else for several days now, and I've reached a final decision. By the same token, I'm going to need more money on which to live. I'm obliged, therefore, to ask for a retirement fee. Considering all that I've done for you and for your father over a period of many years, I hardly think what I ask is too much."

"You've been paid for every job you ever performed for my father and for me. I hope you're keeping in mind that you have collected very large sums."

"Obviously—I've been worth it to you!" Plosz retorted with some heat. "Just as I'm sure that I am deserving of the additional payment."

They came to the creek and stood looking down at the clear water rippling over the stony bottom. Stones covered much of the bank, too, and Martinson stepped several feet away until he was standing on a large rock.

Plosz followed, and they stood side by side. Martinson was still calm on the surface and puffed his cigar placidly. Plosz, however, appeared excited and was losing a measure of his self-control.

Moving casually, Martinson dropped back until he stood about two or three feet behind the other man. "I'm not happy about your asking on such short notice," he said. "I've been putting too much into this project."

"I'm sure you'll find the money," Plosz retorted unpleasantly. "You're like your father that way. You can always come up with large bundles of cash when your back is against the wall."

"How much time will you give me?" Martinson asked. As he spoke, he slipped his long wool scarf from around his neck.

"I'll need an answer at once—today," Plosz declared flatly. "I have no time to lose. I'm planning on leaving Washington permanently as soon as I can."

Acting swiftly, Martinson grasped the scarf by its ends. Looping it over Milton Plosz's head, he used it as a noose. Once it was secure around the man's throat, he kicked out viciously, catching Plosz behind the knees. Plosz's legs gave way, and he fell heavily to the rock on which he had been standing. As he fell, Martinson twisted the scarf, tightening it around his opponent's neck.

The assault was so unexpected, so out of character for the James Martinson whom Plosz knew, that he was utterly unable to defend himself. Lying on the ground, he gasped and tried to pull the scarf away from his neck.

Showing no mercy or remorse, Martinson twisted the scarf still tighter until it was cutting off Plosz's breath. Then he lifted Plosz's head and struck it hard against the rock, repeating this action again and again, using all his considerable strength, until Plosz was thoroughly dazed and helpless.

Plosz moaned and struggled feebly, but in his semiconscious state he was no match for his bigger, determined assailant. Finally he passed out. But even then Martinson kept up the merciless beating for three minutes or more, until he was certain that Plosz was beyond help or hope.

Not until Milton Plosz's eyes stared vacantly up at the leaden sky did Martinson desist. Then he rewrapped his scarf around his throat, made certain that his gloves were not spotted with his victim's blood, and rising to his feet, kicked Plosz's dead body viciously in the side.

"That," he said venomously, "is your final payment, Milton. I make it to you freely in lieu of the money that you wanted." He strolled back to his carriage, still the imperturbable, highly placed official.

Driving back into the city, he headed directly for the Washingtonian, a private gentleman's club located in an old mansion not far from the White House. Among its distinguished members it numbered the President, Cabinet members, high-ranking commanders of the army and navy, and other government leaders. Martinson was active in the club, and it was his intention to use his presence as an alibi, pretending that he had been there since noon.

As soon as he entered, Martinson quickly removed his hat, coat, and scarf and left them in the cloakroom. Then, his luck continuing to be good, he encountered several men who were just leaving the dining room after finishing their midday meal. He made a point of telling a complicated joke to the minority leader of the Senate, and then he repeated the story for the admiral who was the deputy chief of naval operations. If necessary, both men could remember having seen him that day, and both would assume that he, like they, had lunched at the club.

Walking through the oak-paneled rooms, Martinson went first to the bar, where he saw a few acquaintances and stopped to have a drink and to chat with them. Entering the dining room, he chose as lunch companions some gregarious men who were inclined to stay beyond the normal hours. After the lengthy meal, he signed the bill—his signature would attest to his presence that day—and left the table, chatting with the headwaiter to make certain that he would be remembered.

Before leaving the club, he returned to the bar and sipped a glass of ale as he talked amiably with the attorney general and the assistant postmaster general. They, too, would remember his presence, and he made a point of consulting his watch, announcing that he had already spent more than three hours at the club and should return to his office.

He drove back to the Treasury Department building. Few of his associates there had any reason to know how long he had been absent, and he had no difficulty in concocting a little story about having fallen in with long-winded friends at the club. He was confident his alibis would hold up in court.

Two days later, a brief article in the Washington newspapers reported that the body of a man had been found in Rock Creek Park the previous afternoon. According to the article, his skull had been badly smashed, but other signs of violence were lacking except for bruises at his throat. The autopsy had disclosed an infected wound in the victim's right foot, but this was deemed to have no bearing on the cause of death. The police had found no clues as to the identity of the victim except a key to a room in one of the major hotels. A desk clerk viewed the body at the morgue and recalled having registered the man as M. P. Jonas of New York. The article went on to say that nothing else could be learned about him, and in the event that the body was not claimed by relatives within seventy-two hours, Mr. Jonas would be buried in a potter's field.

Martinson read the article and was satisfied that "Jonas" never would be identified. Thus, the trail would not lead to James Martinson.

XII

Dorothy White would always remember the day as the most sustained nightmare she had known or could imagine. It had started like any other, and upon arriving at the office she had busied herself with customary routines until she was called into the office of General Pitcher in midmorning.

He startled her by questioning her, as did an officer from the War Department, about the man in New York to whom she had sent former cadet Henry Blake.

Although surprised and uneasy that the general knew about Hank's defection, Dorothy nevertheless pretended complete innocence. Denying any knowledge of what he was talking about, she managed to stubbornly maintain that position, in spite of their interrogation.

In the long run, Dorothy's intransigence availed her nothing. General Pitcher discharged her, effective immediately, and even cut off what would have been her normal dismissal pay. She was told to leave the grounds of the academy by early afternoon.

She went home to pack her belongings, but before she could leave, a letter arrived, informing her that her sister Wilma had died in Washington.

Badly shaken, Dorothy took a train to Washington, where she arrived in time to take charge of her sister's modest funeral. She stayed in Wilma's apartment, where she could look after young Freddy, her nephew. And there, after the funeral, she took stock of her overall situation.

She no longer would be able to send reports to Martinson, so that source of income had ended. Furthermore, Wilma's death broke off her means of contact with Martinson. Nevertheless, she was determined to try to see the man who had come to mean so much in changing her life-style.

Arriving at his office, she was not in the least surprised when Martinson refused to see her. A temporary secretary informed her that he was "in conference" and could not be disturbed for the rest of the day. Rather than persist in pursuing a hopeless goal, Dorothy abandoned it, at least for the time being.

Wilma had left all her property to her son, and Dorothy was encouraged when she saw that, including insurance policies, her sister's estate surprisingly amounted to more than ten thousand dollars in ready cash. This made custody of Freddy far more attractive to the right person, and after thinking about this for nearly twenty-four hours, she reached a previously unexpected decision. Their bachelor brother, Lem, who had been estranged from the rest of the White family for many years, had occasionally been in touch with her—a penny postcard now and then, sometimes with a plaintive recounting of one more personal disaster, coupled with a request for five or ten dollars "to tide me over." Dorothy, whom he evidently regarded as the wealthiest and softest touch in the family, usually was able to oblige, and so their distant and infrequent cordiality continued. Now, she began to think of Lem as providing the solution she needed to the problem that Freddy posed. The ten thousand would represent a godsend to Lem, and to Dorothy it represented only a small stake in the game she had in mind.

Having made up her mind, she closed Wilma's apartment and bought train tickets for herself and Freddy to the little town in the Allegheny Mountains of West Virginia, where she, Wilma, and Lem had grown up. When they arrived at Lem's home, he was clearly taken aback, but something in his sister's manner and her expensive apparel caused him to relent and give a reasonably warm reception. He even was noticeably sobered by the news of Wilma's death.

That night, after Freddy was safely in bed, brother and sister sat together at the kitchen table in Lem's bungalow.

Dorothy wasted no time in getting down to business. "You'd have no way of knowing this," she told him, "but Wilma left her son quite well off."

Lem moistened his lips and peered at her across the table. "What do you mean by quite well off?" he demanded.

"Freddy," she said, "has inherited about ten thousand from his mother. That's quite a neat sum."

Lem sat bolt upright. "That's a whole damned fortune!" he exclaimed. "Congratulations, Dottie. Even though you'll be responsible to a court for his welfare, I assume you'll be able to use some here and there for your own purposes."

"I would if I were going to be his guardian," Dorothy said, "but I'm not. I'm young, I'm single, and I have my whole life ahead of me. I can't be burdened with responsibility for a little boy. Freddy would get in my way."

"What are you planning to do with him, then?"

Lem had walked into her trap, and she allowed herself the luxury of smiling benignly. "Obviously," she said, "he can't be left in the custody of just anybody. The court would ask for the assurance that he would be in the care of a close relative. So, if I can't take him, that leaves you, Lem."

Lem shifted his bulk in his chair. "Do you mean to sit there and tell me," he demanded incredulously, "that you aim to give up ten thousand? That ain't like I remember you, Dottie. You must have changed. You were such a 'gimme' kid!"

"I have certain plans, very ambitious plans," Dorothy admitted, "and having custody of Freddy would interfere with them, as well as my life in general. As a result, I am willing to relinquish him to you, and let you have first crack at the fortune that he's inherited."

"I think you're loco, Dottie," Lem said, "giving up a sure thing for some wild dreams. You always were kind of crazy, I guess. But you don't have to invite me twice, not with all that money staring me in the face. I accept it. I'm willing to be the kid's guardian, and I want that understood between us, before you have a chance to try to go back on your word."

"I won't change my mind, Lem," Dorothy assured him. "This is a very tidy arrangement that helps both of us and does no harm at all to Freddy. I will give you whatever you need in the way of a sworn statement that should help you in establishing the relationship to a court's satisfaction. In the meantime, you can wish me luck."

In the morning Dorothy said good-bye to her brother and her bewildered young nephew and returned to Washington. She engaged a room at a quiet, inexpensive hotel favored by unattached ladies who worked for the government. In the privacy of the drab little room, she counted her assets.

First and foremost was her appearance. Her face was very attractive now that she had learned to use cosmetics, and lightening the color of her hair had added a distinct flair to her looks. Her figure was good, and when she wore properly cut clothing, which she favored despite the expense, she could create a sensation in many public places.

Thanks in part to Martinson's past generosity, she could live for a reasonable time on the two thousand dollars she had accumulated, without having to work. In fact, she had no intention of seeking employment. Instead, she planned to use Martinson and his fortune to her advantage. She was aware that Martinson's strange conduct had included strewing money around for what appeared to be highly questionable purposes. In one way or another, she planned to do her best to ferret out his secrets and force him to cooperate with her. If he was one of the wealthiest men in America, as his visible wealth suggested, she was out to share that wealth. No matter what she had to do to accomplish her ends, she had convinced herself that she was prepared to do it. Before she was finished with Martinson, he would open his bank accounts to her.

Although Emil Braun loved to strike a bold posture, indicating to anyone who listened that he alone was in command of his camp, the disappearance of the man known to him as M. P. Jonas soon left him facing a potential shortage of funds.

To an extent, he was fortunate: He had enough money in the bank, given him previously by his contact, to pay the salaries of his officers and the wages of his troops for another three months. He needed money, however, to buy munitions, without which he could not expect to function effectively.

As the days became weeks, Braun became increasingly certain that he could no longer rely on Jonas and that he was indeed on his own. He would need to act quickly, to replenish his arsenal. If he could not do so, he would not even be able to hold his men together.

Pondering his problem, Braun realized that it actually was to his advantage that he no longer was dependent on Jonas for his orders. He was acting completely on his own initiative now, and he was glad. His dreams of military glory were such that he actually believed he could initiate his own actions without awaiting instructions as to when and where to strike.

Those who supplied the funds for his entire venture were indeed fortunate, Braun told himself complacently. They no longer had Jonas on whom to rely, for whatever the reason, but instead they could deal directly with a military man who knew what to do and how to go about doing it. Convinced, as never before, of his own military invincibility, Braun began to toy with his own ideas and rapidly expanded them.

Trusting no one, not even his key subordinates, Braun devised complicated plans and began to develop them secretly. As a military tactician, he was justifiably self-confident. Now he left no detail to chance. Acting decisively and swiftly, he selected and segregated two dozen of his most experienced veterans. He told them only that they would be going out on a mission, which he declined to identify or explain. The officers in charge of the unit were also handpicked; without exception, they had served under him faithfully during the war.

The general surprised the officers by taking personal command of the expedition. After supper one night, they left camp under the cover of darkness, armed with rifles and bayonets and carrying a small supply of rations and ample water. They headed east, marching all night, then resting during the day in a well-concealed location. They marched the next night, and by dawn of the second day they were approaching the Tennessee River. Braun called a halt while the men were still concealed on a heavily wooded ridge overlooking the river, and there they made camp.

Through contacts in Memphis provided by Jonas before he disappeared, Braun had been able to locate and hire three boats large enough to accommodate his men. These had been brought up the Tennessee to the rendezvous point where Braun and his men were now camped. Accordingly, shortly after nightfall, Braun ordered his men into the boats for the continuing journey upriver. He also informed them of the destination and purpose of their journey. They were to invade a government arsenal outside Chattanooga, where they were to commandeer all the munitions they could carry.

They made good time upstream. When they reached the vicinity of Chattanooga, the men left their boats about a mile from the arsenal.

Advancing shortly after midnight, they carried out their assault with the military precision that had always been Braun's hallmark. The small night-shift garrison at the arsenal was overwhelmed.

Two defenders were killed, three others were wounded, and the remaining survivors were forced to surrender. The invaders selected gunpowder and bullets suitable for use in their own weapons, piled them into wheelbarrows and carts that they found on the premises, and were gone in less than an hour.

Bound hand and foot, their victims were unable to give an alarm in time to overtake the raiders. The attack was not discovered until the platoon scheduled to relieve those who had been on night duty appeared at the arsenal an hour after sunrise. By that time, it was too late to track down the attackers, who had vanished.

The attack made headline news in the press, but the surviving army troops could provide little useful information about the raiders. They had worked swiftly, responding to softly spoken commands. Editorial writers and politicians speculated in vain about the significance of the attack, and the entire nation was concerned.

Toby speculated and waited for confirmation.

Later, after the expedition had returned to camp, Stalking Horse reported to Toby. "Hank said to tell you," he said, "that Braun personally led a raid on the arsenal and has returned with enough ammunition to pose serious problems. There's talk of another attack soon."

Toby promptly rode into Memphis, where he sent a telegram in code to General Blake.

Thirty-six hours later, a reply arrived, ordering him to proceed without delay to Nashville, where he was to report on all that he knew about the raid to Tennessee's governor, DeWitt C. Senter. The governor, latest in a long line of extraordinary statesmen to add to the luster of Tennessee, received Toby immediately and listened attentively to his report.

"I have other news as well," Toby said, as he concluded his account of the attack on the arsenal. "For whatever reason, Emil Braun seems to be accelerating his whole timetable. According to sources within his camp, he's preparing to follow up his raid with further action."

"And you think he poses a major threat?" the governor asked, his expression grave. "I'm thinking of the long term—over the next few months."

"Braun has raised and trained a corps of Civil War veterans, some of whom are scamps and scoundrels, but also some with distinguished war records. They shape up as dangerous enemies," Toby said. "But now for the important part. As I understand it, Braun is making plans to take over something here in Tennessee. I don't know what, but I'm hoping to learn details fairly soon."

"What's the man's motive?" the governor asked, clearly concerned.

"I can answer to that on my personal experience with him. It appears that he's an egomaniac who, for some reason, considers himself at war with the United States. I know it's a ridiculous idea, but nevertheless, men were killed and wounded by the assault on the arsenal, and the danger is all the greater now that he's obtained munitions."

"The information and analysis you give me," the governor said, "corroborates what I've learned from the federal government. I'm strongly tempted to call up the state guard and challenge Braun, but I hesitate. In the first place, we've had a difficult time rebuilding the state militia, and I'm none too sure how well we could match a trained force of determined and experienced men. Even more important, if he's a madman who has scant regard for human life, he well might order his troops to do battle with the militia, and too many men could be killed."

Toby frowned and shook his head. "The caution exercised by responsible men in office is used by Braun as a weapon to further his own cause. I don't yet know what the answer to that dilemma might be."

"Ordinarily," the governor told him, "I visit the major communities in the state twice a year. I'm due to make a trip to Memphis, and I'll advance my schedule slightly and go there as soon as I can. Before I take drastic action, I want to see Braun myself if possible and sound him out."

"I hardly need to remind you, sir," Toby said, "that it's possible you could be in considerable danger."

The governor smiled. "I'll take my chances," he replied.

Three days after that meeting, the governor arrived in Memphis with his wife. Accompanied by a small party of aides, they took up residence in a state-owned house on a bluff overlooking the Mississippi. The mansion, formerly a private dwelling, was set in dense, parklike surroundings. The governor sent a message to Toby at Violet's cottage telling him of his arrival.

Toby promptly traveled the several miles into the city to pay his respects.

"I sent the 'general' a letter by messenger before I left Nashville," the governor told him, "asking that he come into Memphis and meet with me. I hope to force his hand and bring all this to a head peaceably."

Toby was dubious about the result of such an effort but concealed his reaction. "Did you happen to specify a date and a time for him to visit you?"

"As a matter of fact, I did," the governor replied. "I suggested that he call on me last night, within hours of my arrival. Apparently he was busy, or he decided that it would be wiser to wait a day, so I'm half expecting him this afternoon or perhaps tonight."

If Emil Braun had not already appeared, it seemed unlikely that he would keep any appointment with the governor, Toby thought, but he kept his own counsel. He was presented to Mrs. Senter, and after chatting with her for a short time, he took his leave, arranging to return the following day.

After he departed, however, he did not return immediately to Violet's cottage. Instead, he quietly made a reconnaissance of the grounds around the governor's temporary house, circling and pausing every few feet to obtain a clearer view. What impressed him most was the view he obtained of the drawing room of the governor's suite, located on the ground floor. From the nearby woods he could see in through the french windows and could make out plainly the interior of the drawing room. He made a mental note of this.

Saying nothing about it to anyone, he returned at dusk, armed with his rifle, and stationed himself in the woods. His vigil was rewarded late in the evening. After the governor and Mrs. Senter had dined in the mansion, the state's chief executive retired to the drawing room. There, using two oil lamps on a desk, he sat with his back to the french windows, working on a pile of documents.

He worked steadily and rapidly, poring over each document, making notes in the margins on some and signing others with a flourish. While he worked, a door opened, and the governor's wife, attired in an attractive robe that covered her from the neck down, came in carrying a tray with two mugs containing a steaming beverage.

Just then Toby could hear a faint rustling sound in the brush about thirty yards closer to the house, off to his right. He looked in that direction and saw a figure who seemed to be studying the couple inside. Although the night was dark with heavy clouds overhead, Toby's superior eyesight enabled him to see the intruder plainly. The man appeared to be young, tall, and broad-shouldered. Under one arm, he carried a rifle. He peered at the Senters, planted his feet apart, and brought the rifle up to his shoulder.

As he did, Toby quickly raised his own rifle, sighted his target along the barrel, and squeezed the trigger. As the man dropped to the ground, Toby sprinted toward the house. The governor, hearing the shot, simultaneously moved forward and opened the french windows.

Toby lost no time in crying out, "Take Mrs. Senter and go into another room," he ordered. "Stay there until I've made a quick surveillance of the area. You're too clear as targets in that room." Hurriedly he turned back into the woods.

The governor obeyed with alacrity. He turned away from the window, spoke sharply to his wife, and she preceded him out of the room, bearing the tray in her hands.

After some minutes Toby came in from the garden and joined them. "Your secretary heard the shot and came out, Governor," he said. "He has taken charge of the man's body after I examined it quite closely. My shot pierced his skull, and he must have died instantly."

Governor Senter looked blank, and Toby went on to explain that, having found an intruder aiming a rifle at the governor, he had shot the villain before the assassination attempt could be carried out.

"On the basis of papers in the man's possession,

I'm convinced he was a member of Emil Braun's corps,"
he said.

"You're saying," the governor replied, "that you
don't consider this an isolated attempt to assassinate
me, but rather a part of a deliberate effort by Braun?"

"No question of it, sir," Toby told him emphatically. "His identity is very clear. As I see this situation,
Braun had no intention of accepting your invitation and
still doesn't intend to meet with you. Instead, he chose
to use the occasion to assign one of his thugs to kill
you."

"Although I hate to think that such men are on the
loose in our state, I suspect you're right, Mr. Holt," the
governor said.

Mrs. Senter interrupted. "Won't you join us for a
cup of hot chocolate, Mr. Holt?" she asked.

"Thank you, ma'am," Toby answered with a smile,
"but I really want to have another look around the
whole neighborhood before I'm satisfied that the assassination effort was confined to one man."

"I want to ask you something, Mr. Holt, and I'll
expect an honest, candid reply," she said. "Do you
think it's safe for us to stay in Memphis?"

The governor broke in impatiently. "Dammit, I'm
not going to let anyone scare me out of doing my duty!"

"You have already done your duty by the people of
Memphis!" she retorted. "Now you must think of your-
self and of me and the people of the state at large.
Would you mind answering the question, Mr. Holt?"

Toby smiled at her. "I appreciate and sympathize
with your concern, Mrs. Senter," he said. "To be frank
with you, as you asked, I quite agree that Memphis is
not the safest place for the governor at the moment. A
man who is increasingly showing himself to be irrespon-
sibly warring against the government undoubtedly would
be pleased indeed if the head of the state were re-

moved from the picture. To accomplish that, he obviously is willing to have the governor killed."

"What would you have me do, then?" Governor Senter demanded hotly. "Would you have me run away with my tail between my legs?"

"If I were you, sir," Toby told him, "I'd go to the capital and wait there for future developments. The story of Emil Braun and his mercenary corps is far from ended. A great deal remains to be done in order to subdue them. As it happens, we feel assured that Braun is intending action contrary to this country's interests. Perhaps we need to let the 'general' try to take that action. Then we could nail him to the wall for more than robbing an arsenal."

Governor Senter reluctantly agreed. "You may be right," he said.

"Unless I'm very much mistaken," Toby said, "we won't have too long to wait. For reasons we don't yet understand, Braun is losing his patience and appears to be becoming anxious. This attempt on your life tonight is not at all like the caution that he's normally displayed. He seems desperate, as though he's been cut off from supporters who are important to him and he's being forced to resort to violent action despite his overall plan. If I'm right, hell will really be popping in the near future because he'll feel impelled to move. We must be prepared to head him off—but also to take decisive counteraction."

James Martinson read the confidential daily newsletter written by members of the White House staff for the sole edification of Cabinet members and their first assistants. He was shocked by the confidential account of the attempted assassination of the governor of Tennessee, since no word of the incident had appeared in the newspapers. Staring out his office window at the familiar outlines of the White House, his ultimate goal

in life, Martinson could not help wondering if Emil
Braun could be responsible for the attack on the governor. It would be most unfortunate for precipitate action
to spoil a perfect scheme.

Martinson feared that, with Plosz gone, Braun had
lost the one check that had existed on him. After all,
Braun had been taking orders from Plosz, and now that
Plosz was no longer on the scene, Martinson feared he
would have increasing difficulty in keeping Braun's troops
in line until the proper time for him to disclose the
threat of their existence, and that time was not yet at
hand. His revelations would be useless if he did not
wait until the next presidential campaign, and he was
willing to risk everything on this essential delay.

Martinson knew of only one way to control Braun,
and that way was not open to him. In theory, he could
reveal himself to Braun as his sponsor and demand
obedience. But that would cost him dearly and would
give Braun unlimited power over him. Under no circumstances would he make such a move.

Seething with impotent rage, Martinson recognized
he had no way of controlling Braun. He would have to
watch helplessly as Braun took whatever course most
appealed to him. Braun and his troops were, for all
practical purposes, not only independent but were also
capable of inflicting great harm.

It was at the request of Governor Senter that
newspapers had made no mention of the attempt on his
life. The body of the would-be assassin was buried that
night quietly in the Memphis potter's field. If Emil
Braun was expecting a report from this man, he would
be badly disappointed. This strategy, Toby reasoned,
would exert additional pressure on Braun and would
cause him to begin the military action that he had been
threatening. Toby's theory seemed to be borne out
when Stalking Horse, returning from a day at the mili-

tary camp, said, "Hank wants to meet you tonight at the birch trees an hour after dark. He says it's urgent."

"Did he tell you why?"

Stalking Horse shook his head.

"You don't know what may be going on or what kind of an action may be planned?"

"He gave me no clue."

That night, after dark, Toby went off to the rendezvous, carrying two pistols and a brace of knives, his broad-brimmed hat pulled low over his forehead.

The rendezvous was deserted when he reached it, and he settled down at the base of the clump of birches. Making himself comfortable, he undid the flap on one of his repeating pistols as he listened for any sound that might tell him someone was coming near.

After a wait that would have tried the patience of a man less disciplined than Toby, he heard approaching footsteps, and then Hank's voice floated to him from a distance of only a few feet. "Are you there, Toby?"

"I'm here," Toby replied quietly.

Hank lost no time in getting down to essentials. "The general," he said, "is raising holy hell at last. He assigned someone to murder Governor Senter of Tennessee, but the attempt failed for reasons that nobody knows, and the trooper who had the assignment has vanished. That set the general off, and he's now thirsting for major action."

As Toby had reasoned, a crisis was approaching rapidly. "Go on," he muttered.

"The day after tomorrow," Hank said, "is the beginning of Mardi Gras in Memphis. They'll have a celebration that goes on day and night for forty-eight hours—parades, street celebrations, everybody dresses up. It's quite a time for the whole city. The general," he went on, contempt and horror mingling in his voice, "has chosen to take advantage of Mardi Gras and to seize control of Memphis."

Toby was stunned. "You're joking!"

"I wish I were. He's intending to seize the railroad station, the telegraph office, and police headquarters. Once those three are secure, he feels that Memphis will be his."

"Is he going to turn his whole armed corps loose on the city?" Toby asked, finding it hard to believe what he was hearing.

"No," Hank said, "that's where he's being so infernally clever. He's going to use only one hundred men for the purpose. Every man is a veteran who served in half a dozen campaigns. They're all experienced—devoted to him. They're ruthless, and they'll obey his instructions to the letter. They aren't going into town in uniform. They'll be dressed for the occasion as pirates, and they plan to move so swiftly that they expect virtually no casualties. The general will hold the entire town in the palm of his hand before Memphis even realizes what's going to happen."

"When is this attack going to take place?"

"At dusk on the first day of Mardi Gras. After he takes Memphis and makes the town secure, he plans to issue an ultimatum. Then the rest of the corps will march against Nashville. And after the capital has been taken, we're to be sent north to Louisville and capture that too. Apparently, he sees himself as mastering Tennessee and Kentucky, then using these two states as a springboard to conquer the entire United States. I think he's truly mad."

"You're not taking part in the original assault?"

"No, I'm being held in reserve with the rest of the corps."

"Do you see any way you could be included in the attacking force?"

"Sure," Hank said. "All I'd need to do is volunteer, and I'm sure that I would be accepted."

"All right, do it, then!" Toby told him. "We'll

make contact in town. Don't ask me where or how, but I'll counter Braun and stifle his attack. It seems the time finally has come for real action. We've waited and we've stalled, and those days are ended now. The real climax is actually at hand!"

Now that the time for action had arrived, Toby knew exactly what needed to be done. It was as though he had spent all of his time while keeping a vigil outside Braun's camp, planning his moves for this moment.

First he sent telegrams to Governor Senter in Nashville and to General Sherman in Washington. Then he went to Martha's hotel and called on her.

Martha, simply dressed and wearing no makeup, came to the door. She took one look at Toby and knew instantly from his expression that this was no social visit. "What is it?" she asked quickly. "What's wrong?"

"Emil Braun is about to move," he said, "and I need help. Can you arrange a meeting for me with Red Leary right away?"

"Come along," she said, without hesitation. "We'll go to Red's office right now."

They walked the short distance to the headquarters of the Mackerels. Toby was silent and preoccupied, but Martha was nevertheless highly pleased. She realized, as he apparently did not, that he had turned to her in a time of crisis, and she knew he was depending on her.

Red Leary abruptly terminated another meeting when he learned that Martha and Toby were calling on him, and he ushered them into his office.

Toby wasted no words. "Emil Braun is going to strike in two days, when the Mardi Gras begins," he said. "He has selected his best man to seize control of Memphis."

"What the hell does that mean?"

"As I understand it, he's going to seize the railroad station, the telegraph office, and police headquarters."

Leary whistled softly under his breath. "He has courage, I must say that for him," he said. "How many men is he sending on this little errand?"

"One hundred," Toby replied. "All combat veterans on whom he knows he can rely. He's got to be stopped."

"Obviously," Red replied dryly. "Turn that many armed men loose in this city, and the casualties will be enormous."

"We have problems to face," Toby told him. "I'm going to telegraph the governor, advising him to call up the militia and to be ready to send it in if it's needed. But he's already told me that it's under strength—and mobilizing it will take time in any case. I prefer to act quickly, using other means if possible, so I'm appealing to you for help."

Martha nodded vehemently.

Leary grinned at her, then at the man who sat tensely beside her. "Glad to oblige," he said.

"What size force can you muster?" Toby asked.

Leary sat back in his chair, stared up at the ceiling, and indulged in some mental arithmetic. "I can gather a force of as many as fifty men," he said at last.

"In other words, Braun will outnumber us by about two to one."

"Granted," Red replied with quiet pride. "But our men, after all, are Mackerels!"

"Where it's necessary, we'll meet force with force, shot for shot," Toby said, "but I vastly prefer to use guile and trickery to disarm Braun's men. The more bloodshed that can be avoided, the better it will be for all of us."

"How can you hope to avoid bloodshed?" Red asked skeptically.

"Braun hopes to take advantage of the holiday atmosphere of Mardi Gras. I say we turn the tables on him by using it ourselves."

Leary seemed confused. "How do you mean?"

"According to reliable information that I've received," Toby said, "Braun and his men will be dressed as pirates. Presumably, they'll mingle with the crowds, work their way toward their destinations, then act swiftly to seize them and make them secure. I suggest that we also rely on disguises."

Martha, who had been listening intently, entered the conversation for the first time. "That should be easy enough," she said. "Suppose that Red's Mackerels dress as Indians for Mardi Gras? They, too, can mingle with the crowds."

Red chuckled. "Fair enough," he said.

"I assume," Martha said to Toby, "that you're intending to take an active part. If so, you'll also need a costume for Mardi Gras."

"So I will," he replied. "I've been so busy thinking in strategic terms that it hadn't occurred to me to wonder about that kind of detail."

"Leave it to me," she said. "I'll go to a dressmaker and have something made that would be appropriate for you."

Toby and Red launched into a spirited discussion of the tactics they should employ. They agreed that Jackson Square, about three blocks from the river, was the key to the operation. Only a few blocks from the square stood the railroad station, where most of the lines that served Memphis picked up and discharged passengers. On the south side of the square, the telegraph office and the headquarters of the police department were located, side by side.

"I recommend," Toby said, "that we keep the bulk of our forces centered in the Jackson Square area. We might deploy the men in such a way that they'll be in the various side streets and alleyways that lead into the square. Braun's forces are sure to congregate there, and I suggest that we wait until they have the bulk of their main body on hand. Then we move in as quickly as possible and disarm them. With any luck, I'd like to take them in hand without firing a shot, although I realize that may be too optimistic."

"You're being *far* too optimistic," Leary objected. "Don't you really see any unexpected complications?"

"I do think that we must keep the river in mind," Toby acknowledged. "It could provide a back door for him in a showdown—but on the other hand the river also could turn out to be a barrier he can't pass. In any event, for now, Jackson Square is sure to be the area of our principal confrontation."

After they had reached a rough understanding on what needed to be done and on the steps they would take to accomplish their goals, they parted company. Toby promised to return early in the morning two days later when Mardi Gras was to begin. He walked with Martha back to her hotel, where he thanked her and arranged to go to her suite later in order to pick up the costume she was having made for him. From there he went out to Violet's cottage. Contrary to his custom of recent weeks, he made no attempt to maintain a surveillance on Emil Braun's military force.

Later that day he received a long telegram from the governor. After reading it, he went to find Stalking Horse and Violet.

"Tomorrow morning, after your brother and I have gone into the city," he told Violet, "some men who are in the employ of Governor Senter will arrive with some important packages for me. When the men arrive, tell them to stack the goods very carefully out in the barn, in one of the unused stalls. Don't go near the boxes yourself, and be sure not to let anyone else know of their presence."

Ordinarily Violet would have accepted his directions at face value, but so many strange things had been happening, beginning with her loss of her farm, that she was unable to contain her curiosity. "What will be in those packages?"

Toby smiled. "For your own sake," he said, "it's best if you don't know, and if any strangers should appear and inquire about them, you never heard of them and you've never seen them."

Seeing that he was very serious, Violet swore that she would follow his instructions to the letter.

Toby and Stalking Horse walked off a short distance for a private chat. Toby revealed the plan that he and Red Leary had devised.

"I will go with you," the Cherokee declared.

"There's no need for you to risk your life in battle," Toby told him.

"On more occasions than I can remember," Stalking Horse said, "I went into battle beside your father. Together we fought renegades and outlaws, some misguided Indian nations, and other enemies of the state and of Whip Holt. Always we triumphed. What sort of man do you think I would be if I failed to do for you what I so often did for your father? I would be ashamed and unable to hold up my head. Is it settled that I am coming with you?"

Toby knew better than to argue. "Thank you, Stalking Horse," he said. "We'll do this your way."

The Indian chuckled softly. "I will not need much in the way of a disguise," he said. "I will dress as I did in my youth. You can expect me to appear not in disguise but as myself."

XIII

When Toby tapped on the door of the suite, Martha called out, bidding him to enter. She directed him to the far side of the sitting room, where his costume was put out on a sofa. She apparently was in a bedroom changing into her own outfit.

He smiled quietly when he saw that she had selected a white Pierrot costume for him, the classic garment of the European clown, with a top that featured wide sleeves and a bottom with loose, full trousers. The outfit was decorated with huge dots of dark red and blue. Accompanying it was a cone-shaped hat, also in white, with red and blue dots.

Toby changed into the costume at once and was not surprised that Martha had obtained clothing that fitted him perfectly. Her ability to provide whatever a situation required had by now become a matter of course to him.

He chuckled aloud as Martha entered the room, dressed in a matching Pierrette costume, a clown's dress with a low, square-cut neckline.

"I told Red Leary how we'll be dressed," Martha said, "so all the Mackerels will be on the lookout for us. Here, you'll need this." She handed him a mask that covered his eyes and nose. As he put it on, she adjusted one on her face.

Toby buckled on his holster belt beneath the loose-fitting upper garment of his costume and slipped his two repeating pistols into it. Then he emptied several handfuls of spare ammunition into his trousers' pockets and said, "Let's go!"

Martha had followed his example, buckling on her own holster belt and placing her pistols into it. She concealed the weapons with a cape that she put on over the dress. "I'm ready for anything," she announced.

Toby hesitated inside the front door as they were about to leave the suite. Reaching out, he put a hand on her upper arm. "You have no need to expose yourself to danger on my account," he said. "We're going to be engaged in serious business—nasty business—today, and I wonder if you understand how rough it may be."

She looked up, and her eyes were smiling and soft behind her mask. "As I've told you, I came to Memphis from New Orleans for only one purpose—to help you," she said. "You've been frustrated in your attempts to halt Braun. You finally have the opportunity to stop him permanently, and I wouldn't miss the right to be at your side for anything."

Before he could reply, Martha reached up, curled both arms around his neck, and kissed him full on the mouth.

Her touch electrified Toby, and he responded immediately, instinctively. Sweeping her into his arms, he held her close and kissed her. She clung to him, and for some moments they were lost in a world of their own creation.

Then they drew apart and looked at each other from beneath the shields of their masks. Martha had been about to apologize for initiating the intimacy, but she changed her mind. She was not sorry and refused to say that she was.

Both were well aware that they had undergone no ordinary experience. Their deepest and most sensitive emotions had been aroused, and they could not turn

their backs on what they had come to mean to each
other. Neither had been to blame for Toby's unexpected loss of his wife, and they needed to face the fact
that they were free now to commit themselves to each
other.

"I'm glad we were able to reach out to each other
before we take on Braun," Toby said.

His comment touched Martha enough that she
wanted to be held in his arms again, but she realized
this was not the right time. They faced hard, dangerous
work before they could finally settle whatever issues
remained between them. She turned away and started
off down the corridor.

Toby moved up beside her, and she took his arm
as they reached the street, where large crowds were
walking. Those who claimed that the entire population
of Memphis participated in Mardi Gras apparently did
not greatly exaggerate. Music from many small marching bands lent gaiety to the affair.

The costumes people wore were colorful and varied:
Ghosts and goblins rubbed elbows with Elizabethan
lords and ladies, while Spanish buccaneers and Turkish
pashas danced with milkmaids and Russian princesses.
Jupiter, Mercury, and other figures from mythology
threaded their way among clowns, prizefighters, sailors,
and Indians. Children, also costumed and masked, ca-
vorted freely, while food sellers catering to every taste
hawked their wares, offering an international variety of
delicacies.

As Toby and Martha made their way to Jackson
Square, slowly winding in and out of the dense throngs,
they occasionally caught glimpses of men dressed as
pirates. Almost without exception these were men with
grim, ruthless expressions and with bodies that testified
to hard living. Trying to be inconspicuous with their
weapons, they nonetheless each carried a rifle.

Also noticeable were various "Indians," all heading

in the same direction as Martha and Toby. These men, all wearing dark makeup on their faces and bodies, appeared young and athletic. Closer scrutiny revealed that most of them carried weapons; they were ignoring the Indian custom of being armed only with tomahawks and bows and arrows.

As the couple drew nearer to Jackson Square, a real Indian approached, and a familiar voice said, "I'm here, Toby."

Toby grinned at the lean, tall Indian. "I guess you were told I'd be wearing this costume," he said.

The Cherokee chuckled indulgently. "That is right, Toby. But I would know you anywhere on earth, no matter how you were dressed," he said. "Your identity is plain from the way you walk." He fell in behind them and followed as they entered the square.

Accompanied by Martha and Stalking Horse, Toby made his way around the square, halting at each of the streets and alleyways that fed into it to assure himself that his men were on hand and in place. A number of Indians were loitering near the opening of each street, and Toby was satisfied that the Mackerels had the situation under control.

His first stop was the police station, where he presented himself to the chief of the Memphis constabulary and explained the situation.

"I wish I'd known about all this earlier," the chief said in an aggrieved voice. "I sure would have kept my entire force on hand here at the station house. As you might expect, about half the men are on duty around town, maintaining order and preventing pickpocketing and other crimes."

"They're exactly where they should be, and you did the right thing," Toby replied. "How many men do you have here?"

The chief left his office to count the constables on hand and looked glum when he returned. "I have only eight here now," he reported.

"That's plenty," Toby told him. "Do they have firearms?"

"Ordinarily they carry side arms and nightsticks, and we keep rifles on hand for riot duty."

"Break out the rifles," Toby advised, "and tell your men to stand by for trouble. Do I have your permission to speak to them for a couple of minutes?"

"Help yourself," the chief said with a sigh. "In view of what you tell me, it's better if you take over—just in this one matter, of course."

The constables assembled in the squad room, and Toby spoke briefly, explaining the outlook and the role that he was expecting them to play. First, he made it clear he was acting under the authority granted him by both the United States government and the governor of Tennessee.

"Under no circumstances," he said, "should you fire unless I give you explicit orders to do so or unless you feel your life is in danger. We want to hold down gunfire because of the possible danger to everyone in the square. We think we can disarm these misguided fellows. Only if we find our backs to the wall and discover that it's absolutely necessary will we resort to firearms."

The constables were less than pleased with the arrangements, but they were in no position to argue.

Toby went outside again, still accompanied by Martha and Stalking Horse. Outside the plate glass window of the telegraph office, an Indian approached him. In spite of the man's disguise, he quickly recognized Red Leary.

"My boys are all in place and ready for action," Red said. "From what I gather, Emil Braun must be about set to pull the trigger, too. He arrived in the area a short time ago, so I assume that his men are now gathered in the vicinity of the square. He's just gone down to the waterfront, presumably to check on a small contingent he has stationed there. It seems that he's put them there, along with a small boat or two, to help make certain that the 'door' you were talking about will really be there if he decides he needs that kind of insurance."

Toby nodded, and not for the first time he wondered if Hank Blake had been able to get away from the military camp and join the members of Braun's group. He had seen no sign of Hank.

Toby was pleased a few moments later when he saw a number of Mackerels walk down an alleyway and enter the police headquarters building by a rear entrance. The traps were being set, and he could only hope that Braun's men would walk into them without causing too much bloodshed.

A large group of pirates approached the square and entered it. In the lead was a heavyset man to whom the other men deferred. Even though they all wore masks, Toby recognized Emil Braun.

The group halted, and Braun, speaking in low tones, issued instructions to his men, who listened intently. Then he and one of his men moved off toward the park that filled the center of the square, as if they intended not to participate directly in the upcoming action. The other men headed for the police station's front door.

Toby immediately put Braun out of his mind, needing to concentrate on the opening rounds of the encounter. He would deal with Braun later. Walking quickly, he led his companions up the alleyway, and they entered the police headquarters by the rear door. There they found a contingent of Mackerels on guard, ready for action.

In accordance with Toby's instructions, the constables on duty had been split into two groups. Four officers were gathered in the rear, just outside the squad room. The remaining four and the chief were in an anteroom inside the entrance, along with another force of Mackerels.

Followed by Martha, Toby opened the rear door a crack and peered into the squad room, where fifteen or more of the pirates had congregated, virtually filling it. They were as yet unaware that nearly a dozen Indians had entered behind them, blocking their departure.

All at once the pirates stopped their low conversations. As their fingers toyed with their rifles impatiently, a loud, authoritative voice filled the room. "Where is Chief Constable Dwyer?" the speaker demanded in a booming tone.

The chief constable stepped into the room. "I'm Chief Dwyer," he announced loudly. "Who wants me?"

"I call on you," the masked man replied, "to surrender yourself, your officers, and this building to me on behalf of General Emil Braun."

"General *who*?" the chief asked. "What does all this mean?"

"You ask too damn many questions," the man answered harshly. "Do what you're told and be quick about it. I'm ready to shoot you and every one of your men down like dogs."

A long moment of silence followed the demand.

The time had come to put Toby's plan into operation. He would fling the door open with a bang that would be a signal to the Mackerels waiting in the front vestibule. They would step into the squad room as he and his group entered from the rear, confronting their foes both in front and behind.

Feeling the loyal support of Martha and the Mackerels at his back, Toby flung open the rear door. Immediately the front door also flew open, and other Mackerels started to pour into the squad room from that direction. But before either group could go into action, a youthful voice was heard from within the squad room. "Drop your pistol, Colonel! You're covered. And your men are to throw their weapons to the floor. Now! I'll put holes into any man who doesn't obey instantly. And if you've seen me on the practice range, you know I could do it!"

The combined elements of the show of force startled and confused Emil Braun's men. Quickly they threw down their weapons, surprising Toby with the suddenness of their surrender. He could not help but laugh aloud as he stepped into the room, a pistol in each hand. Martha was close behind.

"Very neatly done, Hank," he called. "You act as though you were in on my planning sessions."

"Hello, Toby," was the cheerful reply. "I told you we'd get together one way or another today. What do you want done with these rascals?"

Toby called out to the chief constable. "I'm sure you have space in your jailhouse to accommodate these guests, Mr. Dwyer?"

"We have ample room for them, and more, Mr. Holt."

"March them to the cells," Toby suggested, "and have some of your men collect their weapons."

"Glad to oblige, Mr. Holt. It's a distinct pleasure, sir." The chief shouted some orders, and his policemen moved in swiftly, shepherding their prisoners off to the cells in the basement. Two constables picked up the weapons.

Toby and Stalking Horse enveloped Hank in a bear hug. "Martha," Toby said proudly, "I'm honored to present to you my stepbrother, Cadet First Class Henry Blake of the U.S. Military Academy."

"Former Cadet Blake would be much more appropriate, right now," Hank said sadly.

"Nonsense!" Toby told him. "By the time this escapade is finished, you'll be readmitted to the academy with full honors restored to you."

"I'm glad you're joining in the fight on our side," Martha said to Hank.

Hank smiled. "Thank you, ma'am."

"Under the circumstances," she said, "you don't want to look any more like a pirate than you can help.

Let me help you get out of some of that silly-looking regalia." She deftly rearranged some of his makeshift apparel, then ordered Hank to remove the bandanna from around his neck. Quickly she folded it. "It's now a headband. Tie it around your forehead and then bend down a little."

Hank obeyed promptly. Martha reached into her reticule and brought out her lip rouge, into which she dipped a finger. Before Hank knew what was happening, she made a number of long red streaks on either side of his face.

"That isn't perfect," she said, examining her handiwork critically,. "but as Stalking Horse will agree, at least you can now pass as some kind of an Indian."

Grinning broadly, Hank thanked her and declared himself ready for any adventure that might follow.

Chief Dwyer interrupted with word that the prisoners had been made secure in cells. "What do you want done with their weapons, Mr. Holt?" he asked.

"Add them to your own arsenal," Toby told him. "You may have need of them before the day ends. Keep the men already on duty at headquarters right where they are. If you should be subjected to attack and can't handle it, get in touch with me. I'll be in the vicinity of Jackson Square." He turned to Hank. "Do you happen to be familiar with Braun's schedule?"

"You bet I am," Hank replied promptly. "While we're here, another group is scheduled to be taking over the telegraph office."

They hurriedly left the station house for the building that housed the commercial telegraph office. As they entered, they could see at a glance that they had come too late. The two telegraph operators and their clerk were bound and gagged and sat helplessly in chairs at the rear. Some ten of Braun's men were in the office, apparently more intent on congratulating one another than on securing the victory. One man, posted as a guard, only belatedly became aware of Martha as she slipped past him.

"Hold on there. Where do you think you're going?" he demanded, as he reached out and grabbed hold of her costume.

"Oh, dear," Martha said, pretending to be flustered. "I wanted to send a telegram—"

"You can't do that now," the man said, relaxing his grip, since he believed Martha posed no threat. "The office is closed."

Taking advantage of the distraction Martha was providing, Toby, followed by Hank, Stalking Horse, and several of the Mackerels, entered the office. The guard turned toward them, to order them out, and as he did so, Martha reached under her cloak and drew her pistols. She aimed one of them at the guard and the other toward Braun's men within the building.

"Up with your hands, every last mother's son of you!" she ordered.

One of Braun's officers reached for the pistol at his waist. He had barely pulled the weapon free, however, when Martha's shot sounded loudly. When the smoke cleared away, the men were astonished to see that she had shot the pistol out of the man's grasp. Toby, who was hardly surprised by Martha's expertise, grinned. "I suggest that you do what the lady says," he suggested, "or somebody is likely to be hurt."

Another of Braun's officers, however, chose to ignore the warning and reached for his pistol. Stalking Horse's tomahawk, thrown with stunning force and great accuracy, flashed through the air and smashed into the man's wrist. The officer screamed in pain, then sank to the floor, trying in vain to stem the flow of blood from his wound.

"I'm running out of patience," Martha called in a warning tone. "My trigger finger is getting mighty itchy. I want all of you to try to touch the ceiling—with both hands! Right now!"

Seeing her as she stood with her feet apart, her twin pistols in her hands, the men knew that this Pierrette meant exactly what she said.

One by one, the men gave in to Martha's demand and raised their hands in surrender. "Keep trying to touch that ceiling!" she warned. "Let's see who's the first one to make it." Then she added more conversationally, "You may collect their weapons now, if you wish, gentlemen."

Toby and Hank moved forward swiftly and confiscated pistols and rifles. In the meantime, Stalking Horse recovered his tomahawk and then undid the bonds and gags that held the telegraph office employees.

Toby went to the front door, opened it, and whistled. A number of Indians appeared from side streets, and he beckoned to them. "Take these prisoners next door," he said, "and hand them over to Chief Dwyer. They're to join their friends in the cells. If they get a bit crowded, that's just too bad. We may have a great many more prisoners to be taken."

While the Mackerels complied and marched the fresh batch of prisoners off to jail, Toby sent a telegram to the governor, bringing him up to date on the favorable developments. He also asked the governor to continue to keep in the state militia on alert. Toby realized that with the assistance of Hank, Stalking Horse, and Red Leary's Mackerels, he would have an opportunity to put a permanent damper on Braun's operations, but it was essential that the chief executive of the state be in charge of keeping law and order in his own realm. In the meantime, however, Toby would take the initiative himself, trusting that sending in the militia was a contingency that would never need to be carried out.

Then, leaving a handful of Mackerels to stand guard at the telegraph office, Toby drew Hank aside. "What next?" he asked.

"Now," Hank said, "we've got to crack a really

tough nut. Braun ordered that the railroad station be captured at all costs. He was to take personal charge there. I understand he was to have at least forty of his best."

It sounded to Toby as though a classical military operation was in the offing. He sent one of the Mackerels for Red Leary, and while he waited, he discussed the outlook with Hank. "I assume," he said, "that Braun's men are all armed with rifles and have plenty of ammunition, as is the case with those we've encountered."

"Right."

"Eventually," Toby said, "the failure to take the first two objectives will cause Braun to retrace his steps and try again. In the meantime, however, I can see that seizing the railroad station is essential to him."

"You're correct," Hank replied. "If state or government troops are sent here by rail, he sees that they could crush him. He's got to hold the railroad station at all costs, in order to keep outside forces from getting behind the heart of his defenses."

"How much time has he allotted for this phase of his operation?"

"The attack on the railroad station was to begin exactly at noon, and he expected the occupation to be completed promptly."

Hank took his watch out and showed it to Toby, who frowned. "That means we have only fifteen or twenty minutes left to prepare an appropriate reception for him," Toby said.

As he spoke, Red Leary appeared on the scene. Toby quickly brought him up to date. "How many men can you assign to this phase of the operation? Apparently Braun has intended to make it the focal point of his attack, and we've got to meet it head-on."

"I may be able to muster as many as thirty men for the purpose," Leary said. "How do you want them deployed?"

Toby thought for a moment. He recalled that the Memphis train station was surrounded on three sides by broad, well-traveled streets, while the depot's fourth side faced half a dozen parallel tracks. Arriving and departing trains could come right up to the station on that side.

"I have a plan," Toby said to Red. "You and your men should cover the three sides of the station that face the streets. My friends and I will take the fourth side, where the tracks are. In that way, we'll effectively encircle the station."

Leary looked at him in astonishment. "My men and I will have no trouble covering our sector. But do you mean to tell me that you can cover the track area with just the help of a pretty woman, an old Indian, and a young fellow who's scarcely dry behind the ears?"

"I'll match my companions and me against any force ten times our number. That includes your Mackerels, Braun's infantry, or the best troops that the U.S. Army can muster."

Leary, who knew Toby Holt principally by reputation, thought that his renown had led him to exaggerate wildly. He kept his opinion to himself, however, reasoning that if a full-scale battle developed, the true picture would become clear quickly.

"The first task," Toby said, "is to clear all civilians out of the station and make sure they keep their distance."

"That should be easy to accomplish," Hank said. "The next train isn't due to arrive until three o'clock and is scheduled to leave again an hour later, so there's no reason to expect civilians to be in the station at this time."

"So much the better," Toby said. "Now then, Red, first of all, we'll let Braun move his men into the station. We'll make no attempt to stop them. When nearly all the troops are inside, my companions and I will go around to the tracks and find our position, using whatever cover we can. When I fire a shot into the air, that will be the signal for all of us to fire on the station. I suggest we shoot over the heads of Braun's men, at the start. By surprising them from all sides, we should be able to get them to surrender without bloodshed. Only if they put up resistance and fire at us should we shoot to kill."

"I'd prefer to shoot to kill from the outset," Red Leary protested. "That's the only way to secure a quick victory."

"That's not the way I operate," Toby replied firmly. "Let them be the first to inflict injury."

Again Leary shrugged. This was not his type of operation, but he had volunteered to assist, not to direct, and therefore he was willing to follow whatever Toby Holt ordered.

Red assembled his men quickly, and the entire party, along with Toby's group, departed to take hiding places inside the buildings along the streets near the station. Once they were in place, Toby himself departed to reconnoiter the track area. He was back within ten minutes and took up his position to await the arrival of Braun's men.

They were not long in coming. At exactly noon Braun's infantrymen, disguised as pirates, began to enter the railroad station, two and three at a time.

Toby, standing beside Red in a building facing the station, watched Braun's men as they stepped into the depot, clutching their weapons. He could even feel sorry for these misguided men who had sold themselves to Braun in return for a dubious future that was about to come to an inglorious end.

After most of them had disappeared into the station, Toby bade farewell to Red Leary, then led Martha, Hank, and Stalking Horse around the building until they reached the area of the tracks. There, as

Toby had discovered while reconnoitering, a short train of three cars on the first track afforded cover. They would be able to move out along the track without being seen from the station.

Leading his party out to the last car, Toby peered around the end of it. To his left he could see into the station, through doors along the platform. Directly in front of him, thirty feet away across two sets of tracks, was an engine. If his party could reach it without being seen from the station, Toby had decided, they could use its high-perched cab as an effective vantage point from which to carry out the next phase of the attack.

Toby could see Braun's men in the station, milling about. They were evidently in a state of confusion, since their leader had not yet made an appearance. Seizing this opportunity, Toby motioned for Martha to follow him and dashed across the open tracks toward the engine, crouching to make himself more inconspicuous. Martha followed suit. They ducked around the coal car in back of the engine, then moved forward to the engineer's cab just behind the boiler. There Toby boosted Martha up the narrow steps. Using the handgrips, Martha was able to scramble up and into the cab. Toby quickly climbed up behind her.

A moment later, Hank and Stalking Horse, having likewise crossed the open tracks to the engine, appeared alongside. They crept forward to the cowcatcher, where they hunkered down, to keep watch on activities within the station.

From high in the cab, Toby had a good view of Braun's men. All forty members of his task force had entered the depot, and their general was now on hand. It was clear that, by great good fortune, no one had observed Toby's party, and Braun's behavior suggested that he believed he had already completed his operation successfully.

The time had arrived to initiate the real action.

Toby drew his pistol, turned to smile reassuringly at Martha, and then fired a shot through the cab window into the air.

The station was transformed into bedlam. A dozen men, including Braun, turned to stare toward the engine. As they did, however, shots from Red Leary and his men echoed from the other three sides of the building, immediately distracting Braun's men.

So far, events were unfolding according to Toby's plan. Braun's men were confused and disoriented by the gunfire on all sides. Toby expected that Braun would soon realize the situation was hopeless and order his men to surrender.

But then the unexpected occurred. Contrary to Toby's orders, Leary's men decided to step up the attack. They seized the opportunity provided by the momentary confusion in Braun's ranks to mount an all-out charge on the building, running across the streets toward the station and firing as they came.

Half a dozen doors gave access from the streets into the waiting room, and determined Indians pushed their way in through every entrance, their pistols blazing. The Mackerels, held in check until now by Toby's orders, were joyously entering into the fray. They seemed bent on violent action as, crouching low, they swept inside the station and took up positions around the wall and behind benches. There, each man dropped to one knee, and as a group they opened fire on their foes.

Emil Braun had been so confident of victory that he had failed to anticipate the Mackerels' sudden attack. Confronted now with a serious situation, though, he lived up to his reputation for clear thinking in times of emergency. His booming voice, which conveyed his courage, quieted his men and ended the near panic. They responded to his order and spread out as best they were able.

The Mackerels totally disregarded Toby's order to

shoot over the heads of the enemy. They took deadly aim at Braun's men, and their fire was effective. Many of Braun's men dropped, but others quickly directed a return fire toward the Mackerels, several of whom slumped to the floor.

Seeing this, Toby knew it was time his group joined in the battle. "Stalking Horse! Hank! Can you hear me?" he called out, during a momentary lull in the deafening din. Hearing their affirmative answer, he ordered, "Commence firing. Shoot to kill."

Martha had drawn her own pistols and seemed filled with the excitement of battle.

Drawing a bead on one of Braun's officers through the cab window, Toby squeezed the trigger. The man staggered backward, a scarlet stain spreading across the front of his shirt, and he collapsed on the floor.

In the meantime, Stalking Horse and Hank were demonstrating their remarkable skill as marksmen. The Cherokee had been second to none for at least a quarter of a century, while Hank had shattered every record for target shooting at the academy. Their task now was made easier by the fact that Braun's elite company was being forced by Leary's men through the depot and toward the tracks.

Martha, too, demonstrated that the many hours Domino had spent teaching her how to handle firearms had been well spent. She had killed one of Braun's followers with a single shot and severely wounded another. Unaccustomed, however, to firing rapidly, she took unusually careful aim each time, and so her toll was relatively small.

As she trained her sights on one fleeing invader, her attention was diverted by an unexpected movement far off to the side. From her vantage point, she could see into the depot, with a view along its northerly wall that extended back from the track area.

There, a small, brindle hound, little more than a

puppy apparently, was nosing its inquisitive way along the wall. It paid no attention to the thundering of the weapons or to the human forms that grotesquely littered the mosaic floor. Even as Martha watched, bemused by the tragically ludicrous contrast of innocent life in the midst of the scene of violent death, she was startled once more.

From the direction of doors opening into the station from the broad street on its far side there came now another intruder. The dim light within the interior made it possible for Martha to discern that the newcomer was a child of not more than three years of age, a little girl obviously intent on only one goal, that of retrieving her wandering puppy. Martha could envision only too well the shock and grief of whatever parent had permitted her to dash after the dog into the deadly area of the station. And now the child, not knowing the danger or at least willing to disregard it in order to rescue her pet, was in mortal peril. Braun's remaining men and Mackerels alike were oblivious to both child and dog as they wandered about, and Martha knew that any stray shot could strike either or both at any moment.

Martha glanced toward Toby and his other companions, but their attention was focused wholly on their targets and the progress of the fighting. If anyone at all was to act to help the little girl and forestall utter tragedy, Martha realized, it would have to be her.

Without a thought for her own safety, Martha dropped from the cab to the flanked area between the tracks and began running toward the depot. She was dimly aware of the intermittent firing, but her mind was solely on reaching the child, finding some way to protect her.

Behind her, a startled and dismayed Toby was shouting frantically to Stalking Horse and Hank to hold their fire, but the order was hardly necessary as soon as they, too, glimpsed the racing figure of Martha. Sporadic firing was continuing, however, as more of Braun's men emerged from the station and headed up the tracks, ignoring Martha.

Martha reached the toddler and scooped her up protectively before turning, in some confusion, to seek a reasonably safe escape route.

She huddled over the tiny figure, looking toward the tracks and the locomotive as if hoping for some direction from Toby. Then she started toward him, moving out of the station into the sunlight. As she did so, Toby could see her expression—determined despite her desperate dilemma. But suddenly he also saw a bulky figure emerge from the darker recesses of the depot's interior.

Without warning, Emil Braun closed in from behind Martha and with the sweep of one arm threw her off balance. She nearly fell on the crying child but caught herself after dropping to one knee.

With the remnants of his shattered force now streaming ahead of him along the tracks in dispirited groups of beaten, wounded men, Braun had no more than a corporal's guard remaining behind, more in fear than in loyalty. Braun was armed with a rifle tucked under one arm; his pistol was in place at his hip.

Now, with the rifle's muzzle prodding her, Martha rose to her feet, turning her head enough to glare at Braun.

Despite her expression of disdain, however, she was well aware of the fact that she was his prisoner. Thus, she offered no further resistance. It was certain that anyone seeking to intervene would immediately put Martha's life in extreme peril.

Toby sized up the horrible prospect and froze. He knew he would have to rely on his wits and on some unpredictable stroke of fortune rather than on direct action.

To Toby, the impending danger to Martha and the

child was of overriding concern. He dismissed from his mind any of the tactical questions of halting Braun, of preventing the wretched man's escape. The "general" had added one more to the list of crimes for which he must eventually pay—and pay he most assuredly would if the honorable tradition of the Holts was to continue to have meaning.

Braun was now shoving Martha ahead of him, poking her mercilessly if she stumbled. Her footing was unsure because the child in her arms partially obscured her vision. And when they started to turn and head northward, Toby felt desperation overtake him. It would be futile to follow Braun and his captives too closely, for it would be too dangerous for Martha and her little ward. Under the circumstances, a shot aimed at Braun would be much too risky.

The tracks curved rather sharply within a few hundred yards of the depot, however, and as the little group began to disappear, Toby jumped from the locomotive and started up the tracks as rapidly as he dared go without attracting attention. Hank and Stalking Horse trailed some distance behind; the Mackerels seemed to be finishing the mop-up of the Braun stragglers.

Though he had not traveled that route before, Toby estimated that less than a mile distant lay the waterfront with the pier where, Red Leary had reported, Braun had stationed men with boats—the general's "door" that Toby had foreseen.

Finally, ahead of him he could see where the tracks approached the waterfront, and there it was that Braun shepherded the hapless Martha. Toby was within a hundred yards of them as they turned to the pier, and by the time they stepped onto it, he was rapidly closing the distance.

Braun, obviously anticipating that he was being followed, turned his face to the tracks and began backing the length of the pier. He held Martha in front of him, still serving as a shield, as he watched Toby approach the pier's end.

Clearly Braun had every advantage, but Toby resolved, nonetheless, to confront him. With time running out, Toby had diminishing options if he was to have any chance at rescuing Martha rather than letting her disappear with the desperate madman.

Accordingly, Toby resolutely took his position at the foot of the pier and surveyed the situation before him. While Braun was painstakingly edging his way backward, step by wary step, Toby's attention was riveted on Martha. Still trying to protect the child, Martha seemed unmindful of the extreme vulnerability of her position. With her back toward her abductor, she was unable to know what he was doing or where, exactly, he was taking her and the child. Because he was bending so low as he stepped back crabwise toward the end of the pier, he was at times virtually hidden behind Martha.

As she crouched, her body completely shielding the terrified child from Braun's view, her face was turned toward the riverbank, her eyes fixed unwaveringly. Unable as she was to make herself heard above the din created by the shouting of Leary's men, who were approaching, Toby sensed that she was trying to convey an appeal or instruction with the fierce directness of her gaze.

With a shock, Toby realized, however, that in this moment of unbelievable horror, she was not looking toward him, seeking to convey hope or love or desperation. Rather, she seemed to be ignoring his presence and looking instead at the knot of Mackerels who were now gathering behind Red Leary some ten feet off to Toby's right. She obviously was appealing to them to withhold their fire if they entertained any idea of cutting Braun down before he might disappear.

Toby swerved sharply in the direction of the Mackerels. A dozen men now stood there, assessing the situation and seeing that their quarry was now only several feet away from the pier's far edge. Within a minute or less, despite the slowness of Braun's progress, he would be in a position to vanish over the edge. A half dozen Mackerels were raising their rifles, fixing Braun in their sights.

Toby took in the new danger even as his glance swung past Leary's men. In that instant he knew that he had been wrong in ever permitting the Mackerels to operate on their own. The pang of self-reproach added impetus to the vigor of his response. He sprang toward the men, arms outstretched and flailing as he shouted, "No, no! You mustn't shoot! Leary, give the order—no firing! We'll let him go if need be!"

Red Leary, mouth gaping in amazement and outrage, regained his balance and his voice simultaneously. "What's the idea, you damned fool?" he demanded. "Let that bastard get away? He's done too much today for us to allow that, you yellow-bellied punk! Why, he's killed a good dozen of my best. And you say, 'Let 'im go'? Never!"

Leary raised his right arm and tried to press it against Toby's throat. Struggling with three other Mackerels who sought to club him with their rifles' stocks, Toby first threw them off, then bent nearly double as he seized Leary's arm and then sent the man flying over his head to crash headlong into his group of men.

Suddenly, from the distant end of the pier, came a single, triumphant shout.

"You thought you could win," Braun was yelling. "But not today! Not ever! I'm going, but you've not seen the last of me."

Preparing to lower himself over the edge, he leveled his weapon in a final act of defiance. Whether he was firing wildly as a diversion or was aiming at Toby or at one of the Mackerels, Toby never could be sure. He might in fact have been taking aim at Martha vengefully, for it was she who felt the bullet's impact. A second after the report of Braun's rifle, she collapsed in a pathetic heap on the pier's rough planking, still covering the child with her body and her costume's full blouse.

Braun's shot revitalized Leary. Disregarding Toby, he shouted to those of his men who had regained their feet, instructing them to return the fire.

"Don't let him get over the edge, whatever else you do," he called out furiously. Four Mackerels dropped to a sharpshooter's stance, sighting Braun's prone figure as he slid, belly down, across the last plank. He had discarded his rifle, but from a pocket he produced a repeating pistol. Under the circumstances, his aim could only be erratic, but with it he was able to create a further diversion.

The crossfire was far from sufficient to prevent Toby Holt's instantaneous reaction as, with sinking heart, he saw Martha's fall. Crouching but running full tilt beneath the bullets, he dashed the length of the pier. A single, riveting thought impelled him onward in spite of whatever hazards existed.

In seconds that seemed an eternity, Toby reached Martha's side. It was at that moment, though he was not conscious of the fact, that Braun at last cleared the pier's far edge and dropped with relative safety into the small boat that awaited him in the water directly beneath. Instantly the officers at the oars sent it shooting into the river's mainstream, following a rough, zigzag course in an effort to foil any shots from the shore. Mackerels' bullets fell harmlessly about the craft.

Toby, as distraught as he ever had been in his life, was bent over Martha. The little girl, too frightened to make a fuss, was placed gently to one side as the firing ceased. All else was forgotten and driven from Toby's mind. Martha lay on the planks, her hair in disarray, a smear of blood at her right temple. All color had drained from her face, and she looked already dead. He could not determine quickly whether or not she was still breathing.

Toby was so shocked, so stunned, that everything else on earth faded from his mind. His whole being was filled with his feelings for the lovely, helpless woman who lay motionless in his arms. She felt absurdly light and tiny as he cradled her, and he looked down with tender, heartbroken longing.

"Martha, my love," he whispered brokenly. "It's my fault, and only mine, that you've been taken from me. I never should have allowed you to take part in our battles with Braun. That was my job, not a woman's."

As a cloud appeared over the face of the sun, Toby's anguish became greater. "It does no good to tell you this now," he said, "but I've loved you for a long time. I've tried to harden my heart, but without success. I loved you as I could never love another woman as long as I live, and I will love you, and you alone, until I stop breathing. Although it's too late to tell you these things now, you're a part of me, and you will remain a part of my mind and my body as long as I live."

When, totally unexpectedly, Martha stirred in his arms, Toby was electrified. She opened her eyes, and reaching up for him, she drew his head down to her and kissed him with all the love and passion in her being. He responded with all his heart, uncertain whether he was dreaming or whether what was happening could actually be real.

At last she released him, and looking up at him with shining eyes, she spoke gently. Touching her temple with one hand, she looked at light smears of blood on her fingertips. "This must have been what happened: A bullet grazed my forehead and knocked me unconscious. But when I awakened, I could hear the sound of your voice, and I heard everything that you said to me. Everything on earth has its purpose." She smiled up at him.

He continued to hold her; he tightened his grip but still did not trust his voice.

"This happened for the best. I'm convinced of it," she said. "For you to show affection isn't easy, and I will never forget these last few moments as long as I live. You know that I return your love. I feel toward you as you feel toward me. The only difference between us is that I recognized how I felt long before you knew it. I have loved you so much, so hard, that I find it difficult to remember the days before you came into my life. You say you love me for all time. I, too, love you with all my heart, as long as we both shall live. That's my solemn pledge."

Again she pulled his head closer, and this time he kissed her with a strength and a depth of feeling that he had not known he possessed.

"As soon as we can get you back to your hotel," he said, "we're calling in a doctor to examine you thoroughly." He stood, picking Martha up and taking the little girl by the hand in a single motion. As they walked down the pier and away, Toby completely ignored Red Leary and the stunned Mackerels, as he turned the child over to an almost hysterical but grateful mother, who had followed from the station, before continuing on to the hotel.

Nestling comfortably in his arms, Martha knew that her analysis of what had happened to her was right. "Yes, darling," she murmured, "whatever you say."

XIV

At Toby's direction Hank sent telegrams to General Sherman and to Governor Senter apprising them of the situation to date and telling them that the final movement against Braun could be expected to reach a climax by early the following morning.

Braun's men who had been taken prisoner during the day were sent off by special railroad cars to Nashville. They were guarded on the journey by a platoon of hand-picked police officers.

Those who had been killed in action were buried after a mass funeral, and the wounded were taken to hospitals, where they were placed in custodial care.

Stalking Horse found a message at the post office from his sister. It sent him scurrying out to her cottage, accompanied by Hank, Leary, and several Mackerels.

Memphis was still in the throes of Mardi Gras, and people were dancing to music in the streets, eating and drinking, and thoroughly enjoying the occasion. Very few knew or cared that an attempt had been made to take over the city. The general belief was that one or another gang, having chosen this time to act up, had been slapped back into place for their pains.

Toby insisted on accompanying Martha to her hotel suite and waited in the sitting room while a physician examined her. Only after that was done was Toby admitted to her bedchamber.

"This young lady has suffered a very narrow escape," the doctor said. "If the bullet that grazed her temple had struck only a quarter of an inch to the right, she wouldn't be here at this moment to recall the experience. She'll suffer no permanent damage, but I want her to take no risks. Therefore, she's to stay in bed for at least thirty-six hours and to obtain all the rest she possibly can.

"Take one of these pills every four hours," he instructed her, "and for the next couple of days, avoid any rich food. Avoid alcoholic beverages as well. You should emerge from this none the worse for wear."

Toby stayed with Martha for another two hours, ordering her a light meal from the hotel dining room and remaining at her side until she had eaten. Then, when she was ready for a night's sleep, he kissed her and left. He had urgent work to do.

His horse had been cared for at the hotel's stable, and he rode rapidly out to Violet's cottage, where he found that the men who had preceded him had uncovered the packages that Governor Senter had forwarded from Nashville. The group was now gathered in a council of war.

As Toby approached, Red Leary stepped forward, his right hand outstretched and a rueful smile on his face. "I lost a lot of my men," he told Toby as they shook hands in a prolonged gesture of comradeship, "but it would have been better if we'd done it your way all along. And you were right, trying to prevent our firing at Braun. Then what you did really opened my eyes. I apologize!

"Now we're trying," Leary continued, "to decide on a plan to get him once and for all. But we don't know what it is you have in mind. We have your packages and found nine strong charges of explosives. What do you propose to do with them?"

Toby held up a hand. "Not so fast," he urged.

"We'll take all this one step at a time. Hank, did you stop off at the print shop and pick up the order I left there?"

"I sure did." Hank reached behind his chair and brought up a neatly tied package. "I was tempted to look inside," he said, "but the way I figured it, if you wanted me to know what the printer had done, you would have told me to examine the contents of the pack."

Toby smiled slightly. "Go ahead and look, all of you," he suggested.

Hank broke open the package and distributed posters, newly printed, conveying this message:

WARNING

YOUR CAMP

IS GOING UP IN SMOKE!

GET OUT—NOW!

BY THE TIME YOU READ THIS

IT WILL BE ALMOST TOO LATE.

EVERY BUILDING HERE IS TO BE BLOWN

SKY HIGH!

SAVE YOUR OWN LIFE NOW!

LEAVE AT ONCE AND GO HOME!

USE YOUR HEAD, AND YOU'LL HAVE A HEAD TO USE.

GET OUT—FAST!

"I'd say the message is very clear," Red said. "Are you prepared to carry out the threat?"

"You bet I am," Toby replied grimly. "I worked out the details of this plan with Governor Senter, who has supplied the explosives. They come from the arsenal the federal government maintains for the state militia."

"It's a great idea, if it will really work," Hank said, grinning. "How do you want these explosives distributed?"

"We've counted eight principal buildings in the installation," Toby said. "Nine, if you include Violet's original farmhouse. We have nine packs of explosives. One pack is to be secreted at each building. Then each will be detonated with a device that goes off ten minutes after it has been set. That will give the person who sets the explosives ample time to take himself elsewhere."

"Who're you putting in charge of this operation?" Hank inquired.

"You and Stalking Horse," Toby said, "if you still have free access to Braun's camp."

"Whatever problem there may turn out to be," Hank answered, "you can depend on Stalking Horse and me to take care of it. We'll be ready for Braun, no matter what!"

Pleased by Hank's courage and confidence, Toby smiled at him and turned to face Stalking Horse. "I may be asking more of you than is fair or even humanly possible," he said to them. "First of all, I'd like these posters to be distributed everywhere in the compound. Every building is to be covered. Emil Braun would shoot on sight anyone he caught distributing these, so you'll need to exercise great caution. What do you think? Can you spread them around without too much difficulty?"

Stalking Horse smiled faintly. "I have waited many weeks," he said, "to obtain vengeance for the wrongs done to my sister. You have known me all the days of your life, Toby Holt. Do you think it likely I would miss this chance to strike back for Violet? Do you think that I would not do anything possible to advance her chances to regain her property? If so, you are mistaken. I will distribute these documents myself, alone. Fear not, my friend! I will not fail!"

Toby was vastly relieved, knowing that regardless of any difficulties, the posters would be distributed everywhere in Braun's camp.

"That leaves the charges of explosives," Hank said. "I assume that there's no way to make them go off at the same time."

"That's correct, Hank. They'll have to be set off one at a time," Toby said with a slight tinge of regret. "There's no way you can connect them so they'll discharge simultaneously. You and Stalking Horse will have to put your explosives in place in advance, of course, then make the rounds a second time to touch them off."

"Hold on a minute!" Red Leary said. "Won't Blake and Stalking Horse expose themselves to suspicion and capture if they're seen going from building to building?"

"Ordinarily I'd say you have a valid point, Red," Hank told him, "but I don't see the situation developing that way. The troops already are so nervous they're certain to be panicky and won't notice what we're doing. You saw how they reacted at the rail station and later at the wharf."

Red was impressed by the young man's response, as was Toby. Hank was displaying natural qualities of leadership.

"This is the beginning of the final act against Braun," Toby said. "If each of us plays the role that's expected of him, we should end the problem by the time most people finish their breakfast tomorrow morning. And I'm looking forward to that hour. After spending weeks chasing Braun, I want to be in at the finish."

"So do I," Red Leary said. "I'll be right there with you!"

Prepared to do whatever was necessary to carry out Toby's instructions, Hank, aided by Stalking Horse, first put the individual packages of explosives in place, hiding them at every building in the military compound. Each package contained several sticks of dynamite.

Distributing the explosives was far more time-consuming and dangerous than had been anticipated. As Hank moved off in one direction, Stalking Horse went in the other. Moving with all the stealth of which a Cherokee was capable, Stalking Horse went from building to building, slipping silently past guards. Once, a guard started to turn in his direction, and the Cherokee thought he would have to silence the man with his tomahawk. But the sentry turned away again without having seen him.

Hank, meanwhile, was carrying out his part of the plan. His last assignment was to place a charge in a flower bed against a side wall of Violet's farmhouse. It was typical of Toby, Hank thought, to make the difficult decision not to spare the building that had been Violet's home, because now it was in fact Braun's headquarters. Sentiment had to give way to the overriding need to defeat Braun with a decisive blow.

Distributing the printed warnings was far easier to accomplish. This task was allotted to Stalking Horse alone. Moving swiftly, he placed two posters in the centrally located mess hall, then one inside each of the barracks. No one saw him, as he moved in and out with his customary stealth, so the warnings appeared in place silently, as if placed there by an unseen hand.

As the men started to move into the barracks for the night, prior to the sounding of taps, they discovered the posters, and immediately the camp was in an uproar. Men gathered in small groups to discuss the warning, virtually shouting at one another, highly excited. The corps and the command were badly shaken by the defeat and the heavy losses that their most elite force had suffered in Memphis. Men weighed their own chances of survival and wondered if they would escape injury or death. This brought up the question of why they were risking their lives. The glamour of membership in the corps rapidly lost its appeal. The message on the anonymous poster, combined with the severe defeats of their elite company, convinced them that powerful enemies were dedicated to their downfall.

Without exception, the troops had been pleased to accept the bonus that Braun had paid when they joined his force, and they gladly accepted their monthly wages. They thoroughly enjoyed the military life and atmosphere of the camp. Few of them had reflected on the possibility that they might be killed, and the thought that their camp might be blown up was enough to immediately cause them to lose their enthusiasm for the cause in which they had enlisted.

Thoroughly agitated and confused by the warning, a few of the men were ready to desert. But most decided on a less drastic course: They would move out of the barracks. Very shortly small groups of men, carrying bedrolls and belongings, could be seen leaving the barracks area and taking up positions on slightly higher ground overlooking the buildings. The movement very quickly became a mad dash, and the barracks were left deserted.

Meanwhile, Braun had retired to his dwelling, following his frustrating day, and he was drinking heavily to forget the humiliation of the defeat he had suffered. Shortly after the first of the posters was found, and while men were leaving the barracks, two of his officers obtained a copy of the warning and brought it to him. Squinting his eyes and concentrating hard to read the document in spite of his drunkenness, Braun finally managed to absorb its message. Color rose to his face, and his voice shook with rage as he shouted, "Damn my enemies to hell! They're trying to scare my troops into deserting. I'll fix 'em! Collect every damn one of these posters that you find on the property and destroy them!"

His two colonels, one of them the adjutant of the entire force, exchanged hopeless glances.

"I'm afraid it's too late for that, sir," the regimental commander said. "The posters seem to have been distributed throughout the post. As soon as the men saw them, they could talk about nothing else."

Braun became even more livid. "Prohibit the men from discussing this rubbish!" he shouted, shaking a fist. "Let them understand that I'll court-martial any man caught heeding this muck!"

"That threat will do no good, General," the adjutant said uneasily. "The damage is already done. Most of the men have in fact left the barracks and taken up positions for the night around the perimeter of the camp."

Braun managed to control himself only with a great effort. "Damn cowards! I suppose they'd desert, except they want to stay and get their pay! I'll go out there and tell them they're to pay no attention to threats, and to move back into the barracks at once!"

"You might do more harm than good, General," the regimental commander said regretfully. "I respectfully urge you to leave the men where they are. If nothing happens, they'll see that the threat was an empty one. But in the meantime, I'd recommend doubling the guard."

Braun weighed the issue. "I suppose you're right," he said at last. "We'll let the men stay where they are. And we'll post extra guards, if that'll make 'em happy. You"—he spoke to the adjutant—"see that it's done."

The adjutant saluted and left. Braun turned to the other officer. "Now then, I suggest you join me for a drink. I won't accept a refusal." He poured liberal quantities of whiskey into two glasses. "Confusion to our enemies!" he said loudly, raising his own glass in a toast. "May they all go to hell!"

Braun's show of bravado did little to quiet the apprehensions of the other man, who joined his commander in drinking, then took his leave as soon as possible. Meanwhile, the camp settled down to a night's rest, though many of the men camped outside were too nervous to sleep well.

Shortly before dawn, Hank Blake and Stalking Horse started on their rounds to carry out the next phase of the operation. Again they divided the buildings between them. Each carried a handful of the new phosphorous matches that lighted at a single stroke.

Stalking Horse, heading in one direction, saw that extra caution would be required because of the doubled guard. He was able once again to slip past most of the sentries, until one spotted him just as he was crossing an open space. Before the man could cry out, the Cherokee had swerved and attacked, smashing the man's skull with his tomahawk. Then he dragged the body off into some nearby bushes.

Meanwhile, Hank was at work. Walking slowly to the rear of a barracks, he squatted down and lit a match and applied it to a length of tapelike cord emanating from the package of dynamite. As soon as he had ignited the fuse, he sprinted to the rear of an adjacent barracks. There he repeated the process.

At the third building, and then the fourth, he again lit the fuses. He had used approximately half the time that was left before the first explosion would go off.

Hank had not estimated having a problem setting off the final charge, which was concealed in the flower bed outside Violet's farmhouse, in which Emil and Laura Braun lived. But a single glance now told him he would have to abandon this plan. Although no sentries were stationed elsewhere on the perimeter, four armed guards patrolled the area immediately surrounding Braun's house. This was a change, made after the day's fiascoes in Memphis. Hank would have no chance to go near the place. This actually was a relief to him because he had no desire either to destroy Violet's home nor to cause harm to Laura Braun, who was innocent of the crimes committed by her husband.

Having completed his task as best he could, Hank put as much distance as possible between himself and the buildings where explosions would occur. Abandoning all caution, he broke into a run, sprinting toward the woods.

As he entered the cover of trees, Stalking Horse, who had been busy at the other buildings, loomed up beside him. The Cherokee's sense of timing was unerring; raising a hand in warning, he threw himself to the ground and covered his ears. Hank hastily followed.

An instant later, a tremendous explosion reverberated through the area. The ground underfoot rocked as though a major earthquake had struck. Chunks of wood and other debris flew through the air. Suddenly a loud crackling noise came as flames leaped high.

More explosions followed in rapid succession, each as devastating as those that had preceded. Stalking Horse and Hank had done their work well.

The walls of several buildings had collapsed, and fires were burning fiercely, flames leaping high and spreading rapidly.

Hank automatically counted the explosions, and when eight had torn at the compound, he knew that he and his Cherokee partner had been successful. With the exception of Violet's farmhouse, every building in the encampment had been blown up.

Dawn was breaking, and men were pouring from the boundaries of the camp. Panic was in the air, as all-pervasive as the fires. Escape clearly was uppermost in every mind.

Rank was forgotten. Officers as well as enlisted men raced beyond the limits of what had been the MacDermid farm, never looking back. Others climbed over the fences or, in their haste, knocked them down and trampled on them. The exodus was universal.

Laura Braun, wrapped in an old flannel robe, wept

hysterically in the doorway of the farmhouse. Her husband was nowhere to be seen.

Lying beside Stalking Horse and watching the debacle, Hank recognized the ultimate wisdom of Toby Holt's plan. Instead of fighting a battle to the death with Emil Braun's followers, a conflict in which federal troops and Tennessee militia alike would have engaged and many would have been killed, it was far more sensible to employ tactics that would result in the dispersal of Braun's force. His threat was being terminated. Thanks to Toby's inspired strategy, it was melting away to nothing.

Approaching footsteps on the hard turf caused Hank to reach for his pistol, but he relaxed when he saw Toby approaching, accompanied by Red Leary. Both were grinning broadly.

"The scheme appears to be effective," Toby said. "We've been watching from the birch trees at the property line, and men are fleeing there and in every direction. Braun can no longer hope to put any kind of fighting force into the field. This means the end."

A final explosion occurred as fire reached a kerosene fuel tank; the noise, abrupt and earsplitting, punctuated Toby's words and seemed a fitting climax to them.

The senior officers of Braun's corps were among the last to depart, carrying bundles of possessions they had removed from their quarters the previous evening. A few had salvaged their civilian clothes and had discarded their uniforms in favor of the more anonymous garb. Some headed toward Memphis, but most trudged off in the opposite direction, looking back over their shoulders for possible pursuers. A long hike and an uncertain future were ahead of them, but they appeared determined to get as far as they could from the scene of their folly.

Braun, who had all but disappeared during the

explosions, as he reverted to his old preoccupation with whiskey, suddenly appeared in the doorway of his home. He had taken time to dress in his uniform jacket, that of a major general, as if that alone would stem the tide of desertion. His decorations were spread on his chest, his sword dangled at his side, and a pistol hung from his weapons belt.

He seemed to have lost all control of his reason, as he rudely shoved Laura out of his path and stepped into the open. Laura fled from his anger, halting only when she reached the fence.

As if to emphasize his disdain for the woman who had so loyally stood by him over the years, Braun pulled out his pistol and fired off a shot in her direction. The shot fortunately went wild, but it so frightened the poor woman that she screamed and fell to the ground, sobbing in panic. Braun, his pistol lowered, looked at her blankly.

At this moment Toby knew beyond all doubt that the issue with Emil Braun would have to be settled by his personally confronting the madman.

Before his companions could stop him, Toby stepped into the open. In his hand he held his pistol.

Braun stared, recognized him, and a look of sheer hatred spread across the man's face. He raised his pistol again, this time aiming it at Toby, thirty yards away.

Before Braun could squeeze the trigger, Toby fired. His bullet creased Braun's left shoulder. Dropping his weapon, Braun cried out in pain and grasped his shoulder with his right hand. He took a step backward as he watched his opponent. Nevertheless, he gave no sign of being ready to concede defeat. Braun, fighting for his life, was prepared to use any trick. Toby, however, would never shoot an unarmed man.

Red Leary became impatient and called, "For God's sake, Holt, put a bullet into the man and be done with it. Don't give him a chance to do more damage!"

Toby made no reply and acknowledged the advice only with a thin smile. He seemed determined to face Braun down on his own.

By this time, Braun had backed himself against the outer wall of the house as he groped inside his uniform jacket with his right hand. The foes who had cornered him were arrayed in a semicircle, and what shocked and angered him beyond measure was the presence in their ranks of Stalking Horse and of young Henry Blake, whom he had commissioned as a major.

It was Hank's presence, above all else, that enraged him. As far as he was concerned, the young man was a traitor, and he held Hank responsible for his terrible predicament. No longer able to apply reason to his situation, Braun made up his mind that if he was going to die, he would take the traitor with him.

His fingers found his second pistol within his clothing and curled around the butt. Although he was not aware of it, an expression of fleeting satisfaction crossed his face. Toby, who was watching him closely, surmised that he had yet another weapon and that he intended to use it.

But as Braun brought out his weapon and shot at Hank, Toby fired. Hank, reacting instantaneously, also drew his pistol and discharged it.

Some said later that what then happened was sheer accident, but others disagreed, insisting that Divine Providence was responsible.

Toby's shot found its mark, while the bullet from Braun's gun flew harmlessly past Hank's ear. Hank's bullet went wild. It plowed into the package of explosives concealed close to the house. The bullet caused the dynamite to explode.

The detonation momentarily deafened those nearby. The entire wall of the house near the dynamite, the roof, and portions of two other walls exploded outward. Debris was scattered over the area.

Emil Braun, who took the full force of the explosion, never knew what hit him. He sprawled on the ground, his sightless eyes facing up toward the sky as the debris rained down on him. He who had courted violence and had lived according to its precepts, unmindful of the rights of others, had ended his own life as he had lived, violently and without mercy being shown to him.

Toby, knocked from his feet by the explosion, scrambled upright again and assured himself that his companions also were unhurt. "May the Almighty deal justly and with kindness," he said, "with the soul of Emil Braun."

XV

Toby led a delegation to Nashville to call on Governor Senter. Of all those associated with Toby in the victory over Emil Braun, only Red Leary declined to participate.

The governor sat behind his long desk of gleaming mahogany, the American flag behind him to his right, the state flag of Tennessee to his left.

"It's my understanding," the governor said, "that President Grant will issue a statement in which he thanks you for the part you played in ridding the country of a dangerous threat to our national security. I want to add my gratitude on behalf of the people of Tennessee. The death of Emil Braun bears out the biblical injunction that 'he who lives by the sword shall perish by the sword.' "

"We're grateful to you, Governor," Toby replied, "for supplying us with the explosives that made victory possible. Braun's force never will be revived. The men who served under him must have learned the error of their ways quickly enough when their barracks and other buildings went up in smoke. I've heard they're using their enlistment money to pay for transportation back home.

"What still perplexes me, and what we may never know now," Toby went on, "is what Braun's purpose may have been. A vast sum of money was spent to

285

recruit and organize and train his corps, and what did he hope to gain? I question that we'll ever find out. Also, we may never know who financed him and for what reason."

"I think it's safe to assume," the governor said, "that whatever forces were responsible for the formation of Braun's corps, they can be expected to make another attempt to carry out their aim. They may not try to raise another armed force, but they might well try something else that will enable them to accomplish their goal."

"I'm aware of it," Toby said. "I think the only possible answer is that the federal government and the various state governments will have to remain alert for a possible conspiracy."

"Vigilance," the governor replied, "is the price our citizens must pay for having the most free and independent government on earth. We must be aware at all times of our liberties and guard them zealously. They're our most precious possession, our richest heritage, the one inheritance that we can pass along to our children in full confidence and pride."

The clatter of hammering and sawing sounded clearly on the air as the volunteers, fifty strong, rebuilt the damaged roof and walls of Violet MacDermid's farmhouse. Others were at work tearing down the remains of the barracks and other buildings, while a third group was sorting out the wood, saving occasional pieces good enough to reuse as lumber and chopping up the rest as wood for Violet's stove.

A group of neighboring farmers toured the perimeters of Violet's farm, removing the sentry gates and the fences erected to keep Braun's men inside the grounds and to bar everyone else. Other neighbors labored behind teams of oxen, plowing the fertile ground and making the farm ready for planting.

While the men of the neighborhood labored to restore the once-productive farm to its previous condition, their wives were at work behind the farmhouse, where several cooking pits had been dug. There, sides of beef and venison were roasting over hot coals, and tables laden with many other dishes were being readied for the company.

Her friends permitted Violet MacDermid to do no work, and she stood in the midst of the bustle looking on with wonder as tears glistened in her eyes. She was flanked by her brother, Stalking Horse, and by her grandnephew, White Elk. Their Indian faces, usually solemn and unreadable, were wreathed in smiles of pure joy at the kindness of the entire region toward Violet, who was surprised at the outpouring of love and sympathy.

As she watched all the activity, Violet could not help thinking of her former employees, the Calloway brothers and Ed Bruton. Though she wished they could be here to witness the rebirth of her farm, she was glad to know, from letters received the week before, that they all had good jobs in Missouri.

Her closest neighbors, the Dalys and the Swensons, who had helped her during the fire, were sharing in the triumph of this day—Elizabeth Daly and Rebecca Swenson were among those cooking the meat, while Frank and Carl were part of the building crew. Jedidiah Maynard, the young man who had called on Violet during one of her loneliest hours, arrived late with his son, Tommy. While the boy went to find White Elk, Jedidiah joined the men who were chopping wood.

When the meat was done and was being carved and the vegetables were removed from the cooking fires, the men were called in from the fields, and the entire group assembled around the tables behind the farmhouse. As a special surprise for Violet, Governor

Senter and his wife had come from Nashville for the occasion, and the governor was prevailed upon to speak.

He extolled Violet's virtues and said that she exemplified the best tradition of the Indians in transition, from the Cherokee and other nations that had contributed so much to Tennessee's past, to those of the present who blended in with modern civilization and had become valued members of the community.

He had high praise, too, for the sense of justice of the inhabitants of the state, pointing out that the land agent responsible for Violet's problems had been removed from office and replaced by a representative of the people who would insure that justice was meted out to all.

Everyone joyously sang out, "For she's a jolly good fellow," and toasts with a fruit juice base were drunk in Violet's honor.

Then, in response to the insistent demands of the entire company, Violet MacDermid was obliged to stand and to make an address. "Be patient with me, dear friends," she said in deep embarrassment. "I never made a speech, and I ask you to forgive me in advance for any mistakes that I might make."

The crowd responded with such a mighty ovation that Violet had to laugh, and her apprehensions dissipated. "My ancestors lived here long ago," she said, "when deer roamed freely through the land and this entire region was a thick forest, as was almost all of North America. When the white men first came into these parts in ever-increasing numbers, my ancestors recognized that it was futile to oppose and fight them, so many Cherokee left and traveled farther toward the southwest.

"Those of us who have remained, however, have worked hand in hand with the newcomers to build a sound future for ourselves and for the generations that will come after us. Those who were brought here before the war as slaves are now free men and women, and they have joined us in our struggles to create a future for all who love Tennessee and work toward a common goal and a bright future.

"I thank you, my good friends, for restoring my property to me and making it possible for me to strive shoulder to shoulder with you toward making this a brighter land and to help make its promise come true."

Tears came not only to Violet's eyes, but to the eyes of many. They knew that the promise that had led the first settlers to cross the mountains into Tennessee and to hew a state out of the wilderness was being fulfilled.

The spectators' seats at the edge of the parade ground on the campus of the United States Military Academy at West Point were filled with relatives and friends of members of the corps of cadets. They rose to their feet in suppressed excitement as the academy band, sixty strong, marched onto the field playing "The Battle Hymn of the Republic." This served as a signal to three distinguished gentlemen sitting in the first row, who rose in reverse order of seniority and walked out onto the parade ground. The first to appear there was Major General Pitcher, the superintendent of the military academy. White-haired and distinguished, with the left side of his chest covered with his many decorations, he took his place on an invisible line with his back to the throng. Coming up beside him to his right was Major General Leland Blake, commander of the Army of the West, who wore even more decorations. General Blake, who appeared to a close observer to be having a hard time maintaining his dignity, turned for a moment and smiled toward two women in the front row of spectators. One was his wife, Eulalia, who looked ravishingly beautiful, as she always did, with her dark hair piled high on her head, her fur-trimmed coat fit-

ting her snugly; as always, she appeared to be wrapped
in a mantle of great dignity. Beside her was her daughter, Cindy, who clutched a lace handkerchief in one
hand. She had been plucking so hard at it that it had
threatened to disintegrate.

Cindy's eyes were shining, and a hint of a smile
appeared at the corners of her mouth, but her lips
trembled occasionally, revealing that she was tense almost beyond endurance as she awaited the coming
scene, the most important that she had ever witnessed.

The last to appear on the field, taking his place to
the right of generals Blake and Pitcher, was General
William T. Sherman, the commanding general of the
United States Army. After President Grant, he was the
Union's greatest hero in the Civil War. He embodied
the supreme symbol of authority, and the crowd fell
silent in tribute.

The music swelled, cymbals crashed, and on the
opposite side of the field from the three general officers, a cadet appeared, wearing his high—plumed, full-
dress headgear over his gray cape and uniform. On his
sleeves were the inverted chevrons that identified him
as the student commander of the brigade of cadets, a
new position that he was the first to fill. He halted
opposite the generals, stood stiffly at attention, and
drew his sword, which he raised in salute to them.

All three returned his salute in unison.

"There he is!" Cindy whispered fiercely, her voice
shaking. "It's really Hank!" She clenched her fists even
harder, then turned to her mother again. "Doesn't he
look wonderful, Mama? He seems none the worse for
the terrible experience he went through, except I guess
he looks older. Don't you agree, Mama?"

Smiling indulgently, Eulalia managed to silence
her. She was holding her grandson Timmy gently around
his small shoulders.

The band struck up another tune, and the corps of

cadets marched onto the field, its regimental and battalion pennants flying proudly.

The gray-clad lines marched with the precision for which they had become justly famous, and applause swept through the spectators. The West Pointers paid no attention. Instead, responding to barked commands of their student officers, they wheeled and marched past the three generals, turning their heads toward the trio of high-ranking officers and saluting with their swords.

Again the onlookers began to applaud, but they halted abruptly in some confusion when the cadets executed an about-face and marched directly across the field.

The long gray lines came to a halt, and the music stopped. The adjutants of the two regiments shouted orders, repeated by the battalion adjutants. The sabers of officers flashed, and the entire corps of cadets presented arms. Brigade Commander Henry Blake was being accorded an unprecedented honor.

Drawing his own sword, Cadet Blake returned the salute and then marched through the lines of his comrades until he reached a point facing the three generals. There he halted and stood at rigid attention, saluting them.

The corps of cadets did another about-face and also faced the generals, who returned the salute.

In awe, Cindy exclaimed, "Mama! They're honoring Hank with a special salute. Can anything like this ever have happened before at the academy?"

Then General Pitcher mounted a platform and proceeded to read a brief document. "By order of the President of the United States," he said, "I hereby restore Cadet Henry Blake to his place in the graduating class of the United States Military Academy and also restore to him the full honors due his rank as a result of his own efforts and accomplishments. I am also pleased to tender to Cadet Blake the thanks of the President, his commander in chief, and to these I add my personal appreciation and approval. Cadet Blake has undergone a grueling experience, for which he volunteered his services and which was kept as a military secret from everyone, including members of his family and the entire undergraduate body of the academy."

General Pitcher descended and was followed to the top of the platform by General Blake. Renowned for being cool under fire, for being collected in a time of crisis, the general found his voice was thick with emotion and threatened to break as he read the order signed by President Grant, which authorized a presidential citation to Cadet Blake. He read the citation, called Hank to the stand, pinned the medal on his son's uniform, and then overcome by his feelings, embraced him.

Eulalia Blake wept and held Timmy tightly. Cindy was happier than ever before in her life. The guests applauded, touched by the emotion of the moment. The corps of cadets, standing at ease, also broke into sustained cheers.

Everyone present fell silent when General Sherman finally mounted to the podium. His dislike of speechmaking was known, and he was famous for dispensing with formalities whenever possible. He looked out over the seated audience and then turned to address the corps of cadets.

"Gentlemen," he said, "ordinarily I would have waited until this class graduates to be present for a review of the cadet corps, but this is indeed a special occasion. I would be remiss to absent myself from the academy at this time. And I have an added duty, a pleasant one. As you know, it is traditional to announce the post assignments of new second lieutenants on the day they win their commissions. Once again, I am choosing to break tradition and to announce that future Second Lieutenant Blake will receive a special assignment. He will be assigned to an intelligence unit commanded by Colonel Andrew Brentwood."

Hank was so elated he could scarcely believe his good fortune. Andy Brentwood, a nephew of Leland Blake's, was the son of Sam and Claudia Brentwood, who had been on the original wagon train that crossed the continent to Oregon; the Brentwoods had stopped in Independence, Missouri, where they had prospered. Their son already enjoyed an outstanding record and clearly was on his way to a distinguished military career. Hank recalled having heard that Andy had been designated as head of a unit that was being organized to perform tasks too difficult or too sensitive for execution by most army units.

It was unusual for a newly commissioned officer to be given such a plum. Hank realized that the army was well pleased with the role he had played in uncovering Emil Braun and helping to get rid of his organization.

The ceremony was almost at an end. Hank took his place at the head of the brigade of cadets and, drawing his sword, called the student body to attention and then marched off the field at the head of the unit. The guests streamed onto the field, and Lee and Eulalia Blake, accepting the congratulations of other parents, retired to their suite at the hotel on the grounds of the academy, accompanied by members of their family and by General Sherman and General Pitcher. Hank arrived soon afterward, and he and Cindy, who had not seen each other since he had taken part in the adventure that had resulted in his supposed discharge from the academy, took one look at each other and, unmindful of the presence of others, embraced and kissed. General Sherman's broad grin indicated that he approved.

Hank presented Cindy to the army's commanding general, and while General Sherman put the young couple at ease, Leland Blake approached them, leading a very small boy by the hand. The child was dressed in a miniature version of an army officer's uniform, and he stood at attention when his grandfather said, "Bill, I want you to meet a future candidate for the academy, my grandson, Timothy Holt."

The child saluted, and then, glancing past General Sherman, he stiffened in excitement and shouted at the top of his lungs, "Papa!"

A smiling Toby Holt was entering the room with his arms outstretched to the boy. Tim ran to his father, who picked him up and hugged him. Everyone in the room, aware that the little boy was manfully trying to overcome his grief at his mother's death, watched as father and son hugged and kissed. Then Toby turned the boy to face Martha, who had quietly come into the room.

"So you're Timmy," she said softly. "I've heard a lot about you from your papa."

Her warmth and her outpouring of sympathy for the child were so great that Timmy could not help but respond. He held out his arms to her.

Martha took him from Toby, and the little boy clung to her as she kissed him.

Toby greeted his mother and stepfather and then proudly presented Martha to them and to other members of the company. "I'm sorry to be late," he said. "Our train was held up. Martha and I were able to observe the ceremony from a vantage point across the field. I can't even begin to tell you how pleased I am that you were able to bring Timmy. We've been separated much too long, and we have a lot of catching up to do. Being with him here is wonderful."

After the excitement over his arrival had died down, Toby had a brief, serious conversation with General Sherman and General Blake, somewhat complicated by the fact that he was again holding Tim in his arms.

"One angle to the whole saga of Emil Braun has confused me in the past, and it still niggles at me now," General Sherman said. "The acquisition of Braun's headquarters, the supplying of arms and uniforms, and the payment of salaries and substantial bonuses to his officers and men cost a fortune. Only a millionaire could have afforded such expenses. Yet Braun was not a rich man. On the contrary, he had almost nothing."

"Are you sure of that, General?" Toby asked, his own mind racing.

"Dead sure," General Sherman replied flatly.

"Then it's plain," Toby said, "that someone stood behind Braun. Someone who had ulterior motives was providing him with large sums of money. Who could it have been, and what reason did he have?"

"I wish I had the answers to those questions," General Sherman replied. "I could sleep a lot easier nights. We have to find some way to get to the bottom of this situation, but I'm not sure how to do it or how to proceed. It certainly is regrettable that we somehow never found that man Plosz. His check was the only real lead we ever had. But for today, Toby, put it out of your mind. This is a day for pleasure, after all. Before long, we'll have to start rooting out the elements of the mystery in earnest."

At the very least, Toby suspected, he had not heard the last of the matter. He was free to return now to his ranch in Oregon, having fulfilled the mission he had undertaken on behalf of the government. If a deeper probe was going to be conducted, as General Sherman had intimated, he would not be surprised if a new call went out for him to take charge and to bring to justice the hidden forces that were behind Braun.

For the present, his heart was too full, and he was torn by too many conflicting emotions to give serious thought to the riddle that General Sherman had raised.

He was overjoyed and relieved at being reunited with his son and at the same time was filled with sadness at Clarissa's death. He was forced to think, however, in terms of the present and future and was eager that his mother and stepfather establish cordial relations with Martha, on whom his future happiness depended.

At supper that evening, Eulalia Blake and Martha sat opposite each other, flanking General Sherman, who occupied the place at the head of the table. Toby watched them anxiously, hoping to see signs that they were establishing friendly relations. He was disturbed, however, to find that both his mother and the woman he intended to marry held themselves at arm's length from each other and were wary and extremely cautious.

Observance of the proprieties made it necessary for him and Martha to occupy separate rooms, so he had no opportunity later that evening to discuss the matter with her. It was still on his mind the following morning, however, when he and little Tim came down to the hotel dining room for breakfast and sat with General Blake. Father and son ordered large breakfasts, and when the little boy became busy eating his meal, Toby addressed himself to his stepfather.

"I wish you'd tell me something," he said. "What does my mother think of Martha?"

General Blake raised an eyebrow. "Should she have an opinion one way or another?"

"Well," Toby replied, with a grin that revealed his innate shyness, "I love her, and I've reached what you'd call an informal understanding with her. I'm going to ask her to marry me."

"Your mother made no mention of Martha," the general said. "She's so pleased for Cindy and Hank that she couldn't talk about anything else. She's just delighted that Hank has been assigned to Sam and Claudia Brentwood's son after his graduation from the academy.

I daresay she'll pay more attention to Martha once she learns what you have in mind."

"What do *you* think of her?" Toby persisted.

The general was taken somewhat by surprise. "Well," he said, temporizing, "she's very attractive. I couldn't establish more than a surface acquaintance with her in the short time we've seen her."

"If it hadn't been for her help and cooperation," Toby told him, "I wouldn't have been able to complete this mission successfully. Martha is the most resourceful, courageous woman I have ever known. On an undercover assignment, she's the perfect partner, and she also saved my life."

Leland Blake's complete attention was captured at last. "Really! How did she happen to acquire these skills? Most women live sheltered lives. That doesn't prepare them for work as intelligence operatives."

"She's the daughter of Domino," Toby explained.

"I see."

"I hope you do," Toby said. "You are aware of how closely he and I have worked in the country's interest. Frankly, I have difficulty in thinking of Domino as a criminal, despite certain of his connections and activities."

It was strange to hear Toby Holt, a symbol of honor and purity of motive to millions of Americans, speaking in defense of a notorious gang leader. Nevertheless, experience had taught General Blake when to keep his own counsel. His grandson was clamoring for his attention, and he turned to Tim, in effect ending the conversation with his stepson.

For reasons that Toby did not quite understand, he shared a feeling of relief that their talk had been ended. Granted that they had reached no definite conclusions, but Toby was not wholly concerned that he needed the approval of his mother and stepfather. He hoped that they would come to appreciate Martha, but even if they did not, that would in no way influence his love for her.

That afternoon, he borrowed a horse and carriage and drove Martha to the West Point railway station, where she was to take a train to New York City on the first leg of her journey back to New Orleans. Toby and Tim would stay on at West Point with the rest of the family until the following day.

"I reckon," he said, embarrassment turning his face beet-red, "that you'll think I'm a darn fool, but it wasn't until this morning that it suddenly occurred to me that I've been remiss."

Martha was mystified and smiled as she replied, "In what way?"

"I've kind of taken our future for granted, and I realize that that's something I must never do. You know I love you, more than anybody on earth, and I will until the day I die. I mean to say, I want you to marry me, if you will."

Martha's light laugh floated out toward the palisades that descended to the Hudson River below. "I guess I was taking you for granted, too, Toby," she said, "but I must admit that a woman likes to be asked. I love you, too, darling, and the answer is *yes*. A thousand times, yes! Of course I'll marry you. I decided that some time ago."

"I've had it in my head," Toby said, "that I wanted you to meet my son before you committed yourself, and have you come to know my mother and stepfather, too."

She slipped a hand through his arm but did not interfere with his hold on the reins. "I lost my heart to Timmy the moment I saw him," she said. "I'd marry you for his sake, if not for your own. I want nothing more than to take care of him and teach him and protect him."

The earnestness of her tone touched Toby deeply, and he smiled at her.

But Martha's expression was serious. "I exchanged only a few words with General Blake, in all fairness to him and me," she said. "As for your mother, I know of no law that insists we be friends. In fact, I don't think we will be."

"Why not?" Toby demanded.

She shrugged. "Who can say? She was cool toward me, so I kept my distance, too. Perhaps she disapproves of me because I'm Domino's daughter."

"Last night," Toby said, "she didn't know you are related to Domino, so that couldn't have been her reason."

"Well," Martha replied lightly, "whatever her motive, it's useless for us to speculate on it. If she wants to keep her distance from me, I'm sorry. But that won't affect my marriage to you in the slightest. I love you, and I'm going to be the best of all possible mothers to Timmy, as well."

"No man," Toby said, "could ask for more than that." And he was satisfied.

They left the plans for their marriage open, arranging to keep in touch by letter and telegraph after they learned whether Domino wanted his daughter's wedding to take place in New Orleans or whether he would prefer to travel with her to Oregon.

Their leave-taking was discreet, and the presence of several other people in the railway station was responsible for their light kiss of farewell.

Martha was going home by way of Memphis because, she said, she had an unpaid debt to settle there. She offered no explanation, and Toby was too much of a gentleman to pry, so she had no need to go into detail with him.

Martha's journey was uneventful, and forty-eight hours later, shortly after her arrival in Memphis and as soon as she had checked into her hotel, she went to the headquarters of the Mackerels. There she conversed earnestly but briefly with Red Leary, and thereafter she departed with Clancy in tow.

She and the diminutive gangster ate a light supper together at her hotel. Then, night having come, they went out to the cottage where Violet MacDermid had made her home during the period she had been dispossessed by Emil Braun. Thanks to Martha's kindhearted intervention, Laura Braun had moved into the cottage after the death of her husband. She had nowhere else to go, and the humble dwelling had become her home. There she existed in misery, frightened and lonely and wishing that her life was different, but lacking the strength and the purpose to bring about a change.

Laura made a practice of taking refuge from her poverty and misery in sleep, so her modest oil lamp was already extinguished when Clancy and Martha reached the cottage. They walked around to the rear, where the bedchamber was located, and Clancy proceeded to give his imitation of an excited dog. The sounds were so realistic that soon they heard Laura stirring and saw that she had lit the oil lamp.

Martha and Clancy had nothing more to do there, so they crept away, rode into town, and went to the house of the Reverend Dennis Dillon. The clergyman was surprised to see them, but Martha offered him only a partial explanation. "I think," she said, "you're going to have a visit from Laura Braun within the hour."

"Really?" the clergyman asked. "I haven't heard from her since her husband's violent death. I've been assuming that she's been too shy and perhaps too embarrassed to get in touch with me again. In fact, I have had it in mind to call on her quite soon."

"Whatever her reasons may have been," Martha said, "she's now had an experience that she considers sufficiently urgent that it overrides anything else on her mind."

"I think she's coming up the walk toward the house at this very moment," Clancy interrupted, staring out the window. "I'd say we got here just in time."

"Just in time to hide," Martha amended. "If you don't mind, Mr. Dillon." Congratulating herself on the precision of her and Clancy's timing, she withdrew with him to the chamber beyond the seance room, where they stood in the darkness behind the thick curtain that separated the two rooms.

Dennis Dillon was uneasy as he went to the front door and opened it. He had been surprised to learn that she was not an heiress, but that the "general" had left her virtually penniless. Dillon had promptly lost interest in Laura and had put her out of his mind, but her sudden reappearance on the heels of the young woman and the man who had impersonated her deceased pet dog made him apprehensive. All the same, he greeted her effusively.

Laura was too distraught to observe the amenities. "Mr. Dillon," she cried, "I have come here as fast as I could. I'm sorry to bother you at night, but Inky was in touch with me this evening, and I know my dear mother is trying to speak to me. She must have a terribly important message to give me for Inky to have awakened me from a sound sleep!"

The clergyman had no real choice, and after inviting her into the house, he sat her down in the parlor for a seance, placing her in front of the small table that he used as a prop and extinguishing the light.

The instant that the minister claimed that he had established contact with the spirit world, Clancy began to imitate an excited dog, barking and yelping furiously. The minister, again having no choice, tried to quiet the animal.

Martha began to speak, muffling her voice with a handkerchief, which she held in front of her mouth. "Darling Laura," she said, "you don't know how happy I am that you've heeded my call. I've been so anxious to get in touch with you and to speak with you again."

"I knew you had something to tell me!" Laura cried. "What is it, Mother, dear?"

"I have two messages for you, both concerned with your welfare and happiness on earth. The first is that you have nothing to fear from the spirit of Emil Braun. He is being punished for the wickedness that he perpetrated in the world of the living. Although I am not at liberty to reveal details, he is harmless and can never again cause unhappiness or damage to either the living or the dead."

"I'm so glad to hear it, Mother, dear," Laura said. "You've no idea how you have relieved my mind. What is your other message?"

"Continue to put your complete trust and faith in Dennis Dillon. He is a wonderful man, but dreadfully shy. So shy that he has been unable to confess his great love for you." Martha had difficulty in refraining from giggling as she continued to speak. "Marry him so that he may continue to shield and protect you for as long as you live."

"I will, Mother, dear. I will!" the ecstatic Laura cried.

Dennis Dillon sucked in his breath. He realized he had been tricked, but he saw no way he could avoid marriage to Laura Braun. If he eluded her, he ran the risk of being exposed as a charlatan, and his entire career would be placed in jeopardy. He smiled bravely.

"I am content to leave you in his care," Martha said. "Come, Inky, our task is completed, and we may rest in peace now."

Clancy imitated a dog for the last time, whimpering joyfully as his voice faded gradually.

Martha could make out in the dark what she had not noticed on her previous visits to the parsonage, that the place had a rear door at the far end of the kitchen. She touched Clancy's shoulder, and together they started toward the back door.

As they crept away, the sound of murmuring voices on the far side of the curtain told them that their mission had succeeded, that Laura would indeed become the bride of Dennis Dillon.

Leaving the parsonage behind, Martha was pleased that she had been able to contribute to the future happiness and welfare of Laura Braun, who had unwittingly worked for the defeat of the forces of evil.

Cabinet members and high-ranking officers of the army and navy, leaders of Congress, and justices of the Supreme Court, accompanied by their wives, mingled in the White House and overflowed into the gardens beyond it. The annual Easter Sunday reception held by President and Mrs. Grant was, as always, a highly successful affair.

James Martinson wandered aimlessly through the crowd. When the disintegration of Emil Braun's brigade dashed his hopes of using it to attain the presidency, Martinson had withdrawn from virtually all social contact while he pondered his next move. Now, lost in self-pity, he was even beginning to regret having emerged for this party. Not only had he lost a great deal of money, but also his carefully laid scheme had totally collapsed. To date, he had not been able to envision any new ideas of how he could gain the presidency. Additionally, his self-esteem had suffered a severe blow.

But his wounded vanity was healing, and his ambition still soared. He would not be satisfied until the White House became his home and the powers and prerogatives of the highest office in America were his.

As he walked through the gardens, a cup of punch in one hand, he exchanged greetings with various acquaintances and tried to stem the turbulent thoughts that raced through his mind. Even in his reverie, however, Martinson quickly noticed the stunning blonde in a snug, white-lace dress. She immediately fascinated him, and he could not take his eyes off her.

Dorothy White felt a vast sense of relief once she felt certain that James Martinson's attention was riveted on her. She had gone to great lengths to arrange to be present at the function, and it was vital to her plans that Martinson see her and be attracted to her.

She raised her eyes to his and returned his stare. Martinson was startled, but it was typical of him not to turn away, not to lower his gaze.

Dorothy took her cue from him and returned his stare steadily. Martinson tried to interpret her expression but could not. Was she smiling at him, perhaps flirting with him, inviting him to a dalliance? Or was he reading elements into her stare that did not exist?

Her eyes still holding Martinson's, Dorothy sauntered forward slowly, her hips swaying, her entire being reeking of erotic promise. When she came close to him, she murmured, "Hello, Jim," softly but distinctly.

Then, instead of halting to converse with him, she moved on, her manner as elusive as the whiff of perfume that she left behind. Martinson turned and continued to gape at her.

Dorothy did not pause to look back over her shoulder. She had accomplished the first stage of her mission and knew she had established a contact that would lead to the goals she had in mind. Still bent on attaching herself to Martinson, to profit from his wealth and his power, she had in recent weeks found her ambitions to be fueled by an additional goal—revenge. Increasingly bitter over all the wrongs that Martinson had inflicted, she was determined to get even. Before she was finished with James Martinson, he would pay for having subverted and destroyed her name and career. He would pay, too, for any wrong done to her sister. He might be a highly placed government official, one of the wealthiest citizens of the United States, but he was just another man, and Dorothy was confident he would ultimately succumb to her charms.

READ THIS THRILLING PREVIEW
OF A BOLD NEW SAGA
FROM THE CREATORS OF WAGONS WEST

AMERICA 2040

BY EVAN INNES

As the author of WAGONS WEST, I love to write about the conquering of the American West and the good folks who brought law, order, and civilization to the unknown wilds. In America 2040, I've found a mixture of all the qualities of WAGONS WEST, but set in the future—courageous men and women forced to flee to the far planets to settle and live, while the Earth teeters on the brink of nuclear war. AMERICA 2040 tells about men and women like you and me, who are determined to carry on American morality and love of freedom and family on uncharted lands light years away. AMERICA 2040 is a terrific exciting book!

Dana Fuller Ross
Author of WAGONS WEST

To American President Dexter Hamilton, entering Greater Moscow in the spring of 2033 was a fifty-year leap into the past, an enigmatic separation from his familiar, changing, bustling world. The impressive modernity of Gagarin Airport, the city's newest civilian and military aviation facility, had not prepared him for the real Moscow.

There was snow in the city, grayed, trodden, piled. Along the motorcade route he and his entourage caught glimpses of real antiques: diesel-powered trucks spouting the contaminants of burning fossil fuel to cloud the chill air. People swaddled in animal furs. Drab, stern, slab-sided apartment buildings that had been built shortly after World War II.

Under a lowering, slate sky, the Kremlin loomed redly beyond the frozen Moskva River. To Hamilton, and to millions, the triangularly shaped fortress housed most of what was evil in the world. The relationship between Russia and the United States remained tense, hostile, suspicious, and dangerous, but Dexter Hamilton wanted to be the American President who halted the eternal arms race and delivered the world, forever, from the threat of nuclear incineration. To that end, he was to meet with the Soviet leader, Premier Yuri Kolchak.

The President was young to be serving in that office, only forty-six, having been born in 1987. His silvering hair—a tight, curled mass that clung to his well-formed head—seemed to be a tacit signal that, although young, here was a wise, experienced man.

Behind the smile-crinkled blue eyes, the classic nose, the upturned mouth, there was the strength that had given him the governorship of North Carolina, then a seat in the Senate, and finally the Oval Office.

When the limousine hummed through guarded gates, past heavily armed and stalwart men handpicked for Kremlin duty from the huge Red Army, Dexter Hamilton was guided from the car by a woman general. He walked with long, quick strides, eager to begin the summit meeting with Premier Yuri Kolchak.

Premier Kolchak was waiting for him behind a wide, gleaming table in a conference room. The Premier was a darkly handsome man, but there was something in his eyes that bothered Hamilton, a quality he'd seen before. Then the memory came back to him: When he was quite young he'd owned a little dog that had wandered into a field and been swept up in a tomato picker. The dying, mutilated dog lay stunned and shocked. In Kolchak's eyes were those same qualities—a pain that seemed to approach madness. Was there truth to the rumor that the Premier was seriously ill?

Several minutes after the meeting has begun, Yuri Kolchak rises abruptly from his seat, obviously taken ill. He is led away hastily, without explanation or apology. Hamilton is escorted back to his suite, where, except for a serving girl bringing dinner, he is left alone for the night.

The next morning there was a knock on the door of his luxurious suite in the Kremlin, and a smiling, dark-haired serving girl in livery appeared. Pleasant aromas of coffee, real eggs, and ham came from the serving cart she was standing behind. A great number of covered serving bowls were on the cart, certainly enough for more than one man.

Just then he heard a deep, resonant voice coming from behind the girl.

"Good morning, Mr. President. You slept well?"

Premier Kolchak was dressed informally in tunic, trousers. At forty-seven his slightly Slavic face was smooth, and his dark and bristly hair showed no hint of gray. He extended a hand. Hamilton took it. Each grip was firm.

"Forgive me for surprising you," Kolchak said as the serving girl disappeared out the door. "But if I had taken time to warn you that I was coming, we'd have to invite our aides and observe protocol." There was no explanation of the previous meeting's cancellation.

"I understand," Hamilton said. Kolchak took a seat and Hamilton sat across the table, and they began to eat.

"My people don't understand your real purpose here," the Premier said.

"Well, Yuri," Hamilton began, "you like straight talk, so here it is: I'm here to talk peace. I want to talk about what we have in common. We're all passengers on a small, increasingly overcrowded planet. It is time we took down the bombs from the space stations and junked the missiles and the space weapons. The men who bring peace to the world will be sung in history down through the ages. Let's make those men you and me."

"I could learn to like you," Kolchak said. "I will give you anything you want from this conference."

The statement seemed simple enough, direct enough, but there was something wrong.

"Because you see," Kolchak said, his dark, hard

eyes boring into Hamilton's, "whatever you achieve in this present conference does not matter." The Premier had finished eating. He leaned back, wiped his lips on a linen napkin, let it fall to his knee. "What matters is what you and I say here in this room." He smiled. "I hope you will be receptive and reasonable."

"I'll do my best."

"For centuries," Kolchak said, "elitist and imperialist countries have delayed the destiny of the masses. We can no longer allow that. Soon, Mr. President, the downtrodden of the world will be free to share in the fruits of their own labors. Within my lifetime, the revolution will be total." He paused. "With one single exception. We will allow the continued existence of the United States as a governmental entity. In time, with the rest of the world's workers freed from their masters and living in equality with their fellows, you will see reason and work with the rest of the civilized world." Ever since the use of the first atomic bomb on Japan, men had dreaded that someday, in some country, a madman would be in a position to push the button. This, Hamilton felt with a despair that made him want to strike out, was the man.

"Mr. Premier, this must be the first time in the history of my country that a President has been so threatened."

Kolchak shrugged. "We can no longer allow you to prevent the legitimate aspirations of the peoples of this world. We have liberated many countries. We will liberate more."

"Are you speaking of South America?"

"That, first."

South America was dominated by the emerging

imperialistic giant Brazil, whose armed forces had overwhelmed Cuba, ending Communist rule there. However, Communist insurgents continued to rebel against Brazilian authorities in the Caribbean and South America. An American fleet was stationed in the Pacific, but as of yet there had been no direct confrontation with the Russians.

"Are you declaring war?" Hamilton asked. "For we will fight you over that continent."

"There will be a war only if you choose to interfere. If both our countries let loose all our military power there will be little, if any, life left on Earth. But that doesn't really matter."

"What, in God's name, does matter?"

Kolchak leaned forward, his face pale, his lips twitching in obvious pain. "The triumph of right."

"Your brand of right, of course?"

"Of course. There is no other. Now will you pull out of South America and let events take their course?"

"No."

Kolchak leaned back, sighed. "Then, Mr. President, prepare yourself for some very difficult decisions."

"We've faced tough decisions before," Hamilton said. "I'll admit that you're scaring the living daylights out of me, but we won't stand aside and let you gobble up what's left."

Kolchak smiled. "Understand this, Mr. President. Before I die, the world will be Red or dead, and quite frankly I don't give a"—he used a Russian obscenity unfamiliar to Hamilton—"which it is."

Hamilton heard himself saying words, inane words. "May you have a long life, Mr. Premier."

"No, my friend, you will not escape the responsibility in that way."

"You *are* ill," Hamilton said softly.

Kolchak, with a cold smile, nodded.

"Perhaps we could help in some way. Our medical research—"

"Is no better than ours."

"How long?" Hamilton asked.

"Fewer than nine years."

"I'm sorry," Hamilton said. "But we have time to think about it, to talk. Yuri, there's no winning a war. My God, man, we've both got enough warheads in space to do the job twice over. If you push the button I'm dead, but I'll have time to push my own button and you're dead."

"But I'm dead regardless of what happens," Kolchak said. With a wicked gleam in his black eyes, he added, "All I care about is that the world is ours . . . or else it does not exist at all."

President Hamilton returns to Washington, where he briefs the head of the CIA and orders him to make the assassination of Yuri Kolchak a top priority. Then Dexter Hamilton and his scientific advisor, Oscar Kost, explore other ways to avert annihilation of the American people and their way of life. Their search takes them to Vandenberg Air Force Base in California, to learn about Project Lightstep, a top-secret operation.

Dexter Hamilton and Oscar Kost were introduced by a two-star general to Harry Shaw, a small, dark man, with a wide forehead and thin mouth that was, nevertheless, capable of a wide smile.

"This is a genuine pleasure, Mr. President, Mr. Kost," Shaw said.

"The pleasure is mutual," Hamilton said. "I have

to confess that I know absolutely nothing about this project. Please start at the beginning."

"I'll try to make it brief," Shaw said. "When I was an undergraduate I worked with platinum metals and their ability to store heat and energy, but it wasn't until I got my hands on a supply of rhenium that I began to make any progress. I decided to hit a few molecules of rhenium with antimatter, and as a result we almost obliterated Los Angeles. The reaction was contained, but just barely," Shaw added.

Hamilton didn't see the significance. A bigger and better bomb would not make Yuri Kolchak take his finger off the button. Nuclear bombs could already destroy all life on Earth, so why bother with something else?

"Harry," Hamilton said, "just tell me rhenium's other applications."

"It's currently the energy source for an experimental space vehicle disguised as a simple planetary probe. It's out beyond Pluto right now. If we've succeeded, that vehicle, propelled by rhenium, has made a round trip to within a few million miles of the star closest to our system, Proxima Centauri. That's thirty trillion miles in a billionth of a second."

Hamilton felt a sudden surge of joy. He glanced at Kost. Oscar's hooded eyes were gleaming. For the first time since his meeting with Yuri Kolchak, Hamilton felt a swelling of hope in his breast. As the countdown clock jerked its second hand closer to the critical moment when the experimental space vehicle's computer-screen transmission would be received by Vandenberg, a fantastic and exciting dream grew inside Dexter Hamilton: If Yuri Kolchak sent the whole world up in smoke and dust and fire, there would be still one last hope for the human race.

"One minute and counting," an amplified voice said, breaking the tense silence.

Hamilton's eyes were on the clock.

"Thirty seconds . . . twenty—"

Screens came to life, flickered, were blank. There was an air of supreme tension in the room, a breathless hush except for the counting voice.

"—five, four, three, two, one—!"

A large screen flickered, static lines flowering, diminishing, and then the screen was filled with fire— harsh, golden, roiling, boiling fire.

"Oh, God, no," Hamilton said. Seen close up, a sun is an awesome furnace, the golden fires of thermonuclear reaction forming slowly roiling masses on its curved surface.

"Wait," Harry Shaw said, his voice cracking with excitement. "We're not on the scopes. We're on radio telemetry."

And slowly, slowly, the screen changed, the fire gradually becoming more distant.

"The camera is changing lenses!" Shaw yelled. "We were too close!"

A cheer went up.

"It worked! Thank God, it worked!" Harry Shaw yelled, doing a little dance. It worked! Man could travel faster than light. With some luck, and some tricky, very secret planning, there could be people, Americans, out there traveling through the far reaches of space.

Now there was hope. At least some would survive. Hamilton would see to that. He could not trust Yuri Kolchak to leave the United States alone. Kolchak would want total world domination, and Dexter would never bow down and live under Communism. There'd be a part of the United States of America alive, out there in space. And if the missiles began to lance down from the orbiting space stations, at least a seed stock of humankind, if the form of Americans, would be alive.

The colossal rhenium-powered spaceship, secretly constructed under the Utah desert over a period of six years, is ready for lift-off. In the interim, Yuri Kolchak's health and the international political situation deteriorate. President Hamilton addresses the nation and the world, on the brink of nuclear war, disclosing at last history's best kept secret, the Spirit of America.

From cameras outside, a view of the White House was flashed upward to satellites, and a band played the "Star Spangled Banner." The anthem was being fed to the sound monitors in the Oval Office. As the last notes of music died, the director stabbed a finger toward Hamilton, who sat immobile, his calm, kind, distinguished face in repose, his eyes looking directly into the cameras. At last his drawling voice broke the almost unbearable tension.

"My fellow Americans. Today, December 24, 2040, this great nation of ours is about to embark upon humankind's greatest adventure.

"Even as I speak, while hundreds of thousands of our servicemen and women are massed in South America because of that age-old curse of mankind—war—other brave men and women are preparing to leave behind family and loved ones, their homes, their native country, even the planet of their birth.

"Today, one thousand Americans will leave Earth to open a new frontier among the stars.

"We Americans have a history of facing and

overcoming the unknown. Our forefathers dared a great ocean and overcame great obstacles to establish this nation, under God, and in freedom. They came to face the fierceness of a raw, vast land, and they established a nation that is unique, a nation wherein each and every individual has equal rights.

"Today our freedom faces its gravest test. Even now, our avowed enemies in South America threaten to overwhelm us, and the largest battle fleet ever to be assembled is massing off the western coast of the South American continent.

"I cannot tell you, my fellow citizens, what tomorrow will bring. But I can tell you this: The spirit of America will not die. The force and the dream that made this country great will live on in those brave pioneers who today will leave Earth to venture into the unknown.

"America now offers hope to the billions of people, citizens of every country. For the great ship that will journey to the far stars can, with international cooperation, bring the blessing of plenty back to our wasted world. American science, American genius, and the American dream have opened up a vast new empire, which can provide us with badly needed living space, a safety valve for our overpopulation, a source of rich, new raw materials to quiet our hunger and restore to us, and to the world, the standard of living we once knew.

"As President of the United States and as your spokesman, I extend the hand of cooperation and friendship to our enemies. The destiny of humankind cannot continue in bitter warfare until there is nothing left but ashes and cinders. No, we have a higher destiny. Our destiny lies among the stars."

Hamilton's face was seemingly at peace, his eagle's eyes looking straight into the camera.

"And now, my fellow Americans, let us experience this great moment together."

The first view was from a distance. Desert. Low mounds in the background, and then, from a hovering helicopter, the first view of the ship. It looked like some fantastic toy buried in a round hole in the ground. Only when the airborne camera pulled back to a long shot and it was possible to see vehicles, antlike people, the temporary town, was it possible to gain an idea of the ship's vast size.

From the top it looked like a huge wheel and had been painted red, white, and blue. On a blank expanse of metal near the core were Old Glory and the words *UNITED STATES*. And on the outer wheel, proudly, in huge letters that gleamed in gold against white, *Spirit of America*.

It came to life slowly. First a billowing rush of smoke pouring up from the circular pit around its sides, obscuring it, and then tongues of flame.

Was it merely illusion or did that impossibly huge mass move?

Smoke. Flames. Rocketry had reached its zenith. Fuels of high mass-to-bulk ratio had been developed during the space-station-building epoch. Combustion times had been extended. But never before had such a mass been lifted from Earth's gravitational pull. Never before had so much fuel been expended in so short time.

The ship crawled upward, and the flames decreased, and *Spirit of America* emerged from them, huge, round, lifting slowly, slowly, and that sound familiar to all Americans was rumbling and roaring, the awesome power sound of bellowing rockets as it had never been heard in such intensity. And now it was accelerating slowly, slowly, too fantastic to be anything but trick photography, and yet it was real.

The ship bellowed straight up for long minutes, and then, as the cameramen began to switch to their long lenses, it tilted slowly and angled off toward the east. It was so big that the longest lenses could follow it into orbit. True, the ship was but a bright speck of reflected sunlight when, after the rockets had ceased firing, it swam through the darkness of near space, a bright star to be seen with the naked eye, but it was there, and after the long tension of watching the takeoff, a billion Americans cheered.